MW01174588

School yard bullying, indeed all types of bullying, has been around for ages, and will continue to be a reality for years to come. While this book is fiction, it is dedicated to all those who have been victims and suffered from this painful and gut wrenching experience.

My thanks to those who have helped make in the publication of this novel. First, my wife Jean, who both encouraged me to write and endured my mood swings as I found myself emerged between one of my stories and my real life. To my sister, Linda Caldwell, who helped me edit. It took a great deal of effort and energy over the past 4 years to complete Adrenalin and she has put as much into this book as I have. A special thank you to Brenda Grant, Niagara Falls, Ontario, who created the cover, I think she did a great job.

Any similarities between this novel and real life are coincidental.

Benny - Thanks for buying my second novel. Don't take it too seriously - - - its just fiction!

Claude W Tiffin

Order this book online at www.trafford.com/07-0380
or email orders@trafford.com

Most Trafford titles are also available at major online book retailers.

Note for Librarians: A cataloguing record for this book is available from Library
and Archives Canada at www.collectionscanada.ca/amicus/index-e.html

Printed in Victoria, BC, Canada.

ISBN: 978-1-4251-1974-4

*We at Trafford believe that it is the responsibility of us all, as both individuals
and corporations, to make choices that are environmentally and socially sound.
You, in turn, are supporting this responsible conduct each time you purchase a
Trafford book, or make use of our publishing services. To find out how you are
helping, please visit www.trafford.com/responsiblepublishing.html*

*Our mission is to efficiently provide the world's finest, most comprehensive
book publishing service, enabling every author to experience success.
To find out how to publish your book, your way, and have it available
worldwide, visit us online at www.trafford.com/10510*

www.trafford.com

North America & international
toll-free: 1 888 232 4444 (USA & Canada)
phone: 250 383 6864 ♦ fax: 250 383 6804
email: info@trafford.com

The United Kingdom & Europe
phone: +44 (0)1865 722 113 ♦ local rate: 0845 230 9601
facsimile: +44 (0)1865 722 868 ♦ email: info.uk@trafford.com

10 9 8 7 6 5 4 3

1

His heart was racing. The sweat ran down the side of his face like blood, and his breathing was thunderous. Alone in the darkness with no other living soul around, he was horror-struck. He got to his feet and surveyed the area. He viewed it differently than he had before. Now he was looking for a way out of this unimaginable act, he needed a cover up.

The sidewalk that he was standing on was going to be extended and would act as a crude burial ground. It dropped a distance of eighteen inches and was filled with pea stone gravel with wire mesh on top. Today being Sunday, the concrete would probably be poured tomorrow. He looked around for something to use to bury the body. There was a portable tool shed about twenty feet away and he quickly made his way over to it, but a padlock secured the door. Not far away, leaning against the wall of the shed, was a round-nosed spade with a broken handle. He grabbed it and walked back passed the lifeless body, reached down and pulled the wire mesh back from the gravel. He etched out a six by three plot in the gravel and began to dig Paulo's final resting place.

His hands were blistered and bloodied. Every inch of his body was aching and drenched in sweat. His mind was reeling, both from the physical and emotional strain of the entire ordeal. He completed the hole in the loose desert sand and stepped up onto the cement slab. Hunched over, panting and gasping for breath he struggled to drag the body towards the edge of the sidewalk. He rolled the corpse face down into the shallow grave and began to shovel sand over the body. He stomped the sand down and with the edge of the spade pulled the gravel back in place as carefully as he could. The final chore was to replace the wire mesh, so that it looked undisturbed.

For a moment, his mind returned to the story of how the casino robbers had been buried in their car in the desert and he wondered just how many secrets this place kept.

He shovelled the remaining sand to one side and levelled it. The mass surge of adrenalin had left his body and he was numb and exhausted. Whether or not any tell-tale signs would be evident to anyone on the job site in the morning, was a chance he had to take. If they were like most labourers, on Monday morning they would not notice and if they did, he would be homeward bound leaving it all behind. He knew that he would never return to this nightmare but the memory of the gruesome killing would be there haunting him for the rest of his life.

He wiped the handle of the spade clean with the tail of his shirt and leaned it back against the shed. He looked down at his clothes they were streaked with sand, sweat, and traces of blood. Getting back to his room undetected would be no small feat.

2

The two boys sat on the well-worn bench in front of the principal's office. One looked frightened and the other looked smug and defiant. The bigger boy turned to the smaller one and said, "When we get in front of this old fart of a principal you'd better not squeal on me, or I'll give it to you good when we get outside and no one's around."

David Rivers was the smaller of the two, twenty pounds lighter, three inches shorter and about fourteen months younger than the boy next to him. He bit his lip and stared straight ahead fighting back tears. He didn't want to cry and embarrass himself. The big red bruise that was now beginning to turn purple was painful enough without having his school friends see him in the Hot Seat crying. That would be the ultimate pain, the kind that lingers long after the scars on the outside disappear.

Joey Gallo, the other boy, didn't mind sitting here at all. In fact, he was used to it; to him it was a status symbol of sorts. He certainly wasn't afraid of the principal and it sent a clear message to all the other boys in this public school not to mess with him. Joey had received this corporal punishment in the past and came out dry-eyed, earning him the tough guy reputation that seemed to feed his ego. This was his last year in public school and he wouldn't have to face Principal Manning anymore.

It wasn't his fault and David knew that but here he was sitting in the spot that he had tried to avoid. Principal Manning had a "no fighting" rule in place but David stood his ground and he was not going to back down from Joey's taunts. Besides, it wasn't him who had gone running to the principal's office for help, one of the student monitors had told Miss Hamilton who ran out to separate the boys. She scolded Joey for fighting with someone smaller than he and brought them both to the office where they were now waiting.

The office door opened and Howard Manning stood in the doorway. He was not a big man but he was solidly built. He kept active in sports at the school often joining in when the senior soccer team was practicing. That was one of the things that most of the students respected about their principal. He supported and participated in the school's activities, glowing with pride when they won and sharing their disappointments when they lost. However today he was not laughing or smiling. One of his rules had been broken by a student, one who was nothing but a trouble maker. He didn't say a word but motioned to the boys to come in.

David had never been inside the office and had only caught a glimpse as he passed on his way to class. The office ceiling was high, almost higher than other parts of the building or at least it seemed that way to David. The room had a cold look to him. He glanced at the numerous pictures that hung on the wall, showcasing past principals and winning sports teams. Howard Manning took his seat facing the boys and for a moment he said nothing. He just sat, eyeing them both intensely, comparing one to the other. The smallest boy was tidy and well dressed although it was plain to see that he was nervous and sweating. He swung his attention to the other boy. He wasn't nervous at all, nor was he a stranger to the office. The larger boy, with black unruly hair and a smirk on his face, got under Manning's skin. Slowly, he turned his gaze back towards David.

"You look like you got the worst of it. How does the cheek feel?"

David's eyes flittered back and forth as if he were afraid to answer. It was a toss up as to who he was more afraid of, but in the end it was definitely Joey. He looked straight ahead as he answered, "It hurts some."

The principal paused and looked at Joey. "This is not your first time in my office is it Mr. Gallo? I don't suppose that this altercation was your fault?"

"He swore at me!"

"Of course he did and for that you thought you'd teach him a lesson, an etiquette lesson perhaps? You think that you are pretty tough picking on boys smaller than yourself. You are older, bigger and an outright bully!"

It was plain to see that Howard Manning was struggling to control his temper. You could see it in his eyes and in the colour of his face. He looked at Joey without saying a word. For a moment the smirk disappeared from Joey's face but it didn't last long. Soon he was defiant again. "I won't let him swear at me. My Dad said I shouldn't let anybody treat me with disrespect."

Manning's attention returned to David. "What's your name, son?"

"David Rivers, Sir."

"Tell me what happened out in the school yard."

David looked quickly at Joey who was biting his lip. His eyes conveyed a look of hatred.

"Don't look at him David, look at me. What happened?"

David looked straight ahead ignoring Joey. "We were out in the yard, Jimmy Allen and me. Jimmy's dad died last year and he has five sisters and his mom can't afford to buy him new clothes to wear to school. He was wearing his older cousin's clothes and they don't fit Jimmy very good. They're too big. Joey and two of his friends started making fun of him and said he looked like a baggy pants clown and he should be in the circus, the freak show circus." He didn't stop to take a breath. "They started pulling at his clothes and shoving him. Jimmy got scared and started to cry. Since his dad died, he's sad a lot and I felt sorry for him. I told Joey and his friends to leave him alone. And..."

The principal interrupted him. "And that's when Joey hit you?"

"Yes sir."

Adrenalin

David was already beginning to regret that he had opened his mouth. He knew he would be looking over his shoulder for some time to come. He had that helpless feeling. This must be what his dad called a 'no-win situation', he thought to himself.

Manning sat back in his chair, removed his horn-rimmed glasses and began cleaning them with a tissue that he took from a box on his desk. He cleared his throat. "You can go for the rest of the day David. Joey and I are going to have a little talk. If he or his friends start picking on you again, I want to know about it. Understand?"

David nodded and quickly got up and left the room. He glanced at Joey who gave him a look that scared the hell out of him. But for now, all he could think of was going home.

Howard Manning stood up and looked out the window. He kept watching until he saw David leave the school yard and head toward home. Joey squirmed uncomfortably in his chair. The principal sat back down and once again faced Joey.

"Proud of yourself are you, Mister Gallo? You and your so-called friends harassing a youngster who has just lost a parent, then beating up someone smaller than you, someone with the integrity to stand up for a friend. I've tried everything with you. Unfortunately, today the strap is not allowed otherwise you'd be at the top of my list. But I *can* expel you and I will." Manning took a breath and tried to restore his composure. "This is the last warning. I'm putting this in your file and the next time you're out for the rest of the year, which means you'll have to repeat grade eight. I have no intention of discussing this with you or your father. We've been down this road before and I'm telling you this is the last time. Do I make myself clear?"

"Yes, Sir."

"If you don't change your attitude one day someone bigger and stronger than little David Rivers is going to make you sorry you ever picked on them."

School was out by the time Joey had left the principal's office and although he was angry, he had lost his usual cocky attitude. That damn Rivers had humiliated him in front of the principal and if he caught him off school property he would give him a real shit-kicking. A deep-seated resentment was festering inside of him. His father had been showing him martial arts moves and he needed someone to practice on. His day would come. Rivers would have more than a red spot on his cheek the next time; that would have been today if Manning wouldn't have let Rivers out of school ahead of him. A tin can that someone had carelessly discarded was on the sidewalk in front of him. He glared at it, in his mind he was picturing David Rivers, as he kicked and sent it flying through the air to the other side of the street. Anyone within earshot would have wondered what he was talking about when he screamed out loud, "It's your ass I'm kicking Rivers, wait 'til I catch you!"

David had hurried along home after the principal let him out early. An unpleasant feeling had come over him. He knew that no matter what the principal said, Joey would come after him, or get one or two of those thugs he hung around with to provoke a fight. He had seen it occur before. Lots of things went on in the school yard that were often unreported, but today someone happened along to stop the fight, next time he might not be so lucky.

The blazing crimson colour of a cardinal in flight caught David's attention as it flew up into a tree and began to whistle. Must be nice he thought, free as a bird, able to leave your troubles behind and take flight. How envious he was at that moment of his feathered friend. He passed the house where Joey Gallo lived. He had to pass it everyday on his way to and from school. It had not been a problem until today, but from here on it would probably be a different story.

That night at dinner, David kept his head down slightly as he picked away at the food on his plate. His mother,

Marilyn, looked at him for a moment and then turned to his father. John was sitting across the table busy cutting a slice off his steak and shoving it into his mouth. He looked up and saw his wife nodding in David's direction. His eyes moved toward their son and it was then that he saw the red mark on David's cheek.

"What happened to your face, Dave? Looks like somebody caught you with a right hook."

David didn't answer. He continued eating.

"Hey, I'm talking to you!"

David looked up and the purple colour of the bruise was in full sight. "I got punched out at school, okay?"

Embarrassed, John's face began to turn red. He didn't like what he considered smart talk. "No, it's not okay. I asked you a question."

"Joey Gallo. I had a fight with Joey."

John Rivers sat silent. "That explains a lot. Like father, like son. I knew it was bad news when they moved into this neighbourhood. As long as I've known Alex Gallo he's always been a problem. He hangs around with all the low life scum drinking and gambling and whoring around."

"JOHN!!" Marilyn's face was red with embarrassment from words that her husband seldom used.

"Well, he does," John said under his breath and although he knew it was wrong he wasn't about to apologize. "Alex always liked to fight when I went to school with him. We had more than one run in and he seems to think that there is something manly about carrying on like a bully. I see he passed that onto his son."

John Rivers shook his head as David told his folks in detail just what had taken place. Marilyn looked at her husband trying to hold back the question that she was anxious to ask, even before David had finished speaking.

"What are you going to do about this, John?"

He looked at her with mild disgust. "Nothing. What do you expect me to do that the principal hasn't already done?"

10

"You have to talk to the boy's father. Let him know that you disapprove of what his son has done."

John looked at his wife in disbelief. "You must be joking. Alex Gallo is a cement head. He would think that was just great for his son to beat up on the son of the man that kicked his ass years ago. Alex would only see it as payback. You don't know him."

Marilyn looked upset. She was not used to dealing with this sort of problem. "Well, I know his mother Ellen Gallo, not well, but a friend of mine does. She came from a good family that didn't approve of Alex. My friend said that Ellen told her that Alex would change his habits if she married him."

John shook his head. "They all say that. How many people have you ever seen change? Very few of them, and Alex sure isn't one of them. His name comes up every once in a while at the plant from people who tell me stories about his violent temper and abusive behaviour. He's still the same. Hasn't changed, never will and is probably proud his son has followed in his footsteps. David did the right thing in standing up for Jimmy Allen." John looked at David as he continued to speak, "Finish your supper David, we'll go out to my shop and have a talk about all of this. Maybe I can give you a few pointers on how to cope with guys like Joey."

Marilyn Rivers looked at her husband. "I still think that you should say something to the Mr. Manning and Joey's parents."

"And make everything worse, I suppose." John rose from the table and headed towards his shop.

John reached up and pulled a cigar box off the shelf behind the workbench. David sat on one of the stools that his father had made and watched as he opened the box and took out part of a cigar, one of many pieces of cigars in the box. His dad put the cigar in his mouth, tore off a small piece with his teeth and began to chew on it. Then he replaced the box on the shelf.

"What?"

Adrenalin

For the first time that day, David smiled as he turned around. "I always wondered how you could quit smoking as quick as you did after your heart attack. Now I know. You didn't exactly quit." David grinned at the expression on his Dad's face.

"The doctor told me to quit smoking. He didn't say to stop using tobacco. Don't you go telling your mother either. What goes on in this shop is my business, just like what I'm about to tell you now." John spat the brown fluid under the work bench.

"I went through all the same bullshit that you are now facing years ago with Joey's father, before I finally grew old enough and strong enough. I beat the hell out of him. I don't think his boy is going to let up on you." David could see the memory of that time in his dad's eyes as he talked. "You might be safe enough in the school yard but off school property; it will be a different story. You're smaller, right now anyway, so you have to be smarter. Don't walk around corners where he or his buddies might be waiting. Practice running and get on the track team. They say a good set of feet never sees its ass kicked. Outrun him if you can, there's no disgrace in it considering the difference in size, I've seen Joey." John began to stand straight as he was about to give his son advice on how to keep from getting beat up. "Another thing, hang around some of the tougher kids at school and go out of your way to make friends with them. Guys like Joey keep their distance from anybody that they don't think they can beat. Finally, if he catches up with you and you have to fight, give it all you got - kick, bite, scratch. Remember, he's bringing the fight to you. Defend yourself."

"Hold your fists up now, in front of your face. Now pretend that I'm throwing a punch at you." John went into a fighter's crouch.

"No, No, No! Don't close your eyes when a fist is coming at you. You can't block a punch with your eyes closed."

"I'm no good at boxing, Dad. I can wrestle some but I can't box."

John Rivers shook his head. "Your reflexes are working against you, that's all. Instead of blinking, duck under the punch and nail him hard in the gut."

"The kids say that you're not supposed to hit below the belt."

"Ya? Well they also say pick on someone your own size. When you're fighting someone like Joey, forget the rule book. He doesn't read it, so forget it. Pound the piss out of him before he does it to you!"

A few houses down the street, another father was having a man-to-man talk with his son. This shop was not filled with tools and wooden projects that occupied a hobbyist's spare time. Here, a series of punching bags hung and suspended from the ceiling were different sizes of boxing gloves. The leather exteriors marked and discoloured from years of use where someone's face or teeth had come into contact with them. Ever since he was a small boy, he had put on the gloves and his father had instructed him in the art of boxing. There were also weights and barbells sitting on racks made especially for them.

The father beamed with pride as he said to his son. "So old Manning stopped you from standing up for yourself with Rivers. He's probably a candy-ass just like his old man. Neither one can fight worth a damn. And that's typical of a principal sticking up for someone like Rivers and looking down his nose at people like us. It was the same when I went to school. I showed them all, today when I walk into a room I get respect. They all know better than to mess with Alex Gallo."

"What you have to do is catch this little snot-nose away from the school. Some place where there's nobody to fight for him. If he's like his old man, he'll hang around with lots of other kinds that run crying to a principal or someone to bail him out. Catch him alone and then show him whose boss."

"I got this magazine the other day. It's all about martial arts. It's a good one. It shows how to use a guy's weight to your advantage, how to throw them over your head and about using your feet. It's out in the car, I'll go get it and then we'll work on some of the techniques. Some that you can use to kick this Rivers kid's ass the first time you catch him alone."

Monday morning Joey stood with two of his tough friends and watched the parade of students walking along the street on their way to school. His old man had been right; David Rivers was always with a crowd of other kids since the day they had been called into Manning's office. Today wasn't much different. Today, he was walking to school with Bobby Freeman, a light skinned black boy. David had been hanging around a lot with Bobby lately. Joey had never seen Bobby fight but he had heard from other kids about his fighting skills. That was the reason nobody wanted to fight Bobby. It was also why Rivers was now his constant companion. Joey bit his lip. He was just itching to get Rivers alone, some place nice and quiet where it would be a one-on-one fight with no monitor to interfere. He saw David steal a quick look at him but before he could give him the finger, David looked away leaving him angry and frustrated. He would have to bide his time.

Two weeks later he got his chance. Bobby Freeman's grandmother had died and Bobby wasn't at school, but David was. The bell ending recess sounded and the students began to file back into the school. David had been playing a scrub game of soccer with some of the others. Last one on the field always returned the soccer ball to the gym and that day it was David. He was sweating as he ran after the ball. He retrieved it and headed into the school but someone was blocking the entrance. David looked up into Joey's face and he could see, Joey wasn't about to move.

"Come on Joey; let me pass before the teacher comes out looking for me."

"What makes you think that she'll come looking for you. You her pet?" Joey screamed.

David's face reddened from the insinuation. He drew the ball back and threw it at the face of his tormentor. The ball slammed against the closed door and took a crazy bounce. David was already angry when he remembered his dad's words, *"Hit him hard before he hits you."* David took a swing with all his might directed at Joey.

The grin on Joey's face was the last thing he would remember. Joey grabbed his outstretched arm and with a quick move ducked under David's body, pulling hard. David flew through the air just like the picture in the book Joey's father had bought for him. His head hit the pavement hard, blood flying from it.

At that same moment, Howard Manning came through the door. He had witnessed most of it from his office window. He had moved quickly, but not quick enough to prevent the incident. Moments later, David was being transported to the hospital in Howard Manning's car. Manning had thought of waiting for an ambulance but right or wrong he acted on his own. He could have the boy at the hospital by the time the ambulance arrived. He would deal with Joey later.

Pain, like the prongs of a fork being shoved up his nose, brought David around. He moved with a start.

"It's all right son, just a jump start by way of some smelling salts." The man who spoke was dressed in green hospital clothing and wore a stethoscope around his neck. David looked around in a daze.

"Where am I?"

"Public General Hospital. Seems you were on the short end of a fight. How are you feeling?"

"Dizzy, like I'm going to pass out."

The doctor placed his hand behind David's back steadying him. "You'll be all right son. What's your name?"

"David."

"Oooh," as David ran his hand up to the back of his head, "It hurts like crazy."

The doctor smiled, his young friendly face giving small relief. "You'll live. I've put stitches in some of the hockey players from your school. They all made it and you will too. Let me have a look at that injury."

David could feel the doctor gingerly touching around the spot that felt like a burn. He looked at David, smiled and said something to the assisting nurse. Fifteen minutes and five stitches later, David was wheeled into a hospital room and put into bed. The doctor was keeping him over night for observation.

"You can't kick my boy out of school just for hitting that Rivers kid. He told me all about it. The kid threw a football right at his head. He was just defending himself!"

Howard Manning looked at the man sitting across the desk from him. He was over weight, slovenly dressed, in dire need of a shave and the odour of stale beer emitting from Alex Gallo was repugnant.

Manning's eyes were solemn as he looked through his horn-rimmed glasses. "It wasn't a football that David Rivers threw at your boy. It was a soccer ball. The students had been playing with it during recess and David was responsible for the return back inside. Joey was blocking his way, attempting to cause a fight which eventually he did. I was just returning to my office and looked out the window when I heard the voices. The voices of your boy and young Rivers, I saw it for myself. I tried to run out and stop it but I wasn't quick enough. By the time I got there, David was lying on the ground unconscious, thanks to Joey."

Being a principal had its down side and dealing with men like Alex, with sons like Joey, made his job frustrating and tiring. As he began to speak his voice became louder, "We don't want him at this school anymore. You were here in my office less than six months ago and I warned you then what the outcome would be if Joey didn't stop picking on kids. It wasn't David Rivers that he was targeting then, so this is not an isolated incident. Joey's out!"

Alex blinked and tried to swallow the lump in his throat so he could speak. Ellen had sent him here after they received the letter from the school that Joey was being expelled. She was going to be mad at him again for encouraging Joey to be tough, not that it would be anything new. She seemed to be mad at him half of the time anymore.

"Give the kid another chance, I'll talk to him and straighten him out." Alex begged.

Manning shook his head. "That's what you said last time. I gave him another chance and he didn't take advantage of it."

Alex felt a moment of panic. "Well what am I supposed to do with him? He belongs in school."

"Not this school." Manning stood up and moved towards the door. "Good day Mr. Gallo!"

Alex was furious as he walked back to his car. He needed a beer. He didn't want to face Ellen just yet so he headed to one of his most comfortable hangouts – Sully's.

Joey had a good reason to wish that he was still in school, his mother and dad had gotten into a real shouting match after he was expelled. His father had always given the orders around the house and his mother was always the quiet one but that night his mother exploded. There was only one month left of classes and now due to the irresponsibility of Alex and the stupidity of her son, it was a year of school lost. Joey had never seen his mother so angry.

"I hope you're satisfied Alex Gallo! What are you going to do now, you know or should know how important an education is to a man."

He remembered how surprised his dad was that his mother was speaking to him in that tone. Alex's face was red as he shot back. "I never went to high school and I turned out all right."

"Really? You work on a production line and will until you die, whether you like it or not. Drunk half the time, in fights in the bars, friends and neighbors shunning us because of the way you act and you passing all of this on to our son like a prize. You certainly are no model to your son."

Adrenalin

"You better shut your mouth," Alex said as he tried to gain control but she had been saving this anger for too long and she wasn't about to give in.

"Me? Me shut my mouth? I have kept quiet for too many years. My mother told me not to marry you and that's the biggest mistake I ever made. I can tell you one thing, Joey isn't going to lie around this house and do nothing." She glared at Alex and didn't even stop to breathe, "If he's not in school, first thing tomorrow he can take our lawnmower, and after he finishes cutting our grass, he can go around the neighbourhood, find lawn cutting jobs and earn some money. He can find out first hand what life is like without an education, he might like it! By the way, you both left me to cut the grass and just so you know, I have cut grass for the last time. I do too much around here and it's over!"

This was the first time that his father wasn't the violent one, yelling or threatening to hit her, as he sometimes did. Today wasn't the day, she wasn't going to back down, in fact she probably had a lot more to say but he didn't want to hear it. So the best thing to do was to keep quiet.

Since his mother had laid down the law, Joey had found himself working more than he ever had in the past. It wasn't all bad though, his dad had taken him aside and told him to just cut enough lawns to get some spending money and then hang around the pool room, until it was meal time. Good advice he thought, but if it wasn't for Rivers he would be out having fun. He still owed him and one day it would be pay day.

3

"How are you enjoying your summer holidays, David?"

David looked across the table at his dad. This wasn't just polite conversation, there was more and he knew that he probably wouldn't like it.

"Good. Real good."

"So how do you fill your day?"

David put on his best smile. "Swimming, playing ball at the park with Jimmy and just hanging out."

"Interesting," said John Rivers, "thought anything about earning a bit of money this summer?"

So that's what this is about. "Maybe when detassling corn begins, Jimmy and I have talked about going."

John smiled the kind of smile that let David know this wasn't the end of the conversation. He glanced over at his mother who was unusually silent, He could see that his parents had already discussed summer work.

"I drove to the place where they hire students for the summer, yesterday. A bunch of kids were just getting onto a small school bus. They were all carrying lunch bags and hoes. I want you to go down there tomorrow and see if there's any work for boys like you and Jimmy, or just you, it don't matter."

"We were going to wait until…"

"No. Tomorrow, You and Jimmy have played around enough."

It was the next evening at dinner, as John Rivers passed the potatoes, he asked the same question. "So, how did your day go, David?"

David knew where this was leading. "Me and Jimmy went and checked out the summer employment place."

"And?"

"And, we start tomorrow. We have to supply our own hoe and lunch and be there by seven o'clock in the morning."

John was more thrilled than his son, as he winked at his wife. "That's good. Right after we eat we'll go out to the shop and sharpen a hoe up for you on the grindstone. Has Jimmy got one?"

"Yes, I asked him yesterday. His mom's got one that she uses in the garden. He said it was sharp enough. Can you give us a ride in the morning?"

"Yup. It's right on my way to work. Call Jimmy and tell him if he wants a ride to be here at quarter to seven, at the latest. How much an hour are they paying?"

David made a face. "The going rate. That's what the man at the centre said when Jimmy asked him. We're just not sure what the going rate is, but we'll get whatever the rest do."

"Good."

Promptly, at seven o'clock the next morning the two boys, clutching their tools, watched as a small school bus pulled up to the curb. They climbed in along with twenty or so other kids. The noise inside the bus sounded much the same as it did at school just before entering class, only happier. Judging from the conversations, most of these kids had done this the day before.

It was a short ride on a paved road to a farm, just a few miles out of town. As the bus drove up the driveway, David could see the rambling farm house, the well kept yard and a line of mature maple trees leading up to the door. Behind the house were drive-sheds and barns. A solitary tractor sat in front of the drive-shed. The bus came to a stop; the door opened and out filed the kids into the morning sun. David noticed that they all left their lunches on the bus, taking only their hoe as they exited. He and Jimmy did the same.

A tall thin figure, that looked much like his grandfather, emerged from the house. He was dressed in denim bib overalls and he wore an old straw hat pulled down on his head so that it stayed in place. The boots were the same colour as the black loam soil in the field where they were headed. As the farmer got closer, David could see that he was probably younger than he first thought. The way he was dressed, the grey hair and the weather beaten face were a bit misleading. His smile was friendly and showed a full set of white teeth. He slowed as he came up to David and Jimmy who were trailing the other kids.

"Morning boys, you two must be new kids. I don't recall seeing you here yesterday?"

"Yes sir, we are. I'm David Rivers and this is my friend Jimmy Allen. We're just starting."

"Ever hoe beans before?"

"I have but this is Jimmy's first time."

The farmer looked down at David's small friend. "I'm sure you'll do fine Jimmy. You boys should have worn hats though it gets hot in the afternoon," he said as he wiped his own brow just thinking of it.

The rest of the boys stopped, lined up one at the end of a row, probably just where they had finished the day before. Some were standing wriggling their feet back and forth, like runners waiting for the signal.

"All right boys, just like yesterday, don't miss any weeds. When you finish your row, come back and help those who haven't. We'll take a break every two rows."

It was like a production line starting up, as the chopping action of the hoes shredding the weeds began. David noticed that it wasn't too bad. The weeds were relatively few and the loam ground was soft. He had hoed in clay before where the ground was hard and the weeds more abundant. Jimmy caught on quickly and in spite of his size, was keeping up. He even seemed much more enthusiastic about the job than David did.

"How much a day do you think we'll earn?"

"Not as much as detassling corn. They said they paid the going rate. I see some of our school friends and I'll ask them at lunch. You mostly get paid every day, cause some kids don't always come back. I think we should be making a little over two bucks an hour."

Jimmy's face lit up. "Oh boy. That's sixteen bucks a day, if we work eight hours! I can buy some new clothes for me and maybe something for my mom."

Jimmy was more excited about the prospects of money than David but after a day of hoeing in the sun, Jimmy might lower his expectations. They went along, managing to keep up with the other kids without too much trouble. The morning went on and soon the two were separated as they didn't always end up side by side when the next row began.

It was after eleven thirty and David was beginning to get hungry. They would be stopping for lunch when they finished the row. He was concentrating on his work when suddenly he felt someone next to him.

"How's it going?"

David looked over to see the farmer. "Oh, I didn't know it was you, mister."

The smile was generous. "Ross, Charlie Ross. They didn't tell you who you were working for?"

"No sir."

They worked along side by side and talked as they neared the end of the row. The sound of a car coming up the gravel lane caught David's attention. He looked up. "It's the cops!"

Charlie Ross began to laugh, a full rich laugh, "Don't worry. He's not after you. That's my son Richard. He's with the Provincial Police and when he's close to home, he stops in for a meal. Well that's about it for this morning, time for lunch. Most of the boys have their lunch under those maple trees on the front lawn. It's shady and a little cooler. See you later, keep up the good work."

Jimmy was just finishing his row and coming towards him. They met up and headed for the bus to get their lunches and enjoy a well deserved rest.

It was cooler under the shade of the trees, just as Mr. Ross has said it would be. They lay down, their tired bodies sinking into the soft grass. It was hard work in the hot sun and their arms and backs were sore. Some of the boys were playing a game where each boy took turns flipping a jack knife until it landed point down sticking in the ground. There were ten various positions that had to be accomplished and the first to do so without missing, was declared the winner.

David looked at his watch, the dreaded time to go back to the fields was approaching, and it was going to be a long afternoon. He saw Charlie Ross and his son coming out of the house. His son was in uniform, a flat rimmed hat, light blue shirt and navy pants with a wide belt supporting a leather-cased revolver and a set of handcuffs. Slightly behind his back, where he could easily reach it, was his nightstick or 'billy'. Richard Ross was not as tall as his dad, and his hair was blonde and closely cropped. His shoulders were broad and his arm muscles were large and could be easily seen beneath the cotton shirt. David watched as he waved to the boys sitting beneath the trees, said goodbye to his dad and drove out of the yard in the patrol car. With a wave of his arm, Charlie Ross summoned the boys back to work.

John Rivers looked across the dinner table at his tired son. "How did work go?"

David could see from the look on his face that his dad was happy that he was working.

"Ya, it went okay. Jimmy was all excited when the farmer handed him a twenty dollar bill and said he'd see us tomorrow."

"And how did you feel when he handed you twenty? He did hand you twenty and you are going back tomorrow, right?"

"Of course he did. The money's all right, I gave it to mom to keep for me. I don't like hoeing though, as a matter of fact, I hate it. It's hot, boring, and it pays less than detassling. I'd rather be swimming."

Adrenalin

"Would you now? Get used to it Dave, this is what life is all about, not always being able to do what you want but sometimes doing what you have to do. And David, you have to do this."

David was sullen for a moment until his mother got up from the table, cleared the dishes and brought the pie that she had baked for him in celebration of his first day of work. She sat a big piece of it in front of him and he enjoyed every morsel while his dad carried on explaining the facts of life to his son.

"Cheer up, you'll probably have a few days off to go swimming and goof around between the time that the hoeing ends and the corn detassling begins."

The next morning, the two boys were early for work, David's dad had seen to that. They boarded the bus and sat near the back. Jimmy was happy and talked on about all the things he was going to buy. This was the first time that he had ever worked and gotten paid for it and he liked it. David had come to accept the fact that he might as well make the best of it since it wasn't going to change, which made him speculate how he would spend the money that his mom was holding.

As David stepped out of the bus he wasn't thinking of who else was on the bus, until he looked up and saw Joey Gallo looking straight at him. Being at the back of the bus and busy talking, he hadn't noticed Joey get on at the last minute. Even if he had it wouldn't make much difference, his dad had already made that clear.

They started for the field, hoes in hand. David felt a tug at his sleeve, it was Jimmy. "Did you see who was on the bus?"

"I saw him, our old pal Joey. Don't worry, Mr Ross won't put up with his fighting. He'll fire him and make him sit on the bus until quitting time, if he starts anything. I heard he did that to one of the kids who got into some trouble last week."

24

David and Jimmy had ended up on two of the worst rows in the field as lunch time approached. The rest of the boys left them behind and headed for the bus to get their food. David was hot, hungry and angry as he realized that he and Jimmy would have a much shorter lunch hour than the rest.

The police car was parked where it had been the day before as David and Jimmy finally made their way to the bus. Jimmy reached up into the overhead compartment of the bus and got their lunches. They walked towards the rest; some had already finished eating. As they headed over toward a shady spot to sit down, from out of nowhere David felt someone tackled him around the legs, sending his lunch flying.

"Joey!" yelled Jimmy, his eyes wide with fear.

Joey rolled and sprang to his feet. A vicious grin on his face as he glared at David. "There's no one here to protect you and you're going to pay for me being expelled, I'm going to beat you to a pulp you scrawny little bastard."

David was hot and already angry about the extra time in the field, all he needed was Joey to add to his day. David charged Joey hurling his body straight at him. They hit the ground with a thud rolling over and over until David landed on top, his fingers closed around the throat of his enemy. The boys who had been sitting quietly jumped to their feet, as they watched the fury of the fight now taking place. Joey's eyes quickly began to bulge from their sockets as he struggled to breathe. He delivered a series of fast and furious kidney blows to David's back, but to no avail. The look on David's face told a different story. The boy who was usually calm and quiet was now possessed and totally unaware of those who watched. Joey's body was limp as David towered over him.

Down the steps of the house came Charlie Ross and his son. The officer passed him as they ran towards the boys. David seemed possessed and he tightened his grip even more. Joey had blacked out by the time Charlie Ross had grabbed him, while his son struggled with David, trying to make him loosen his hold. Breathing heavily, David had broken into a cold sweat, and his arms were covered in bumps. His strength was more than the police officer could handle and as Joey was turning blue, in a last attempt to break the hold, Richard Ross took his billy and struck him. David slumped to the ground, his grip broken as the police officer shouted instructions to his father.

"Call an ambulance quickly dad, tell them to step on it!"

Turning Joey on his back, he checked and could see that he was no longer breathing. He quickly blew air from his mouth into that of Joey Gallo, stopping briefly to press rapidly on his chest, as he tried to revive him. The blare of sirens could already be heard from the city a short drive away. Charlie came running out of the house over to his son. "Is he coming around Rick?"

Between breaths, the officer felt for a pulse as he continued his life saving attempt as Joey lay still on the ground. Finally, the ambulance raced up the drive. Two men got out and ran over to Joey, and quickly administered the proper attention. When Joey's breathing had returned, they loaded him onto the stretcher and put him in the ambulance. David was lying on the ground, away from the crowd.

Charlie Ross looked anxiously at his son. "They found a pulse, a strong one. Do you think he'll be okay?"

"I think so. Get the name and addresses of the kids that witnessed this fight dad. Have you had trouble before with the boy I hit?"

"I've never had trouble like this before with any of the kids. That boy you hit, I was working beside him yesterday and he seemed like a real nice boy. I can't imagine what would make him go crazy like that."

For the second time in less than six weeks, David was shocked back into consciousness by the sharp pain shooting up his nostrils from smelling salts. He groaned as his eyes flew open and he looked around. He tried to struggle to his feet, but a force was holding him down, not letting him move.

His eyes fluttered again and an unfamiliar face came into focus.

"Easy, boy. Take it easy. See if you can sit up."

David sat up feeling weak and weird at the same time. He didn't recognize the person behind the voice. "Who are you? Where am I?"

"I'm a friend that's helping you at the moment."

The friend held up two fingers. "How many fingers am I holding up?"

David wobbled back and forth still feeling woozy. "Hold them still."

"I am holding them still. Let's try again. How many fingers?"

David squinted. "Two." He looked around. No one was there but him and this stranger. Further away, in the laneway was a police car with a policeman speaking into a hand held mike. He looked around again, this time into the face of the stranger. "Who are you?"

"I'm a paramedic. I came in the ambulance they called after the fight."

David looked around again and felt his head. He squinted again as the intensity of the sun seemed to blur his vision. "What fight?"

"You don't remember getting into a fight?"

"Who with?"

The paramedic walked over to the policeman who was walking towards them. David listened, only catching part of the conversation.

"He's had a concussion. I think he's all right, just kind of out of it. Says he can't remember the fight and I believe him. I've seen this sort of thing before, they just draw a blank."

David watched as the policeman shook his head. He still wasn't sure who they were talking about.

"That kid was going at the other one like a tiger. I thought for a minute that he had killed him. If I hadn't stopped him with my club, I believe he would have. He looks harmless sitting over there now, but you should have seen him in action. Like nothing I've ever seen before. I called the station. Do you think he's all right?"

The paramedic looked over at David and shook his head. "If you mean will he live? I'd say so. He's still sort of dizzy but I'm sure he'll come out of it. Might take a little time before his memory returns, but it probably will. He's young and tough."

Richard Ross raised his eyebrows at that last statement. "I can testify that he's tough all right. I phoned the station and they said that if he seems physically able, for me to bring him in, and put him in a holding cell. Just until it's decided what they will do with him or where they will take him. I'm going to put the cuffs on him. He's too much to handle if he decides to act up."

David's memory was starting to come back. Now he knew where he was and he remembered Jimmy and all of the kids that were sitting on the lawn. Beyond that, he couldn't remember much. The cop was coming over. He reached down quickly and David felt the cold hard steel handcuffs being placed on him. The voice was soft but strong. "Stand up. We're going for a ride."

He felt a hand being placed on his head as he was shoved down and into the back seat of the patrol car. He felt the car sag slightly from the weight of the two that got in and then the sound of gravel, as they pulled away and headed for town.

As the officer opened the door of the holding cell, he shoved him into the cage, turned the key and locked the door. From behind the officer, Richard Ross spoke.

"Take it easy and relax. A doctor has been called and he'll be here within a short time to examine you. How are you feeling?"

"Sick to my stomach and my head aches," said David, as he placed his hand on the bump on the back of his head. It was not very far from where the wound he received earlier has just healed.

The cop made a face. "If you feel like you're going to throw up, do it in the toilet. Don't make a mess in there."

"How long am I going to be here?"

"Make yourself comfortable. You'll probably be here for a while. If the kid you were fighting doesn't come around, you could be here for quite some time or more than likely, somewhere else in custody."

Constable Ross walked into the Police Station and headed for the Chief's office to give a report.

Daniels shrugged his shoulders. "We'll have to wait until after the medic sees him, then if he's all right, I want a judge to rule on this one. Exactly what was going on out there?"

Chief Roy Daniels sat back and listened as he ran his fingers through his thick white hair. He had heard enough and seen enough during his thirty-seven years on the job and almost nothing shocked him anymore. Still, for two boys of this age to be going at it as hard as this, was extreme. He reached down and picked up the phone while Constable Ross was still talking and dialled the hospital.

"Yes, this is Chief of Police Daniels calling. The ambulance brought a patient in about an hour ago, a Joseph Gallo. I would like to check on his condition." He sat back saying nothing for several minutes, before the person on the other end of the line got back to him. Then, the faintest of smiles crossed his lips.

"Oh that's good. Yes, yes. That is good news. So you did notify his parents and they are there? No, no. We'll take it from here. Thank you." He hung up and looked across at Richard, who was trying to listen to half a conversation.

"You can make out your report. I'll have the desk Sergeant call the boy's folks, the one that we have in custody that is and then I'll call Judge Harding after I talk to the doctor. Do you know the boy's name?"

"Yes, it was in his wallet. I believe that the desk Sergeant has it. I can ask him to call the boy's parents if you like."

"Do that."

It was the first time that Ellen Gallo had seen real fear in her husband's eyes. The call from the hospital that day to his work place had brought immediate panic. That Joey was in the hospital in imminent danger was in itself a shock even impossible! Joey could look after himself, Alex had seen to that. They rushed along the corridors of the hospital, a real sense of urgency as they hurried towards the emergency room.

A great sigh of relief escaped Ellen's lips, as the doctor came up to them and told them that their son was out of danger. At first, it was the same with Alex, although it didn't last long once he realized the danger had passed.

"I want to see my son, Doc!"

The doctor was dressed in a green surgical gown with a stethoscope hanging from around his neck. His eyes darted back and forth from one parent to the other, noticing the relief in the mother and the apparent anger that now seemed to be coming from the father.

"We're just going to keep him here for another hour or so Mr Gallo, to observe him and make sure that he is still breathing all right and that all of his vital signs are normal before we release him. Come along, I'll walk you down to him."

Alex began to quiz the doctor almost immediately. "How did this occur? Did the other kid hit him with a club or something, because Joey can really handle himself? I taught him how to fight and how to look after himself."

The doctor shook his head. "The police have all of that information. We just evaluated him when he was brought in."

"Did he have any marks on him? Like I mean a bump, where the other kid hit him?"

The doctor stopped and looked Alex Gallo in the eye. "From our assessment Mr Gallo, he had stopped breathing. There were bruises on the throat, especially in the windpipe area."

"You mean he was choked?" Alex gasped.

"That would appear to be so."

Alex turned bright red. "Someone tried to kill him?" He grabbed the doctor and screamed, "Tell me the damn truth, who did this?"

"Take your hands off me and keep your voice down Mr Gallo, this is a hospital. There are other patients, so calm down. Don't upset your son, he's had a harrowing experience and doesn't need anymore excitement and I'm too busy to put up with you." Doctor Howard spun on his heel, his large frame shaking with anger as he walked away. He paused at the nurses' station, giving brief but firm orders to the nurse who looked surprised at the gentle giant's tone today.

Joey didn't even want to talk about it. He knew how his father was going to react and at this moment, he dreaded it more than having that scrawny Rivers get the best of him. Slowly, he looked into his father's eyes. "Let's just forget it pop. I'll get even with him. He won't catch me flat footed next time."

"Who won't?" Alex screamed.

Joey hesitated. He was lying there, trying to think of some way to work around this. The truth would get out one way or the other.

Alex didn't get to finish the sentence, the nurse that appeared out of nowhere was adamant. "Doctor Howard left firm instructions Mr. Gallo. I am to escort you back to the waiting room, if you cause any kind of disturbance. Mrs. Gallo can stay with your son but you'll have to leave, now."

The look that Alex gave her was incredible as first his mouth dropped open and then sprang shut like a trap. "You can't order me..."

"I'll call security and you will be arrested if you don't leave at once."

As he was leaving Alex looked over his shoulder and made one last pass at the nurse - "Bitch!"

Adrenalin

David stood looking through the bars of the holding cell wondering how he had gotten there. He was still confused and somewhat disoriented. As he paced the perimeter of the cell he saw another man escorted to the end of the hall. This cell was smaller than his room at home with only a small cot and a blanket. The cement walls made the room cold and damp. He wondered how long he would be there. He was tired and exhausted from the fight. He only wanted to go home. It seemed like forever until he heard the heavy door open and footsteps quickly approaching. The guard and a small man with thinning grey hair dressed in casual clothes carrying a satchel stopped at his cell. The guard inserted the key and spoke to David as he turned it. "Step away from the door and move towards the back of the cell." He turned to the small man and in a more moderate tone of voice said, "He's all yours doc, just give a holler when you're done."

The doctor who examined David was not that friendly and David sensed that he didn't like jail cells much more than David did. Maybe it was the fact that he didn't like the kind of people that occupied them; hostile, drunk and disorderly like the one that had just been led in cursing and swearing at everyone, particularly the officer that had him in tow.

He looked at David with that evil grin and yelled, "You'll be popular in prison boy!"

David stared at the medic with quizzical eyes. "What's he mean?"

The doctor looked grim. "You don't want to know. Jail is a bad place for anyone. Don't worry about his kind, you won't be going where he probably will be anyway."

"Where will I be going?"

"You're just a kid. They don't put young offenders with those hard cases, not unless you make a career of breaking the law. If you do, you'll find out what he means and believe me, you won't like it. Besides being molested, you'll spend all of your waking hours counting the minutes until you're released. Sound like the kind of life that you would like?" The doctor looked around for a moment as if dreading the thought himself. "These places give me a bad feeling. Anyway, you check out all right, medically anyway."

Richard Ross arrived at the home of John and Marilyn Rivers, just down the street from the Gallo's residence. He knocked at the door and John opened it with a look of surprise.

"Can I help you?"

"Are you John Rivers, David Rivers' father?"

"Yes, what's the problem officer? Is something wrong with David?" the tone of his voice started to rise in concern.

"Well, actually there is, may I come in?"

Constable Ross proceeded to tell John and Marilyn about their son's encounter with Joey and that David was in jail waiting for a decision on what to do next. They were distraught and in shock.

"Your son is well and will be evaluated by a doctor. I believe that he will be seeing other people concerned with his safety and well-being tomorrow. I'm going to need a short list of some of David's school chums. I would like to interview some of them before the hearing in order to get a clear picture of what prompted this unfortunate incident. I would also like to ask both of you some questions, such as how long your boy has known the other lad and so on."

Fifteen minutes later, Constable Ross left the River's home with two pages of notes and four names and addresses of fellow class mates of both the boys involved in the altercation. The first on the list was Jimmy Allen. He lived a few blocks a way. Richard Ross looked at his watch; he would leave that chore until tomorrow. It had been a full day.

That night alone in the cell was one of the longest nights that David ever spent. This was what it was like to be a criminal. But how could he be considered a criminal, he was just a boy and it wasn't his fault, Joey had provoked the fight, as always.

He was checked on frequently by a guard who monitored David on suicide watch, something that David had not even thought about but apparently they had. David was scared and only wanted to go home. Where were his parents, he wanted his mother and father.

He slept intermittently, trying to figure out what made him react so violently. Then a horrible scream woke him, just after he had finally got to sleep. He ask the guard about it and his reply was, "Nothing, and if you stay in jail you'll get used to it." Afterwards, David lay there thinking about jail. It was a lonely place filled with horrible people and there was no way that he would ever be back to any kind of jail, not for any reason. After some time, he finally drifted off, turning and tossing all night on the rock hard cot.

The next morning, David was hustled into another patrol car. He wasn't restrained by the handcuffs that had bit into his skin. There was another officer in the car along with Constable Ross. Bernie was a young muscular police officer, larger and taller than Ross.

The morning traffic was light. They wheeled into the psychiatric wing of the hospital that was set apart from the main building. David and his friends from school used to refer to the building as the 'nut house'. Although they didn't know what that meant, it scared them and they stayed away from the building, not knowing what to expect from crazy people.

He had once asked his father why the kids called it that and his father said, "Some people have illnesses that are not visible, but are just as real as other problems. There are many reasons for mental illness, like stress or trauma, or sometimes it is just in their genes. You have to show more understanding and compassion for those that are being helped there. The word nuts, is cruel and is a word that people who don't understand mental illness, or are afraid of it, use."

Today, David was about to find out exactly what it was that his father had been talking about. The officers escorted him through the door and up the stairs to a waiting room, filled with empty chairs. David quickly scanned the room but it looked like any other waiting room in any hospital. The difference was the secretary, that sat in the small glassed-in office, had to unlock the door leading into the interior of the building. There, they were met by a male nurse who led them down a hallway into a large office, with gold lettering on the door that spelled out the word 'Administrator'. Beyond the office, was what appeared to David to be a lunch room with half dozen tables and four chairs at each table. One table was occupied by two male staff, having a coffee break.

Constable Ross turned to Bernie. "You and David can wait in there, while I deliver the paper work and see where we go from here."

"Do you want something to drink kid, a pop or milk?"

"Do they have chocolate milk?"

Bernie gave a broad generous smile as he looked down at the boy. "They probably do. Grab a chair and I'll be right with you."

David sat down at one of the tables as the officer walked over to the counter and moments later, walked back carrying a tray with a coffee, chocolate milk and a couple of Danish deserts. He smiled as he watched David devour the pastry and gulp down half of the glass of milk.

"Didn't they feed you at the lockup this morning?"

David shook his head. "I don't like porridge, and they just had white milk which I'm not too crazy about." He noticed the cop raise his eyebrows at the mention of the word crazy, as he quickly looked around for a response from the two at the other table. There was none.

Bernie relaxed as he ate and sipped slowly on his coffee. He was used to killing time, waiting for his partner to reappear.

As they sat there, a small balding man, a little older than David's father entered from the other door, at the far end of the cafeteria. At the same time as David spied him, so did the two male nurses. They both turned their attention towards the man and one of them said, "Henry, you're not supposed to be in here. I thought that you were in your room."

One of the male nurses glanced over at his colleague and said, "Go get a jacket Herb, I'll try to keep his attention until you get back. Hurry!"

Herb made a hasty exit; the eyes of the small balding man followed him. David noted the glossy distant stare and the disoriented look in Henry's eyes, as the male nurse began to talk to him.

"Come on over and sit down Henry and have some breakfast." There was no response. Only the same strange stare, that really didn't focus on anything. David heard the rapid beat of approaching footsteps as the other nurse hurried in holding the straight jacket. He looked over at Bernie who was taking it all in. Both male nurses drew closer to the small man as if he were an aggressive animal. Herb shook out the straight jacket, so that the arms of it faced the man as he spoke to him.

"Come on Henry, put your arm in here like a nice fellow."

The material of the straight jacket merely touched Henry's outstretched hand, when suddenly he went wild. Screaming and kicking at the nurses who were trying to put the restraint on him. He lunged forward knocking both of them off of their feet. Bernie jumped up and put one of his powerful arms around the neck of the frantic patient.

As the male nurses scrambled to their feet, Bernie let out a howl. "Geez, he bit me!" Out of the office came Constable Ross, followed by another man. Ross went for the crazed man's feet taking him down. The straight jacket was immediately brought into play as all four men, each bigger than the man that they were trying to restrain, as he put up incredible resistance. Biting, kicking and screaming he was finally brought under control, as one of the male nurses slipped behind him, away from the teeth that were snapping at him and fastened the strap of the straight jacket.

The man that had come out of the office with Constable Ross looked towards the two male nurses. "You'd better place him in one of the secure rooms for the time being. I'll see to it that his medication is increased for a few days. We're going to ship him out to St. Thomas. We just don't have the capacity to hold him here."

Subdued in the straight jacket, the man looked nothing like the maniac that had been there just moments before and he was easily led away. Constable Ross brushed his hair back in place with his hand as best he could and picked up his hat and put it back on his head.

He walked over to David and motioned with his eyes to the man in the suit and said, "David this is the doctor that will be in charge now."

David watched as the two police officers walked away and the doctor said, "Come with me David." David obediently followed him into his office and sat in the leather chair in front of his desk. David's eyes began to scan the office; the walls were bare, except for a number of diplomas and a few landscape pictures. David sat there, not knowing what was going to happen next.

"My name is Doctor Harry Hammond and I'm the chief psychiatrist here at General Hospital. I'm going to have our newest doctor work with you. I think you'll like him David, he's closer to your age than many of us. He should be here shortly."

In a few moments, two men entered the office. One, David recognized as one of the male nurses and a younger redheaded fellow in his thirties, with the beginning of a goatee probably hoping it would give him the distinguished look of a psychiatrist.

Hammond looked at the redhead as he spoke, "Doctor Armstrong, this is your next patient David Rivers." He looked over at the male nurse and then at David. "Jake here will take you to your room, while Doctor Armstrong and I have a little chat. He'll be down to see you in a few minutes."

As they passed two corridors lined with rooms with closed doors, Jake explained that these rooms held the more difficult patients. David had already seen one of those difficult patients.

"Doc Hammond must have felt that you're not a flight risk or that violent, so you get to go down with the general population."

They made a right turn, passing a large room with lounge chairs, where two middle aged men sat watching a television that was securely fastened well above their reach. "You can probably come down here and watch TV, if Doc Armstrong says that its okay, but stay in your room until after he speaks with you. Here we are."

David waited until the nurse pushed open the door of a small room, that contained a single neatly made bed, a toilet and a basin.

"Just relax David, sometimes these doctors take a while."

Doctor Armstrong appeared shortly after and sat down on the bed beside David. "So you and this other boy had quite the encounter?"

"I guess so."

"And you really attacked him."

"If that's what the report says. No harder than he's attacked me many times before."

Doctor Armstrong was busy with his pencil, taking notes. He smiled as he looked up, a kind of plastic smile, as if it had been rehearsed several times in front of a mirror.

"You were anticipating this fight then?"

David squinted, unsure of what he meant. "What?"

"You were ready to pounce on..." he looked down at his notes, "Joey Gallo."

"I didn't start it, he did. I just defended myself."

"It says here that you almost strangled him."

David said nothing for a moment. He wondered if this guy was here to help him or to try and keep him in here. He thought, before he slowly answered.

"Yes. I guess I just lost it for a moment, my temper that is."

"How often have you experienced this loss of control when you're angry?"

David smiled ever so slightly. "First time."

The psychiatrist wrote quickly. "Did you get the feeling of being ready to explode just before this incident?"

"To tell the truth, I don't even remember becoming angry. All that I can remember is walking past Joey with my lunch, him tackling me and my lunch go flying. The next thing that I remember is waking up and the sting of smelling salts in my nose."

"Is that the first time that you were revived with smelling salts?"

"Once before, when Joey threw me over his head and split my skull. That was the first time."

"Do you think that subconsciously you were waiting to get even with Joey?"

"No. He came after me."

Doctor Armstrong lay his writing pad on his knee. "How do you feel at this moment David? Are you tense? I want you to hold your right arm up over your head."

The doctor stood up, laid down his pad and gently ran his fingers over David's uplifted arm. "Just as I thought. You're all tensed up, just thinking about your encounter. I think that you were angry when you saw that boy and that is why you reacted so violently. You have an anger management problem and I'm going to work with you on this. You won't be allowed to leave here until you can manage it. If you had killed this boy, you wouldn't be here at this hospital. They would have moved you to a maximum security hospital and you would be waiting trial for manslaughter. I'll see you tomorrow David and I will help you. We will do it together."

The next day about three o'clock, the same male nurse that led him to his room the day before, now brought David into the cafeteria. To his delight, his parents were waiting.

The hugs and kisses that his mother gave him were most embarrassing, especially with the male nurse seated a short distance away, watching.

"Good to see you son," said his dad as he grasped his hand. "How are they treating you?"

"Good, real good. I thought that you and mom would have been here to see me before this."

"They wouldn't let us. We haven't exactly been sitting at home. As a matter of fact, we just came from seeing the Justice of the Peace. He cleared it so that we could see you."

David's mother burst into the conversation. "Why is it that you and Joey Gallo have to carry on like this David. His mother is very upset at this behaviour. You could have killed her son!" Out came the handkerchief as the tears started. "Is there a washroom handy?"

The male nurse heard her and stood, directing Marilyn Rivers to one just around the corner. John Rivers turned to his son.

"Your mother is taking this hard. She doesn't understand the Gallos like you and I do. What kind of treatment are they giving you?"

"They've turned me over to this young doctor that is bound and bent that I have an anger management problem and he insists on curing it, before I have any chance of getting out of here."

John Rivers nodded. "Well the good thing is that Joey is all right. You must have beaten the hell out of him. I know I told you to do whatever you needed if he ever came at you again, but I didn't tell you to try and kill him."

David shook his head vigorously. "Didn't happen like that dad. It was as if something took over my body. I don't even remember most of it. It wouldn't have mattered what you said, so don't blame yourself. It probably was anger that was bottled up and the bottle exploded. Maybe this doctor will help me some. I don't know."

"Well even if he doesn't, play along with him. We both know that you're not crazy. We're going to be moving if we can sell the house and get as far away from the Gallo's as we can, at least in this city. As long as you two stay away from each other, I don't think that there will be a problem. Alex is half the problem, the biggest half."

At that moment, the male nurse reappeared with David's mother. He was polite when he said, "Five more minutes folks, David has an appointment."

Over the next four days, David had daily sessions with Doctor Armstrong that lasted for an hour, sometimes longer. They took place in the confines of the doctor's office. The first one David would remember most vividly, thinking afterwards that perhaps there was something to anger management. The session began with David laying full out in a prone position on the famous 'psychiatrist couch'. Dr. Armstrong asked David to conjure in his mind a picture of his nemesis, Joey and then to begin to tell of how they met and when they got into fights. At first, it produced the desired effect that the counselor wanted. David's body began to react in an extremely stressful way, full of tension, in spite of the fact that David tried to suppress those feelings.

Dr. Armstrong would then attempt to show David how to redirect his anger through exercises. One exercise included lying flat out with his eyes shut and clearing his mind of all negative thoughts. Then the doctor focused his thoughts on deep breathing, taking a large amount of air, filling up his lungs with oxygen and then slowly exhaling all of the air in his lungs. He made David repeat this, until it became easier. Next, he started to concentrate on relaxing his body. First, David's arms taking them from tense and hard to limp and rubber like. Then the legs, feet and the back to the neck and head until David's body was so relaxed he was almost asleep. The doctor talked to David about his ability to fight the feeling of tension and anger and how to put his thoughts in a mental place to relax his tension.

At the end of the session, David was amazed at the calming effect it had on his mind and body. David realized how much better he felt, but also realized that as he thought back to that day, it was more than just anger. There was something stronger, even sinister about the person he had become during the fight. A built in protector unfathomable, deep down inside that couldn't have been stopped with mere relaxation exercises. That inner being that seemed to have sprang forth and engaged Joey Gallo on that day. He was not going to confide that to the psychiatrist. How could he, he didn't even understand it, nor could he remember enough about that day to talk about. As his dad had said, 'play along with, him we both know your not crazy'.

After the second day, Dr. Armstrong would take David down to the cafeteria where they could talk easily. David would have chocolate milk while the doctor had coffee, and sometimes cookies which they shared before David went back to his room.

On one of their sessions, after the doctor was finished David had something he wanted to know. "Mind if I ask you a question, Dr. Armstrong?"

"Of course not David, that's what we are here for."

"That first day that I arrived here, right here in this cafeteria, the male nurse and those cops that brought me in had to put a restraint on a small man."

"I remember. Henry. Yes, we sent him down to a long term care facility in St. Thomas. Patients diagnosed with severe illnesses don't stay here."

"Well, I wasn't really asking where he went. I was just curious how come it took four strong men to control him? Like without being angry, I could probably handle him myself."

"Now we're getting into his mental state and the complication of his illness."

David shook his head negatively. "No, no. You're taking this wrong. What I want to know is where did he get all of that strength?"

"Probably the same place that you did. You see, picture the human body as a small factory. The food that you eat is the energy that drives the engine. The waste that it doesn't use, is flushed down out. The heart pumps the blood to every vital organ of the body, including the brain that orchestrates every movement that you make, follow me?"

David showed remarkable interest as he said, "Yes."

"Good. Now, the nerves of your body react to pain. If you're cut or burned, those nerves send the message to your brain that tells you to move your hand away from the fire, or to cover that cut with a band aid. Within everyone, there are body defense mechanisms to protect us. One of these is a chemical known as adrenalin. Sometimes it is produced on demand, like when something frightens you suddenly, or if you're in danger. In some mysterious way, adrenalin brings to the surface superhuman energy and abilities that are conventionally inaccessible. Adrenalin produces all sorts of responses, sometimes called the fight or flight reaction. It prepares your body for the extra effort required if you need to defend yourself, or run away from a predator."

David thought about the times Joey attacked him and began to wonder if Adrenalin had that affect on him.

The doctor continued, "Adrenalin will make your heart beat faster. It will make you breathe more deeply. It will bring you out into a cold sweat and your skin will be covered with goose pimples. It may even make you vomit and it can cause your bladder or bowel to lighten the body in readiness for escape or defense. All these reactions are designed to help you survive a dangerous situation."

David's mind went back to times when he had gotten angry, like when Joey jumped him at the farm. He could vaguely remember some of those feelings taking place during these periods of anger. David looked at the doctor and said, "Does it make you stronger?"

"There have been examples where a man was working under a car and it fell off the jacks and trapped him. People who came to help have been said to physically lift the car up by themselves, while someone else pulled the trapped person free. Adrenalin gives the body tremendous strength, but only for a short time." The doctor paused and looked at David; he was quiet and deep in thought. "That's where Henry got all of that power. While we don't really know what sets him and those like him off, we do know the strength comes from within. I think that is what happened the day that you overpowered the boy that you couldn't handle before. What I haven't figured out is why you can't remember. I don't think that you're mentally ill, or you'd be in here for much longer."

By their last session, David was beginning to understand where the power in his body lay. That day in the cafeteria, the doctor wasn't having anything to eat or drink, although he had gotten milk for David. Just before they completed the session, David glanced over at the female psychiatrist who had come in and sat down at the table across from them. David watched the woman and unless he was wrong, she was reading Armstrong's lips as he spoke.

"Well David, the nurse will take you back to your room. You're out of here tomorrow and I may not see you, so I'll wish you goodbye and good luck. I believe that we have made some real progress on learning how to manage your anger. You don't want to end up in some institute like poor old Henry for the rest of your life." He smiled at David and then his face turned serious. "If the public feels that you are a danger to society, because you cannot manage your rage, you could be institutionalized to protect them as well as yourself just like Henry. But I'm sure that you'll be able to cope out in the world and that we'll never see you back here again."

David reached over and shook his hand as he smiled. "You won't Doc. Thanks for all your help." He walked towards the male nurse that would take him to his room.

Doctor Armstrong walked up to the counter, got a coffee and a chocolate chip cookie and walked over to where Doctor Joan Smith had sat watching him. "Mind if I join you?"

She smiled. "Not at all, although I'm almost finished my break. I have to be at the administration office in five minutes. How's it going with your patient?"

"Great. He's going home tomorrow. It's very rewarding knowing that you've had a positive effect on someone."

She smiled again. "I've been observing you both from a distance."

"So what do you think?"

It was the smug look that puzzled him. "I was watching him as you described that if he couldn't control his rage he could be permanently confined."

Surprise was on the face of Doctor John Armstrong. "How did you know what I said?"

"I spent part of my internship in a deaf mute ward where I learned how to read lips, at least good enough to get the general drift." she said raising her eyebrows.

"And?"

"Either you've done a wonderful job, or..."

He looked pensively at her. "Or what?"

"Or he's still hiding something. I saw a look of panic in his eyes at the thought of being confined in a hospital."

Dr. Armstrong's mouth dropped in disbelief as the cookie snapped in his fingers. He watched her get up and gracefully walked away. Who did she think she was? David was his patient and he knew more about him than her smug diagnosis.

4

It was four days after the incident at the farm that a black and white patrol car pulled up in front of the Gallo house. Alex heard the sound and saw the officer approaching on foot. Quickly, he set his beer down and buttoned his shirt over his large belly. He hurried to the door, opening it at the same time that the officer's fingers pressed the bell.

"Come in, I was expecting someone to come around. This is about the kid that tried to kill my boy isn't it?"

"In a way Sir, I have a court order with me that I am now presenting to you. You are Alex Gallo and your son's name is Joseph Gallo, and your wife's name is Ellen Gallo?"

"Yes."

"Then you are hereby served. You are to appear before the Justice of the Peace at the county court house on the specified date, place and time. Furthermore, Joseph Gallo is under house arrest, until after the arraignment. In other words, he is not to leave this house until after he appears in court."

Alex turned white. "What the hell do you mean he can't leave the house? He's the victim, damn it! Me and him were just going over to Sully's, I mean Sullivan's garage, after he gets dressed."

"Not today Sir, nor tomorrow. Not until the court day arrives, and even then not without the presence of both your wife and yourself."

"But ..."

The officer was already half-way back to his car by the time Alex slammed the door and hollered at his wife, "I'm going to Sully's."

John L. Sullivan Sr. had been named after the famous boxer and in 1934 when he opened the garage; the name was a big draw. The station was large with four bays and two pits, where cars were driven in for oil changes and grease jobs. And while the maintenance of vehicles generated much of the business, so did the sale of White Rose gasoline pumped by attendants from shiny glass pumps. John L. had installed a canopy roof that extended over the gas pumps, keeping both the attendants and the drivers dry. John L. did everything to meet his customer's needs.

John senior was a big man with jet-black hair and an infectious smile and was all business. He was well-liked by his customers and it was his pleasure to keep them happy. Business was good, very good until he passed away in 1964. It was then that his son and present owner John L. Sullivan Jr., or Sully as everyone called him, took over the garage.

Sully was of average height but slight of body. His hair was prematurely grey and the generous smile possessed by his father was non-existent, but instead a sly grin sometimes presented itself. Sully had not inherited his father's ambition or personality.

The gas station pumps were now empty and they had been since Sully took over from his dad. The White Rose brand of gasoline had disappeared long ago and the company that bought them out had wanted to upgrade the station with modern electric pumps. Sully turned their offer down. He had no desire to pump gas. Now the grass grew up around the pumps and under the canopy sat the cars waiting for repair, blocking the view to the garage entrance from the public.

Sully made his living, if you could call it that, by fixing cars in the old bays inside. That was the legitimate part of the business, the part that he filed income tax on. Just enough to keep the tax man from the door. The rest of his income came from the cards and crap games held in the back room. That and the booze that he bootlegged, kept him living the easy life that he enjoyed. But the sale of illegal alcohol had started to fade in the past few years with the extended hours of the local bars. A group of local bikers had begun to frequent his place. Here at the edge of town, here where the noise of the motorcycles, the leather garments, tattoos and long hair of the bikers were to a degree, out of sight and out of mind.

Sully's new friends introduced him to a new source of income, but with the potential of more danger. It started with white powder, but soon turned to all kinds of drugs. Sully had made contact with a friend of a distant cousin that had been in jail and knew where to buy all that he needed. Before long, Sully had a thriving business using the bikers to help move the stuff. He was always looking to expand, but he needed another runner he could count on.

Just as Sully was working on one of the motorcycles, he looked up and saw his old school friend Alex Gallo approaching. "Alex my man, how you doin'. What are you drinking? I'm buying today."

Sully sat back, that sly smile showing. "Looks like you have a full head of steam on today."

"Ah. The cops just dropped off a summons for me to appear before the Justice of the Peace day after tomorrow. Told me that my son couldn't leave the house, not even to come over here with me! That damn Rivers kid nearly killed him and it's us being treated like criminals. When I get in front of that judge, I'll give him a piece of my mind!"

Alex twisted the cap off of the bottle of beer that Sully handed him. He put it to his mouth and chug-a-lugged until the bottle was empty. Reaching into his pocket, he threw a five dollar bill on the scarred and cluttered desk that Sully used in his office.

"I need another," barked Alex. Sully handed him a frosty bottle and Alex attacked it like it was his first.

Sully sat looking at Alex. "Don't go off half-cocked man. You're not just up against one man, you're up against the system. They don't give a fuck about you. Use your head and play dumb. Try to get this guy, this Justice of the Peace on your side. What's this all about anyway?"

"I don't know what to think, it's the first time I've heard of it."

"I was going to tell you," Alex said as he looked annoyingly at his wife. "Sully, I mean John Sullivan just told me about it yesterday."

It had caught Ellen by surprise and before she knew it, she heard herself saying, "It's all right with me."

"In that case, I will give permission for your son to go to work. That's all though. For the next thirty days, after work he is to remain at home. The house arrest still applies in that regard. In thirty days, we'll see how things are working out. One other thing, from here on your son is to have no contact whatsoever with David Rivers. The same thing will apply to David. Is that clear to all parties?"

The 'yes' that came from John and Marilyn Rivers were the first words that they had spoken since entering the room.

"Then you and your wife are excused, Mr. Gallo. I will see you back here in thirty days. An officer will deliver a summons to you before then. I wish both you and your son success in this endeavor. John and Marilyn Rivers, I ask you both to remain so that we can discuss your son David."

The Justice of the Peace watched as the Alex and Ellen left the room. His demeanor quickly changed. He smiled as he laid his spectacles on the table and relaxed as he turned to John and Marilyn. "Just maybe a full time job for this Joey Gallo might be a good thing. I have read the report that Howard Manning sent over and being around adults, instead of younger people might be exactly what the boy needs. It might be what it takes for him to get away from this bullying. After meeting his father, I can see where the problem begins. I see that you are neighbours. How long have you known each other Mr. Rivers?"

John glanced at his wife before he spoke. "A long time for me. Alex and I had our problems, similar to the animosity between our sons."

"And was Alex Gallo the aggressor?"

"You could say that."

Adrenalin

"Ah, yes. I think I get the picture. The report from the hospital indicates that it was pent-up anger from being harassed by young Gallo that precipitated the incident. The attack on Joey was indeed serious, very serious. I guess that our main concern is whether this is an isolated incident or not. The long range possibility of this happening again is of great concern naturally. I have studied his school records and behavioural patterns leading up to this. On the surface, I hope that this is a one time thing and all things considered, I believe it is. The part about those two staying away from each other, I trust that you will monitor your son and if there is an infraction to contact the authorities. Do you have any questions?"

"We have decided to put our house up for sale," said John. "It's just going to be too hard to keep the two of them apart, as long as we live as close to each other as we do. When we move, it will probably be to the other side of town. We were thinking of moving before this got out of hand, in part for this very reason. Of course we didn't think that it would escalate to the degree that it has."

"No, of course not. I think under the circumstances though, that you are making a wise decision."

5

John Rivers cleaned the grill of the barbeque with the scraping tool from the barbeque set. He didn't like cooking food on a surface that had set for the past few weeks with residue still clinging. As the match met the escaping gas, there was the usual boom that occurred as ignition took place. He closed the cover, sat down and had a cool sip of beer. He waited and when the thermometer on the cover of the barbeque reached 400 degrees, he decided that it was hot enough to put the steaks on.

John heard the back screen door open and looked up to see his son walking out onto the patio. He had grown taller than his father, but the resemblance was unmistakable. David was smiling and that was a good sign.

"So how did it go?"

"Went good, real good. They asked to see my high school diploma and then I got in to meet with the personnel manager."

John Rivers was impatient. "And then?"

David's smile broadened, he could see the anticipation in his father's eyes. "I have a one o'clock appointment with the manager tomorrow. If he likes me, I'm in and I'm almost sure that I've got the job by the way the personnel manager spoke. Apparently, they were looking for an apprentice in the tool room. I guess that they had been advertising for a certified die maker and none of the applicants were qualified enough and so they decided to train their own. Lucky for me."

"Oh that's good news. Go tell your mother."

"I already did, she's happy for me and is going to make me a pie."

"Well I'm happy too, but go in and bring out a platter for these steaks, it's time to eat."

The next day it was around twelve-thirty and David was just leaving the house when Jimmy Allen yelled, "Wait up David."

"What are you doing in this neighbourhood, Jimmy?"

"Schools out and it's hot enough to go swimming. We rigged up a swing in a tree down by the river yesterday. You can swing out and drop right into the water. We must have spent a couple hours or more there. It's neat and lots of fun. I just want to know if you'd like to go."

David shook his head, "Can't, not now anyway, maybe later. I think I've landed a job and I'm on my way to an interview."

"Gee that's great. I had some good news too. My oldest sister Shirley got in to St Joseph Hospital as a candy stripper. It don't pay anything, but it's the first step into becoming a nurse. I got a job there too. It don't pay much, just spending money at first. I'll be helping out cutting grass and trimming hedges, but if I work out good, they say that there might be an opening later on in the lab, when I graduate next year. The priest put in a good word for us. Actually, I think that we got the jobs because of Father Labelle. He's been real good to our family ever since dad died."

"That's great Jimmy. I got to get going. I'll give you a call after supper."

David was about to enter the Personnel Office of the Atlas Stamping Plant when he heard the roar of motorcycles and then saw them come racing into view. The plant was located on the same side of the river, as Sullivan's vintage gasoline station. David had heard that Joey Gallo was working there and one of the bikers looked like Joey, as the group raced past. If it was Joey, he hadn't seen David which was the way that David liked it. He hadn't seen or talked to Joey since the hearing.

About the same time that David sat down for his interview, Jimmy Allen and two of his pals were peeling off their clothes at a small beach on the banks of the Thames River, called Sandy Bottom. The bikers had passed by the beach and Jimmy had also seen Joey riding with the others. They had seen Jimmy too, but had kept riding away. Jimmy was always leery of Joey Gallo, so when he heard the sound of a motorcycle, warning bells went off in his head. But the sound came from the other side of the river, back behind the bushes that lined the other bank. Then, all was quiet once more.

The boys couldn't wait to cool off and Buddy Rodgers was first to grab the rope and swing as far as he could out over the water and then dropping into the middle of the river. Moments later, he emerged and all you could hear was, "Eeeh yow! That first plunge is cold!"

Martin Cole was next and reacted in much the same manner and so it went with Jimmy Allen being last. They had played their game for about fifteen minutes.

"This is my last swing Buddy," said Jimmy as he grabbed the rope and prepared to swing out over the river. "We should get going pretty soon."

He swung out high and was about to let go when from the far side of the river, Buddy and Martin heard what sounded like a fire cracker, but Jimmy didn't hear it. The bullet that tore into his body would forever end his hearing, as he dropped straight down and into the muddy Thames.

Across the river, Joey 's grin was evil as he broke down the twenty-two rifle, sticking each one of the parts into his saddlebag, as he and his partner revved up their bikes and rode away, unseen by a living soul. He had settled a part of a long standing feud. Someday, he would settle the other half.

The police officer that broke the news to Jimmy Allen's mother almost broke down in tears himself. This was the worst part of the job he thought, as he watched the widow lady and her girls weep for the only man that was left in the family. The police had no suspects and no one had seen anything until the bullet hit. It was not going to be an easy case to solve.

Friends, relatives and neighbours attended the graveside ceremony that week, including David and his folks. Jimmy had been a good friend for a long time. As the coffin was lowered into the ground, the undertaker threw a handful of dirt onto the coffin, as it came to rest on the cold hard earth. Life wasn't fair. Jimmy should have been around much longer, enjoying life. The sorrow David felt for his friend, was unimaginable. David felt guilty. Jimmy had asked him to go with him that day, but David had to go to the interview, otherwise it might have been him who was being laid to rest. His body trembled, as he hugged Jimmy's mother and sisters at the graveside. The joy of finding a job the same day as Jimmy was killed, took away all the pleasure that he would have experienced.

As David and his parents walked away from the grave, he saw someone in a black leather jacket moving away from a group of trees, in the far corner of the cemetery. David couldn't make out who it was, but there was something familiar about the way he walked. David wondered if the police would ever find the bastard who did it.

Ellen Gallo read the headlines in the newspaper and gasped as she read the front page. She new that name, Jimmy Allen. As she read on, her eyes became moist. It was all in there; how the three boys had been swimming, how the shot came from behind the bushes on the other side of the river. She read how Jimmy was supposed to be getting a job, to help out his widowed mother and his sisters. Suddenly, she stopped reading and gazed off thinking; wasn't that the name of the boy that David Rivers had stood up for when Joey got into trouble at school. Joey had never gotten over that whole situation. Her heart started to pound and her mouth filled with saliva, she had trouble swallowing and her breath came in rapid succession.

She put her hand to her mouth, oh no she thought; Joey wouldn't have had anything to do with this, would he? She went back out and read the paper again, the part about the kind of bullet that killed him. Her heart skipped a beat, a twenty-two caliber. That was the same caliber as the rifle that she had bought for Alex the first Christmas that they had been married. She knew where it was kept and she hurried to see if it was still hanging there. Her heart was pounding as she opened the closet door and looked in. It was gone.

She started to shake uncontrollably and then began to cry. Maybe she was wrong. It just couldn't be. On the other hand, there was too much coincidence. Joey was a changed person ever since he had begun to work for Sully. She hated that name. Every night Alex headed over to Sully's and Joey practically lived there. Joey was only home occasionally and that was so she could do his laundry. His clothes were dirty and smelled of things other than oil or grease. He was also treating her with the same disrespect that Alex did and what was worse, was the fact that Alex thought it was funny.

Neither one of them knew that she had overheard a conversation just a few months ago, when both of them thought that she was at the grocery store.

"Ah, that kind always tries to trap you. What did she say when you told her to get an abortion?"

"She screamed and hit me. I told her that I didn't think that it was mine and you should have heard her howl then."

They had both started to laugh and Ellen had nearly been sick to her stomach, but she continued to eavesdrop.

"So now she's in the place for unwed mothers that the church runs. She can adopt it out or keep it, I don't care. She was a good roll in the grass anyway pop, but now she's as big as a cow and twice as ugly."

Ellen couldn't listen to the rest. She was ashamed and bitter. Alex was too stupid to know that the child that would be given away would be his grandchild, but neither would make great role models for any child. She was well aware that the child would carry her blood and in her heart, she knew that where ever the little one was placed, it would be better off. She would try to keep track of the whereabouts of her grandchild. Ellen knew the girl that Joey had gotten pregnant and she would do whatever it took to help when the time came.

For some time now, Ellen had been saving very small amounts of money from the grocery allowance. She hid it where neither Alex nor Joey would ever look, where the dish soap was kept. Some day, they would come home to an empty house. She was truly afraid of Alex though and what he would do to her if she tried to leave. Now, she was afraid of her son as well. Joey had crossed the line.

6

After four years of apprenticing in the die trade, in May David finally became a certified journeyman Tool & Die maker. His first purchase was a Ford pickup truck; it was dark green in colour with a camper top. He also moved to a rented apartment at the back of a house on Water Street. His apartment faced the river and in the summer, provided a serene and private place. For David, life was looking up. He even had a girlfriend, Jennifer and at twenty-five, it was time to start thinking about settling down.

But there were times he found his mind drifting back to Jimmy Allen's tragic death. Although the case was still open, the police had never solved the crime. In his own mind, he was certain of who was responsible. He was sure Joey was the man who walked away from the grave sight that day, and the shadow haunted David like a nightmare he just couldn't shake.

David did not think that he would ever need to resort to the anger management counseling, but lately he found that it was the only way he helped calm his inter-self. In the quiet of his room he would lie stretched out on the bed, breath in slowly through his mouth, exhale through his nose and attempt to ease the tension in his body. He would descend into a meditated state until he fell asleep. But like an obsession, it would not leave, it just kept reoccurring. It was something that would have to learn to live with and try to control.

Adrenalin

That year David had gone to the company Christmas party. The big draw prize was a trip for two to Las Vegas. David's buddies all started talking about what they would do if they won but David really didn't give it much thought, as he wasn't big on travel. They were about to announce the winner. The room was silent and the Plant Manager put his hand in the big drum, pulled out a ticket and announced in a loud voice the winner's name: David Rivers.

The table went wild. The guys were all over David to take them with him on the trip. At first, David didn't care but the more they talked the more he got excited. But who would he take? Would it be his new girlfriend or his best friend at work, Donald Summers? He had not been dating this girl for a long time, whereas Donald had been his best friend and he was convinced he would be able to do more and see more if it was with another guy.

Once the word was out that David and Donald were going to sin city, it wasn't long before two of Donald's friends decided that the trip would be fun and wanted to come along. David thought why not, the more the merrier; and so on one cold day late in January, they flew off to Vegas escaping all the ice, snow and dreary days.

For David's first flight, it was good. The plane was a wide-bodied jet which made it possible for all four to sit together. David sat on the aisle seat, next to Donald who kept up a constant chatter with the two buddies, Steve and Allen, who had come along. The sound of excitement filled the plane like a bunch of kids all wound up going to strike it rich in Vegas..

An older grey haired gentleman in the seat ahead had been to Vegas before and could be heard telling his travelling companion about the trip. "It's always the same on the planes headed for Vegas. Everyone chattering like magpies excited about the prospects of big winnings. Most of them are all cleaned out by the time they return and the entire plane is quiet. They swear they'll never go back to that place. Then less than a year later they're off again, this time the plan is to win back what they lost the year before. Just a vicious circle."

His travelling companion laughed. Donald just rolled his eyes and looked at David for a moment. It must have made him think because he leaed forward in his seat and pulled his wallet out of his pocket. David grinned, watching Donald's lips move silently as he took inventory of the contents of his wallet. He separated some of his cash putting it in a separate part of his wallet, probably enough to see him safely home.

"Hmm," David thought 'maybe I'd better take a page out of Donald's book and protect my own assets.'

It was ten o'clock as the plane began its descent towards the airport. The pilot's voice came over the intercom telling them to fasten their seatbelts while giving the time and weather conditions in Las Vegas. The plane bounced slightly as it broke through the clouds and into the bright sunlight that shone over this Mecca in the desert. It was not exactly the barren desert that he had expected. Instead, he was surprised to see the mountain ranges that surrounded the city and the wide stretch of highway lined with buildings and palm trees. Hotels with large lighted marquees dominated the strip and beyond lay the urban sprawl. David had no idea how it could continue to transform itself into the magic attraction that would take place after the sun went down.

A loud cheer went up as the wheels of the plane touched the runway. The sound of the wing flaps dropping and the brakes brought the DC-10 to a stop. David looked over at Donald and the others and said, "We made it. Our first flight! How did you guys like it?"

"Great! And it's only going to get better Dave!" It was time to party.

The white taxi cab whisked them along Las Vegas Boulevard. The sights were amazing, things they had never seen before; magnificent hotels and casinos, palm trees, people, cars of all kinds including Rolls Royce and Jaguars.

More sights than four country boys could have ever imagined.

The taxi was Donald's idea. David was all for taking the shuttle down to the Phoenician where they were staying. But as they rode in the cab, they knew it was the better choice. It turned out, of course, that the driver was a Las Vegas veteran, having lived there since the place started to boom, although they never did hear just when that was. He gave them a guided tour as he kept pace with the rest of the traffic. Grey hair stuck out from under his faded cap as his head swivelled from one side to the other while he described the city and how it had changed.

"The strip, as it's called, was just a dirt road when my dad first moved here. All of the action used to be up on Fremont Street downtown, when I was a kid. Then Bugsy Segal moved out here and built the Flamingo, it brought a lot of the business here from uptown. Boy, if I had been smarter and invested in property 20 or 30 years ago, I wouldn't be driving this cab now, no sir."

"Course you had to be careful back then, there were a lot of gangsters here and you weren't sure who you could trust. I kept my nose clean. It is different now though, the government and the gaming commission began to change all that. Big money moved in to some of the other big casinos, like the Phoenician where you guys are staying, and everything changed. Property right here along this strip is worth a mint. There's lots of land for sale around Vegas, some not a bad price but not right here. They've even started to tear down some of the old casinos and build new ones costing millions. It's location that makes the difference. It's where the action is. How long are you boys here for?"

David spoke up, "Four days and three nights. Where is the best place to eat and see the shows?"

The old man shook his head. "It's all good here. Caesar's Palace has a great buffet. Lots and lots of food, anything you can imagine, champagne too, all you can drink. For entertainment, right where you're staying is good. Bobby

Black's show is always sold out but if you're a paying guest they can probably get you in. Then in the big show room there's a show called Hallelujah Hollywood. Me and my wife went to see it. They have a big stage production with a whole ship that comes right up out of the floor. Lots of dancing gals with bare breasts."

David looked over at his friends. The last statement that came from the cabbie caught their attention. Yes, it was party time all right.

They wheeled into the long driveway leading into the Phoenician coming to a stop under the canopy and, just like in the movies; the door man opened the car door for them. The opulence and the glitter, the sheer magnitude of the Phoenician hotel and casino literally blew them away. It was beyond their wildest dreams. Four boys from a small town suddenly found themselves in a place where the world came to play and it was overwhelming. David could see it on the faces of his companions as they entered the Casino. Even at noon it was filled with people and was beginning to come to life with the dinging sound of the one armed bandits.

After checking in they went up to their rooms. The palatial rooms were way beyond their expectations. David and Don were sharing a room with two beds while Steve and Allen were just down the hall from them. They had been busy laying plans for that evening before they had travelled down stairs. It was decided they would first try to get tickets for both of the shows that the cab driver had told them about but it was confirmed on the marquee of the Phoenician, the Bobby Black show was sold out for the week. No chance there, but there were tickets for Hallelujah Hollywood.

David was spokesperson for the group. The first woman they were about to encounter was at the ticket counter. A generously endowed blonde, who wore more than her share of makeup, smiled when David asked for four tickets for the Phoenician's premier show. All smiles, she pushed the tickets forward as she batted her false eye lashes.

Adrenalin

"The show starts at two. Please be in line at least fifteen minutes before show time."

David turned towards the other guys thinking that he had heard her wrong. They had the same stunned look on their faces that he must have had on his. He turned to face her. "No we don't want matinee tickets."

She chewed her gum even faster. "Those aren't matinee tickets honey. This is Vegas. That's two o'clock in the morning. It's not passed your bed time is it?"

David could feel his face getting hot and could guess that it was probably pretty red as well. "No, it's not passed my bedtime and yes, I shave and drink too!"

The guys were all having a pretty good laugh at him and momentarily, he began to laugh as well.

"What do you expect from a hick?" he said, as he handed each one their ticket putting his own in his pocket. David had taken inventory earlier in the room. Like Don, he had set aside fifty dollars, ace in the whole money, and was in good shape for some fun on the town.

All four of them stood in the doorway of the casino absorbing all of the wonderment. The room was large and huge chandeliers hung from the high ceiling. Rows and rows of slot machines filled the room. The bright lights made the room sparkle. The loud sounds, from all the people and the machines, were deafening. All kinds of noises came from those machines; bells, whistles, music and the sound of coins jingling in the trays as they fell. Hundreds of players squealed with delight if they were lucky enough to make the bandits cough up money. All these stimulations added to the excitement of the room. Not to go unnoticed were the cocktail waitresses in their scanty colourful costumes, dutifully handing drinks to patrons and smiling sweetly to those who tipped, sometimes handsomely if the player had a lucky streak running.

Donald's blue eyes were always sparkling and never quit moving around the casino. Donald was the first to come back to earth. "Okay guys. What are we going to play first?"

David answered, "Let's just spread out and play the slots for a while. It's going on four o'clock Vegas time, which is actually seven o'clock back home. We'll play for a couple of hours and then get something to eat. How about we all meet back at our room in two hours and then we'll wing it from there. If that show doesn't start until two in the morning, we're going to have a lot of time to put in."

David had been playing the slots for about an hour winning some and then losing it back again. He was hovering somewhere around even when suddenly Donald appeared wearing a grin from ear to ear.

"Come on Dave, I just hit a machine for a hundred and fifty bucks! I know where the other two are, so come on, supper is on me. Let's go over to Caesar's Palace and see if that cabbie was right about that buffet."

David followed Don as he rushed past the hundreds of people who filled the casino. It was natural that Steve and Allen were ecstatic with the news that Donny was buying. From the looks on their faces, fortune had not smiled on them.

They rushed out into the warm sunlight. Although it was warmer than the weather back home it was beginning to cool as the desert sun went down. The traffic began to pickup as they hurried across the street towards the Palace. Vegas was beginning to come alive and the overwhelming feeling, that generally affects anyone seeing this gambling Mecca, began to infuse the four of them. They walked quickly up the driveway leading to the Palace past towering ivory white statues of Roman gods. It all seemed so surreal, they knew they were in the twentieth century and yet the surroundings looked as though they were back in the land of the pharaohs.

David was walking alongside Steve with whom he hadn't really spoken to that much. Don and Allen were walking much more quickly as if they were walking towards a mirage afraid it would disappear before their eyes.

"Kind of takes your breath away doesn't it David?"

"It's something else all right. Like walking back in time or onto a movie set."

"Ya, it's all pretty terrific, these statues and the Palace that we're about to walk into. Thanks for letting us tag along. I had no idea this city was anything like this. Don got lucky in a hurry, lucky for all of us. I tried to budget each day and I'm not too far off of my limit for today after paying for my show ticket. That machine that I was on swallowed twenties as if it was starved to death."

Ahead of them Don and Allen had already walked through the massive doors leading into the Palace. It was Don who was impatient. The big win must have pumped him up. Looking back as David and Steve caught up he yelled, "Come on you two, your dinner awaits!"

After passing more slots and tables, they finally found the line leading into the buffet, strategically and poetically placed not far from Cleopatra's barge. Allen was the first to comment.

"Transcends the ages doesn't it. I mean the way that two people two thousand years ago let us dine at their place tonight. We're about to experience the golden age of Rome as we dine. I wonder just how close to those ages of antiquity we really are."

Steve laughed. "Speak a little louder, Al some of these people will never guess that you majored in history at college."

As they stood in line something caught David's attention, out of the corner of his eye. Someone had just exited the elevator and was walking so fast that one would have to run to keep up to them. Then he recognized the person, as did others, but not quickly enough for them to interrupt his line of travel.

"Hey there goes Jarrod!" All heads turned. It was Don who said, "It sure looks like him." The small figure disappeared before an ocean of people closing like the waters of the Red Sea.

"It was him all right" David said. "He walked through the crowd so quickly that if people recognized him it was too late for them to mob him for autographs and pictures. We actually saw a rock star in person; or rather we saw the back of his head. I'm the only one that actually recognized him."

"Right. You're not sure and neither are we," Don quipped.

At that moment the buffet line began to move forward and from behind them someone commented, "Did you see Al Jarrod? He walked by me so fast that at first I didn't recognize him. Women were trying to grab him as he walked by. Man was he ever going!"

David just smiled as the other three looked in his direction tongue in cheek.

That night and the next day would be one of the best and most memorable for David. The old English saying of 'eat drink and be merry' didn't even come close to the lifestyle that they experienced. Caesar's Palace had done a great job trying to recreate the splendour of Rome.

The show at the Phoenician didn't end until the wee hours of the morning. It was orchestrated in the same manner as the legendary movie studio whose name appeared on the marquis outside the casino. The costumes, the music and the beautiful women were all dazzling and the boys had the time of their life. As part of the show package, each had four drinks, alcoholic or not and so they tried everything; beer, Southern Comfort on the rocks, and martinis. The boys weren't used to drinking and luckily it was only a short walk to the elevator. None were fit to drive or even hail a cab.

No one was up early the second day. After all, it had been closer to daylight when they finally stumbled into their rooms following the show. They all slept until sometime in the early afternoon when it was time to get up and start the party all over.

The next day began much as the day before. They ate more than they should have at the buffet table at the Phoenician and then headed for the slot machines. David hung back a bit from the other three. The seven's just wouldn't line-up on the one armed bandit that was robbing him blind. After losing forty bucks, he decided to move away from the cash hungry machines. He didn't have to meet back at the room until about seven to plan the evening, so he thought he would explore the casino.

As he sauntered slowly along observing the tables of Craps and Black Jack, it felt good to be on his own for a few hours to be free to do as he pleased. After all, he was the one that won the trip. It was time to enjoy and savour the city, if even for a short time.

He moved along past the roulette tables and observed the people. A tall man with thinning hair and colourless eyes smiled slightly while neatly stacking the pile of chips in front of him. A huge black man, in his middle to late thirties, wearing a black bowler hat covering a bald head cursed loudly at losing another fifteen hundred It was far more money than David would ever consider gambling at any time in any place. David continued to walk towards the far end of the casino. He almost felt guilty about wearing shoes on the plush crimson carpet.

In a room off to the side of the slots, a baby grand sat on a small stage and a talented pianist coaxed a low sweet sound from the keys. Tables of men and women sat and enjoyed a drink away from the casino. Back behind a polished mahogany bar was a movie on a large screened TV silently showing one of the Phoenician's old classic musical productions. David walked over finding a stool a bit away from the crowd. The bartender quietly moved towards David. "Can I see some I.D.?"

David grinned confidently. It was the first time that he had been asked as he handed the bartender his birth certificate.

"Canada, eh. Where's Lambton County located?"
Again David smiled. "Are you familiar with Canada?"
"Should be, I was born in Oshawa."
"Then you probably know where Chatham is."

70

The smile widened. "Down near Windsor isn't it?"

"You got it."

"Well what are you drinking David?"

"Rye and coke."

The bartender slid the drink to David, cashed the bill and placed the change in front of him. David pushed a tip towards him. The bartender wiped the money onto the small ledge know as bartenders territory.

"Thanks. First trip here David?"

"Yes. My money began to disappear too quickly, so I thought I would take a break from those machines."

"Sam's my name, Dave. I'll tell you what I do when my luck's down. I head into the Sport Book right through that arch behind you. You can bet the ponies for a couple bucks a race or bet a hockey or football game and have a little fun. You'll find that your money won't go as fast. You might even get lucky and win a bit. Anyway, have a nice time here and good luck. I have to get back to work," he said as he moved to serve another customer.

The pianist started to play another show tune that he recognized as he quietly sipped his drink. Two people moved down the bar towards him a man and a woman. The lady, walking ahead sat down next to David and smiled. She was probably early thirties, blonde, that long silky kind and she was wearing a black dress cut low in front. The man, swarthy in complexion with dark hair greased close to his scalp sat down next to her. He was not as friendly almost resenting David's presence. Sam the bartender took their drink order, served it and moved on glancing at David's still almost full drink. He said nothing as he moved on. The young woman talked to the man beside her loud enough that David could hear. She turned her back to David, the dress was cut low in back as well as front and her skin was smooth and silky looking.

"One hundred dollars!" David couldn't make out the subtle tones of the man.

A low and sexy laugh came from the woman who was still speaking loud enough for David to hear.

"You'll see the best body that you ever saw for that hundred."

David choked nearly spilling his drink. No, this wasn't Chatham. It also wasn't a conversation that he wanted to eavesdrop. Quickly with drink in hand he got up and headed towards the huge arch leading into the sports book.

The sports book was much larger inside than he expected, although most things at the casino did defy the imagination. Televisions hung on the walls above a row of wicket counters each screening a different race or sport's event. It was a busy place; some patrons were standing, some looking upwards towards the TV's and all were placing bets or collecting their winnings. He glanced around, cigarette and cigar smoke filled the air along with the hum of voices scattered throughout the theatre-like setting. There were several rows of tables and chairs where men sat with their noses in some kind of newspaper.

David selected a chair near the back. On the table beside him was one of these newspapers. The wrinkled pages were turned and folded obviously someone had been sitting reading it. David thought about picking it up and browsing the pages, then decided against it not knowing if someone would return. Moments later, they did.

The grey haired gentleman pulled back his chair and sat down with a nod and a pleasant, "Howdy."

David choked a bit as he spit out a "Hello" that nearly caught in his throat on the way out of his mouth.

The old gentleman picked up his paper, took a pencil and began to doodle on the page, all the while looking over his bifocals peering at a television. A group of thoroughbred horses were being loaded into the starting gate. David summoned up his courage.

"Excuse me sir, but could I ask a few questions about what goes on here. Like, how do you bet, how much do you bet, how little can you bet, what's that paper..?"

"Shush boy, the race is about to start!"

David's gaze followed that of the old man's at the television screen and the dozen or so race horses that burst out of the starting gate. Down the back stretch they flew changing positions and finally entering the home stretch when the old gentleman jumped clear off his chair and began yelling.

"Come on number seven! Move up that rail!"

The race finished and the old man sank back down to the seat of the chair.

"Blast it! That jockey could have won that race if he'd have taken that horse to the outside instead of getting trapped on the rail!"

"Did you have a bet on that horse?" David asked.

The old fellow looked thoroughly disgusted. "Why the hell do you think I was yelling for him to win?"

He calmed down a bit almost immediately after gaining his composure and began to laugh. "I guess I get carried away too much with these races. You'd think I'd had a bundle bet on that race. I guess it's why I bet the ponies, gets the adrenalin flowing, brings out the excitement! You'll have to pardon my manners; I guess that I stay away from the mainstream of humanity for too much of the year. What was it you asked me anyway?"

David scanned the outward appearance of this cowboy. He wore a modified western Stetson on his head and his bifocals were perched on his nose with the same hawkish look as a bird of prey. His face, wrinkled and aging, was well-tanned as though he had spent much of his time in the sun. His western style shirt, with pearl snaps, looked new and crisp. The bolo tie that he was wearing caught David's eye. It was shaped like an arrow head with a peculiar gold coloured lump of metal fastened to it. A smooth black calf skin vest fit as if it had been custom tailored and his trousers rested on Ostrich skin western leather boots.

"I was just asking how this betting works. This is my first time here, first time anywhere other than Canada."

73

David held out his hand, momentarily forgetting about the races. "My name's David Rivers."

A broad smiled accompanied the hand that David shook with enthusiasm.

"From Canada is it. I've seen lots of Canadians. My name is Calvin Sparks. I live up in Idaho. Ever hear of Idaho?"

"I know where it is. I've seen it on the map. Just where in Idaho do you live?"

The old man paused for a moment before he answered, his eyebrows rising slightly.. Slowly he answered, "A place that you probably never heard of, a small place in the Rockies, about seventy miles from the Canadian border. Where 'bouts in Canada are you from?"

"A place called Chatham, about fifty miles from Detroit, Michigan. We would be quite a bit south of where you are."

Calvin Sparks looked at David with great scepticism. Over the top of his glasses his pale blue eyes studied David for a moment before he spoke. "Who are you trying to fool boy? I've lived close enough, long enough, for me to know which direction Canada is from Idaho. Canada is north!"

David just grinned. He began to relax even though Calvin seemed to be upset at the moment. "Here, let me see that pencil that you're using to pick your horses."

David turned the racing form over and on the back of it in a blank space he quickly drew a map of North America. He put in detail of the border boundaries between the U.S. and Canada and particularly the Great Lake region. He placed the hastily drawn sketch in front of the man from Idaho and with a smile David pointed with his finger as he spoke.

"Now this is the U.S.-Canada Border, this line across here. This is roughly Idaho, although I don't have all of the States nor the provinces identified. Where I'm placing this 'x' is approximately where you claim to live. Way over here, and far south, as you can see here at the base of the Great Lake basin where I'm placing this other 'x', is where I live. So you see neighbour, I do live south of you."

The old man looked with wonder as he stroked his chin. "Well I'll be damned. You know, you're showing me something that at my age I never knew, never even wondered about for that matter. I'm still sceptical, I'm going to go into the next library that I come to and get one of their maps and have a look see for myself. Anyway, for the time being, I'll take you at your word. What do you do for a living down south in Canada?"

"I work at one of the automobile plants. I'm a machinist. The plant that I work for had their Christmas party and I won this trip. A couple of my buddies came along. We'll meet up later today. I'm not sure just where they are at the moment. Tell me, what do you do in Idaho?"

The old gent smiled. "Guess."

"From the way that you're dressed, I'd say a rancher."

"Not quite. Not a bad guess though. I just dress in my fancy duds when I come down here to spend the winter. You wouldn't believe how cold it gets where I live. No sir, I'm not a rancher. I'm a gold prospector."

David laughed. "Now it's my turn to be sceptical. I thought gold prospectors died out before the turn of the century. You mean that you work for the mining company as a geological engineer?"

"No. I mean I pan for gold."

"Like in the old days when you gather stones from the river bottom with a pan and swish it around until the gold dust settles to the bottom?"

The old man shook his head. "The same way and just like in the old days you don't advertise where you find it. I have a cabin way down in a valley where you seldom see anyone. I leave my car at a relative close by to where I go. He keeps his mouth shut. I pack in on horse back with two mules carrying all of the supplies that I need from April 'til November. I pan gold all that time and then I come down here and on to L.A., where my brother lives, and spend the winter. Not a bad life."

"I didn't think that there was any gold left like that anymore."

"You and a lot more think that way. You can't strike it rich like years and years ago, but if you know what you're doing, and I do, you can make a good living. Look here at my bolo tie."

"What, that old lump of stuff on that arrow head?"

Calvin snorted. "That old lump as you call it is a genuine gold nugget worth over a thousand dollars! I panned it myself! I do good and live a good life. Enough of that though. You already know more about me than most people. Let's educate you about betting horses and see if we can make some money, young feller."

"Let's start with this thing that you called a newspaper, where you drew your map, to either educate me or fool me, it's called the Daily Racing form." With that, he once again peered over the top of his glasses this time smiling broadly.

"You might say that it's the bible for those of us that wager the ponies. It gives you all of the past performances, how they finished in their last several races, and how much you would have won had you bet on them."

The rest of the afternoon, David spent in absolute comfort in the company of his new found friend. They wagered together, won together, lost and laughed together. They conversed with other bettors, some who boasted about their winnings and many who groaned when their horses got beat at the wire. Finally, David looked at his watch.

"I've got to go and meet up with my chums Calvin. I have one more day in Vegas. Maybe I'll see you here tomorrow."

The old gent stretched out his hand. "Been a real pleasure meeting you and sharing the day, David. But, by tomorrow this time, I could be track side at Santa Anita. I'm leaving right after supper and driving to Los Angeles to meet my brother. I'll be thinking of you. Good luck the rest of your stay partner."

David headed back towards his room, almost a hundred dollars richer than when he had arrived at the Sport Book. Calvin Sparks knew how to pick winners right enough. It had been a good afternoon. Actually one that he would remember as time went by.

Las Vegas was an exciting town. They sat down for supper in one of the casino's smaller cafes. All four took turns hitting on the waitress. She had with long legs and big breasts. She seemed to enjoy the attention as much as she did the bubble gum in her mouth. "So what can I get you guys?" She took her time making sure she talked directly at each of them. Once she was finished writing, she winked at them and left. They all watched with great enthusiasm as she strolled back to the kitchen to place their order.

Donald was pumped with excitement as he described the events of the afternoon with his two friends.

"We went downtown on the bus. Down to Fremont Street where the cabbie said Vegas began. You should have come with us Dave. A country guy and his band were playing ragtime music. It was a blast. Ten bucks buys two drinks and the show is free. We sat with this guy that was older than the cabbie and the stories he told! He claimed at one time, way back when this Bugsy Segal ran the Flamingo, some guys tried to rob the place." Donald leaned closer, his eyes wide with excitement as he went on. "This guy says that as the robbers left the casino, some of Bugsy's boys met them and they had machine guns. This guy said the car with the robbers came flying out the driveway and Bugsy's men fired and killed every one of them, Four, I think he said. Then they got hold of a tow truck and, according to him, they hauled the car out into the Desert and buried the car, robbers and all in a big excavated hole. They wanted to send a clear message to any body else who thought they would try to rob the casinos!"

David looked over at both Steve and Allen. The guy who told the story must have been convincing by the looks on their faces. David grinned. "Just like the movies, eh. You don't think for a moment that this guy was stringing you along?"

Donald answered, excitement still causing his voice to quiver. "You would have believed him had you been there. I believe him." He looked over to the other two. "You guys believed him?"

"I believed him all right. What do you think, Al?"

Allen wasn't as sure as Steven. "I did at the time. Maybe he was stringing us along so we'd buy him more booze, which we did."

"Bull. You believed him just as me and Steve did. I wish I would have been there to see it. Just like Bonnie and Clyde."

The waitress sat their food down. Steve looked at his food and then towards Donald. "What's on for tonight?."

It was Sunday morning about eleven o'clock as the sound of the cleaning crew in the next room woke David. He looked over at the other double bed. Donny had the covers pulled over his head and his bare feet were sticking out near the foot of the bed. David sat up and took his pillow, and threw it full force at what he figured would be Don's head.

"Oh!" The form beneath the covers came alive as the bare-chested Donald sat up, his hair looking as if he had been out in a wind storm. He looked around for a moment, yawned, and then looked at David through blood shot eyes.

"What time is it?"

"Time to get up, it's our last day in Vegas."

Don rubbed his eyes and yawned again. "Seems like we've been here longer than two days, don't it?"

David grinned as he threw the covers back and climbed out of bed, still wearing the same briefs as he had when he arrived, his chest bare. Like a dog, he sniffed under his arm. "I'm going to shower. You want to use the bathroom first?"

"You bet. I have to piss the moment my feet hit the floor."

"Hurry it up then." An hour later all four of them were dressed and lined up at the buffet table of the casino for brunch.

As they ate, Don looked at David. "This was a good trip buddy." The other two began nodding their approval as they crammed food into their face. "Tell you what. My trip was on you so tonight is on me, that is, yours and mine." With a look at the other two he said, "You two can pay your own. What we were talking about last night Dave, you remember?"

"Not really. After the forth drink my memory went bad."

"Right. We all want to go out big the last night. We figured that tonight we'd go down to the Tropicana and see the Follies show."

David put down his fork and wiped the corners of his mouth with his napkin. "Call for tickets yet?"

Don grinned. "I'm on it," as he raced away from the table. Moments later he returned. "The ten o'clock show. Come on, we might as well go down and get our tickets now and play the slots some."

It was six o'clock as David looked at his watch and then his buddies. "Any of you guys want to go and sit in the Sports Book and bet the horses?"

It was negative all around. "We're going to play the slots for a while. We can all meet out front about nine thirty and catch a cab down to the Tropicana," Don said.

David turned on his heel. "See you guys then."

There seemed to be about the same amount of people in the Sports Book as there had been the day before. In all probability, many of them were locals that came on a regular basis to bet the horses. David scanned the area looking for a familiar face. It wasn't there. Calvin Sparks must have split. David spied a racing form lying on one of the desks. It looked used, wrinkled and deserted. Someone had probably left it there from earlier in the day. He sat down and picked up the form. He glanced up at the screen and the post parade for the tenth race at Santa Anita was live. He looked over the horses on the program and quickly walked to the betting window.

"Give me an exactor box please, one and three at Santa Anita." The cashier looked up and smiled as the machine spit out the ticket. "You just beat the bell pal. The horses have just left the gate." David took a step back and without time to return to his seat, he stood looking up at the monitor. The horses were already racing down the back stretch. One and three were out front and in a head-to-head duel as they rounded the head of the stretch pounding down the homestretch. David could feel the excitement building inside. Another horse pulled up along side of the two that he had bet on and just before the wire the five horse stuck his nose in between. David waited impatiently for the photo to separate the winners. It was a while before the results were posted and David made his way back to his seat.

Someone else was sitting in the chair next to where he had been, a dark swarthy individual with a large upper body wearing a florescent pink shirt and a satin black tie. His hair was curly and jet black. He looked Spanish, Greek or Italian, David didn't know or care. The new arrival was first to speak as David sat down. He flashed a big smile in David's direction.

"Having any luck, Amigo?"

The Spanish ordinarily would have established his heritage, but then a lot of the native Las Vegas people, that David had encountered, used Spanish phrases when they spoke. It did not necessarily mean that they were of Spanish descent.

"Not on that race. I'm kind of new at this pari-mutuel betting. I received a short lesson from an old gent that I met here yesterday. He was a good teacher." David paused watching the reaction on his face.

David held out his hand. "My name is David Rivers. I'm from Canada."

"Friends just call me Paulo. I live just outside of Los Vegas in Henderson. Know where that is?"

"Not really. How close to Vegas?"

"About five miles, someday it will probably be a part of Vegas if this town keeps spreading its wings. I see the thoroughbreds are all done running at the tracks in the east. Ever bet the dogs?"

David gave Paulo a curious look. "What dogs?"

"The greyhounds, they chase the rabbit. Where you been man? You never seen the dogs run? They're easier to pick than the horses. There's nobody on their backs holding them back. They race dead out. I'll go get a couple programs, be right back."

David watched as Paulo moved towards the cashier window, moments later returning with a new program. In the next five minutes, David got a crash course in betting the dogs. Not unlike the one he had received from Calvin Sparks the day before and hopefully he would be as lucky.

After three races they still hadn't picked any winners. His dark skinned friend complained that his dog ran 'up the track.'

David studied the form, remembering what Paulo told him about handicapping.

"What have you got picked Paulo?"

Paulo shook his head as he turned to face David, his grin still showing but with less enthusiasm. "I've got to get some of my bread back. I'm going to box the track-man's selections and bet a triactor."

"What's that cost?"

"Twelve bucks. All three dogs have to hit the board, but they can be in any order."

David glanced up at the screen. The dogs were just being paraded. Looking down at the program he said, "I'm going to bet a triactor too. There's a dog named after my dad and one called David's Delight, I'm going to put them with the track-man's selection and see how my luck holds."

Adrenalin

Paulo exhaled air sounding like a giant balloon deflating. "You're blowing your money man. No way those two long shots are going to be there."

David laughed. "Probably not but it's my last bet and it's only twelve bucks. I have to go soon and meet my friends." He hurried to the window and returned to his seat, ticket in hand.

It was the luck of the Irish, according to Paulo as David headed for the payout window. Moments later he returned with his winnings. The dogs did come in, long shots do win occasionally. But the look in Paulo's eyes didn't seem to hold the same light of companionship as he watched David put the fourteen hundred dollars into his wallet.

"I have to get going Paulo. I'm meeting the guys that I came down here with out front at about nine thirty. We're going down to the Tropicana to catch the show." At that moment, a scantily dressed cocktail waitress came along. The blonde pony tail was as eye catching as her provocative smile.

"Can I get you boys a drink?"

David began to say no but was interrupted by Paulo. "Stay a moment and have a parting drink pal. Give me Jack Daniels on the rocks. What are you drinking Dave?"

David took a quick look at his watch, ten to nine. He wanted to go up to the room for a quick shower but what the hell, what difference would fifteen minutes make. With a smile at the attractive girl he said, "You can bring me the same." He watched as she disappeared among the patrons flooding the Sport Book as the evening began to come alive.

Paulo smiled again. "Good, one last drink. So you're off to the Tropicana. I've seen the show. Lots of skin it will rouse you all right. Taking a cab down?"

"It's too far to walk."

"Next time you come to Vegas and stay here you won't need a cab to go to the Tropicana." Paulo was interrupted by the waitress who appeared with their drinks. David fished a five dollar bill out of the pocket of his trousers and placed it in the outstretched hand.

"Thanks honey," he said as she moved on.

He raised his glass to Paulo who had initiated the toast saying, "To new friends."

"What's this about not having to take a cab next time?"

"You wouldn't know it but there building a monorail, out behind this casino. It will run all the way down the strip to where they are building a new casino. It'll be free transportation from here all the way down. They've already begun to build it, come on out back and have a look." Paulo got up and began to move.

"I haven't got time. I've got to get back to the room."

Paulo grinned. "You got time. Nobody is ever on time in Las Vegas. Com'on, it'll only take a minute. Be something to tell your buddies."

Paulo was already heading towards the rear of the casino. David hesitated, and then thought, what was a minute. Courtesy rather than curiosity compelled him to follow Paulo, who was now a good four or five steps ahead. They passed the elevator that he should have taken to his room. He felt the coolness of the desert breeze as he moved outside and into the darkness of the night. Paulo slowed his walk, grinned and waited for him to catch up. All over Vegas people were moving about in a party like atmosphere with neon lights blazing with colour and the sound of the city that never shut down. Here behind the buildings, behind the bustle of activity, it was deserted. Paulo came to a stop alongside of a huge concrete column that looked like a giant whose arms sloped out and away from his body.

"See, I told you. There will be a whole series of these stretching out for almost two miles. This is the first support arm that's been erected. Just like a train in the sky"

David was looking up at the shadow of the giant structure and following its path behind the hotels. The noise of the city seemed to disappear and a strange stillness surrounded him. He wasn't sure what he was feeling as he quickly turned and glanced over his right shoulder.

Paulo's demeanour had changed. The smile that had been on his face was gone replaced by a sinister stare. David saw the flash of the long bladed knife in Paulo's hand.

"Come on, fork it over or I'll slit your throat. I know how much you won!"

The over head the sound of a jet taking off from McCarron airport blotted out all other sounds. Fear began to make David's skin crawl.

David's fear was soon replaced by anger. He could feel it, like a volcano that begins to rumble just before it spews forth lava. He started to breathe heavily and sweat profusely as he felt the force within him grow. He couldn't stop it, he was being threatened and the need for survival was uncontrollable. He took a deep breath as he looked at Paulo with hatred in his eyes. "You want it, take it."

Paulo lunged forward, the blade sweeping in an arc towards its victim. The judo move, that Joey Gallo had used to throw him through the air and onto his head that day, was about to be used again, but this time by David. Like lightning, he grabbed Paulo's outstretched wrist and ducked under his arm. Lifting him clear of the ground he sent him screaming through the air as the blade flew from his hand. David knew he should leave before it was too late and as he turned to make a hasty exit, he heard the wind expel from his would be assailant and a cry as his body hit the ground.

Confusion with his exact bearings at that moment worked against David. His foot slipped off the edge of the newly poured cement and he floundered, tripping on the wooden barrier in place for cement that would be poured the next day. Down he went, scraping his knees on the wood and cement as he fell to the ground. He got up as quickly as he could and looked for the door into the casino. He saw the light and, at the same moment, the form that suddenly blocked it from sight. Paulo! He had recovered quicker than David thought and had found a weapon, a length of pipe about three feet long and two inches in diameter. In the light from the full moon, and reflections from the distant marquis, David saw the blood running down Paulo's cheek.

"You fucking hay seed! I'm going to kill you!" he screamed as he swung the pipe at David. It slammed into David's ribs sending unbearable pain through him. Paulo raised the pipe high over his head, intent on slamming it down on David's skull. For the second time in David's life, the combination of fear and rage manifested itself. It was not David Rivers that Paulo was about to confront but a hidden warrior created by a massive surge of adrenalin. David sprang at him like a thunder bolt, one hand going for his throat, the other for his groin. He was hoisted into the air and then driven head first into the concrete. Paulo's scream of terror could not be heard on the busy thoroughfare on the strip but here in the back lot it was terrifying. Again and again, the warrior slammed the now lifeless body of Paulo onto the concrete slab.

David Rivers sank down onto the pavement beside the warm corpse lying limp and bleeding on the cold hard cement. David could feel the rage and violence that had suddenly possessed him moment's earlier begin to ebb away like the tidal waters of the ocean. His body and mind began to return to normal along with the fact that he was responsible for the sight that lay before him. The battle that had taken place, so fast and furious it was like an out of body experience. Almost as if he had been standing back watching, but he knew better. This was the same problem that had placed him in the psychiatric ward years before. Doctor Hammond had warned him, *"If you are perceived by the public to be an imminent threat or danger, you could find yourself spending the rest of you days in a facility like this one."* David knew he would lose his most basic need, freedom.

Paulo's head was completely shattered, a mass of blood and brains oozing out of what remained of his skull. Society would not accept this as mere self defence. He could almost hear the words of a prosecutor. *"Here we see the work of a madman."* He would end up in mental institutions for the rest of his life even though this thing was not entirely his fault.

It seemed like hours digging Paulo's final resting place and covering his tracks. He had to ensure no one would find it until he returned home or possibly ever. The back of lot of a Vegas casino might be an appropriate burial ground for him to spend eternity. Perhaps some of the tourists that Paulo had taken money from and no doubt scarred to death might someday walk over his cold dead body. He had missed meeting his pals but getting back to his room, away from this place, was all he could think about

He headed for the door and walked towards the rear of the casino, his mind rushing trying to come up with a reasonable solution. Al Jarrod had breezed through the casino almost unrecognized that day. If it worked for Al, it might just work for him. He entered the casino at a walk, like a run. The elevator door had opened and a couple dressed in a tux and an evening gown stepped out as he slid through the closing door.

In the elevator, David fumbled in his pocket for his room key. It was in his hand as the door flew open, and he left the elevator with as much speed as when he entered it. He saw no one in the hallway, much to his relief, as he turned the key in the door. He stepped into the sanctity of his room and for the first time felt safe from prying eyes. He stopped in front of the mirror and caught sight of his image. He was a mess, his hair in disarray and his stained clothing showed the obvious signs of a struggle.

He slid open a drawer and tossed the contents of his pants pocket into it. His wallet was full of money that would ordinarily have excited him but now it felt more like blood money. He glanced at the small travel clock on the dresser. It was eleven-thirty and his friends were no doubt partying in the place where he should have been. He would have a couple of hours to himself before they returned, asking him questions that he couldn't answer truthfully. He went into the bathroom, removed his shoes and let his clothing sink to the floor.

The hot water and soap that ran down his body carried away the unwanted residue he had accumulated. His body was coming clean but the image of the body that he slid into the shallow grave could not be wash away. He leaned against the wall of the shower and trembled with sorrow. What was going on? David hit the wall as he screamed, "Why is this happening?! What is wrong with me?" He wasn't a monster, but he couldn't explain the man within. There was no answer to help David's conscience only regret.

He emerged, water dripping off onto the bath mat, and he dried on one of the large towels. The feeling of luxury that he should have enjoyed was lost. He was tired, bone weary, but his mind was still working overtime. The clothes, he would have to get rid of the cloths but how? He walked from the steamy bathroom out into the main part of the room. Opening up the suitcase, he withdrew the clothes that he would need for the trip home and placed them in one of the dresser drawers, the same one that held his wallet and room key. He put on a clean pair of jockey shorts, the ones that he would sleep in and wear in the morning. The dirty clothes he laid in the bottom of the suitcase covering them with the other shirts and under wear that he had brought. He would dispose of the clothes that might incriminate him, at home. He wanted nothing that could be traced back to him. The shoes! He almost forgot his shoes all covered with sand, the sight of which would cause questions. He used one of the wash cloths to clean the shoes; the suede material would be dry by morning. He placed them just under the edge of the bed where they would dry and not be seen. He picked up all of the towels and facecloths and took a final look around making sure that nothing looked out of place, and then he rolled back the covers and slid his weary body beneath the covers.

At about the time that David was falling asleep his buddies were finishing their third round of drinks down at the Tropicana. The chorus line was on the stage and showing enough skin to ruin the eye sight of all of them. A mist of pale blue smoke rose slightly behind the gals as they performed to the Can Can music of the Moulin Rouge.

Steve looked over at Don, who was sitting there, his mouth gaping like a city slicker seeing the New York skyscrapers for the first time.

"Rivers doesn't know what he's missing. I wonder where he got to? I thought maybe he'd show up but it don't look like he's going to."

Don came out of his memorized stare for a moment and looked at his two companions. "I know. We waited until the last minute before we left. I've no idea where he is. It isn't like him not to show. He's usually the first one ready when you're going somewhere."

Allan turned away for a moment, a brief moment, before his eyes swung back to the floor show as if they were pulled by a strong magnet. He spoke while still watching the performance. "Maybe he ran into a hooker. Maybe he's doing what we're just thinking about doing!"

Don shook his head negatively. "Not David. Maybe one of you two would do that but not David. I'm hoping that he might have got on a hot slot machine and wouldn't leave until it cooled."

His two chums answered almost in unison. "That's probably it. His tough luck, he's missing a great show."

Donald turned his key in the lock hoping that David would be in the room. It was a relief, even if it was a surprise that David was in bed. He walked over and looked down at the sleeping form of his friend. He noticed an abrasion on the side of his face that he hadn't seen before. Gently he shook him. David groaned as his eyes fluttered open. Don stared at him for a moment before speaking. "You all right?"

David sat up in bed. "Yes I'm all right."

"So how come you weren't waiting out front at nine-thirty?"

David threw the covers back and sat on the side of the bed. "I guess you could say I nearly got mugged. This guy that I met asked me to go outside and look at this thing called a monorail that is being built out behind the casino. When we stepped outside, he hit me with something in his hand, a piece of pipe or something. I fought back and started yelling and he took off on the run."

Donald's eyes went wide with surprise. "Did he get your wallet?"

"No. That's what he had in mind though he saw me win at the races. I guess he figured that he would share the wealth, or rather take it all. My ribs are still sore where he hit me."

Donald's eyes grew large. "We should call the cops."

"Where do you think I've been? Security at the Casino called them. It seems that this is a regular occurrence here. Anyway, I gave them a description and they're on the look out for him."

"Maybe we should…"

"Maybe we shouldn't. I learned my lesson and I'm all right. If we start making a lot of noise we might have to hang around, like to I.D. the guy and I don't want to, so that's it."

Donald looked for a moment as if he was going to argue and then thought better of it. "I guess you're right. You feel okay? Can you stand up?"

"I'm all right."

"Well I'm going to slip down the hall and tell Allan and Steve that you're all right. I'll be right back."

David heard the door close and that was all he heard until he woke up next morning.

The plane back from Vegas was a 727. The guys couldn't all set together so they sat two and two. David took the window seat while Donald sat sandwiched between David and a rather boisterous self professed entrepreneur that was educating Donald on everything about franchising, investing and a host of other business opportunities. David's mind slid back into the depressing events of the previous night. In a way, it was good that gabby sat in the aisle seat beside Donald. David didn't feel much like conversation.

The 727 thundered down the runway and the sensation of the lift as they became air born lost some of the excitement that he had experienced in his initial flight. The plane hovered over Las Vegas for a few moments before banking and turning towards the flight path and as it did the wing dipped giving a perfect view of the strip. David's eyes zeroed in on the Phoenician and the workers at the site of the new monorail. A cement truck with lights flashing as he backed up came to a halt at that instant in the exact spot where Paulo was now resting. He was about to get a permanent headstone, his reward for a bad decision. David was beginning to wonder about the life-form inside him and questioned if he was ever going to be able to have any real control. He had to find a way.

7

Sully's underground operation was growing in size and he now had 20 bikers who pushed the illegal substances for him. His business was thriving and while he didn't flaunt his wealth there was little doubt that he prospered from the enormous profits runners earned. The police were suspicious of his business but they could never prove anything. Sully's employees were very discrete and trustworthy and for this he paid them well. The best deal Sully ever made was getting Alex to agree to bring his son into the fold.

Joey was making quite a name for himself. He could be seen flying down the streets on his Harley with the other bikers trailing behind. Joey had grown physically powerful, as well as notorious. He was now over six feet in height and exceeded two hundred pounds. His greasy black hair hung below his shoulders, well beyond a socially acceptable level. Weathered and hardened like some comic book character, his muscular body was quite impressive. But the most ominous sight was the multitude of demonic tattoos that covered his burly arms, making the entire package frightening. Day by day he was slowly becoming the lead within the biker's tight knit community.

Joey's name was associated with all kinds of criminals, and although he had never been caught, he was well known and feared by his peers as well as other dealers in the trade.

Drugs had become a growing concern in the city and to Joey it didn't matter who used them or what lives they ruined, to him it was all about money and power. The little boy that was a bully was more treacherous as an adult. He liked the power and fear he saw in people's eyes when they encountered him. The dealers never cheated Sully, they knew that Joey would be calling and the result could be deadly. Jimmy had been the first that Joey killed and the thrill of taking a life excited him. He could still see Jimmy fall into the water like an animal; his shot had been right on target. The best part was that he was never caught and this only made the game more exhilarating.

Sully had run into a small business problem, one of his suppliers had been arrested and he had to look outside of his territory for another source. This problem demanded immediate attention and he knew just the person he could trust.

He heard the sound of an approaching motorcycle and recognized the Joey's bike coming in the driveway. Joey walked in and threw a small cloth bag on the desk. Sully grinned and placed the bag in one of the drawers. Sully's smile was different this time not his usual sly grin.

"Joey my man, I've got something to show you, follow me." Sully slid out of his chair and headed towards the far end of the garage where the light was dim. Still smiling he reached over removing a canvas cover hiding a brand new Harley.

Joey's face lit up like a four year old kid at Christmas. "Wow looks brand new. Where did you get it?"

"That's not important. It's the fastest thing around, even has a special muffler on it so that it runs quieter than any other bike. It's my bike but you're the one that gets to ride it."

Joey's knew there had to be a reason why Sully offered him the bike but he didn't care, he just wanted the bike. He listened as Sully went on, "My supplier ran into some trouble with the law and he's going to the penitentiary as a guest of the government. I found another supplier down in Windsor. The thing is there are some motorcycle clubs down there that don't like anyone else anywhere near their territory. While we are doing business, we need to get in and out quickly and quietly. We'll also be buying in larger quantities so that we don't need to make as many trips. That's why I invested in this Harley. Think you can handle it?"

Joey beamed. "I can handle any motorcycle!"

The grin covered Sully's face. "It wasn't just the bike that I was talking about. I meant the pickup and delivery.

"Never let you down yet have I?"

"Not yet. Another thing, some guys have contacted me recently, bikers from B.C. They're trying to set up some people like myself across the country, it would be coast to coast and we're talking serious money both for me, you and the boys. What do you think, Joey?"

Joey's eyes had never left the new Harley. "Whatever you say, Sully, when do I start?"

"Soon, real soon."

8

The bushings fit tightly on the guide posts of the die that David had just built. He took the grease gun and gave them a final shot making sure that they would slide up and down nicely in the press. He could see the foreman waiting for the dies completion. The parts were supposed to be shipped by the end of the week as promised, that always seemed to be the case. David took a clean rag and removed all the excess grease that had shot out of the bushings and gave the die a final wipe.

"How close are we Dave?" the foreman asked anxiously.

"She's all yours, Harvey."

"About time."

David passed the remark off with a laugh. Harvey had been working in the tool room when David had started as an apprentice and he had worked under the supervision of the little Scotsman. Harvey had been promoted, and sometimes regretted the move. Occasionally, there was more pressure at the top, especially if a die wasn't finished and the customer was being put off until it was. Today, he wouldn't have that problem if the die was right the first shot.

An hour later, Harvey returned with the blank that the die had produced and David could tell by the grin on his old friend's face that it was all right.

"Checked out good. Got another rush job for you."

David grinned. "Aren't they all?"

"So it seems. We just broke a section in a trim die. Same customer and supposed to ship the parts the same day.

They're sending a truck from Tennessee to pick up the parts. Can you stay tonight and finish it pal?"

"Oh, pal is it? You buying the beer, Scotty?"

"Sure, Saturday night at the social club dance, as long as it's done by morning."

David wiped his hands on a rag and threw it on the bench. "Where's the die?"

"The setup man is pulling it out of the press now. By the time you finish your break, the die will be on your bench."

It was past midnight by the time the die was repaired, put in the press and a part run before David packed it in. He was ready to call it a day, a long day. Out in the parking lot, he jumped into the Ford pickup and turned the key. Nothing started. He hit it again. Nothing. He pulled on the light switch and as he glanced at the instrument panel he realized that it hadn't lit up.

"Damn it! Just like my old man always said, a twelve volt battery don't give no warning when they're going to die. They just do."

David sat there for a moment. He could go phone for a tow truck, but then they would probably give him a jump start and in the morning the battery would be dead again. He got out and slammed the door.

He began to walk along Grand Boulevard, towards the railroad bridge to take the shortcut home. The night air was cool. June was always a nice month with weather that was as comfortable as it gets. David liked walking late in the evening; the cloak of darkness gave a feeling of privacy. Ever since Vegas, it seemed almost as if a dark figure strolled along with him. The phantom figure shaped by his imagination, manifested itself through the windmills of his mind. It constantly disturbed him and clung to his subconscious, especially when he was alone with his thoughts as he was now.

David thought of the Catholics with their confessional of absolution. He wasn't sure just how it worked. Would a person confess a murder to a priest, even if that murder was in self defense? Having someone else share his secret would probably lighten the load, but then maybe not. Maybe it would just be some other mortal that would know what monstrous act he had committed. He had prayed silently to God for forgiveness, but the memory of that night would not leave.

The incident with Paulo had been much different from the one with Joey, where there were huge gaps in his memory of what actually took place. With Paulo, it had been different; he could clearly remember everything. The problem was that once the fight began, he couldn't control himself or his rage. Had he been able to, Paulo might still be alive and he would not have these frightening dreams that woke him in the night. All of these things kept him from having any type of normal life. The uncontrollable amount of adrenalin that consumed his body and came to his defense acted like a barrier, to what judges and lawyers referred to as reasonable defense.

David was brought back to reality by the barking of a large watchdog and the racket it made, as it railed against the fence that confined it. Other sounds captured his attention; he heard the mournful sound of a train whistle and then tires on the pavement from the first car that he had encountered since he left the plant. Then another noise, it was the sound of a motorcycle coming from the direction of Sullivan's garage. This sound made him stop and his heart start to pound. It was still about a half mile to where he would turn to cross the track and he hoped that the rider would not be Joey. He didn't need the hassle that a confrontation might result in. The bike pulled even with him as he passed the worst possible place, directly beneath a street light. He was almost afraid to look. He could feel his breathing start to quicken as he turned his head.

He was relieved to see that it wasn't Joey. But the relief was short lived, as the rider was another biker that David had seen with Joey the day Jimmy was shot. The sound of the brakes on the motorcycle filled the stillness of the night.

David looked over his shoulder as the biker turned and raced back towards Sully's. David felt a sense of urgency and picked up his pace. It was a pretty good bet where the biker was heading.

Joey was just coming out of Sully's, he turned the Rotwieller loose in the shop and locked the door. He was headed home when Alfie Turner roared into the driveway.

"Thought you left, I locked up and turned the dog loose."

"Just seen something, or someone, that I thought might interest you, Joey."

"Get fucked, it's been a long day. Who are you talking about?"

Alfie's grin was wide as he watched the expression on Joey's face. "David Rivers is walking all by himself along Grand Boulevard, about half a mile from the railroad bridge."

Joey had already jumped on his bike and started it up. "I've been waiting for this and I won't need no help. This is private. I'll see you tomorrow." he said as the Harley fishtailed on the loose gravel before skidding out onto the pavement.

David had reached the point where a right turn would take him across the railroad bridge and once over it, he would be close to his apartment on Water Street. At almost the same time, he heard the roar of a motorcycle rapidly approaching. He didn't have to guess who would be riding it. He ran faster, his feet hitting the wooden planks of the footpath alongside the bridge. The floodlight of the Harley shone around and past him, forming images like a wild dancer. He turned to face what he knew would be his attacker. "Joey!" he yelled.

Joey sat under the lamp post at the approach of the bridge, defiantly looking at him. The light illuminated his figure, making him look awesome in his black leather vest and the long hair. The smile was evil, and the flickering shadows only made the scene more terrifying. From beneath his vest, he withdrew a large hunting knife with a brass knuckle grip holding it in a forward position, he screamed,

"Time's up Rivers, just like it was for that candy-assed friend of yours. He didn't know what hit him but you will! I've been waiting years to catch you just like this, with no one around to help you. I'm going to run this blade clean through you and listen to your screams!" He revved up the bike and threw the weight of his body back until the front wheel left the ground and came thundering towards David, the knife held straight forward like a jouster's lance.

David froze with fear, standing there with no weapon and no practical path of retreat. He looked across the guard rail on the opposite side, where suddenly a train had rounded the corner and was fast approaching. The engineer leaned on the whistle as he saw the figures on the bridge. David's fear had begun to fade when Joey confessed to the murder of Jimmy. Now, as Joey was almost upon him David began to react in a familiar pattern. The fear turned to rage as he sprang onto the guard rail, giving him the advantage of height and placing him on the opposite side of Joey's knife. The scream of the whistle was getting closer as David now wild with rage, hurled his body at his assailant as he passed. David's unexpected move brought a look of surprise and confusion on Joey's face and in an instant, the clash of their bodies rocketed through the wooden guard rail. The two combatants and the Harley flew through the railing and down into the waters of the cold muddy Thames.

Water splashed high into the air, as the vortex caused by their entry swallowed up man and machine and they plunged towards the bottom. As the men entered the water, David ended up beneath the motorcycle, while Joey surfaced gasping for fresh air that quickly filled his lungs.

Far below, David had been pulled along by the Harley's spinning wheels and only the incredible strength could push the motorcycle away. The rage still consumed him as he squatted on the muddy river bottom and then recoiled like a missile heading towards the surface desperate for air. Together, they spotted each other at almost the same moment. Joey still had the bowie knife clutched in his hand

and as he drew even with David, he struck out driving the blade through the palm of David's left hand. The sight of first blood brought a look of victory to Joey's face. It was short lived, as he felt David's right hand grasp the back of his neck and his mouth open wide, while his teeth suddenly tore into Joey's throat like a tiger's fangs. Joey's eyes flew open as he felt his life slip away. Blood poured into the river and Joey's lifeless body began to sink almost immediately, towards the same river bottom that had once held Jimmy.

The adrenalin still rushed through David's body, as he spat the mass of flesh that had been Joey's throat out across the water. Still feeling the immense surge of power that continued to rush through his body, he headed for shore. The fast current of the water carried David swiftly, resisting his attempt to swim ashore. Almost as fast as it came, the adrenalin began to leave his body leaving him weak. His work boots were heavy and the pockets of his pants filled with water, making it difficult for him to swim. He took a deep breath and went under the water, undoing his boots and pulling them from his feet. He resurfaced gasping for air and treading water for a moment, before he went under again after loosening his belt and shedding his jeans. It was easier now for him to swim, although now he was tiring quickly.

He began to swim for shore as hard as he could, and with the shore finally in sight he began to feel the murky bottom. Here along the shore, the bottom was soft and the mud deep, he began to sink into the mud unable to keep his head above water. His body began to shut down; entirely fatigued he began to hallucinate. His mother was scolding him for being in the river, a place he wasn't allowed to go as a child. Then visions of his father filled his mind and he found it was easier to let go than to struggle to survive. The life that flashes through your mind before the end was starting to play out. Suddenly, his flailing hands caught a root and like a lifeline he took it. He pulled himself into the mud shallows of the river still tugging at his feet as if to hold him. It would have to let go, it had claimed one victim tonight. This one would crawl away; it was not his time to die.

When David finally dragged his body out of the muddy Thames, he was streaked with mud and dripping wet, as he stood up clad only in his briefs and sweatshirt. He looked around. He had come ashore about two hundred yards from his apartment; the eerie yellowish light of the moon allowed him a dim view, as he headed for home.

He reached the porch, only realizing then that his keys together with his wallet were at the bottom of the river. Above the door on a ledge, his hand touched the spare key that he had kept for emergencies. He inserted it into the door and let himself in. It was good to be home, so good. The whole ordeal had left him literally dead on his feet.

He made his way to the bathroom. The hot water from the shower that cascaded over his body felt incredibly good. He looked at his hand where Joey's knife had cut through and it was throbbing. The water, with residue from the river and his hand swirled towards the drain. He dried himself off and then found gauze to bind his hand. It would have to heal on its own; he could not explain this easily to a doctor. When he finally dropped into bed, he was asleep before his head hit the pillow.

He thought that it was the ringing of the alarm that jolted him out of bed. It took a few moments for him to realize that it was the telephone. He got up on wobbly legs and picked it up on the fourth ring.

"Hello," he managed still trying to wake up and get his bearings.

"David?" the voice asked.

David's thoughts came slowly. Was last night a bad dream? He looked down at his naked body. This was not normal, he always wore pajamas. He saw his bandaged hand and shuddered. Last night was real. He looked down at the phone in his hand. He was slow to react; his mind would not kick into gear.

"Scotty?"

"Who else? What's going on Dave? This is the first time that you haven't shown up for work on time. I thought you were already here. I pulled my car right up alongside your truck in the parking lot. What gives?"

"When I came out of the plant just after midnight, my battery was dead. I was going to call for a boost but changed my mind and walked home. Is the die running all right? Did you get the parts out that needed to be shipped?"

"Dies are working fine. Both dies as a matter of fact, the one you repaired and the one that you made. We'll have the parts ready when the truck arrives. Do you want me to send someone over for you?"

"No. I guess I just tired myself out. All of this overtime has finally caught up with me. I'm going to take the rest of the day off, have some breakfast and then get a cab to get a new battery. I'll see you first thing tomorrow."

"Sure you don't need any help?"

"I'm sure. If I do, I'll slip into the plant and get you."

"Okay Dave, see you tomorrow."

David hung up the phone and looked up at the image in the hall mirror. There was no colour in his skin and his eyes were red from the polluted water. Suddenly, he realized that he was looking into the face of a killer. He was going to have to protect himself against this wild surge of adrenalin. It was something he couldn't control, something that possessed him and took control. He stood there transfixed just staring into the mirror.

The words of the psychiatrist came back to him, 'If society fears you, they will lock you away.' What was it he feared most, death or incarceration? He had fought against death and for now, he had won. From incarceration, he would have to flee far and fast. One look at Joey's lifeless body and the police would be looking for a maniac. He could still see Joey's eyes bulging from his head as he watched him slip below the surface of the river. How long did he have before a search for Joey began, or when the body would come floating up, giving up the river's secret? He had only one choice; to run and run quickly.

He pulled on clean underwear from the laundry his mother had done. It was then he realized one of the hardest things that he would have to do, leave without saying goodbye to his parents. The police would question them first, after Joey was found, or possibly sooner. Someone would see the broken railing on the footpath of the railroad bridge and then a search would start.

David yanked on a pair of Levi's and a long sleeved shirt, ramming the shirt tail into the waistband. He searched for a moment for a spare belt, finally finding one after wasting precious minutes. All of his personal accessories were gone, his wallet and keys were at the bottom of the river. He was lost without them but he would adjust. At least he had hidden a spare key for the pickup in the front wheel hubcap, in case he forgot or lost his key, lucky for him that he had.

He hurried to the fridge and poured himself a glass of orange juice. It would have to hold him for a while. Actually, he wasn't really hungry. The images from last night made him sick to his stomach and he threw up the orange juice he had just swallowed. He returned to the bedroom and spied the carry on bag that he had used when he went to Vegas. He put several pairs of underwear, socks, a couple of t-shirts, and three pairs of blue jeans into a bag. The empty pocket on the outside would have to become his wallet.

On his way out he stopped and locked the door. He thought of taking the key with him but if he did the police might break down the door. If they found the key there, they may assume that he might still return and that may buy some time for him. He reached above the door and replaced the key.

David hurried along on foot, towards the downtown core. His mind was still racing, sometimes confused. He should have cleaned up the apartment before he left. The police would find evidence of the crime, such as the dirt and water that he had tracked from the river. For a moment, he thought of going back then decided against it. The police would have enough to go on to start looking for him even without evidence that they might find in his apartment. Speed was of the essence, the more space that he could put between him and the city, the better. He hurried on, passing the jail house just down the street with its grey stone wall, twenty five feet high, and a wall that he might well find himself behind or another one just like it. The thought sent a shiver through him. No thanks he thought, as he continued on with his escape.

David reached the end of Water Street and walked through the park towards the footbridge that crossed the creek. Workers were busy in the park this morning, creating flower gardens. The beautification of the park meant the loss of the old ball diamonds. Briefly, he thought back to happier times when he played ball with his high school friends. Moments that he would cherish forever, now gone. He crossed the creek and walked up beside the bank and then through the front door to the teller.

"Could you tell me my bank balance?" David asked the young male teller.

"Do you have your book sir?"

"No, I forgot it but my account number is 204030."

"Do you have some I.D?"

This was what David was dreading. "I forgot my wallet along with my bank book." Fate had smiled on him, for as the teller began to shake his head in a negative fashion, Beth Hunter who had been in the same class as David, walked towards the vault. Her smile was sweet, but her words even sweeter.

"Hi Dave, haven't seen you in a long while. How've you been?"

"Great Beth. Nice to see you." David could see the teller relax.

"Your balance is twenty-five hundred and forty dollars, Mr. Rivers."

"I'd like to make a withdrawal."

"And how much?"

"Twenty-five hundred even." With a forced grin he added, "I've got a good deal on a car for cash. Could I get it in fifties and twenties?"

"Certainly."

David's hand was shaking as he took the handful of money. It was larger than he thought it would be. At a desk inside the bank, he put the money into the outside pocket of the carry on bag. He shoved a hundred dollars in twenties into this pocket. He glanced over to see if the teller was watching and wondering what he was doing, but he was already busy with another customer. At the reception counter in the bank, he stopped and asked the young lady to call him a cab.

David watched as the dark-haired girl made the call. How cruel life had been to him, he hadn't really had time for women in such a long while. She interrupted his thought. "They'll be here in five minutes."

He stepped out of the bank and into the bright sunlight. Traffic on Main Street was beginning to pick up. A young mother walked by pushing a stroller with an infant sucking on a bottle, while at the same time holding the hand of a whinny little fellow about three years old. She trudged along looking down at the youngster pulling back at her side. "Stop it Jeffrey. You be good and momma will buy you a treat." Life was so simple for them, but not for David. He frantically waited for the cab that would take him to the store where he could get a battery for his truck. After that he would leave but where he was going to go, he wasn't sure, but it would be far and fast. The sight of the cab coming down the street broke his chain of thought. It pulled alongside and David climbed into the back seat.

"Where to pal?"

"The Canadian Tire store."

The cab pulled in front of the store. "Just wait. I'll probably be about five minutes."

The driver shook his head. "You leave twenty bucks with me if you want me to wait. I'll be here until the meter reads that much."

David passed him a twenty and rushed into the store. Luckily for him, the store wasn't that busy and in less than five minutes he returned to the waiting cab with a new battery. He had enough tools in the truck to change the battery.

The Ford pickup was right where he left it last night. A lot had transpired in that short time. The cab pulled along side. "That's fifteen bucks even pal," the driver said as he handed five dollars back.

"I forgot my keys and my spare is in the hubcap. If you have a wheel wrench and can pry it off, you can keep the five."

With a big grin, the cabbie got out and popped the hubcap in seconds. The magnetic box holding the spare key fell out on the ground.

Five minutes later, the new battery was in and working perfectly. David was ready to leave. He put the old battery in the camper cap of the truck, threw his travel bag inside at a respectable distance from it, took a last look at the factory where he had worked for the past six years and sped off without a word of goodbye. That was the painful part. Joey didn't have a chance to tell his folks goodbye, and neither would he. He knew the police would question his folks and so when they said that they hadn't seen him, it would be the truth. Just how much of a lead he would have on the law, he couldn't know.

Luckily, he had just filled up with gas and had the oil changed two days ago. He wouldn't have to stop until he hit Toronto. David sped along the highway, carefully watching his speed. The last thing he needed was for the cops to stop him. With no wallet, license or insurance certificate, they would haul him in for sure. His current situation had evolved quickly. At least he had enough money for a while, but before it ran out he would need a job and that would require ID. It would only be a matter of time before his name would be in the system.

A service centre was coming up and he was hungry. He pulled onto the exit ramp and dropped his speed. He drove through the pickup line and ordered his food. The hamburger tasted good as did the fries. He tore back the spill proof tab and sipped his coffee as he drove along. His mind reverted back to where it was before he stopped. Not being able to look for suitable work was going to be a real problem. He would have to look for some alternative way, something where no one asked too many questions. What was it that old man he met in Las Vegas did? Oh ya, he panned for gold. What was his name? Calvin Sparks. Calvin said that sometimes he didn't see a soul for weeks, even months. He thought for a moment trying to search his memory for the name of the place. It was in Idaho, someplace east of Pocatello, wherever that was.

David looked at the gas gauge; soon he would have to fill up. It was about thirty miles to Toronto. He would look for another Canadian Tire store where he would get gas and pick up some things that he needed. He would need an atlas so he could decide where he was going and better yet, how to get there. A comfortable sleeping bag, then he could sleep in the camper cap of the truck. Not only would it save him money, but he could avoid contact with others.

Using drive-through restaurants kept him out of long conversations and face-to-face contact. He could slip into washrooms fairly undetected and slip back to his truck. Being a fugitive was a new experience for him. He would have to get used to this life since it was either this or institutions of one kind or another for the rest of his life. There was no choice as far as he was concerned. Freedom was what wars were fought over and he wasn't going to lose his if he could help it. Why was he always a target? First Paulo had found out the hard way. He wondered if anyone ever reported him missing. Now Joey, and like Paulo he brought it on himself. David knew that what he did was horrendous but it was kill or be killed. It was all about survival, his survival.

9

The sound of a motorcycle coming into the yard caught Alex's attention. Joey must just now be coming home. His hours were erratic. Often Sully had him making deliveries and pickups into the wee hours of the morning. Alex knew what was going on and what was in those parcels but Ellen didn't know; at least he didn't think she did. She would have been furious if she did, or maybe not. She had grown very quiet and the way she looked at both him and Joey at times disturbed him, but what the hell, who knew what a woman was ever thinking anyway.

The doorbell rang. "That's funny," Alex thought. "It can't be Joey; he would just walk right in." Alex walked over to the door and opened it. He recognized Alfie from Sully's.

"Is Joey home?"

"No, he ain't here. I heard the bike and thought it was him coming home. Isn't he down at Sully's?"

"Nope. Not today, not yet anyway that's why I thought he might be here. Sully hasn't seen him either, he sent me over to get him."

"Well he didn't come home as far as I know. I didn't look in his bedroom but if his bike ain't here then he ain't either."

Alfie stood in the doorway. "Maybe. I saw him just after midnight. I told him I saw that Rivers guy that he don't like heading over towards the railroad bridge. Joey jumped on that ole Harley and took out like a shot. Said he had a score that he'd being waiting to settle one that he could handle by himself."

A big grin broke out on Alex's face. "Joey's been waiting a long time to give that kid a good shit kicking! I'm glad to see that he finally got the chance. He always wanted to catch him alone. He probably headed over to one of his girl friends afterwards. He's been banging that blonde girl whose husband is in jail."

"Sally Martin?"

Alex thought for a moment. "Could be. Do you know where she lives?"

"I think she's over on Maple Street. Her number's in the book. Give her a call, Sully sounded like he wants to see him right away."

"There's the phone and the book. You call her."

Moments later Ellen came up the steps carrying a bag of groceries from the corner store. Alex hadn't heard her leave the house. She walked in, sat the bag on the kitchen table and looked at Alfie on the phone. She looked back at Alex curiosity written all over her face. "Where's Joey?" Looking in Alfie's direction she continued, "What's he doing?"

"He's just calling one of Joey's girl friends. Sully's looking for Joey and can't find him."

The look on Ellen's face caused Alex to ask, "Why the look?"

"Oh probably nothing but I just saw the fire truck heading down the street and a police car following. Probably nothing but when you said Alfie was looking for Joey...well mothers always worry about their kids when they hear sirens."

Alfie put down the phone and walked over. "No Sally ain't seen him. Last I..." Alex shook his head motioning Alfie to stop.

"Me and Alfie will go find him. I'll be back at dinner time." The troubled look on Ellen's face was the first time in months that emotions of any kind had passed between the two of them. Alex hoped the warning bells going off were unnecessary.

Outside the house Alex caught the sound of a siren giving its final drone. He looked over at Alfie. "We better go over to the railroad bridge and see if there is any sign of Joey. Maybe he racked that damn Rivers kid up pretty bad and the cops got involved. Maybe they even have Joey in jail."

"Wouldn't they give him a phone call?"

Alex looked disgusted. "How the hell would I know. I know he didn't call so we have to start checking things out. You follow me on your bike; we'll get to the bottom of this."

Alex could see that something was going on by the number of cars that had pulled up and parked all over the lawn. People were standing there talking as he drove up and got out of his car. Alfie parked his motorcycle just behind him. The walkway approaching the bridge was blocked off by yellow police tape.

"What the hell's going on?" Alex asked a bystander.

The man looked up. "It looks like someone or something went through the guardrail and into the river. The railings all splintered but you can't see much from here. The fire department rescue unit is on the other side of the river. Oh, oh the diver is coming out of the water, see him over there? He's pointing to the middle of the river. He must have found something or someone down there."

"My God," said Alex, his face turning white as he looked around for Alfie. Spying him he yelled, "Let's get over there Alfie!"

Alfie shook his head. "They put yellow tape across the path. You can't pass it."

"Well, we'll walk across the train trestle. I'm going over there you can't see nothing from here."

They crossed the track in spite of the cop who waved them back. A tow truck was trying to make its way to the river. The same cop was busy trying to keep people away from the area so he could make it down the steep bank. All eyes watched as the tow truck operator got out of the cab, went to the back where he released a cable and handed it to the diver. The diver grasped it and then disappeared beneath the muddy brown water. Everyone stood breathlessly waiting to see what the Thames would give up. There was a gasp from the onlookers as something slowly emerged from the river. The object was covered in reams of chocolate coloured mud and water gushed as it swung around. As it rotated on the cable, the mud fell off it until finally it became recognizable to all. It was a motorcycle.

Alex stood there unable to move, it was Joey's. No doubt about it, it was his bike. The saddlebags with the skull emblems helped with the identification.

Suddenly Alex gasped, grabbed his chest and staggered backwards. His colour began to change and his eyes closed as he started to sink to the ground. Alfie quickly stepped forward catching him under his arms.

Alfie yelled at the cop, "Help, help over here. Get a medic or somebody from the rescue unit."

Soon, Alex was surrounded by ambulance personnel who examined him, fastened oxygen equipment on him and loaded him into the ambulance. They turned on the siren, parted the crowds and raced towards the hospital.

Corporal Ross walked over to Alfie who was still standing there in shock. "Whose bike is that?"

"How should I know?"

"I assumed that all bikers knew each other."

Alfie shrugged.

"We can go down to the station and have a nice friendly conversation if you like. Maybe your memory will come back."

Alfie squirmed a bit uncomfortable with all of the questions. Sully didn't like anybody talking to the cops about anything. This was probably different though it had nothing to do with Sully. "It might look like Joey Gallo's bike. I ain't sure though?"

Constable Ross looked hard at Alfie. "Joey Gallo? That name sounds familiar. Hangs out a Sullivan's garage doesn't he?"

Alfie gulped unsure of what to say. "I guess he might."

"You guess. Don't you 'guess' that sometimes you hang out there too?"

Alfie just looked at him but said nothing.

"You're just full of information aren't you? Who was that guy that was here with you, the one that they just took away in the ambulance?"

"Alex Gallo."

The police officer, who broke the news of Alex's heart attack to Ellen, drove her to the hospital. She wondered about Joey but hadn't asked; the news about Alex was stressful enough. He always seemed so strong. Alex having a heart attack was the last thing that ever entered her mind. The officer left her at the nurse's station and they asked her to wait in the sitting room. While she waited, they brought her hospital forms to complete including information concerning his insurance coverage.

There was no one else in the waiting room and time dragged. It had been over an hour and from where she was sitting she could see nurses coming and going. She leafed through a few of the magazines but couldn't concentrate enough to read. Finally, she approached the lone nurse at the station.

"Is there any news yet about my husband? I've been waiting so long to talk to someone."

"What is the name?"

"Alex Gallo. Dr. Jerome Martin is our physician. I don't know if he is the one that is looking after him or not."

The nurse smiled, picked up the intercom and used the paging system. "Dr. Martin will you please call extension 201, Dr. Martin extension 201." Putting down the intercom she said, "Please have a seat and I will call you as soon as I hear anything."

Minutes later a young blonde nurse stuck her head around the corner. "Mrs. Gallo? Please follow me."

Ellen had to almost run to keep up with the nurse through two large doors and into the emergency ward. It was full of single beds on wheels for ease of movement. Curtains acted as temporary walls surrounding three sides of the bed; some were drawn and some not. Patients laid or sat waiting for service of one kind or another. The nurse turned her head and spoke as they hurried along. "I hope you weren't waiting long, this place has been a zoo today. Ah, here we go."

Ellen never got a chance to answer. The nurse pulled back a curtain and ushered her in where Alex lay. A breathing mask partially covered his face exposing just enough to be recognizable. His hair flowed out against the pillow; his skin had lost much of his colour. For once, this blustering hulk of a man looked completely helpless. He blinked his eyes in recognition and held out his hand. Gently she took it. It was the first physical contact between them in months.

Half an hour later, Dr. Martin slipped into the emergency room. Alex had dozed off, releasing her hand as the medication began to work. The doctor motioned her outside the emergency confine.

"How are you, Ellen?"

She blushed slightly. She was always uncomfortable talking to the doctor although she never knew exactly why. "I'm all right doctor. How bad is Alex?"

"It's a little too early to tell. I'll know better in a few days, lucky for him that there was a rescue unit right at the scene. By the way, the police officer that brought you here is waiting to have a word with you. I'm going that way so I'll walk along and we can talk. I have a feeling that Alex will respond to treatment fairly quickly. His vital signs have stabilized and that's good but he'll probably be here for a week at least. Can you manage on your own?"

Ellen was about to say that Joey would be around but suddenly she had this strange feeling and wasn't sure. What had caused Alex to the point of having a heart attack? And why did the policeman want to talk to her? Suddenly her heart began to race and breath came in gasps. She didn't know what was going on but she had a bad feeling.

All she remembered was Constable Ross escorting her to the waiting room. It was all so surreal and the words seemed to make no sense. "And so at this point we're not sure just where your son is, Mrs. Gallo. We are hopeful that he will turn up all right but you may as well hear it from me rather than read it in the paper. At this moment the fire department is dragging the river for your son Joe and another person."

The officer gently put his arms around her as she broke down sobbing; all of this was just too much to bear.

Chief Roy Daniels looked up as Constable Ross walked into his office. "Good morning, Rick. Go get a coffee and sit down, I want to go over this incident at the PM Bridge yesterday."

"Do you think that it was drug related?"

Constable Ross stifled a small grin. The chief was getting paranoid he seemed to think that drugs were somehow related to everything lately. Of course, in this case it could have been but he seriously doubted that it was.

"Just before the rescue unit quit dragging the river last night, they found a pair of blue jeans with a wallet in them."

"Who's wallet? Gallo's?"

"No, David Rivers. I know Dave. He's a nice kid from a good family but a few years back he and young Gallo got into quite a fight. I was there when he rendered Gallo unconscious. Joey Gallo has been in a lot of trouble since then but I never heard anything about David until they found his wallet in those pants. I think that this may be more of settling an old score than drug dealing."

"You mean Rivers went after Gallo?"

"More likely it was the other way around. That's what went on the first time. Gallo had been bullying Rivers and the kid finally turned on him. I'm wondering if something like that happened again."

"Did you check on Rivers?"

"I was just about to Chief."

Ross pulled up in front of John and Marilyn Rivers' house. He took a deep breath and tried to get the thoughts straight in his head. This part of the job was one of the harder things that he had to do, investigate situations where disturbing news about loved ones could have a negative impact on the family.

John Rivers opened the door and faced the officer with a look of surprise. "Yes officer?"

"Good morning Mr. Rivers, I wonder if I might step inside a moment and have a word with you."

John opened the door wide and stepped to one side, his gaze somewhat puzzled. "Certainly, is there a problem?"

Once inside Ross removed his hat as his eyes panned the neat interior of the bungalow. "I'm afraid there is." Behind John, Marilyn Rivers appeared her eyes growing wide with curiosity.

"Have either of you seen the morning paper yet?"

John managed a smile. "Our paper doesn't come until after four."

"Well there is an article on the front page about an incident that happed yesterday over at the PM railroad bridge. We pulled a motorcycle belonging to Joseph Gallo out of the river after it was brought to our attention that something had gone through the guard rail. We sent a diver down and he recovered the motorcycle."

Marilyn's hand flew to her mouth her eyes wide. "Was Joey found in the river as well?"

"No, he wasn't. In fact, we found nothing but the bike. We dragged the river and what the rescue unit found was a large Bowie knife with what we call a brass knuckle grip. There was something else we found...a pair of Levi's with a wallet in the pocket belonging to David."

The look of shock on the faces of the two seniors was very real. They both sank down onto the sofa. Ross waited for a moment before proceeding. "Have either of you spoken to your son today or in the last few days?"

Adrenalin

It was John that answered, his face white and his voice trembling. "When you mentioned the name of Joey Gallo my heart skipped a beat, he and our son had more than one run in going way back to when we lived in the same neighbourhood. David has his own apartment over on Water Street. We haven't seen him in a couple of days. I could call him."

Constable Ross silently waited as John Rivers dialed the number. His hands were shaking and his eyes were growing misty as he waited hoping for an answer on the other end, but there was no response. "I'll call his work and see if he's there."

John finally replaced the phone his voice trembling. "They haven't seen him either. The foreman said that he worked late the night before last and didn't show up for work yesterday or today. He said something about David having trouble with his truck but I wasn't listening close enough to understand. I don't know what to say."

"He never called or came around during this time?" Ross was now writing that all down in his notebook.

"He was over here last Sunday for dinner." John said. "We haven't seen him since. He doesn't check with us every day. He's a good boy and wouldn't hurt anyone but if that Gallo boy is involved, it can't be good. I can just feel it."

"He lives in the rear apartment and he keeps a key over the door, a spare key if you have to get in. I could go with you if you want."

"No, that's okay, I have some other things to do. I'll check it out later. Thanks for your help and I'll be in touch if I hear anything further."

Constable Richard Ross walked back to his cruiser. He had declined John Rivers offer to go over to his son's apartment. If this was a crime investigation you never know what you might find and he didn't want them to be a part of that.

He stopped at the address on Water Street, walked around to the door of the apartment and knocked. No answer but then he wasn't expecting any. He ran his fingers along the top of the door. They came to rest on the key. He used it to open the door and let himself in.

"Hello. Anyone here?" Still no answer. He took out his notebook and continued writing. The trail of brown silt that ran to the bathroom was easy to follow. The underwear on the floor was still damp and the bed was unmade and wrinkled badly. He had better get someone from the lab down here to go over the whole apartment.

After he made the call to the station, he went out to the trunk of his car and pulled out a roll of yellow tape. He would have to designate it as a possible crime scene before he even tried to contact the people that lived in the front of the house. A hunch told him to walk out to the bank of the river and look for signs, and they were there. The brush had been broken and pieces torn out of the ground. There were also signs of foot traffic on the bank where someone had recently come ashore. He looked down towards the railroad bridge where a train was now rumbling across. He could see the new boards that replaced the splintered ones.

Like a puzzle, things were falling into place. Two important pieces were still missing though, Joey and David.

10

Marie and Jean-Claude St. Clair sat on the dock at the back of their farm fishing. The crops on their hundred acre farm had all been planted and this was Sunday a time to relax. Their farm was located in the small French speaking community of Jeanettes Creek, about five miles from the mouth of the river where it emptied in the lake, and about 14 miles from Chatham. Here fishing was good, anything that could be caught in the lake could be caught here or so Jean-Claude always claimed. The huge muskie that he had caught off this dock hung on the wall of his den as proof. The spring run of pickerel had been over for some time; still the odd one was caught along with perch and bass, all good eating.

Today, the fish were not biting. They sat on the Adirondack chairs just enjoying the warmth and the quiet. Marie's pole gave a little bounce. She came back to life as she waited for that second tug. There it was as she set the hook. She reeled it in, the small perch fighting back as it came to the surface. She unhooked it studying whether or not to put it on the stringer. Her short stocky husband began to laugh.

"Da fish she is so small. You not going to keep dat?"

Marie didn't appreciate the dig. "Mister smart guy! The big fisherman! What you caught so far, eh?"

Her husband smiled he knew just how to get a rise out of her. "Dats not a fish, dats a minnow. She's just good for bait."

At that moment, his pole bent and he quickly set the hook. The black bass put up a real battle as it broke water several times. He reached down with the net and brought it in. Smiling broadly he turned to Marie. "Now dats a fish for sure."

"Too bad you can't keep it Jean-Claude. Da season she don't open 'til a week from tomorrow."

From a willow tree jutting out of the bank a short distance away, a kingfisher made his high pitched scream as he left a branch darting straight down coming out of the water with a small fish in his beak. Jean-Claude hooked over at Marie. "Dat kingfisher he catch one bigger dan da one you have on da stringer." And he laughed loud as he lovingly watched her face in disgust.

Marie began to curse her husband in French when suddenly her pole bent deep into the water. Something had hit hard. The drag on the reel started to slip.

"Set the hook! Set the hook!" yelled Jean-Claude caught up in the excitement. "Tighten da drag. Not too much, don't loose 'im!"

Marie was excited and busy as she yelled back, "Shut up old man I know how to fish just as good as you! Maybe I catch a muskie dat puts da one you hung on da wall to shame!"

Jean-Claude watched closely waiting for the fish to break water. But the fish wasn't surfacing, nor was it diving for the bottom, but it wasn't a snag either. It was still coming in, once in a while the brake on the reel would slip but it was not continuous like when a fish puts up a fight. He said nothing. She had snagged something, but what?

Suddenly Marie screamed and dropped the pole. Jean-Claude grabbed the rod just before it went off the end of the dock. He reeled it in some more. Almost instantly he saw what made Marie scream. What Jean-Claude didn't know was that they were bringing Joey Gallo to the surface. That nightmare would keep him and Marie away from the fishing dock for many years to come.

11

The sun had gone down over three hours ago. At this time of year it must be close to midnight. He should have bought a watch but he didn't and he could turn on the radio and listen for the time, but it didn't really matter. He had put a lot of miles behind him and still had a long way to go. He pulled off of the Trans-Canada Highway and into the service centre. He drove back to where the 'big rigs' parked, where the drivers were catching twenty winks in the comfort of their sleepers, before heading back out racing to their destinations.

It felt good just to stop, although he felt as if he were still moving, he had been traveling that long. At first he had thought about heading for Idaho, maybe even meeting up with Calvin Sparks, although that would really be a long shot. That wasn't what stopped him. It was the border. He had spent precious moments scanning the atlas that he had bought along with the sleeping bag that he was about to put to use. Remembering from his youth the stories of the Klondike gold rush in the Yukon Territories, he had decided to head in that direction and see just where it took him. British Columbia was where he was heading and he was a good part of the way along the road now.

He reckoned that he was close to Thunder Bay. Lake Superior's cool breeze would make for good sleeping he thought as he climbed into the camper cap and into his sleeping bag. How long he slept, he wasn't sure. The sound of one of the big eighteen wheelers pulling out must have awakened him.

The sun was just beginning to break in the east as he climbed out, locked the cap, and headed for the washroom at the rear of the restaurant. He avoided people, not wanting to stop to talk for fear someone might remember him. He went through once more what was becoming a routine. He pulled up to the drive through, got a breakfast sandwich and a coffee, then made his way over to the full service gas pump, where he pulled his hat low, paid the attendant for his fill-up and wheeled back out onto the highway.

David had expected heavy traffic around Toronto, everyone in Ontario knew that driving there was a nightmare, but Winnipeg caught him by surprise. He had a false impression of the city from looking at outdated school books. Thinking back, those books showed pictures of old traders with wagons loaded with buffalo hides in front of a Hudson Bay store, funny how that had stuck in his mind. This city was as modern as Toronto and the traffic nearly as bad, compounded by the fact that he didn't know where he was going. He couldn't take his eyes off of the traffic long enough to read the signs. He was becoming bewildered when suddenly a transport with Alberta licence plates driven by a man who knew where he was going passed and David was about to follow. Horns blared as he pulled over behind the truck. Keeping him in sight, he followed close, perhaps too close. He didn't want to rear-end him so he dropped back a little. Luckily, the transport was high-balling it.

They had nearly cleared the city as darkness set in and what might well be the last food stop came into view. David went through the drive-through, got his food and pulled around back into the parking lot.

As he ate, he surveyed his surroundings. At the back of the parking lot was a commercial garage. The neon sign over the large doorway said Mac's Towing. Half a dozen decaying cars sat in the lot; they appeared to be heading for the wrecking yard. Two had front ends smashed, two had flat tires and the others were just rusted out.

Adrenalin

Reaching under his seat, David pulled out a multi-bit screw driver. The Ontario plates on his truck were beginning to turn heads and that was the last thing he needed. He wanted to blend in to the western culture, not stick out like a sore thumb. Five minutes later, the Ford had a set of Manitoba plates, and he was on his way again.

He cruised along the highway until just after the twelve o'clock news. He pulled into a truck stop, fuelled up, and then pushed on through the night. It would be a couple more days of driving until he could start to relax far way from his nightmare.

A small herd of goats was standing on the road as David past the 'Welcome to British Columbia' sign. He stopped the truck and got out to breathe in the fresh clean mountain air. The sight was more than he could believe. The mountains rose out of the ground and peaked into the clouds. These stone giants covered the landscape and the scantily treed boulders lived up to their name, the majestic Rockies.

He laughed softly as the goats watched him. "This must be the welcoming committee," he mused. They stood looking curiously at him. There were several small kids among them, one began to bleat and the rest stared at him as he moved towards them. He had never seen wild goats and as he neared them, they practically exploded in every direction, bounding over the rocks rapidly disappearing down the side of the mountain. What a peaceful scene, if all of British Columbia was like this, he would enjoy it.

There was not a soul in sight. He pulled his truck safely off the road, grabbed a left-over sandwich and a coke and found a place to lie in the sun. Looking at the atlas, he had just passed Lake Louise in Alberta and with his finger traced the jagged red line of the highway until it intersected with another highway running at right angle to it. He traced that one north through towns with unfamiliar names. Finally, he came across one that he knew, Dawson Creek. Why that name stuck in his mind he wasn't sure, but it did and it was as good as any place. In the back of his mind it seemed to him that Dawson Creek had once been a gold mining town or was that Dawson City. On the map still looking north, he could see Dawson City. Ah well, he would have to drive through Dawson Creek to get to Dawson City. What was it his grandmother said about fate?

12

"Good Lord! What's this world coming to?" said Chief Roy Daniels, his eyes wild with disbelief.

"This is like something out of one of those horror movies like Dracula. This kind of thing isn't supposed to take place in this one-horse town." He stared down once more at the coroners report lying on his desk.

"The victim's throat tore completely out and supposedly done by human teeth! Come on Ross, let's take a ride over to the coroners. I want to see this for myself. Maybe the coroner, old Clarence Newburg, has hit the bottle again, not that I'd blame him. I never could figure why anyone would want to be a coroner, I thought that my job was bad enough."

The coroner drew back the sheet from the face of the corpse. "Good God. I never seen anything like it. Can you cover the throat of the victim with a cloth Clarence so that when we ask the next of kin to I.D. the body it won't look so gruesome?"

With a weird grin Clarence said, "You should have seen him before we cleaned him up Roy. His eyes were bulging out of their sockets and his skin was a ghastly grey colour like one of those monsters from a Frankenstein movie and..."

Chief Daniels shuddered from head to toe. "You have a distorted sense of humour Clarence."

If the sight of Joey's mutilated body upset him, he didn't want to be the one to tell the boys mother.

He turned to his officer. "You can drop me off at headquarters before you head over to the Gallo's house. I understand that Alex is still in the hospital."

Walking out towards the patrol car Corporal Ross was not happy. "It might be better coming directly from you Chief, a show of compassion from someone besides an ordinary cop."

"You're probably right Rick and I would, but I have an appointment with the mayor and then the school board has been after me about..."

And on and on, thought Corporal Ross. This trip was going to be a whole lot worse than the last one. He let the Chief off at the station and headed for the Gallo's house. He couldn't get this over quick enough.

Clarence Newburg had put a white sheet right up to the chin of the corpse. Ellen Gallo stood close by trembling. It was one thing to kid along with Roy Daniels, but quite a different thing to show no sign of remorse to a family member, especially a mother. His whole demeanour changed as slowly he pulled back the sheet showing only the face. A wail escaped her lips as she recognized the body of her son.

"Oh, Joey!" she said as she began to weep. The coroner gently replaced the sheet. There was no need for a formal statement. Under his breath, Corporal Ross cursed, the Chief should have had this chore instead of him.

Chief Roy Daniels was on the phone, his hair in disarray as he brushed it back with his free hand as Corporal Ross entered his office. Whoever was on the other end of the phone line was irritating him to no end. His face was a glowing shade of pink.

"Now don't go printing something like that in the newspaper. You'll have every nut in the country calling this office! No, I don't think that there is a maniac on the loose. Who told you that there were teeth marks on the victim?"

"Oh he did, did he? Well sometimes he exaggerates. You saw them yourself? And you're an expert I suppose. Now listen, the boy's next of kin are taking this hard, show a little compassion when you write the story and tone it down for their sake. Listen, we have a suspect in the case. You play ball with us and we'll give you an exclusive on the case, Bill. Don't go scaring people with this Dracula thing."

"As soon as we're sure...You bet."

The chief looked at Ross. "Reporters. Anything gory that sells papers they want to sensationalize."

Corporal Ross levelled his gaze on him and thought 'looks good on you.'

"How did the meeting with the mayor go?"

For an instant Roy Daniels drew a blank. "The mayor? Oh, he ah, he cancelled at the last moment wouldn't you know. This phone hasn't stop ringing since I got back. How did Mrs. Gallo take it?"

"She's a brave lady. I felt real sorry for her. Too bad her husband was in the hospital, she could have used the support."

Chief Daniels leaned back in his large swivel chair. Usually this was a quiet little town, almost boring to some residents. But not to him, he liked it that way. He reached up and wiped the sweat away from his brow with the palm of his hand. He sat for a moment deep in thought just looking at Ross.

"Where is the investigation into this Rivers kid going?"

"We put an all-points bulletin out on him as a 'person of interest', haven't heard anything yet. I had forensic go over his apartment. They found what I did. A pair of jockey shorts and a T-shirt both stained with river water and mud. The shirt had traces of blood and they'll compare it with that of Joey's. They made casts of the hand and foot prints along the river bank. So far, no trace of him. His parents haven't seen or heard from him, nor has his workplace. A couple of other things, his dresser drawer was open and it looked as if clothes were missing, as if he'd left in a hurry. Also, he took $2,500 out of his savings account. I checked at the bank. A taxi driver said he drove him over to the Canadian Tire store to get a new battery for his truck. He waited and then he drove him over to the plant where he worked and dropped him, and the battery, off."

"And when was that?"

"The same day they pulled Gallo's bike out of the Thames."

"That's enough for me to believe that he's still alive and our number one suspect. Upgrade that all-points bulletin to include 'flight to avoid prosecution'. I want this David Rivers found right away!"

"I'll get right on it. There are a few other loose ends that I want to clear up in the event that he is our man, and to make sure that we have all of our facts straight when, and if, we go to trial. I'm going over to the psychiatric unit and have a talk with Doc Hammond. Have you discussed any of this with the Crown Attorney?"

Chief Roy Daniels face showed just the slightest trace of disgust. He was the man in charge and he wasn't too keen on Ross' initiative. He preferred to give the orders and come up with the ideas; maybe Ross had his eye on the top job. Still he was right, you wanted all the facts before you were called to testify. He sat erect and cleared his throat. "I was just going to suggest that. When you finish your report officer, give me a copy, I'll see that we stay right on top of this."

Dr. Hammond listened intently to what Corporal Ross had to say.

"I remember arresting David Rivers some years ago and bringing him here for evaluation. At that time, he had gotten into a real battle with Joey Gallo, the boy they found in the river. Could you dig up the file for me?"

Dr. Hammond pressed the intercom. "Mary, would you see what we have on a David Rivers. His file would be somewhere between six and eight years old."

It wasn't long before Mary brought the file into the room. Dr. Hammond sat there for a few minutes, his lips moving slightly as he read the file to himself. "Yes. He was one of Dr. Armstrong's patients. Armstrong was green when he worked here. He has since gone to Toronto and set up practice. According to his report, the only thing that he found unstable about Rivers was that he seemed to get an extraordinary surge of adrenalin, more than normal, much more, when he was either frightened or angry. Armstrong seemed to think that this surge of the body's defence chemical seemed to override all sense of reason, even the difference between right and wrong when it took control. Armstrong put him on medication and we had no problem with him here. I seem to remember him now. What you describe though Rick, this savage attack could be the result of one of these adrenalin charged attacks. I've seen things emerge here that you wouldn't believe unless you saw it for yourself. Sometimes it takes several of the staff to restrain them, and narcotic injections to tranquilize a patient, until we can get a straight jacket on them or some other form of restraint."

"Okay, hypothetically, if Rivers was defending his life or thought he was, could he get off with a self-defence plea?"

"Are you defending Rivers actions, supposing that it was him?"

"Just wondering."

"You've probably been in court more than I have Rick. What do you think? If you were on the jury, would you feel secure with someone who had torn the throat out of another man, walking around loose?"

"I see your point. Actually you're only confirming my own beliefs. Rivers probably figured this out himself, eh?"

"Doctor Smith, who was also familiar with the case, seemed to think that he was quite capable of drawing that same conclusion. There was one thing anyone who had anything to do with David Rivers stressed, that he would rather be dead than incarcerated in any way, shape or form. I know it sounds melodramatic, but you might have trouble taking him alive if he thinks that his freedom is in jeopardy."

Corporal Ross sat in his patrol car. He had one more stop before writing out his report, a stop that he really didn't want to make. Events this week began to make him think more about his dad's offer to take over the family farm and leave police work to others.

Slowly he approached the Rivers' house, notebook in hand. He heard the squeak of a door and looked up to see John closing the front door behind him. "I've kind of been expecting you officer. My wife is taking this hard, so I thought that we could talk out back."

A nice rose garden sprawled out along the back porch where the two men sat down on Adirondack chairs. "Can I get you anything to drink?"

Ross smiled. "No thanks. This won't take long. You know why I'm here?"

"As I said, I was expecting you. The news that Joey Gallo's body was pulled out of the river was on the radio. Obviously, you think that David had something to do with it."

"I'm not going to beat about the bush, Mr. Rivers. At this point, David is our prime suspect, all of the evidence points to him. Personally, I don't believe that David had much choice in the matter. I know first hand how Joey Gallo hounded him. It looks as if David may have gotten pushed into a corner and took the only way out. The trouble is, that after someone, like Joey gets killed all of their faults seem unimportant. David's running certainly makes him look guilty. Have you heard from him?"

"Nothing, no phone calls, nothing."

"Do you have any relatives that he might seek out?"

"What kin we have live in this vicinity. I'm sure that we would know if he had contacted any of them. I was always afraid that something like this would happen." Tears began to fill John Rivers' eyes and the look of sadness on his face was hard for Ross to watch.

"What made you think that?"

"David always was a good boy, but Joey wasn't the only one that ever picked on him. Those other times, according to his mother, he would come home and go up to his room and scream and holler and beat on the walls. Once he punched a hole right through the plaster and the lath. I know, because I had to fix it. He has an uncontrollable temper when someone

129

comes after him. Otherwise, you wouldn't find a nicer person. I'm not surprised. Did you see the remains?"

Constable Ross stuck his notebook in his pocket before answering. "I saw Joey and it will probably be a closed casket."

As Constable Ross walked towards his patrol car, the curtains inside the house moved slightly as Marilyn Rivers watched him go. She slipped out the back door to where her husband sat, his face buried in his hands. Gently she asked. "How bad does it look for David?"

The weight of the world seemed at that moment to rest on John's shoulders as he looked up. "It looks real bad dear. We may well have seen David for the last time. He can't risk trying to contact us and I think he knows it. We'll just have to remember the good years that we spent with him. Ever since he came back from that trip to Las Vegas, he acted different. Did you notice it?"

"Yes, but I didn't say anything. I thought that maybe it was just my imagination. Even hoped that it was, but there was a coldness about him, as if he was hiding something. He wouldn't look straight at us and seemed to avoid even coming over to supper when we invited him. You noticed it to?"

"Oh yes, probably more than you did. Something took place, something terrible that he wasn't sharing with us or with anyone."

They sat quietly in the rose garden, both fearing that their son had been taken from them. Not in the same way that Joey Gallo had been taken from his folks, but almost as unbearable. John put his arm around his wife and pulled her close. It was a time of grieving.

13

It had been just four days since David had left Ontario. Four days since his life had been turned upside down. It was hard to keep his mind off of the grisly events that put him on the run. Here in British Columbia, it was easy to find places to stop, pull his truck off of the road and relax. He would find himself beside peaceful streams with mountains rising up behind providing spectacular scenery. It was different at night as he slept in his warm sleeping bag, secure in the camper cap in his truck. It was then the past memories would come stealthily into his dreams. They would evolve into ghoulish reflections, mainly of two arch-rivals of the past, Paulo and Joey Gallo. Sometimes one, sometimes both and sometimes just an unidentifiable form would pursue him. He would try to flee on legs that wouldn't move, with arms that would not rise to protect him, or let him flee from the monsters that chased him relentlessly. He would wake screaming. Fortunately, the locations he found for himself were far away from other people. When it was too much for him to bear, he would drive trying to flee what he could not; his own subconscious.

He stopped at Quesnel for a bite to eat and to fill up with gas. "How far to Dawson Creek?" he asked the elderly fellow filling his tank. He saw him reading his licence plate and thought how lucky that he had changed it. The old man didn't comment.

Again he asked, this time a little louder. "How far to Dawson Creek from here?"

The old fellow turned looking in the direction of Dawson Creek before answering. "Long way, five or six hundred miles. Take you most of the day to get there. You won't make it on this fill up and there ain't too many gas stations along the way, so if you see one, run on the top end of your gas gage."

The old man was right. There hadn't been many gas stations along the way and David stopped when he saw one. It was late when he finally rolled into Dawson Creek. The lights of the city were a welcome beacon. He had spent plenty of time thinking over the first move that he would make when he arrived. A motel would be good; he was tired of sleeping in the cramped quarters of the camper cap, tired also of waking up and having to look for a bathroom or even less suitable accommodations. Then it hit him! He would have to sign a register. He thought – a new start – a new name, but what? He would stay with David. It was a common name and one that he would answer quickly to, but the last name? Something that wouldn't pop up on a computer should be something like Rivers, the water part so that it would connect. Maybe David Lake. Hmm, too bland, he thought for a minute. Lakeworth? He said the name again. It didn't sound that bad really – 'David Lakeworth, from Manitoba.'

Frontier Motel was the marquis that first caught David's attention and it had a vacancy sign. Having arrived this late, he might still be lucky enough to get the local paper from the box in the lobby. He would also be able to watch the eleven o'clock news on the television to see if there was news of any kind about him. He was reasonably sure that there would not be, but being on the run was something that he was going to have to learn – and fast. There might not be a second chance if someone in this area was alerted to the fact that there was a killer in their midst. If nothing showed on either one of the media, he would try to fade into the fabric of the city.

The lone male clerk smiled as he walked up to the front desk. "For how many nights sir?" he asked as he shoved the registration card towards him.

"Just one," said a weary David.

Again the smile. "Will that be cash or credit card?"

"Cash," as he handed him the proper amount.

Looking at the registration card, the clerk smiled once more. "That will be room forty-six, Mr. Lakeworth." He quickly brought out a sheet showing the layout of the place. "Your room is located here on the south side of the building downstairs. You can park right in front of the door. Anything else that I can help you with?"

"I'll manage thanks," as he picked up the room key and headed for the door. The coin box contained the last copy of the Dawson Creek Sentinel. Lucky he thought. Outside, he found that he hadn't really parked that far from his room and the truck was all right where it was. With bag in hand, he turned the key and walked into the room. The nice large bed was a welcomed sight. His back was getting sore from the long drive and the hard flat box of the truck where he had been sleeping.

He read the paper and watched the news and it was a big relief not to see any mention of his name or the incident. The hot shower felt great and it felt every better sliding between the sheets of a comfortable bed. This night he would have a good sound peaceful sleep.

David imagined that it was much later than it was when he woke up. He looked at his watch, ten o'clock. The sound of the garbage truck outside must have shaken him from his slumber. Pulling the drapes aside, he could see the signs of the early birds beginning to move about. It was then that it dawned on him. The time difference! He had forgotten all about it. He had noticed the time difference once or twice at different intervals along the way but hadn't taken the time to change his watch. Flight and speed had been his only concern up until now. He turned on the television as he sat in his last clean pair of shorts. The world news was just ending as the local announcer came on beginning with, "Welcome to the seven o'clock news. Today here in Dawson Creek and the neighbouring areas of Tumbler Ridge, we are in for a gorgeous day…"

Adrenalin

David changed his watch to Pacific Time. He yawned, stretched and rubbed his eyes. He listened to the news for a few minutes more hearing nothing earth shattering, and nothing about the outside world, just local news including the mainland, Vancouver. He looked about the room, pulled open one of the drawers in the dresser and found what he was looking for, a plastic garment bag and a phone book. He searched for Laundromats. Noting the address of one that he would check out, he emptied the dirty clothes out of the carry on bag into the garment bag ready to do his laundry as soon as he could.

He looked at himself in the bathroom mirror; five days of not shaving had left him looking scruffy. He ran his hand over his chin; it was almost as if that rush of adrenalin had stimulated the growth of his whiskers and his hair. A razor and some shaving cream would have to be purchased and put to use before he gave up his room.

He dressed pulling on a T-shirt that would probably not be warm enough this far north, and a pair of blue jeans. He reached into his pocket feeling his keys and a crumpled twenty dollar bill. This was no good, he would need a wallet. The thought of where his old wallet was sent a chill up his spine, a thought he quickly decided not to dwell on. He would have to carry a decent amount of cash with him and stash some in the truck. Just for an instant he thought about opening up a bank account but then there would be all those questions and papers to sign and then if he had to suddenly flee. He decided against it, a money belt along with a wallet might be the smart way to go.

He zipped open the compartment of the carry-on bag and withdrew some cash. He took time to count it, just short of nineteen hundred dollars. Pretty good actually considering the expenses he had getting here. Not bad. Then he wrinkled his brow, the money wasn't going to last. He could not afford to stay in the motel or for that matter, to pay rent anywhere without some sort of income.

"First things first," David thought. He had already determined that all of his money should not be kept in one place. Five hundred he stuffed into the pockets of his jeans. The rest he split into two piles. The one pile he stuck back in the zippered pocket of his carry-on bag. The other he would hide near the spare tire inside the camper cap. Leaving the bag in his room, he took out his room key and locked the door as he was leaving. Checkout was eleven o'clock and it was now just ten after eight. Walking over to the pickup, he unlocked the cap, reached inside the spare wheel cover and deposited the money. Carefully he looked around; no one was paying any attention to him. About half dozen cars were parked alongside the motel where his truck was parked. At one of them, a man was getting instructions from his wife on how to pack luggage in the trunk of a car that was already overloaded. After satisfying her, he slammed the trunk down, got into the car still cursing as she hurriedly jumped in and closed the passenger door before he took off.

David reached down into his pocket and came out with a twenty dollar bill. By the number of cars and trucks pulling into the Caribou Restaurant across the street, he decided it must be a good place to eat, and he was getting hungry.

The diner was rather small and crowded. A lunch counter ran the length of the place. The cash register was strategically placed at the front so that no one could leave without paying. Beyond the arbourite top of the counter and the barstools sat a half dozen tables each with four chairs. Two of them occupied, while a man sat alone at one of the others. At three of the bar stools sat local construction workers, their hard hats giving their profession away. They were in the process of wiping their plates clean and swallowing down the rest of their coffee as David walked past them and sat at an empty stool at the far end of the counter. The trio got up and paid their bill as he picked up the menu.

The cook had his back to David and busied himself scrapping the grill with a chrome-plated spatula. The bacon sizzled as he threw it on the cleaned surface and filled the air with the aroma it gave off. The lone waitress was busy ringing up the cash, taking orders and delivering food. She finally made her way down to where David was sitting. She looked to be in her forties with more than enough makeup on a face that probably didn't need that much. Her hair was red and frizzy and she was chewing gum a mile a minute as she took the pencil from her hair.

"What will it be honey?"

David really hadn't made up his mind. "What's the special?"

"Two eggs, any style, with bacon, ham or sausage, with home fries, sourdough toast and coffee, for three dollars."

David smiled. "Sounds good." The aroma of bacon helped him make up his mind. "Eggs scrambled and bacon."

She turned to the cook, who had already heard the order and was busy scrambling two eggs. "Got that Harry?"

"Got it," he said as he carried on.

The waitress moved down the counter picking up the change left for tips, dropping it into her apron pocket as she gathered up the dirty dishes. David felt in his pocket. Yes, he had some change for a tip.

The waitress brought him a cup of hot coffee. It wasn't long before she brought the overloaded plate with his breakfast and set it down in front of him. She grabbed the ketchup bottle from down the counter and placed it within reach. "Anything else honey?"

"Not at the moment." He took a sip of the coffee; it almost burnt the skin off his tongue. He poured more milk in it and took another sip, then grabbed a piece of toast and attacked his breakfast. At first he didn't notice the person who slid onto the stool next to him, until he spoke.

"What's this I hear about you selling this little gold mine, Harry? You getting tired of running this diner or what?"

David looked over at the fellow on the next stool. He was old with grey hair sticking out from under the battered old hat perched at a rakish angle on his head. His rumpled sport coat looked comfortable with suede patches on the elbows. He was peering through a pair of wire rimmed glasses and wearing one of those 'dickey bow ties'. The tie reminded David of his father who used to say *you should always buy a coffee coloured tie so that the stains wouldn't show*. He thought about his father and how he would never see him grow old, and there was an empty feeling in his heart.

The cook turned and eyed him slowly, his grey moustache contrasting against his reddening face. "Word of mouth seems to travel faster than 'The Sentinel' in this town, Ken." Harry said dryly.

"Is it true?"

"I wanted to keep it quiet until the papers are signed."

"When will that be?"

David could see Harry becoming annoyed by the inquisitor. "This afternoon about two, since the paper won't hit the street until three, I should be all set."

His remarks hardly fazed the old fellow. "Now don't be testy, Harry. It's the worst kept secret in town. You know I have my job to do. Who is the buyer, just for the record?"

Harry smiled for the first time. "Come around after closing and I'll tell you."

"But you don't close until after ten o'clock at night!"

"I know that's one of the reasons that I'm selling this 'Little Goldmine'. The other one is that I hate the cold winter's here, so I'm going back to the mainland. You can print that too if you like."

Harry turned around and went back to tidying up the grill before the next flow of customers arrived.

Ken turned towards David. "Howdy stranger, new in town?"

David was just wiping his plate clean, hoping to get out of the diner without being interrogated. He saw the outstretched hand coming at him, what he was about to hear was already a foregone conclusion.

"I'm Ken Davis, reporter for the Daily Sentinel, and you are?"

"David Lakeworth, from Winnipeg Manitoba." It was strange hearing what he had rehearsed, coming out in a conversation. The last one that he had expected to use it on was a local news reporter.

"What brings you to Dawson Creek, David?" he asked while bringing a dog-eared notebook out of his coat pocket and licking the end of a pencil before beginning to write. David could feel his stomach churn.

"I'm just at loose ends right now, nothing noteworthy."

The old man's pale blue eyes lit up. "Everything is newsworthy my boy. It's surprising what interests' people. What did you do in Winnipeg?"

Damn the questions, David thought, as he began to perspire. He remembered what his dad once said, 'the best way to keep from answering a question is to ask them one.'

"I came to Dawson Creek thinking that maybe there was still a little gold prospecting around this area. Is there?"

"Oh the gold all played out a few years after the 'Klondike rush of '98. They still do a little mining down near Barkerville, the site of the Caribou gold rush of the 1860's. You'd have better luck, if any, down that way."

"Well I'm here with time on my hands at the moment. So could I just buy a pan and hunt around anywhere?"

"No, I didn't say that. Some of this area still has claims registered. You would have to check first."

"What difference would it make if there's no gold here?"

The expression on Ken Davis's face was almost comical to watch. Obviously he was better at asking questions than answering them.

"Well, ah, there is still some gold found in these parts but very little, certainly not enough to get rich on or even make a decent living."

"Who has these claims?"

The old man rubbed his chin, puzzlement clouding his face. "Well off hand, the only one that comes to mind would be Jim Hawkins. He bought up a bunch of them old claims for pennies some years back when no one wanted them. They say he makes a buck or two on them. Hmm, you know that might not be a bad story angle. Maybe I should interview him myself. On the other hand it might just be a waste of time, Jim's not big on giving out information on himself."

"Where would I find this Jim Hawkins?"

"He lives down towards Tumbler Ridge. Name is on the mailbox. It's a big ranch type house with a veranda running all the way around it. You'll see a half dozen or so mules in the pasture. He guides pack trips for big game. He also does fishing trips and runs some trap lines. He has his fingers in a lot of enterprises and land deals, anything that turns a dollar, nice fellow though, real easy to get along with."

"Maybe I should have a talk with him," said David, happy now that Ken's focus of attention had turned away from him. His dad had been right.

"Well, if you go out there, you can tell him that you were talking to me. That way it won't sound like you're a stranger. By the way, if you drive in the yard, sound your horn and wait a minute before you get out, and wait for him or his wife to show. He sometimes has some pretty mean dogs that'll snap right on to you."

David reached into his pocket and slid some change under his plate for the waitress. He looked up into the face of the old reporter. "Thanks for the advice Mr. Davis. I think I'll take a run out and see this Hawkins fellow."

"Well give him my regards. It was nice to meet you, Lakeworth was it?"

"David Lakeworth, from Winnipeg."

The variety store next door had the shaving soap and razors he would need, the stubble was beginning to itch. Shaving before he checked out of the motel would be a good idea, no telling when he would get another chance.

He turned in his key, threw his carry-on bag in the camper cap and pulled out of the Frontier Motel's parking lot. Two blocks down the main street he spotted the Laundromat and pulled in.

Adrenalin

The dryer was still running as David walked to the front door and looked out. Across the street, and a few doors down, was a sporting goods store. He stood there looking out as a woman with a basket full of laundry pushed by him. In a few minutes she would have the place all to herself he thought as he pulled his briefs and socks out of the dryer.

The sporting goods store window displayed a small tent and some sleeping bags. Beside it was a mannequin dressed in waders, a shirt and a vest loaded with all of the paraphernalia that a fisherman should have. He was also wearing a hat with trout flies covering the surface. In his hand, he held a fly rod and on his face, a realistic smile. What caught David's eye was the fishing vest. It would work better than a money belt and not look out of place worn over a t-shirt.

Twenty minutes later, he emerged from the store. He wore a vest, one like in the window, over a plaid shirt that he also bought. Even though it was June, it was still cool here. He picked up a collapsible fishing rod and reel in a small compact carrying case, along with some flies and casting bait, and a small hunting knife in a sheath that fastened to his belt. Catching fish and cleaning them could become a very necessary means of survival. He placed the money that was left in a new wallet.

David unlocked the camper cap, reached in and retrieved the money that was in the carry-on bag. In the privacy of the truck's cab, he slipped off the vest and deposited the cash in the pocket in the back, the one meant to carry fish. He started the truck and headed down towards Tumbler Ridge.

He kept his eye on the odometer. Three miles rolled up and he spotted what looked like the house the reporter had described. The mules in the pasture were the first landmark. They would catch anyone's attention. The ranch house held a commanding view from the top of the hill. A large red hip-roofed barn was located a hundred yards or so from the house. A large fenced yard contained two dog sleds and several husky dogs that began barking as he turned into the drive. David had noticed that dogs and dogsleds were quite prevalent in this area, giving the north a distinctive difference from landscapes far to the south.

He stopped adjacent to the path that led to the house. A large Siberian husky came running towards the truck, barking loudly, the hair on his back bristling. This dog must have been the watchdog or a special pet that was not confined with the rest of the pack.

David sat there a moment debating whether or not to risk stepping from the safety of the truck. That decision was made for him, the door of the house opened and out stepped a man that David was sure must be Jim Hawkins. He was six feet plus in height, dressed in Levi's, a plaid shirt and shiny western boots. His face was tanned and he had that capable confident look. A full head of rich brown hair framed a face with penetrating blue eyes and a neat handle bar moustache.

"Lay down, Wolf!" he said, directing his stare at the husky. The dog retreated to the large veranda where he laid down, head between his paws, those wolf-like eyes never leaving the stranger.

"Mr Hawkins?"

"I'm Jim Hawkins. What can I do for you?"

"Ken Davis from town said that you might be able to answer some questions for me."

"He did, did he? Most of the time Ken asks the questions," he grinned. "Are you a reporter?"

"No. Nothing of the sort, I just came up here from Winnipeg. I thought I might try my hand at panning for gold. Ken said that you might shed some light on where I could or couldn't pan."

Jim threw his head back and let out a hearty laugh. "The gold rush petered out in the early part of the century. You're a bit late."

David relayed the tale that the old prospector he had met earlier in Las Vegas had told him. As he finished, the expression on Jim's face changed slightly. "Did you ever pan for gold?"

"No. But I understand that it's not to hard, learning it that is."

"Come on up on the porch and sit down."

As David settled down into one of the comfortable rustic chairs, Jim hollered towards the open door of the house. "Hey Judy, we have a guest, bring out some refreshments will you honey?"

From inside the house came the high pitch of a woman's voice. "What do you want, beer or root beer?"

David laughed. "Just make mine root beer. I'm still feeling my way around here."

Over his shoulder, Hawkins roared. "Two root beers, Judy."

It wasn't long before Judy appeared with drinks in hand. She had dark hair and appeared to be about the same age as Jim. She was pretty and had a good shape, and the higher pitch of her voice had led David to think that she would have been tall and thin. Her smile made David feel as if they had met before, the kind that probably made everyone seem welcome right off. The two frosty mugs that she was carrying looked good as she set them on the table.

Jim turned and said, "This is... I guess that I forgot to ask you your name?"

"Oh, I'm sorry, I should have introduced myself. It's David, David Lakeworth, from Winnipeg."

Judy's eyes lit up. "My cousin lives in Winnipeg. Where 'bouts in Winnipeg did you live, David?"

It was something that he hadn't anticipated. He had to think quickly remembering what little he could of a city that he had just buzzed through. He was trying to remember the billboards on the roadsides and what they were advertising, or the marquis with neon signs that flashed by while he was trying to keep up with the trucks. But he was drawing a blank. The only one that might be legitimate flashed into his mind. "We lived on a small farm out by the Assineboin."

"The racetrack or the river?"

Think fast; think fast. "The racetrack. Where does your cousin live?" He began to sweat waiting for the answer.

"She lives in a condominium downtown. I'm not sure of the street. Emily Jones is her name. I could look through some old Christmas cards and get her right address?"

"No, don't bother. Her name is not familiar. I didn't often go downtown anyway. The farm kept me busy. I probably wouldn't even know the name of the street either." David was about to panic. He hadn't anticipated all these questions. He should have known that only a woman would ask so many questions, men would have quit after the first. He glanced over at the mules in the pasture and hoped that Jim didn't start asking him farm related questions. From now on, he wouldn't mention Winnipeg and he certainly hoped that no one else would bring it up. He looked at Judy who just smiled.

"No, maybe you wouldn't. Winnipeg is so much larger than Dawson Creek, isn't it David? Oh well, it was nice to meet you." With that, she disappeared back into the house.

Jim took a big drink and sat down the empty glass. He sat there looking at David sizing him up. He raised his eyebrows and said, "You look like your more into fishing than panning for gold."

David laughed. "I just bought these articles of clothing and some fishing equipment this morning before coming out. Me and my dad had a falling out and I had to get a way from everything and everybody for a while until I get myself straightened out. It's just a family matter. The fishing stuff, well, I have to eat and it looks like there's lots of fish around here."

"There is that, but if you didn't pick up a licence you'd better. There's lots of work in this area though, jobs that you could make a whole lot more money at than panning for gold."

"Maybe later but for now, I just need some space."

There was something in the way that David spoke, the look in his eyes that stirred feelings deep within Jim. Maybe what he said about his dad was true – maybe not. He had seen more than one man come to this area to escape the cares of the world or other things. Maybe he was on the run. He didn't look the type though. Whatever it was, up here-you didn't ask a lot of questions. He drummed his fingers on the arm of his chair as he looked quizzically at David.

"What exactly did Ken Davis say that sent you looking for me?"

"He said that you had bought up most of the old claims in this area."

"Ah, so that's it. I did some years ago. I thought that there might be something still worth mining, something that the rest had missed. The gold washes down from the mountains above and I thought if I could find a spot where there was even a moderate amount of gold, say a small concentrate of it, that it might be worth getting a geologist to examine the rock formation above that area. If I went to all that expense and trouble, I wanted to be sure that it was me that had the mining rights."

"And did you have any luck?"

"Some, but not enough to bring in a geologist. I make a buck or two, but nothing big. What I did was find a person like you, only older, much older, someone who just wanted to be left alone and didn't need to make a lot of money. He pans the claims. At the moment, he's working one about forty miles from here over towards Jasper Park. There's an old cabin on the place that we fixed up a little so that it doesn't leak, and he cuts enough firewood to keep warm in the winters. That is when he stays there, which isn't always. I generally take him some potatoes and vegetables and some elk or deer, when I shoot one. He makes us both a little money. He knows what to look for in the rock, but so far, there hasn't been enough to get excited about."

"Do you think he could use some help up there?"

Jim looked long and hard at David. David could feel he was deciding whether or not to trust him. He finally seemed to satisfy himself. "You see, the thing is, he's temperamental as hell. He's not a big man but he's full of fight. He weighs about a hundred pounds, eighty pounds of temper and twenty pounds of man. I'm not sure that he'd even let you stay there and if he did, you might be working for nothing. We really aren't finding that much gold. Sometimes though, I worry about him all by himself there's no one around if there's trouble. Judy's mentioned that more than once. Still, he don't seem to mind."

David shrugged. "I got nothing to lose. Can we take a run up and see him? What's his name?"

"Andy, Andy Jackson. Well I can't go today or for the next few days. Some people want to pack in and go fishing up in the mountains and I'm supposed to act as their guide. When I saw you drive up with that new fishing vest on, I thought that you were part of the crew."

"Nope, not me."

"So I see. Nonetheless, their spokesperson said that they would be here today. I'll tell you what I'll do though Dave, I'll draw you a little map. You can go up and see Andy yourself. See if you can get along with him, if you want. You can tell him that you talked to me and that the decision is his. Or, you can hang around Dawson Creek until I get back, and I'll go up with you. He'll be testy. I can almost guarantee either way. He don't cotton much to strangers."

It didn't take long for David to decide. Right now, he didn't 'cotton' to strangers or anyone else. It would probably be easier to deal with one cranky old man than a city full of curious people. "Thanks a lot Jim, I think I'll drive up and see this Andy. I'm sure that we can work something out."

Jim looked at him rather sceptically. "Don't get your hopes set too high. There might not be anything to thank me for. Come on in the house first though, you might as well have some dinner before you strike out."

The drive down to the claim site was refreshing. The scenery was a bit different here, more exposed rock and fewer trees but all of it breathtaking scenery, as sparkling streams

145

and rivers flowed far below the roadway. Wildlife was evident wherever he looked, from the whiskey jacks in the trees to the white flags that seemed to shoot up out of the bushes as white tailed deer spooked by the vehicle bounded away. The six days since he left home seemed light years away. This was the new beginning that he needed. It felt right, away from the eyes and ears of the world, blocking out the past. Jim felt that he would have trouble getting along with this Andy fellow, but he was determined to make it work, whatever it took.

He glanced down at the odometer; forty miles would be about sixty kilometres, about six to go. He pulled over to the side of the road. The sketch that Jim Hawkins made left much to be desired. Somewhere up ahead, according to the sketch, was a hill, then a curve, and then a narrow road running down towards the creek. Occasionally, it could be seen paralleling the road. The terrain was hilly and full of curves in the mountains; however he had not seen many narrow roads leading away from the main one that he was travelling. Once back on the road, he slowed down; at least there was no traffic. Since he left the Hawkins place, he had seen only four cars. Finally, he came to the small roadway leading down towards the creek. David glanced at the odometer, sixty-three kilometres. He turned off the main road proceeding carefully. The assent down to the creek was steep. Dropping the transmission back into first gear, he let the truck creep along. Suddenly, a whitetail deer darted out in front of the truck, startling both the deer and David. It was a near miss. Moments later the ground flattened out and David pulled into a large clearing.

Over to the left sat the old cabin. There was no doubt it had been erected a long time ago. The original structure had been logs. Part of the back wall had been patched and covered with John Mansville brick siding, dating that bit of repair to the nineteen forties. The roof had been covered with corrugated steel, some of Jim Hawkin's handiwork no doubt.

The whole place had the comfortable look of a patchwork quilt.

An old Chevy pickup, ravaged by rust was parked nearby. He didn't know if it was still used for transportation, perhaps not. As David stepped from his truck, he looked around, his eyes sweeping the entire landscape. The cabin was sitting on a piece of real estate fit for a millionaire. There was a small waterfall at the edge of the clearing, spilling its crystal clear water into a large pool. At that moment, a fish broke the shimmering surface as it leapt for a bug. A large buck stood at the edge, sipping from the stream. He lifted his head, looked in David's direction, and then calmly took another sip from the stream.

As the deer walked off into the woods, David heard the cabin door open, and he got his first look at Andy Jackson as he came down the steps. It wasn't the size of the man that caught David's attention. He had been prepared to see a small man. It certainly wasn't the way he was dressed, rubber boots, a pair of overhauls and plaid shirt, topped by a well worn hat, similar to the one that the mannequin in the store hat been wearing. It was the thirty-thirty rifle that the old man was pointing in his direction. This was certainly a long way from any greeting that he would have received back in Chatham. This, of course wasn't Chatham and for that matter, this wasn't exactly a greeting.

"What the hell do you want?" he roared with his back humped up like a Halloween cat.

"Jim Hawkins sent me up to see you."

The barrel of the rifle dropped slightly but his gaze still held its intensity.

"Why?"

"He thought you might be able to use some company and some help," David said putting forth his best smile.

The old man never batted an eye nor showed any interest in making new acquaintances with anyone, least of all, the one that he was facing. "Well I don't need either! I get along just fine. Besides, if Jim Hawkins was going to send someone up here he should have checked with me first or at least come up here with you."

"I just showed up and told Jim that I wanted to learn how to pan for gold. He would have come up here with me but he has a fishing party that he has to take up in the mountains. He said he would be busy for a few days."

The hair that stuck out from under the hat fairly bristled. Small and defiant, his huge grey handlebar moustache made him look like a character out of a Disney cartoon. He wasn't to be taken in the same comical manner though, not with that rifle in his hand. His eyes narrowed below their bushy eyebrows. "You go back and tell Hawkins that I'm not wet-nursing any kid! If he wants to, he can!"

David decided to go the sympathetic route. "Have a heart man. I had a fight back home with my old man and he kicked me out. I got no money to speak of and no place to stay. Just let me give it a try."

"Listen kid, that ain't my problem and I'm not about to make it one, so haul your ass out of here now!"

David stood for a moment, the two of them facing each other down. David wasn't going to take no for an answer, this was exactly what he wanted. "No. I'm not going back. I'll stay here until I'm damn good and ready to go."

The old man was beginning to show signs of an impending fight as the rifle barrel tilted upwards in his hands. "Maybe I should just dust your tail feathers with old Betsy here. You won't be so sassy then," he roared.

"You'd shoot an unarmed man?"

It did seem to take some of the steam out of Andy. "You do what you want, but if you come within three feet of my cabin, you'll find out that I'm not fooling, unarmed or not." With that, Andy Jackson turned and walked back up the steps of the cabin slamming the door behind him.

'Well, we're off to a great start,' thought David. He could still picture Andy in his mind. The battered hat, the denim overalls, and dusty rubber boots that went up to his knees, reminded David of the gold prospectors that he had seen in history books. What he lacked in size, he made up for in force. It would be foolhardy to provoke him anymore at this time, maybe anytime.

David didn't move from the spot for a full five minutes. He was deep in thought. Somewhere in the back of his mind, his father's advice about the tool and die trade came back to him; *'Patience and perseverance usually pays off.'* This was as good a place as any to wait it out.

Out of the corner of his eye, he saw the curtain in the window move ever so slightly. He was a watched man. No doubt, Andy was expecting him to leave. He was likely thinking that when David climbed into his truck he would have won. David started the truck up, turned to head out the same way that he had come in, moved a few yards, put it in reverse and backed up close to the creek. He was not about to leave.

The first thing that he would need was firewood. About half an hour of hauling branches and twigs gave him what he thought would be enough to do him the night. He gathered some nice flat rocks, just like he had seen them do in the movies and placed them in a circle. In the absence of someone else to talk to, he talked to himself.

"Oh damn. I forgot matches." He looked towards the cabin; he had seen the curtain move once or twice. He thought of asking for matches and then remembered the warning, *'you come within three feet of this cabin and I'll dust your tail feathers'.* Bad thought, it was better, and safer, to leave old Andy alone. Wasn't he supposed to be panning for gold? Maybe he would have if David hadn't come along. At the moment he was watching his claim, David mused. He walked over to the truck and rummaged through the glove compartment. His hand came to rest on a single pack of matches. One of his smoking buddies must have put them in there. He made a mental note to get some the next time he went to town. Six precious matches later, along with the help of some paper from the clothes that he'd purchased, he had the fire blazing.

Adrenalin

In the hour that it took to burn down to a nice hot bed of coals, he put the fishing equipment that he bought to the test. As he sat on the tailgate of the truck reeling line onto the casting reel, he could see the odd trout jumping for flies. He had heard the splashing while he gathered wood. Now, as he sat watching, he could see the large circles left as they disappeared below the surface. It excited him. No doubt there were few that fished here, not with that old man around. The first cast of the Mepp's spinner drew a strike that he missed because he didn't set the hook quickly enough. He didn't make that mistake on the next cast. The water came alive with the fish jumping, fighting and splashing trying to get away. Moments later, he removed the treble hook from the mouth of the rainbow trout. It must have weighed at least two pounds. He marvelled at the colour that gave the fish its name. He was amazed at all the wildlife that he was now seeing up-close for the first time. Another cast, another fish, almost the same size. This one he released and watched as it swam away. One would be all that he could eat.

He quickly took the hunting knife from his belt and began to clean the fish. He was surprised at how little gut there was to a trout, the fish was very meaty. He laid the fillet on the tailgate.

He trimmed a nice four foot branch from a live willow tree. He cut it so that there was a 'Y' where the branches separate allowing the fish to be impaled in two places so that it didn't fall off and into the fire. He sat there slowly turning the fish, like roasting marshmallows over the glowing hot coals. As the fish began to slip away from the stick, he quickly withdrew it and rearranged it on the stick. He thrust it back over the fire for a few more minutes before he decided to try it. With no plate, he began to eat it as he would corn on the cob. It was delicious. Hot, but delicious, especially the first few bites. Along with matches, he would have to buy a frying pan and some plates.

David licked his fingers clean. The fire was burning low and the coals still a bright cherry red. He threw the bones, along with the head and entrails, into the fire. He sat back throwing a few more sticks on the fire. Small sparks drifted harmlessly up before extinguishing themselves in the air. Here on the banks of the creek, there wasn't much danger of the fire spreading; the shore line contained more flat rock than anything else. He sat there long into the evening just watching the birds that flew into the trees and listening to the sounds and the movement of all the forest creatures. In the quiet of the evening he could hear the distant sound of a moose or a bear splashing in the water. He was certainly not alone. Finally, the campfire nearly burnt out and David decided to turn in. He left the rear window of the truck open so that the breeze would flow through. He snuggled down into his sleeping bag and drifted off to sleep.

The loud sound of a rifle shot snapped him out of his sleep. It was Andy's voice loud and clear. "Get the hell out of here!"

"My God, the old man has snapped," was David's first thought. Maybe staying hadn't been such a good idea.

Another shot rang out, close to the truck. David raised his head high enough to see Andy, rifle smoking in his hand. He was dressed in those same overalls with the suspender straps holding them up over his long johns. The rifle was not pointed at David's truck, but in the direction of a full grown bear and cub as they scrambled away from the gun shots heading for the cover of the woods. Apparently, it was the bears that Andy had been yelling at and not David. He rolled out of the back of the truck.

"Up early hunting, Andy?"

The old man's look was anything but humorous. "No I'm not," he snapped. "Did you leave any food around last night?"

"Just what was left of the fish, the bones, the head and the guts. I threw them all in the fire before I turned in."

"Jesus! You can't leave food around where there are bears. It draws them like bees to honey. You have to bury that stuff you damn greenhorn. You'll end up getting yourself killed or both of us."

"I always heard that bears would leave you alone as long as you left them alone."

"Bullshit! These grizzlies are unpredictable at the best of times. We're on their turf here. If you'd have stepped out of that truck and got between that female and her cub, you wouldn't have to worry about anymore tomorrows. One swat of her paw and your head would have gone flying. You don't get two chances with them."

David looked rather sheepish for a moment before responding, "I guess I should say thanks."

"You're welcome," said Andy in a voice that was beginning to lose its biting edge. "Maybe I was a bit short with you yesterday," as he lowered the business end of the rifle. His voice was still gruff though. He wasn't going to do an about face too quickly. "Since you're bound to stay here, I might as well take you under my wing. I'd feel bad if you got yourself killed through ignorance." Andy took a good look around. "It looks like the bears have left. Come on in the cabin and I'll rustle up some breakfast for us."

A few new boards on the steps leading into the cabin were evidence of work that had been done recently. The blend of old and new was testimony that no more than was necessary was being spent on the place. A hasp had been placed on the door, so that a padlock secured the cabin in Andy's absence. In all probability, Hawkins would have a key as well.

As the door opened, a stale and musty odour greeted David. It was unlike anything that he was used to. The log walls had stood the test of time considering that the place, originally built during the gold rush, was now over a hundred years old. At some time, the floor must have been replaced with plywood but it had turned to a blackened grey from the boots that walked on it. Soap and water had been used sparingly here. A large cook stove sat in the middle of the room, serving all of the cooking and heating needs. A wooden table with three chairs sat in the corner, at one time there had probably been a fourth. Two beds lined the wall; one made, the other apparently just slept in. In one corner, a wooden pantry held all of the cooking utensils along with a variety of canned goods and other kitchen essentials.

As David looked about Andy spoke up. "It ain't much but its home. Me and Jim fixed it up so it's liveable. We fixed the roof and the steps, put up new stovepipe and if you notice, we put wire mesh on the windows to keep them damn bears out. Sit down, I'll rustle up some grub. Do you like beans?"

14

With Alex still in the hospital, all of the funeral arrangements had fallen on Ellen. It was difficult, extremely difficult for her to cope under these conditions. Alfie, and the rest of the motorcycle gang including Sully, had offered their immediate help. The thought of six pallbearers dressed in Levi's and leather repulsed her. Not wishing to offend them, it was with great relief that she accepted the same offer of compassion from the social club where Alex worked. Pallbearers dressed in suits and ties conjured up a more presentable picture in Ellen's mind.

The sensational press coverage had led to a large turnout at the funeral. The gory details brought people that Ellen had never seen before, all offering sympathy and condolences. The coffin was closed. The array of flowers that filled the room was at least of some comfort. She kept up a brave face even though her heart was heavy. She comforted herself by looking at the picture that had been placed near Joey's coffin. It was one taken just before he had started to walk. He was holding a large beach ball in his hands and a wide enthusiastic smile on his face. It was a memory that she tried to hold onto.

Home alone, after the funeral she tried to come to grips with one of the most devastating weeks of her life. The thought of losing her only child so early in life was something that she had never envisioned. Carrying a child from conception to birth was something that only a mother could know, a feeling far stronger than Alex could ever understand. The sorrow would last forever. Joey had been a disappointment in the way that he had matured, but that was Alex fault, and deep down she would never forgive him. As long as Joey lived, there was always a wisp of hope that someday things would change. That hope was now dead along with her son. A very real sense of defeat lived within her and she wept as nature's relief of emotions flowed through the teardrops.

Ellen looked at the plants and flowers that had been brought to the house after the funeral. They were displayed in containers decorated by birds and butterflies, efforts of the potter to bring beauty and joy at a time of sorrow. The cut flowers were nice, but their life would be short lived as was her sons. As she rose from her chair, she picked up the sympathy cards that sat among the flowers. One of them caused a stir of emotion. The family had not been present at the funeral; no doubt their thoughts had been though. It was from John and Marilyn Rivers. She knew that their lives had been changed forever as well. How quickly the normal pace of life could change, she thought. The ring of the phone brought her back to reality.

"Hello."

"Ellen? This is Alex. They are letting me out of this damn place today. Can you come and pick me up?"

"I guess I could. It's been a long time since I drove the car though."

"Well, it still drives the same way. You still have your licence don't you?"

"Yes. I still have it."

"Well then get down here about two o'clock. I've got to get out of here. This damn food is getting to me."

So that was it. Alex seemed to have weathered Joey's passing better than she had. He was in a foul mood, so he must be on the mend, she thought.

The nurse pushed the wheelchair out the doors of the emergency exit. Ellen opened the door of the car as he got to his feet, manoeuvred his way into the car and sat in the passenger seat.

"Take care, Mr. Gallo", the nurse said with a wave.

"Ya thanks," he said as he sank into the seat.

Ellen drove slowly out of the hospital. It had been a long time since she had driven the car. The fact that Alex did not begin to complain indicated to her that he was still not himself in spite of the gruff way that he had talked to her over the phone. She drove into the yard and shut the car off.

With help from her, Alex slowly climbed the steps. As they passed through the front door, he headed over to his favourite chair and collapsed in it. The plants and flowers sat not far from his chair. The picture of Joey in his youth immediately brought tears to Alex's eyes.

For a moment, she studied her husband's face. He was finally showing some emotion. Perhaps he had been in denial much of the time, and now, the fact that he had missed his son's funeral and that he would never see him again, really hit home. Alex took a look at the commemorative setting and began to weep in earnest.

It was the first time that Ellen had seen Alex express such emotion; he had always considered it a weakness in others. For all of his faults, the feelings between Alex and his son were very real. If he had any regrets for the way that he raised his son and what it had finally come to, he would have to live with them. She laid her hand on his shoulder and he reached up, touching it softly. It had been many years since they had felt any intimacy towards one another. What a shame that it had taken such a terrible tragedy to expose the frailty of human emotions.

For the next month, Alex was very quiet around the house. He even took his medication without complaint. The heart attack had affected his mobility that is until his doctor told him to start walking some if he ever expected to get better. The first few days, Ellen walked with him. They were short walks, just around block and then later a couple more. At first he was civil, the conversation scant, but pleasant. Alex never brought up Joey's name. He held the grief inside and let it fester. During those first few weeks, Ellen had the feeling that Alex was blaming himself for Joey's death, but it didn't last.

It was the beginning of the second month out of the hospital when Ellen noticed his old ways beginning to make an appearance. Alex got up from the dinner table and put on his sweater, even though it was reasonably warm outside. "I'm going for a walk."

Ellen jumped up. "I'll come with you. Just give me a minute to pile up the dishes."

She could see the hard line and the determined set of Alex's chin. "No. I'm going down to Sully's. I haven't been there for quite a while. I want to see him. I'll be back after a while."

Ellen watched as he walked away. It was a fairly long walk to Sully's but Alex looked determined. Someone would probably give him a ride home. She had a feeling that he would begin driving the car by the end of the week. All of her premonitions proved to be right. Things began to fall into an old predictable routine.

Sully had that same shady smile on his face as Alex entered the room. He slid into the swivel chair behind his desk, took a drink from his beer bottle and sat it down. "Good to see you up and around Alex, my man. How is the wife making out after what you and her went through?"

Alex took a long drink from his beer and ran the sleeve of his sweater across his mouth before setting it down and eyeballing Sully. "You know women. Well, maybe you don't, being's as you're not married. I know that she misses the kid, but she's all full of this 'milk of human kindness' bullshit. I even woke up Sunday and she was just coming in from church. She's all full of this forgive and forget stuff. I'm telling you Sully, if I ever get the chance to get that skinny little bastard Rivers in the crosshairs of a rifle, its goodbye asshole. I'd shoot him in a minute!"

Sully looked through half-closed eyes at Alex as he tipped his bottle towards him. "Amen to that. You could give him one for me. Joey was a good kid, my right hand man. I was just getting set up for a big deal making him my head courier. I'm branching out Alex, going nation wide. We're joining up with some others looking after all the small towns that the 'big guys' haven't been bothering with and Joey was going to do the run from here to Winnipeg. Then this happens." Sully's train of thought drifted to his own loss.

"Oh. That reminds me."

Alex watched as Sully reached into his desk drawer, pulled out a roll of bills and tossed it towards him. "That was what Joey had coming. He's gone, so I guess it's yours. I'd rather be giving it to Joey though."

Alex leafed through the roll of hundred dollar bills, his eyes wide, slightly confused. "How come?"

"Cause he earned it. Right now, Alfie is out west doing the courier work that Joey would have been doing. This is big man, but I'm telling you because I know you won't talk and maybe someday, I'll ask you to keep a package for me at your place, you know. Nice and quiet like."

"Anytime Sully. Anytime. Guy's like you are rare."

Sully's eyes were like slits. "I'm bringing a few more bikers in and getting rid of some of the others. You'll get used to seeing them. One is a Russian, a big tough guy by the name of Giorgio Svetlana. 'Sweat' for short. Another guy just goes by the name of Mercury. I don't know what his right name is or care, but they are good guys that can keep their mouths shut, just like you Alex."

Alex smiled. "You got that right Sully. Hey, you couldn't give me a ride home could you? I shouldn't have walked so far. I'm going to start driving again to hell with all of this walking."

"Sure thing, Go get in my car, I'll be right there."

It had been just over two months since the grisly discovery of Joey's body. Chief Roy Daniels looked up from his desk and saw Alex's bulky form making its way towards his office. There was no way to avoid him; he had already seen the chief. Daniels put on his best smile and came around the corner of the desk, hand outstretched. He had known Alex since their school days.

"Good to see you Alex. I've been thinking about you and wondering how you were getting along. How's the wife. You people have really had a rough time of it and I want to offer my condolences."

Alex flopped into the uncomfortable wooden chair that sat in front of the chief's desk. It was uncomfortable for a reason; Roy didn't encourage long visits from anyone. Alex looked at him. Alex wasn't smiling. "Took you long enough to offer those condolences. This ain't no social call. What the hell have you done about that goddamn kid that murdered my son?"

Chief Daniels face reddened. "If you're referring to David Rivers, we have an all points bulletin out on him and have had since your son's body was found. We're still not sure whether or not David Rivers actually killed Joey. At this point, he is still just a person of interest."

Alex shook his head in disgust. "I don't know how you find the door to go home at the end of the day, Roy. What other suspects other than Rivers is there, answer me that?"

"Now don't take that tone with me Alex. The letter of the law must be followed. We're trying our best to locate the Rivers boy. We've spoke to his parents..."

"Who wouldn't tell you if they knew!" Alex bellowed.

Perspiration began to break out on the chief's forehead. "Now look here Alex, I don't have to take this. We traced David Rivers as far as Toronto. That's where he was last seen. We have an all points bulletin out on his truck, the licence number and his description is in every police computer across the country. I don't know how much more you expect from me. The kid has vanished. There's no trace of him anywhere but we're still looking. Sooner or later, he'll slip up and we'll nab him."

"And then what?"

"Then we'll have done our job. The rest will be up to the courts."

Alex was getting ugly. Suddenly he slipped his hand inside his sweater and Roy Daniels thought he was going for a gun. Daniel's body stiffened as he began to panic. Alex's hand emerged with a puffer and held his mouth open giving the metal container a few quick presses before replacing it beneath his sweater. Apparently, the heated exchange had worked against his hypertension. It hadn't done much for the police chief's either.

Alex paused for a moment, just staring at the chief before he spoke. "You know Roy, as bad as the state of my health is right now, I'll bet that I could find Rivers and bring him to justice myself before you dumb bastards could. My kind of justice, that is."

Daniels was getting frustrated. Sure, Alex had lots to bitch about, but Roy had known Alex long enough and well enough to know where much of the blame lay. "You had better be careful about making any wild statements or trying to take the law into your own hands. David Rivers hasn't been found guilty of anything. If you know where he is, or find out where he is, you had better let us handle it."

Alex braced himself on the wooden arms of the chair as he stood up, a dark scowl on his face. "You better catch him before I do, Roy. Don't worry about me or my wife or my boy's killer. I'll look after all of those things by myself, I always have."

Alex sat across the supper table from his wife in a frustrated state. "The doctor said that I'm almost ready to go back to work. I won't have much choice because they'll cut off my insurance payments if I don't. I was hoping that either the police would have a lead of some kind on that Rivers kid, or that I would have word of where he is by now, but nothing."

Ellen looked at him in surprise. "Why is it that you think that you would find out where he is?"

Alex looked up saying nothing as he wolfed down his food. Ellen didn't know that two weeks earlier, he had gotten a recent photograph of David Rivers, one that had run in the local paper. He had the picture, along with a description of David, printed on a flyer and a reward of one thousand dollars for information on his whereabouts. One of Sully's bikers distributed the flyers across the country, wherever his couriers went. Even out to Winnipeg and beyond, as far as the west coast. Somebody somewhere had to have seen him. He looked up at Ellen as he quietly said, "I have my ways."

It was the way he looked, the sudden change in his voice that gave her cause for alarm. She had been around Alex long enough to know that when he put his mind to something he wouldn't stop until he had his way. But this change was different, somehow sinister; she could see it in his face.

"It's best left to the police, Alex. Sooner or later they'll catch Joey's murderer."

Alex didn't respond. He finished his supper, got up and said, "I'm going over to Sully's. Don't wait up."

Ellen watched him go. She knew the signs. Alex had mourned for, and missed, his son for those first few months after he died. Now, it was something else, what Alex called 'his pound of flesh'. It was revenge that he wanted, pure and simple. Ellen was sure that he would get it, one way or another.

15

That first day, Andy merely tolerated the presence of the damn tenderfoot hoping he would get tired of the lonely way of life. He tried to go about business as usual. After breakfast, he got out his pan and announced, "I have to get to work. You can stay here and keep out of trouble, follow me, or haul your ass like I told you in the first place. I don't care."

David could see that this wasn't going to be a quick thaw. Andy was letting him know in no uncertain terms that he wasn't at all welcome here. Too bad, David thought, this is exactly what I want. He smiled as Andy put a plaid shirt on; stuffing the shirt tail into his pants and raising the suspenders back up over his shoulders. Next, he pulled on the old boots. Andy was now ready for work.

"I think I'll tag along. I never seen anyone pan for gold."

The old man locked the door behind them and silently set off along the river bank with David a few steps behind. Finally, they came to a spot where Andy seemed satisfied. David watched as the old prospector waded into the fast rushing water. He began to swish the gravel around in the pan looking for the illusive flakes of gold. David watched and asked annoying questions like: "How do you know where to pan? How come all of the gravel doesn't wash out? What does the gold look like?" until he finally got a response.

"Damn it! You ask more questions than a two year old kid just learning how to talk. How do you expect me to get anything done with you badgering me? Come over here and see for yourself."

That first day was a long one. One David enjoyed more than his host did. To Andy, David was plainly a pain in the ass.

"Now pay attention 'cause I'm only going to show you once. After that keep your mouth shut and watch. First, look around until you see a likely spot but it has to be gravel. That's what washes down from the mountains carrying the gold with it, that's if there is any in the first place. Now scoop it up gently like this. Swish it around tipping the pan slightly so that the water carries the gravel with it. There, see that little bit of glitter, that's gold."

David became excited as he saw gold in the raw form for the first time. "How much would that much be worth?"

Andy shook his head. "Not enough to buy a can of beans. That's the trouble. I don't know why Jim sent you out here anyway, there isn't enough gold here for one, let alone three."

"Jim said that you were really looking for the source, where the gold was coming from."

Andy looked very disgusted. "Jim talks too much, especially to a total stranger. He's going to get an ear full from me when he shows up here."

Andy probably worked harder than he had before with David by his side. David could tell that he was a thorn in the old man's side. He watched as the old man would take a leather pouch, hung around his neck, and scrape the gold from the pan carefully into the sack. He saw David watching and quietly offered an explanation. "This here is my poke. As you gather the gold dust, you place it in one of these."

"How much will it hold?"

"A hell'uva lot more than I'm going to get today," he paused looking at the sun high overhead. "Maybe we'll call it a day. Look, maybe we didn't get off to a very good start. If you're determined to stay and waste your time here, I've got another pan in the cabin. I'll give you a hand to get started tomorrow. Maybe after a day or two, you'll find out that this isn't as easy or as exciting as it looks. At any rate, we'll give it a try. Let's go get some supper," he said as he waded out of the water.

The walk back to the cabin was more friendly. David ventured a question. "What's for supper?"

The old man actually cracked a smile. "Beans any style, boiled, baked, or fried."

"How be I catch us some trout for supper?"

"I guess that would be all right. I could fire up the stove and put some tater's on to fry. Hmm, sounds better than beans now that I think of it?"

And so it started out, slowly at first without any trust, but things did get better. In the evening, they sat on the back steps until dark. The whiskey jacks would fly down and take peanuts in the shell out of Andy's fingers. Chipmunks, Andy had named Charlie and Daisy, would scamper about the step scrounging for bits. Together, Andy and David would watch waterfowl spread their wings and drop their tails, braking to a stop before dropping into the water where they would spend the night. Deer would walk out of the edge of the forest that surrounded the cabin and sip from the cool clear water of the creek.

"People think that I get lonely here. I know that Jim does. That was probably the biggest reason that he sent you up here. But it ain't that lonely, not for me. Look at all the company that visits me every evening. Best of all, they don't expect anything in return, well, all except those chiselling chipmunks," he said with a chuckle. "A man could do a lot worse. I know I have. It's the peace and quietness that I love. Lord knows I don't do it for the money. We haven't struck nothing that's really worthwhile. What went on between you and your old man, Dave?"

David expected this would come up sooner or later. He had been thinking up an answer. "My dad didn't like the girl that I was going with. Neither did my mom. The girl could feel it and she ran off with my best friend. I guess that I said some things that I shouldn't have. Time will probably heal the wound though."

Andy looked at him, those blue eyes peeking out from under the bushy grey eyebrows. Did he buy it David wondered? He hoped that Andy wouldn't ask him again. Lying was tough for him. The problem with lying was that sometimes he forgot what he had told people. The truth was always the same. Lies were always different, always changing, always tripping you up.

The next day was a complete reversal of the day before. Actually, it was whistling that woke David up, Andy's whistling. He was already dressed and banging the lids of the stove about as he got the cook stove roaring. For a moment, David lay there surveying his surroundings. Yes, this was the same cabin that he had gone to bed in the night before. He threw back the covers and jumped out of bed.

"Morning, I thought I was going to have to wake you. If you want to learn how to pan for gold, you better get a move on. I always start early, well, almost always. You'll have to settle for bacon and home fries, from some of those taters that we had for supper last night. Maybe Jim will bring some eggs and flour for flapjacks and some syrup when he comes here in a few days. 'Till then we'll have to rough it."

The food still tasted a lot better than what David had on the way here from those fast food restaurants. He devoured it and burnt his tongue on Andy's black coffee.

"Where are we panning today? Same place?"

"Guess so. If the battery wasn't dead in my old truck, we could try farther along the creek. This area is pretty well worked out."

David grinned inwardly, Andy wasn't going to come right out and ask him to drive, but the hint was broad. Maybe even the reason for the change in attitude.

"I could drive, how far we talking?"

"Oh not far, a mile or so, just too far to lug the pans and a lunch, if we take one."

"Well make up some kind of a lunch and we'll be off."

They pulled off the road, into a small clearing and took the food heading down towards the creek. Here, the creek was wider and the bank more sandy. A dead tree laid off to one side, its bark completely gone, the limbs looking like brown bones, its roots still clinging to Mother earth. Not far from it, Andy sat down the lunches as did David with the pans he was carrying.

Andy grinned as he looked at David. "Today you start to earn your keep, boy."

David returned the smile. "I'm ready, willing and able."

"We'll see just how able you are."

"Have you and Jim found anything worth while?"

Andy shook his head. "Not really. Often times the gold is washed down from an old mine that petered out. We always hoped that we would hit something worthwhile. It's like the carrot in front of the horse's nose, it keeps us going. The temptation is always there, seemingly just out of reach. I keep finding some gold, enough to make a few bucks for me and Jim. But the big one, well we're still searching. I got kinda lucky last year. I probably found half a dozen nuggets, some had a bit of size to them. We split them, Jim and me. He gets a third and I get to keep two thirds. That's the way it'll work if you get lucky my boy. If we find anything that amounts to much, we'll take the picks and some chisels and go up above into the mountains and check it out. Lets get to work."

David looked back over his shoulder in the direction that Andy had looked while talking about the mines in the mountains. "Have you checked any of those old mines out?"

"Oh ya. There's an old mine shaft just above that outcrop of rocks, over there to the right. See that dark spot just bellow the ridge, that's the mine entrance. I checked that one out a couple weeks ago but it's pretty well played out. It was just a waste of time. I was thinking of going about ten miles east to some other spot that Jim has the claim rights to. I checked it out before the battery went dead in that old truck of mine. The creek down there has a real good gravel bottom. I don't think that there's been anyone down there panning in a long while from the look of things. It's the last claim that

Jim has down this way. If you was of a mind to drive us down there, like maybe tomorrow, we could have a look see."

David grinned, they seemed to be hitting it off together and that was fine with him. Whatever it took to keep the old man happy, maybe they would find something. While panning for gold was slow, finding the odd bit of glitter excited him. It was easy to see just how gold fever could begin to possess those who prospected for the elusive metal. They stopped at noon and ate the cold bacon sandwiches Andy had made, and drank from the clear water that gushed by. The creek cleaned and polished the water as it rushed along.

"I got another poke bag, back at the cabin that we'll fix up for you, Davey. It's got a little hole in the bottom but I got some linen thread that I can sew it up so that it'll do until we get you a new one. Then, whatever you get you keep two thirds and Jim he gets the other third, just like me."

They worked away until the sun had started its descent in the west before packing it in for the day. "Ah, that's enough Davey," Andy said as he waded out of the water, set his pan down and drew the back of his hand across his sweaty brow.

"How much you reckon we panned today, Andy?"

"About a spoonful, remember boy that spoonful would probably weigh about an ounce, and an ounce is worth maybe three hundred dollars. Today this would be split three ways between you and me and Jim. Like I say, it's wages but damn poor wages."

"Well today you can keep my share for teaching me the ropes. I'll get that poke bag that you said you'd patch up and then I'll start in earnest to try and fill it."

Andy's face cracked in a big grin as he chuckled for the first time. "We'll see that you fill her, Davey. Who knows, maybe you'll bring us luck and we'll find a mine that still has something worth while in it."

The next morning at sunrise, they put their pans and lunch in the back of David's pickup and headed east. Around

David's neck hung the poke bag that Andy had patched up for him.

"This sure is a nice pickup, Davey. I like that thing that you got on top of the bed of the truck, whatu'ya call it?"

"Just a camper cap. What I like about it, you can lock it up so that nobody walks off with anything. It keeps things dry and you can even sleep in it. I did when I came out here. I would just pull off into a campsite and climb right into my sleeping bag."

"Sounds great. If I ever strike it rich, I'm going to buy one just like it."

David began to laugh. "You don't have to be rich to buy a truck like this one. Maybe we'll find enough nuggets today so that you'll be able to buy one."

The old man's eyes gleamed. "Wouldn't that be great. You never know when it comes to gold. Them nuggets are worth more than regular gold you know. Some people use them for jewellery just the way that they're found."

About ten miles down the road, Andy said, "Pull over here as far as you can off the road. There's no road down to the creek, so we'll have to hoof her in. We'll get our gear and then you better lock her up just in case some hunters come along."

They got their gear out of the truck. David wasn't too comfortable about having to leave part of his money in the truck, but there was little that he could do about it. The fishing vest held a third and there was just a little less than a third in his wallet, so he wouldn't be broke anyway if someone did pilfer the truck.

From the canvas bag containing their lunch, Andy pulled out a couple small bells with shoelaces attached to them. "Here, tie one of these around your neck," he said, as he looped the laces over his neck beside his poke bag, like a crucifix.

"Is this supposed to ward off evil spirits?" David quipped.

"No. It's supposed to ward off bears. If they hear you coming, generally, they'll get out of your road. You never want to startle one, especially a grizzly. They'll come right at you. Then you'll need one of these," he said as he dropped his hand to his side and came up with a bowie knife about a foot long.

David had noticed the knife before, but had never seen it drawn. The wicked blade gleamed in the morning sun light.

"Wouldn't a gun be better?"

"Sure it would. Trouble is they're awkward when you're panning for gold. You can't carry a rifle with you when you're working. You should have bought a real knife instead of that toothpick that you carry around. That thing wouldn't stop a bear. It would only make him mad"

David shook his head in despair. "I wasn't thinking of fighting any bears when I bought this knife. It's still something that I wouldn't look forward to doing."

"It generally isn't something that you get time to think about, boy. You have to be prepared for danger all of the time when your up in this part of the country. You might be surprised what you'll do if suddenly it's you or a bear. We'll have to slip into town and get you a real knife. I'll lend you some money to get one if you haven't got enough. It just might save your life."

They started down the game trail. It was the only path that led down to the creek. There were lots of bear droppings along the way and suddenly David took great comfort in the jingle of the little bells that hung round his neck. Andy's respect for the creatures was probably brought on by experience, the greatest of all teachers.

The game trail levelled out. A grove of evergreens ran almost to the water's edge and the creek itself. A closer inspection of the water's edge revealed a gravel bottom. Near the shore, the bottom of the stream was visible for about the first ten feet before it dropped off and then the visibility was lost.

Andy set down the canvas bag with their lunches and carefully looked about, always vigil. There was no sign of anything or anybody, for the time being they were completely alone. Andy waded into the water. About eight feet from shore, the water came right to the top of his boots, and from there it dropped off quickly.

"Damn it. I thought that the creek was shallower here. Maybe I got my bearings wrong, maybe I was downstream some when I checked it out some time ago, I don't know. The old mind isn't as reliable as you get older. Oh well, we're here anyway. We may as well give it a try."

It wasn't long before David, standing in the cold running water, began to see traces of gold in the bottom of the huge round vessel. He ran his fingers around the rim scooping up the shining metal. He waded to shore and set the pan down. Opening the drawstrings of the poke hanging around his neck, he placed the precious metal within.

"Looks good here, Andy."

"Not bad. I don't think that anyone's been down here for a long time. There's only a few fools like us around here anyway. Most make more money working at other things."

They stopped briefly for lunch. David, caught up in the excitement of finding gold, was more anxious to get back to work than was his partner. Andy grinned at him through yellow stained teeth. "Relax for a few minutes, Davey, you're getting gold fever. This stuff does that to a man, especially in the beginning."

"Yes, it does. How much do you think we'll make today?"

"I don't know. I got a scale back at the cabin. It don't take too much to make an ounce. I'd say that we're going to make real good wages today if it keeps up like it has this morning. Remember, Jim gets a clear third of what we get. You know, he should be showing up in a day or two and bringing us some grub. We're starting to run low."

"He told me that he would be guiding those guys up in the mountains fishing. It'll probably be another day or two before he shows up. Well, let's get back to work old timer."

Andy grinned at the words 'old timer', as he struggled to his feet, picked up his pan, and followed David back into the creek.

By the time that they had quit for the day, there was a considerable amount of dust in David's poke. He could feel the weight even though the volume was not great. Andy, with his experience, had gathered much more, but they both seemed happy with the results.

As they drove back towards the cabin, David couldn't contain his excitement. "Are we coming back to the same spot tomorrow?"

Andy grinned, the point of his chin thrust forward as he smiled. "Oh, we'll pan there as long as it shows promise."

David was still pumped up. "How much do you think we made today?"

"There should be enough for a nice sized payday for each of us."

The next three days were equally as prosperous. As they arrived back at the cabin, Andy headed in to light the stove and begin to prepare for supper. David grabbed his pole and headed for the creek.

"How many fish do you want for supper?" he yelled at the old man.

"I'm plenty hungry, you've been working the tail off of me. Three or four good sized fish will be great, what we don't eat today, we'll have tomorrow."

As David stood attaching the lure to the line of his fishing rod, he saw another fisherman approaching, far overhead. The osprey swooped down; talon's extended as he skimmed over the glistening water of the creek. A sudden drop and the talons found their mark. The osprey rocketed upward, the fresh caught trout wiggled in its clutch.

The sound of a vehicle coming down the grade towards the cabin caught David's attention. The truck came to a stop and David recognized Jim Hawkins smiling suntanned face.

"I see old short and fierce didn't run you off like I thought he would," he laughed.

David shot a glance up towards the cabin looking for Andy before he answered.

"It wasn't because he didn't try. I thought at first he was going to, especially when he greeted me with his rifle, but I toughed it out. We're getting along just famous now. Hopefully it will last."

Andy had heard the truck and was now hanging out the door. "Jimmy," he shouted. "It's good to see you. I hope you brought some food up. We're almost down to eating shoe leather."

"I did. How are you and the new man getting along?"

Andy began to stammer and then quickly recovered. "We're getting along great. It might take a while to break him in though."

"You're just the man for the job, Andy. I thought you might be getting tired of beans, so I brought enough beef steak up for three hungry men. Have you got the stove fired up yet?"

Andy's eyes lit up. "I will have by the time you bring the stuff in and wash up. What else did you bring up?"

"What do you need?"

The old man looked in amazement. "What do I need? Bacon, eggs, taters, lard, sugar, flour, you name it, we need it."

"Well, I brought most of that stuff and maybe more. Get that fire going, David can help me bring this stuff in."

Andy quickly forgot the fatigue that he had been complaining about. Soon the sizzle of steak against the hot frying pan was something he had missed. "Boy oh boy, just listen to that steak frying. I was just thinking the other day how good a steak would taste, you must have read my mind, Jimmy."

They all dug in, the steak was thick and juicy, and Andy had cooked it perfectly. The inside was still pink, cooked enough so that it was still tender and flavourful. There wasn't much conversation at the table while they were busy eating. They washed it down with hot black coffee, the kind that David was beginning to get used to. Andy drew the back of his hand across his mouth.

"Boy that was good. You don't usually bring beef steak up here. It's mostly elk, deer or moose. This was a welcome change."

"Well enjoy it, the next time it probably will be game, but it's a little early in the season. Another couple of months and I'll be hunting again."

Andy shoved his chair back and picked up his plate. "You and Davey go out and get some fresh air, while I do the dishes up."

Out on the small porch Jim laughed heartily. "It's good to see you and the old man hitting it off. I really didn't think that he would let you stay here. He's a crusty old bird. I'm glad it's working out though. I was always a little leery having him stay here by himself, although that's the way he likes it."

David shoved his hat back farther on his head. "He didn't take to me right off. I just dug in my heels and told him I was staying whether he liked it or not. It got pretty intense for a while but then he began to mellow some. He kind of puts up a wall between himself and strangers it seems. Down deep, he's a good person."

They sat talking for a while until finally the door opened and Andy came out of the cabin. Jim looked up. "David says that the panning has picked up the last day or two."

"Ya. It's showed some promise. I think maybe tomorrow, we might take some tools and go up the mountain behind where we've been panning. We'll check the rock, see if there's a mine. There is supposed to be one, ain't there, Jimmy?"

"Supposed to be one that has been worked out. It's about the only one that you haven't checked out. Maybe it will be the lucky one."

Andy chuckled. "I'm not getting my hopes up too high. We haven't been too lucky yet. Tell you what though. We do have enough dust to settle up some. I'll go set up the scales and give you guys a holler when it's ready and we'll see just how rich we are, or aren't."

Adrenalin

David sat there, looking at the same type of scales he had seen on T.V. balancing the scales of justice. The two chain triads each held a brass plate about the size of a small pie plate. A hand, similar to that on a clock pointed to zero. Carefully the old prospector withdrew the standard weights while Jim and David watched. Satisfied that he had put the proper weights on the scale, he got out his poke bag and poured the gleaming gold onto the pan. It outbalanced the coin sized weight on the opposite pan. He smiled and added a weight. Andy paused for a moment, shifting his watery blue eyes towards David.

"Get your poke bag Davey, we'll make this an even split," he grinned.

To David, it was a good feeling. The added value that Andy was giving him was welcome. One never knew how much money would be needed, but more than that was the feeling of being accepted as an equal. That meant much more to him than the wealth.

"Where do we cash it in?" David asked eagerly.

Jim looked at him and grinned, he could hear the excitement in David's voice. "Not in Dawson Creek. There's no one here that handles it, but I have some business up at Dawson City in the Yukon, in a month or so. We can all go up there and have a bit of a holiday. How much do you figure the gross worth?"

"Somewhere around fifteen hundred. Split three ways, that's about five hundred a piece."

Jim sat back for a moment and looked at the pair. "Maybe we can make a bit more before we leave for Dawson City. I got into a poker game on the weekend. I had some luck and in my winnings, I picked up a couple of claims down the other side of Barkerville. One of them has a cabin on it. Maybe in a week or two, we could slip down and have a look at the place. They still have a Klondike type of celebration each summer and pan for gold. We might have better luck down that way. How about it Andy, could you use a change of scenery?"

"We could go have a look see, after we check out that old mine. So far we haven't hit a bonanza, still, I like it here."

"Yes, I know you do, but there isn't much that you haven't worked over. You might like it there too. Nobody says that you have to stay if you don't like the place anyway, especially if we don't have any luck there. Personally though, I think it will be better. Or, I could send someone else down to Barkerville and they might get lucky."

Andy's eyes grew wide. "We'll go. Week after next, I want to check out a few rock formations before I leave here though."

"Good. I have to get going now, Judy will wonder where in the world I got to. We'll see you in about ten days then."

"Yes that ought to be good, maybe we'll even have some good news for you by then."

"That's what I like about you Andy, you're always optimistic, just like most prospectors. Well, I'll see you boys later."

They watched as Jim pulled out of the yard and drove up the grade.

"Maybe you just showed up at the right time, Davey. They always said that prospecting was better down at Barkerville. By the way, carry your share of gold in your vest, you never know who stop here and break into the cabin. I should have given Jim his share to take with him but in all the excitement, I forgot, so I'll carry his with mine. One good crack with a hammer and that old lock would crack open like a nut."

By Thursday of the next week, the gold panning began to dwindle. It took several pans and hours of hard labour to produce even minute traces of gold. David could tell that Andy was becoming very frustrated.

"Darn' it anyway. We're just wasting our time here Davey. Let's call it a day. Tomorrow, we'll just bring down some mining tools and leave the pans at home. We'll see if we can find out where this gold dust filtered down from."

Adrenalin

The next day David got his first taste of geology. Andy rubbed his head several times as he squinted towards the sun and looked up towards the rocky face of the mountains.

"Jim says that there is a worked out mine up there some where's, but I can't see it. Can you?"

David shook his head. "There are too many shadows for me to say for certain. What about up there, off to the right, it's a shade darker there."

Andy stared in the direction that David pointed. "Hard to tell ain't it. That might be it though. That little stream that trickles down the mountain comes out not far from where we found the most gold. Its work getting up there, but we might as well get started. Lock the truck up and let's go."

They followed the little stream upwards into the mountain. David's canvas bag was heavy, and the sharp point of one of the tools dug into his back, as he shifted the weight around trying to avoid the aggravation. Andy's was probably just as awkward to handle but he didn't complain, and so the two of them made their way up the side.

"There she is!" Andy exclaimed. "You were right on the money. It's an old mine shaft, probably dug out over a century ago. Somebody probably dug a fortune out of it. Let's hope that they left some. Ah, my back feels like its breaking. We'll set these bags down here. At least it won't be so bad carrying them down."

Andy unzipped the bag that David had carried up. Reaching in, he withdrew a pair of hardhats with a lamp attached to the front of each. He grinned as David watched. "Miner's hats, we'll need them to see inside."

David put his on his head and started forward.

"Wait a minute, where do you think you're going?"

"Into the mine, isn't that what we came up here for?"

"When it's safe. You got something to learn boy. You don't know just what's inside that mine and neither do I."

Gently, Andy reached into the bag and pulled out a stick of dynamite. David knew what it was and how much respect it commanded. He had seen his uncle blast stumps with it on the farm years earlier. He gave Andy a curious look.

"What are you going to do with that?"

"Just watch."

With a pair of pliers, Andy attached a cap to a length of fuse. He cut the fuse to the right length, and then turning the pliers upside down, he thrust the handle into the dynamite, causing David to jump away in fright.

"Jesus! That stuff will blow up."

The old man grinned wickedly. "Not if you know what your doing and I do."

David watched as the old man packed the dynamite firmly around the cap. Then drawing a match out of his pocket he called out. "Get over behind those rocks and keep your head down 'cause now this stuff is dangerous and you never know just what might come out of those old mines. Sometimes it's just pieces of rocks, and then other times it looks like somethin' straight from hell."

Andy looked towards the entrance to the mine and yelled at the top of his lungs, "Anyone in there. Hello...dynamite coming in. Three, two, one."

Hearing nothing, he lit the fuse and hurled it as far as he could into the entrance. He made a beeline for the rocks where David was already crouched down waiting for the blast.

There was a loud bang that echoed across the valley. A belch of smoke and two full grown coyote's erupted out of the opening. The coyotes raced down the side of the mountain escaping the shock.

Andy stood up laughing, his long grey moustache blowing in the wind as he turned and looked at David. "See what I told you? You never know what's holed up back in them mines."

"Maybe we should have brought a gun," said David.

"Just something else to carry, the dynamite generally brings out anything that's in there. They don't like that stuff. We'll give it a few moments for the smoke to clear away and then we'll take our tools and get some rock samples. Maybe that blast did some of the work for us and we'll just have to pick up gold."

Inside the mine, the acrid aroma of the dynamite was still strong. The urine, left by the departing coyotes, had not done much for the smell either. Without the lamps on their hardhats, it would have been impossible to see. A few pieces of rock had been blow out on the floor, but not many. Andy took out a chipping hammer, selected a spot and began to chip away. Fifty yards or so further into the mineshaft, he took a few more samples.

"How does it look Andy?"

The light shone upon the rock and David could see a glitter or two.

"There's a little showing. Not much though. It played out no doubt. I don't know how deep this mine is, probably two or three hundred yards. They didn't have modern equipment when these mines were developed, so as soon as they quit showing promise, so did the miners. We're here though, so we'll check it out good."

They explored the mine for about five hours, David chipping on his own. They threw the fragments into a sack and finally headed out into the daylight where Andy dumped the contents out on the ground. Carefully, he turned the rocks over in his hands mumbling to himself.

"Not much here. You can see some glitter but its low grade ore, costs more to get it out of that rock than it's worth. God knows how long it took old Mother Earth to wash down as much as she did into that creek. It's just like most of the others that we checked out. I'm going to take a half dozen of the best pieces back to the cabin. When we go up to Dawson City, we can have it assayed, but it probably is a waste of time. You keep hoping that you'll strike it rich. Mostly though, its fool's gold...this old fool's gold."

"Why don't you quit?"

"And miss all this fun? Hell with that, maybe we'll strike it rich in Barkerville."

David had been caught up in the search for gold ever since coming to Dawson Creek. He had completely put past events out of his mind. Each night when he put his head on his pillow, he fell asleep immediately and slept peacefully. This night, he fell asleep quickly, but deep in the caverns of his mind, the shadows of monsters lurked. The faces of those that had caused him great anguish in the past were surfacing. The shadowy figures of Paulo and Joey Gallo haunted him once more. He tried to run but his feet refused to propel him as the ghostly figures closed in on him. He screamed for help as the long arms of the banshees reached for him. They were closing in on him and he could not get away. He screamed but it felt like there was no sound to be heard. Louder and louder he shrieked hoping someone would come to his rescue. They were now within reach and he could feel the hot breath on his neck and hear their voices calling his name. He couldn't move, he was engulfed in fear, and escape was hopeless. He screamed with pain as they jumped on him pushing him onto the ground.

" Davey, Davey! Wake up. Jesus, let go of me!"

David rose up from his bed. He was sweating profusely and it was Andy that was yelling, "Let go! Let go! You're having a bad dream. Snap out of it."

Partially awake now, David struggled to get his bearings in the darkness.

"I'm going to light a lamp David. Take it easy, you're all right. Get a hold of yourself boy!"

The flame cast a ghostly glow about the cabin. As he sat up in bed still shaking, David could feel the perspiration that soaked his body. He could see Andy, his face drawn; his eyes larger than normal. "Ah, that's better. You've got one hellu'va grip boy. I'm sure glad that you don't dream every night. What were you dreaming about?"

David just sat for a moment trying to gather his thoughts. Neither Andy nor anyone else was going to hear the truth from him. It was too hard for him to think about let alone someone like Andy.

"I've always had bad dreams. I found out that a boy died in the room at home where I used to sleep. After that, I would often have nightmares and wake up screaming. When I told my dad about those dreams, he moved me into a different room, but those dreams followed. I guess that they still do, although I haven't had one for a long time. Maybe it was just going into that mine that brought those dreams back, I don't know."

Andy put the lamp on the table and sat down. "You scared the daylights out of me. You were yelling and cursing something fierce."

"What was I saying in my sleep?"

"Nothing that I could understand, it was just a lot of mumbling that woke me up. I walked over and shook you to wake you up and you grabbed me and started screaming to let go. Next thing I knew, I was screaming the same thing when you grabbed me. You're a lot stronger than what I took you to be. I guess that we're both wide awake now. You feel all right?"

"Oh ya, I'm okay. Sorry I scared you."

"I've been scared worse. I'll get over it, although I'm keeping my distance when you're sleeping. I'm going to fire-up the stove and put some coffee on."

It seemed to take a while for the brightness from the lamp to saturate the darkness and completely illuminate the room. David pulled on his Levis while Andy lit the fire and placed the kettle on to boil. Andy turned around facing him.

"So you and your old man had a falling out and that's why you came up this way was it?"

It took David a few moments to realize what Andy was talking about. Then, he recalled the story he had told him that first day that he had arrived.

"That's how it started, actually, there's a little more to it than that." He watched while Andy pulled on his coveralls.

"I kinda thought maybe there was. Want to talk about it Davey? Might help you sleep better."

"Maybe someday Andy, but not right now. There's too much anger that I have to work out." He knew he was lying and was afraid of getting tripped up. He decided to change the subject. "What brought you to these parts, Andy? You didn't always live in Dawson Creek did you?"

The old man drew up a chair and sat down. He cast an eye towards the stove as he waited anxiously for the kettle to boil. "Nope, I used to live in Vancouver. I was married for over thirty years to the same woman. My job demanded a lot of my attention, lots of overtime, and lots of travel. One day, I came home early and caught my wife with my neighbour." There was a catch in the old man's voice and the glimmer of a tear in his eye. "He was a bachelor, and I guess she just got lonesome with me gone as much as I was. In the end, well she left me for him."

He paused for a moment, got up and, lifted the lid on the stove and with the poker stoked the fire some and placed another stick in it before closing the lid and sitting back down. "Anyway, I became very angry and vengeful. I bought that rifle in the corner there. I thought real hard about killing both of them and then myself. I had that gun and some shells in my car and I was driving towards home when I had to stop for a funeral procession that turned into the cemetery. Traffic was blocked, it was a big funeral, and as I sat there, I realized that at the rate I was going, in a few days that hearse would be carrying me, my wife, and our neighbour to our final resting place."

He paused and wiped his eyes. David suspected that what he was hearing was something that no one else had ever heard. He went on, "I guess that was a twist of fate, a message from above perhaps. I drove on thinking about how many men end up in jails or cemeteries, and that they could have avoided it all if only they put some distance between themselves and their problems."

181

He paused again, maybe regretting what he was saying, but realizing that someone needed to hear it, someone he could trust.

"Anyway, when I reached the house, I just drove on by and got a motel room. The next day, I went to see a lawyer. He looked after all of the details. He filed for divorce, put the house up for sale, and divided the assets. After that, I just drifted. I quit my job of course. But after a few years, I began to run out of money. I didn't want to go back to working around people or even being around people. Finally, I came up here."

"I ran into Jim Hawkins in the hotel, just by chance. We got to talking and he told me about these claims that he had just bought. One thing led to another, the rest you know. We divvy up just like now. He gets his third and I get two thirds. Jim keeps me in grub and I live in the cabin that we fixed up for free. I cut my own firewood and if it's a day that I don't feel like doing anything, I don't. I have a little money in the bank now. Some winters I run trap line for Jim and some I go down and visit my brother in Yuma, Arizona. I just can't imagine living the rest of my life anywhere else. There's so much freedom here and so little stress, that all of the old anger and hatred is long gone."

In the soft glow David could see Andy's eyes take on a gentle look. "Having you come here and work along side me has been a real pleasure. It does get a bit lonesome at times. That's been the only drawback. It's good having you around Davey, but don't have any more of those bad dreams," he grinned

The coffee was bubbling and percolating on the stove as Andy got up, took two cups from the sideboard, and poured. The steam was rising from the cup as he sat David's down in front of him.

"When we go to town, I'll get some of that powdered creamer."

"No need, I'm beginning to get used to drinking it black."

Andy took a sip and looked across at David. "Tell you what, tomorrow will be one of those days when we don't do nothing, nothing serious anyway. I'll get out the old washtub and wash our clothes out so we can be clean when we go to town. You can catch a mess of fish for our dinner. The next day, we'll drive into Dawson Creek and meet up with Jim. Now let's turn in again. This time, have a pleasant dream. We can sleep in."

By noon the next day, the clothesline was full of David's briefs and Andy's long johns, along with a couple pair of Levi's and a shirt a piece. As David fished away, he had time to think of some of the things that he needed in town. The dream the night before helped bring him back to reality. It would only be a matter of time before someone came looking for him. It would be wise to have a cache of survival items stashed somewhere. Possibly even more than one spot, just in case he got cut off from one supply. Mentally he began to make a list; matches, candles, and maybe a couple lighters would be first. Also a frying pan and some first aid supplies like Band-Aids, ointment and alcohol. Maybe some needles and thread, just in case he had to stitch himself up, one never knew. Some sealskin bags to put stuff into to keep the moisture away. A large Bowie knife like Andy's, a small saw, and a hatchet along with some more line and fish hooks. Last but not least, one or two nylon backpacks to store the stuff and carry supplies.

His chain of thought was broken as Andy yelled. "Hey, have you caught our dinner yet?"

"Yes, I caught some nice ones. Give me fifteen minutes to clean them."

22222222222222222

16

The sun was high in the July sky, as David and Andy piled into the Ford pickup and headed for Dawson Creek to meet with Jim Hawkins.

"I'm going to have to gas up when we get to town, Andy."

"I'll pay for it Davey. I'll have to go to the bank first though."

David grinned. "I think I've got enough on me to fill up. Thanks anyway." If Andy knew how much cash that David had in that fishing vest that he always wore, to say nothing of what he had in his wallet, the shit might hit the fan. He looked over and could see Andy screwing his face all up slowly thinking things over.

"I thought you said that you were broke when you first came to the cabin?"

A smile spread over David's face as he said, "I just thought that there was more of a chance of you feeling sorry for some poor soul down on his luck and broke."

Andy's moustache bristled slightly. "That part about your old man throwing you out was that bullshit too?"

David's face grew more sober. It was clear that Andy resented being taken in.

"It's a little more complicated than that. Someday, I'll tell you all about it. Then you'll see why I haven't said much about it."

They rode in silence for a while. Finally, Andy must have run it through his mind and come to a conclusion that he could live with. "I guess every one has some secrets. Like the one that I told you the other night. That's the first time that I ever told anyone." He sat silent for a moment and then began to laugh. "Maybe I would have put the run to you if you hadn't looked so pathetic standing there that day." Andy's face brightened up. "On the square, do you need any money from me before I go to the bank or not?"

The tension eased and David felt much better. "I'm fine for now, at least until I cash in some of my gold dust."

They were coming up to Dawson Creek. The small houses built on a few acres were surrounded by snowmobiles sitting high and dry waiting for winter snow. Dog sleighs parked at the back while the teams of grey and white huskies ran loose waiting for their work to begin.

They pulled into the gas station and David filled up. It was about ten o'clock and people were moving about. The hustle and bustle was probably much greater than it would be in the winter when the Arctic winds began to blow. He paid, got back in the truck, and drove up and parked on Main Street.

"I'll just go to the bank and then meet you at the sporting goods store Davey," Andy said as he headed across the street.

David was in luck. The bank must have been busy, he had time to slip into the hardware store next to the sporting goods store and get most of what he needed. He placed the supplies well back in the camper cap of the truck before Andy came out of the bank.

"Damn it all, I always manage to get behind someone in line that either knows the teller, and wants to visit, or someone that's just been to the doctor and has to tell them all of their medical history. Come on Davey, let's get you set up with a real man sized knife."

David had already been in the store once and was fairly familiar with the layout. This was frontier country, and the display of guns and knives was probably as large as, or larger than, in any other part of Canada. There was everything from the smallest pocket knife up to huge Bowie knives. The handles were made of wood, bone, leather and you name it, they had it.

David looked up and saw one just like the one that Joey Gallo had used that night, the one with a brass knuckle grip. He remembered how the knife stayed put in Joey's hand.

"What do you think of that one Andy?"

Andy shook his head. "Too big and clumsy, it wouldn't be what I would want."

"Well I like it. Once your hand's locked in, nothing will pull it loose."

"I guess there's that about it. It does have a good blade, and as you say, it wouldn't get knocked out of your hand. You'll have to get a clerk to unlock that case. They lock up everything anymore. Time was you could leave anything lying around. Not anymore, they walk away with anything."

The clerk smiled as he handed the knife to David. "That's our best seller, finest Sheffield steel, finely honed to keep an edge. The grip won't let it slip from your hand. Feel the balance?"

"Sure do," David said as he turned the knife over in his hand. He slipped his fingers into the holes, it felt good. The light hit the gleaming blade, it shone wickedly.

"How much?"

"Tax and all, ninety dollars, and it comes with a genuine leather sheath."

David hefted it again. "That's a lot for a knife."

"Think of how long it will last, sir. No one was ever sorry for buying quality."

"I guess I'll take it. Don't bother wrapping it."

As he threaded the sheath through his belt, Andy smiled with approval. "You look like a mountain man for sure Davey. I hope you never have to use it, but if you do, you picked a good one."

As they headed for the door of the store, Andy stopped for a moment near a display of hats and took off his old worn hat and began trying new hats on. With each new hat he would watch in the mirror to see which one best suited his outdoors image. David mused at the faces he was making as he tilted his head at different angles trying to decide which one looked best. But none seemed to be making Andy into the rugged woodsman that he wanted to project. David stood off to one side of the mirror, smiling at the antics of the little old man. Andy's sense of humour was never very predictable, so David stayed out of sight as Andy reached up and placed a western styled Stetson on his head. The big hat made him look like a character out of a comic strip. David lost it and had to leave the store before Andy saw him. As he walked out through the front door he heard the sound of a motorcycle coming to a stop.

The biker sat for a moment looking around, then focused on the store and David. His identity was partially concealed by goggles. It was difficult to tell whether the mean look on his face came natural or whether he was just trying to give his bad-assed image a little help. Whatever it was, it brought back memories that David was trying to forget. The man stepped off his bike and walked towards the store entrance. He was well over six feet tall, with a barrel chest and the beginning of a beer belly. He wore a nickel studded vest, exposing tattoos that covered his body from the waist up.

Andy bumped David's arm as he walked up. "Ready to go?"

"Just waiting for you."

They headed for the door just as the biker was approaching. David thought that it was his new knife that was attracting the biker's attention. The man looked David in the eyes with a strange stare. But the biker said nothing. After he passed David, he shoved Andy into the door casing as he shouldered his way past. The old man reacted wildly.

"Watch where you're going you ugly bastard," the old man screamed.

The biker turned slightly looking in the general direction of Andy as he gave him the finger and said, "Fuck you Grandpa."

Adrenalin

Andy, now out on the street was about to throw a fit. Jim Hawkins description seemed to be fairly accurate: eighty pounds of temper and twenty pounds of man. His face was beet red and his hair streaming wildly from his head as he screamed, "Why that ignorant son of a bitch. Shove me around like that, will he. Give me your knife for a minute Davey, I'll teach him some manners!"

"Calm down Andy, we're supposed to be going to pick up Jim Hawkins, that guy's not worth the trouble. Forget about him."

"I don't give a shit! I'm not scared of him or a dozen like him!"

"I know you're not, but let it go for now. You'll probably never see him again."

Andy looked for all the world like a terrier wound up and ready to take on a bulldog. He was still full of fight.

"He better hope that he doesn't run into me again. I'll be wearing my own knife the next time that I come to town. I'll let his guts out."

Andy was still steaming as they drove into Jim Hawkins place. Jim was sitting on the veranda, apparently waiting for them. He got up, turned and yelled something through the screen door to Judy, and then walked down the steps towards them. Wolf moved from his resting place, yawned, stretched and began to follow.

"Stay Wolf," Jim said.

The dog cocked his head to one side, let out a low cry and then laid back down again, his grey and white eyes following his departing master.

"Just park your truck over there David, I'll drive."

Back through town they drove. As they passed the sporting goods store, the biker emerged and looked in their direction.

"There's that tattooed bastard that shoved me around!" exclaimed Andy, still angry from the confrontation.

"What's wrong, old timer?" asked Jim.

Andy was still fired up. "Me and Davey were just coming out of Massey's sporting goods store, when that ignorant son of a bitch shoved me." Andy recalled the meeting and got angry all over again.

Once in a while, Jim looked over at David to confirm what Andy was saying. Jim shook his head, his voice steady and calm as he said, "Some of those bikers show up here in the good weather. They don't all belong to gangs, but some do. It's best to put some distance between yourself and them. Some bikers are just regular guys enjoying themselves, others can be downright dangerous. David steered you right Andy. No one's questioning your courage. It's just better to avoid that guy."

Andy eventually let it go as Jim changed the direction of the conversation, "Have you ever been to Barkerville, David?"

"Nope, but the name is familiar. Maybe it was on one of those roadside signs that I passed when I first came to Dawson Creek. How big a place is it?"

"It's not very big. We turn off at Quesnel and go east for about half an hour. It's more of a tourist place than anything. At one time in the eighteen hundreds, it was a gold rush town, just like Dawson Creek. The townsfolk restored it to its original size and décor, well, maybe a little bigger and probably better built now than it was then. They painted it up real pretty and they have live theatre presentations and stagecoach rides. They also have a big festival every year and pan for gold in the Cottonwood River."

"Do they find any gold in the river that amounts to anything?" asked David, his eyes suddenly wide with interest.

"Do they find any gold there? Well, they find enough to bring people back year after year, and attendance seems to increase every year, so they must find something." He grinned. "Probably about as much as you and Andy were finding down at the cabin at Dawson Creek. Hopefully though, you'll have better luck if you decide to come down here."

Andy spoke up. "So how far from Barkerville is this claim you bought Jim?"

Hawkins shot a glance at Andy out of the corner of his eye. "About twenty minutes east. The guy that I won it from didn't bother with the claim, he didn't do any panning. He just used the cabin for hunting and fishing. His dad willed it to him and the cabin is supposed to be in real good condition, but you never know. We'll see when we get there."

It was after two o'clock when they finally rolled into Barkerville. David looked around; Jim had described it rather well. The buildings ranged from the old siding that showed the weathered age of time, to the theatre that was all spruced up in eye catching colors with a huge gold lettered marquis. As they watched, a stagecoach pulled up in front of the theatre and began letting off passengers. Jim Hawkins looked over at David who was enjoying the images of past gold rush days.

"As you can see, Barkerville caters to the tourist. That's the real gold in this town, helping folks relive the past. But I doubt that old prospectors back then were treated in the same manner as today's tourist. This is the old West 'Hollywood style', roughing it in comfort. When the festival takes place later on, this little town swells to about five times the population and you can't find accommodations within fifty miles of here."

The smile on Jim's face widened as he pulled up in front of his new piece of land. The cabin he had won in the poker game was better than he imagined. It was not a large cabin and had been built within the last five or ten years. The exterior was of whipsawed boards with narrow strips of wood covering the cracks where the boards were put together. Asphalt shingles covered the roof, black in color, and the whole cabin was a far cry from the dilapidated one at Dawson Creek.

Andy looked over the outside of the cabin. "How much was at stake in this poker game?"

Jim laughed, his perfect set of white teeth contrasting against the deep tanned complexion of his face. "The stakes were high enough, but I was holding four aces and a king. As I told you earlier, the guy inherited this place from his old man. Easy come, easy go. If I hadn't won it from him, someone else would have. It didn't seem to bother him that he lost it. I was really just after the claim rights. And if they turn out to be as good as the cabin, we might have hit the break that we've been looking for old timer. Let's go inside and have a look."

The interior of the cabin was even better. It was finished in knotty pine with a modern set of kitchen cupboards laid out in an open concept kitchen–living room style. There was a small bedroom and a two piece bathroom. Andy's eyes lit up when he saw the inside facilities. "Gee look at that, an inside bathroom finally. I sure won't miss that old outhouse and freezing my ass off in the wintertime. There's no electricity though. Without an electric pump, how do you flush it?"

Jim thought for a moment. "There's a hand pump in the sink, just like at the other cabin. I guess you just draw a pail of water and pour it down. Maybe we can buy a generator and get some electricity for you boys, if it works out. Think you want to move down here Andy?"

"Are you kidding? We've worked the other place dry of any gold that I could find. The sooner we move the better, eh Davey?"

"You bet, let's have a look around outside."

17

It was hard to believe that Andy had accumulated so much stuff in the two years that he had stayed in the cabin at Dawson Creek, but as he said, " Most of it's junk Davey, stuff that ain't worth hauling anyway."

Much of the trash went up in smoke in the bonfire. Some stayed with the cabin for any hunters that might want to rent it. Still that left enough of Andy's personal belongings to fill Andy's old truck and David's.

Andy stood beside his beat-up old truck, pulled off his hat and squinted towards the cabin in the glare of the morning sun. "I guess that'll about do it Davey, I think we've got everything loaded. If there's anything that I missed, I'll just get Jim Hawkins to fetch it down."

David looked at him for a moment, a look of concern on his face. "What truck is the dynamite in, mine or yours?"

Andy's sides shook as he laughed. "Relax, both the dynamite and the caps are in my old truck. Don't look so nervous, I've been handling that stuff for years. I know what I'm doing. Back your truck up in front of mine and I'll hook up the tow chain and we'll say goodbye to this place."

It took a few days to get settled. What a change, new bedding on Andy's bed and for the pullout couch where David would sleep. An assortment of dishes, pots and some pans as well as groceries and other necessities had to be bought at the local hardware. It was the morning of the forth day and it was time to find out what the mining prospects would be. It didn't take long to find that while the pickings were better than where they had left, it was still not great. But there was enough to make wages for David and enough to keep Andy prospecting.

Each day they roamed a little further down the Cottonwood River, always looking for a source up above in the mountains that might be worth looking into. They worked the river down to where it narrowed and a rocky cliff on each side of the river forced them out into deeper water than they could pan.

Andy looked up at the grey coloured rock. "That's it Davey, we can't go any further on this side of the river. We'll have to go around it. No telling how far that ridge goes before the river widens out again. We can check it out tomorrow or start back down this way on the other side of the river. What do you think?"

Slipping his hand into his pocket, David felt the comforting weight of his poke His brow wrinkled as he peered down the river, smiling he said, "I think its supper time Andy, we can talk it over later."

It had been almost a month since they had come down to the Barkerville Place. They pushed back from the breakfast table just as the sound of a vehicle pulling into the yard caught their attention. It was Jim Hawkins. His smiling face was always a welcome sight as he came walking up the steps.

"Morning boys, how's it going?"

Andy's jaw dropped. "You sure must have gotten up early to get here at this time in the morning. It's a good five-six hour drive down here."

"Don't I know it, but if I didn't get started early, I wouldn't be home 'till midnight. I was just wondering if you two wanted to go for a little trip and cash in some of that gold dust that you've been collecting."

"Where to, Jimmy?"

"Dawson City, up in the Yukon. I have a little business to take care of and Judy doesn't want to go, she suggested that you boys might want to go. How about it?"

Andy quickly became excited, "Sounds good to me. How about you Davey? We could cash in some of our earnings and have a good old time."

David grinned and thought before he answered. He was beginning to get a funny tingle up and down his spine. The fewer people that saw him the better. Not only that, he wanted to find someplace to cache his getaway supplies in case he had to depart in a hurry and he hadn't been able to do it with Andy here night and day. "Maybe next time, I would just as soon stay and hold the fort. You and Jim can take the gold and split it as you see fit, I trust you guys."

"Ah, this place can look after itself Davey, you never been up to Dawson City have you?" Suddenly a gleam appeared in Andy's eyes. "They got a dancehall there with pretty gals all dressed up like they was way back when the gold rush was on. There's gambling up there too. Boy it's a roaring place. You'd really like it."

David laughed. "You two can check it out real good. I'll go next time. I want to do a little hiking around on my own. Both of you have lived here at least long enough to be familiar with the whole territory. It's still pretty new to me, there's a lot I'd like to see for myself. I often look up into the mountains and wonder what the view is like. I'd like to hike up and see."

"I know what you mean," Jim spoke up. "When I go on hunting trips, I still get the same feeling as I used to. The air is different up there, different animals, like the mountain goats that seldom descend down to these levels and birds that seek solitude. Just be careful, you're all alone."

They measured the gold out in three equal amounts. As Andy brought out his battered suitcase, David asked, "When do you think that you'll be back?"

Andy looked first at Jim. "How long do ya figure?"

"Four or five days. It's a long haul up there and it depends how long my business will take me, but we'll probably be back within five days at the latest."

194

Andy turned to David. "You be careful Davey. Lock the cabin and your truck. If you leave the cabin, don't forget to wear those bells so that you don't surprise the bears."

"I'll be fine. You two have a good time and keep Andy out of trouble."

David watched as the truck pulled out of the laneway. It was the first time that he had the opportunity of having the place to himself. There were things that he wanted to do in private, now he could. The backpack with his emergency supplies was still in the back of his truck, untouched since the day that he and Andy had gone to town. There were some other items that he wanted to add and now, he would have the time to get it all together as it should be. He sat down with a pencil and paper and began to make a list of all that he would need:

- Fifty feet of small diameter rope
- Two forty foot lengths of plastic covered clothesline wire (It would be as strong as steel cable that size)
- A hand-held propane torch
- Sealed cans of emergency rations (spam, salmon, sardines, beef jerky)
- A large plastic groundsheet
- Collapsible shovel
- Hatchet
- First aid kit, needles and thread, alcohol and iodine as well as some ointment
- Fishing gear (independent of what he kept in the cabin)
- Cooking utensils and frying pans
- Sleeping bag and gym shoes
- Matches, candles and flares.

He read the list over. He would probably miss some things but his backpack would only hold so much. Some of those things he had already purchased from the sporting goods store, the rest he would pick up at the general store in Barkerville.

Adrenalin

He sat there trying to mentally organize all of the things he required. He would have to find a secure hideaway nearby for his backpack and gear. Maybe if he found a good place, he could store some blankets and extra clothing as well. At least now, with Andy gone, he would have enough time to examine the area thoroughly. Somewhere out there among all the rocks, caves and old mine shafts, he should be able to find a suitable spot.

David locked the cabin and went outside. He looked around. Satisfied that everything seemed safe and secure; he jumped into his truck and headed for Barkerville.

Very few places had authentic styled general stores in this day and age, but Barkerville did. This was probably due to the fact that they had tried to restore the town to a replica of what it had been at the turn of the century. At the store, they tried to keep one of every item that anyone could possibly need. They had all the items that David needed and more –much more.

David walked out into the street loaded down with his purchases. The stagecoach rolled by as he unlocked the camper cap and the driver spat a spew of tobacco in his direction. "Howdy stranger", he yelled. The driver grinned and rubbed his hand across his whisker-cover mouth. He cracked the lines on the rumps of the horses. It was just like a scene out of the old West thought David as he hollered back.

"Hi yourself, you look like you've got it made."

"Best job in town!" he said, as he rambled on to pick up another load of tourists.

David walked over to the restaurant that the three of them had eaten the first day they arrived in town: A half hour later he emerged, his hunger satisfied.

Armed with only his hunting knife and wearing the bell around his neck, he set out. He went to the place where the rocky cliffs that had stopped their panning activities along the river. That would be a good place to start.

It was almost two miles down to the spot. It was peaceful and while he liked Andy's company, the solitude of the day was pleasant and unobtrusive. He looked at the brilliant colour of the evergreens, the Aspens and other trees whose leaves were beginning to turn colour slightly. A small herd of elk took flight running through the long grass as the bell sounded his arrival. He hadn't seen any bears, although there were signs. Overhead, a flock of geese were already heading south. The subtle signs told of colder winter weather approaching.

He came to the spot where he and Andy had finished the day before. Upwards he climbed. The scrub brush and rocks tore away at his clothes and it was difficult to manage. It was steep and David was puffing hard by the time he reached the top where it levelled out. He could hear the rush of the Cottonwood River far below and see the white water as it dashed against the boulders in the river.

David picked his way along the rocky ridge. Suddenly, a rock gave way under his left foot and a sharp pain shot through his ankle as he began to fall. He reached out wildly catching a small evergreen that had anchored its roots deeply into the rocky surface. It had been like stepping into a groundhog hole, but David had seen no groundhogs in this region since he had arrived. Marmots perhaps, but this hole was much larger. The tree had saved him from falling. He withdrew his foot from the hole at the base of it. The foot was painful, and at first he thought that he might have sprained it. He gingerly put his weight on it. It was not a sprain; he had experienced a sprain before and had once broken a bone in that same foot. He knew the difference. He sat down and removed his stocking. The foot was red and there were abrasions where the skin had been removed when his foot slid into the hole, but that was the extent of the damage.

He looked down into the hole, the branches of the evergreen brushing the top of his head. He could see only blackness. Looking around, David found a rock, roughly the size of his fist. Dropping it down the hole, he listened. The sound of rock hitting rock came back to him. He dropped a couple more down the hole. By the sounds of it, the hole was not all that deep. David looked around for something that would burn, something that would illuminate the hole. He found nothing suitable. What he needed was a flashlight, the one thing that he hadn't thought to buy. There were a couple of miners hats back at the cabin. He would have to go back and get one.

Quickly he finished his dinner, he wanted to get back to the rocky ridge and explore the contents of the hole. He located the miner's hats and made sure that the light was working. Armed with a three-quarter inch rope, a shovel and a pickaxe, he set out. He had all that he could carry as he struggled back up the grade to the top of the ridge. Finally, he arrived at the spot, huffing and puffing.

Tying the rope securely to the harness inside the helmet, he switched on the light and gently lowered it down inside the hole. The helmet, swung back and forth as it was lowered and David let it slide until it hit bottom and the rope went slack. He tied a slip knot to mark the spot and then withdrew the miner's helmet and light. He looked at the length from the helmet to the knot. The hole was somewhere between fifteen to twenty feet deep. Still curious, he lowered the miner's hat back down into the hole. Lying on his stomach, he peered as far as he could down into the depths of the hole. The opening was large, that much he could tell, beyond that though, he could not make any other judgements. He would have to enter the area.

He stopped and looked around. There were several rocks and boulders scattered about, probably the way that nature had positioned them. The hole itself was roughly twelve inches wide, at the widest point. Grass and vegetation had grown around the hole and the base of the evergreen tree. David decided to clear it so that he could enlarge the hole. He took the pickaxe and began to hammer away at the rock. The roots of the tree gave way. David hauled it over to the edge of the ridge and shoved it off into the river below. He returned to the opening which now was growing ever wider and continued to work away, intent on making the opening large enough to be able to enter into it. With the shovel, he pried some of the rocks loose and they fell into the hole echoing as they landed on the rock below. He steadily worked away until finally, a huge piece of rock let go falling into the emptiness.

He looked about to see if anyone or anything was watching what he was doing. There wasn't. He was sure that there were no humans around and the sound probably frightened away any animals. He decided to take a little rest. Even though he had been living in the outdoors for some time and was in reasonably good shape, this effort was most fatiguing. He began to talk aloud inasmuch as there was no one here that would think him crazy.

"Phew," he panted. "This is too much like work. If it wasn't for curiosity and maybe finding a good hiding place for my emergency supplies, I wouldn't be doing this."

Finally rested, he returned to the task. Soon his persistence paid off. He had a hole that he could easily pass through. He fastened a rope securely to one of the huge boulders nearby; making sure that the rope was down near the base of the giant rock so that it wouldn't slide under it. Pulling the rope out to its full length, he tugged on it mightily. What he had in mind might prove to be foolhardy. Going down into unknown territory without backup of any kind could have dire consequences. Still, it might prove to be the secluded spot that would eventually save him from capture or a worse fate.

He tied several hand loops at various intervals on the rope, so that he would have something to hold onto when he had to climb back up. He secured the rope around his body put the miner's hat on his head. He took one last look around and then descended down into the hole. The depth of the outer rock was a good four feet thick before the light shone out into what seemed to be a very large cave. David descended another full twelve feet beyond before his feet hit the floor.

He looked around, amazed by what he had discovered. The cave was huge reaching back to depths where the light would not penetrate. It had to be at least sixty feet across. The most astonishing aspect however, was a stream about twenty feet wide flowing at a fast pace. It must have been the flow of water that caused the erosion that created this subterranean cave. David walked over, bent down, and touched the water. It was warm, very warm to the touch. It was a thermo stream, similar to those around Banff, and was thought to be therapeutic ecstasy. The outside air in those particular baths in all probability cooled them more than what this underground one was. He looked around, still hardly believing what he had found. How long had it been here undetected? Probably centuries, kept secret by the stone faced cliff alongside the river. The only visible entrance was the very small one that David had stumbled onto, and now enlarged.

As his eyes adjusted to the darkness, he could see the shaft of light from the entrance. Looking on the floor of the cave, he saw skeletal remains of small animals, probably rabbits or marmots that had fallen through the small entrance. With no means of escape, they had met their demise. They were the only signs of existence.

The floor of the cave was rough, with a rather scalloped look to it, bumpy, yet smooth. The erosion caused by water rushing over the rock, left nature's sculptured pattern. He remembered his studies in the die trade when one of his teachers referring to the fine finishing of steel had remarked, "Only by abrasion can a smooth and accurate finish be obtained." This was nature's work, probably the original teacher of the primitive man who adopted nature's method to suit himself.

David examined the walls of the cave. They were fluted; concaves and convexes that ran the entire length of the wall, or at least as far as he could see. He ran his fingers across the surface. It occurred to him that this might not be rock at all but limestone, which was a much softer material. The steady abrasion of the water had cut easily into the limestone and was now just a wide stream that flowed through out into the river. It had taken Mother Nature thousands, if not millions of years to work her wonder and carve out this cavernous cave.

Once again, David looked around in wonder. He was not a strong believer; still, it seemed as if a guided hand had brought him to this spot. It was perfect. He had found his shelter, his refuge if need be, from those that might track him. He would bring his backpack and supplies here right away. The fact that Andy and Jim would be gone for at least another three days gave him lots of time to complete his plans. He would keep it a secret from all.

18

The doctor's advice to Alex Gallo about changing his lifestyle and giving up drinking had fallen on deaf ears. An additional six beers a day corrected any lingering affects of the heart attack as far as he was concerned. Ellen expressed concern that the drinking might impede his recovery but this only brought the answer she expected to hear.

"My nerves are getting the best of me. This business about Joey just won't leave my mind. The booze calms me down. I still can't believe what happened. Joey was twice the man of that damn Rivers. Somehow, he must have got the jump on Joey. He could NEVER have taken him in a fair fight. And what have the cops done about it, zero."

Ellen said nothing. She accepted things as they were. She had grieved for her son. At first had blamed herself for not stopping Alex's constant encouragement of violence that in the end, led to Joey's death. She had started to go back to church to help her cope with her guilt, remorse and depression, and it had helped. Alex, on the other hand would not let it go. It festered and manifested itself inside of him and now Ellen was beginning to see a side of Alex that frightened her even more than it did before. It was an obsession, one that had taken over, one that would only be satisfied by David River's death. Alex's only reference to religion was a quote from the bible - 'an eye for an eye'.

Alex had now returned to work. It had been three months since his heart attack. Three months since that night that Joey had disappeared and David Rivers had gone missing. He was still drinking heavily and had been called into the office over being intoxicated on the job. They gave him a leave of absence to further recuperate. It only drove Alex into a deeper depression.

The root of the problem ran much deeper than anyone knew. Even Ellen couldn't know the rage that simmered within. It had festered there for many years, all the way back to when David's father, John, had humiliated him at high school by beating him in front of his friends. Friends that had looked up to him as the tough guy at school until that day that John had fought back and won. He had never forgotten it, and when his son was born, he was determined to have his boy grow up fearless – ready to take on all comers and win. While he had kept his feelings to himself over the years, now, they hounded him. Deep down, he was doing what he felt his wife Ellen was doing, blaming himself for the death of their son. It was something that he couldn't live with. Somehow, someway, he would find David Rivers and make him pay, and David's father John, the cause of the problem, would get to know just what loosing a son was like.

Ellen was probably also unaware that two weeks earlier, he had gotten one of David River's pictures from the newspaper. He had to go to the local library and look at some old micro files before he ran across the picture. Next, he had several hundred copies of the picture printed. He asked Sully to have his bikers distribute them all over the country. Alex was determined to do what the police could not, locate David. He offered a reward of one thousand dollars to anyone who could provide information to the whereabouts David. Then he waited, thinking that he would hear something from someone within a week. He was still waiting. Maybe it hadn't been such a hot idea after all.

Alex pulled his car up in front of Sully's garage and went in carrying a twenty four box of beer. A couple motorcycles that he hadn't seen before were parked near the door. Sully had picked up a couple more bikers to take Joey's place. He made his way back towards the office where Sully could almost always be found. Two burly bikers were working on their bikes. One was the guy called Sweat; the other he had never seen before. Both of them glanced in his direction and then silently continued on with what they were doing.

At the moment, Sully wasn't around and so he ripped open the pack and began filling the fridge. The sound of the door opening caused him to turn around as Alfie came into the office. Alex simply opened a bottle and thrust it towards Alfie and opened one for himself.

"Ah, that went down good. It's hot out there today." He flung himself into a chair. "What's up, Alex my man?"

"Not a lot. Where's Sully?"

"Out. Tell me something Alex, that thousand dollars you said you would put up for anyone that could finger Rivers, is that still standing?"

Alex sat up straight, his senses overpowering the effects of the alcohol. "Has someone spotted him?"

"Maybe, maybe. Is it still standing?"

"Hell yes," he said as he came to his feet. "If you've got some information lets have it."

"Not so fast Alex. We got a call from one of our boys. He says that he's not saying anything until he gets the money."

"How sure is he that it's Rivers?"

Alfie brushed his long hair back out of his eyes. "He says he's seen a guy who fits the description."

"And where was this that he says he seen him?"

"Well that's the one thousand dollar question, isn't it, Alex."

"Don't fuck with me Alfie, out with it. Where is he? I'm not paying anything out to anybody until I'm sure that it's Rivers."

Alfie's eyes got big. He remembered that Alex had a heart attack, and he didn't want him to have another. "Okay, okay, take it easy man. The guy that saw him is in British

Columbia right now. He said he saw Rivers and he's pretty sure it's him."

Alex stood up and came closer. Alfie could smell the stale odour of his breath, he was that close. "I want to see Rivers for myself first hand before I pay anybody anything."

"Didn't you hear me? He's out in British Columbia. That's probably why the cops haven't found him."

Alex sat back down. The colour in his face began to return as he sat in silence thinking. "Figures. If I was him, I guess that I would have travelled far and fast as well. The guys a wacko and he should be spending the rest of his life in the nut house."

Alfie put his feet back up on the desk and took a drink. "So what are you going to do? I hope that you're not going to get me in shit. I wasn't supposed to tell you until you anted up the dough. What are you going to do with the information? Turn it over to the cops?"

"Hell no. I'll pay the guy the money myself just like I said when I see Rivers with my own eyes. I'm on a leave of absence from work. I'll go to British Columbia myself. Screw the cops. It wasn't them that found him, it was me."

It should have come as a surprise to Ellen, but it didn't. So many things had happened in her life lately that she felt like a combat soldier. After the first few battles, the soldiers are considered seasoned, ready for more. She wasn't ready for more but she was seasoned to the point where she could endure more than she ever thought she could.

"So you're going to take a month off and go find David Rivers, even though you're not positive that it's him. You know that it's a police matter now. Why don't you call Chief Daniels and turn the information over to him?"

Alex snorted. "That fat ass couldn't find a pimple on his nose! I'm the one that found Rivers, not these local cops." His voice suddenly took on a menacing tone. "Don't you go telling the cops or anybody else what I just told you. If the law catches Rivers, there would be a trial first off and he would probably plead self-defence. Then a jury might let him off. No damn way, Rivers is going to pay in full for what he did to my son! I'm going to try to talk Sully into letting Alfie come with me. Alfie is just as interested in finding Rivers as I am, him and Joey were pals."

Ellen began to tremble. She knew that she should be quiet, yet she said it anyway. "Alex listen to me, if you take the law into your own hands, you could be the one that spends the rest of his life in jail, and I won't..."

His fist made her nose bleed profusely. Alex's hands closed around her neck. "Don't make the mistake of running to the police. You hear me! Nobody is going to stand in my way, not you, not anyone! You hear me now. I mean it. Rivers is just going to disappear. The police won't even know it. So if they do question me, I'll know where it came from. Don't make the mistake of crossing me!"

It was a relief when she heard the car pull away that morning. Alfie was with him when they left. Good riddance to the pair of them, she thought. It crossed her mind about calling Chief Daniels, but this time, she really was afraid of Alex. She had seen him wild and threatening before, but not like this. He seemed possessed. He had been brutal and she was more afraid of him than ever before.

She looked in the mirror. He had hit her so hard on the nose, that her eyes were turning black. It wouldn't be the first time that she would have to wear dark glasses out in public, but it would be the last. She had been hiding away money over these past months and now she had enough to get away. She had given this a lot of thought over the years and had options; moving to a different city and look for an apartment and a job or perhaps start at a shelter for battered women. But this was the last straw, she had made up her mind, if Alex came back, it would be to a cold and lonely house, one that she wasn't coming back to.

John L Sullivan sat in the office going over some figures, very impressive figures from a ledger that the internal revenue would like to see, but wouldn't. It was after eleven o'clock and Sweat was doing the run to Windsor on the bike affectionately named 'The Silent Knight'. They had been very successful slipping in and out of Windsor picking up their supplies without ruffling any feathers. Alfie normally rode Joey's old bike but now Alfie had gone with Alex hunting for David. Sully didn't really want Alfie to go at first, but then he heard about a drug contact in Vancouver with connections. So he had given Alfie a fistful of dollars, told him to have a good time, and not to come back without a deal of some kind with this guy. It would tie-in good with the bikers that he was set up with in Winnipeg. Besides, lately Alex Gallo, had become a real pain in the ass around the garage, drunk all the time and obsessed about David. Sully wondered if Alex really thought about what he was getting himself into; David had already put one Gallo in the ground.

Out front, a car pulled up by the empty gasoline pumps. Sully looked up in disgust. But the car just sat there, the motor running. He got up and walked to the front door. It was still warm as he stepped out in the yard. The window slid down in the car, on the driver's side.

"We're closed! We don't pump gas here at this station anymore." yelled Sully.

The car door of the new Lincoln opened and a short man, neat in appearance, walked towards Sully carrying an attaché case.

"I told you, we don't pump gas here anymore." Sully said.

The stranger moved silently as he walked up. "I know that. I'm well aware of who you are Mr. Sullivan and what you do. Lets step into your office shall we."

A cold clammy feeling come over Sully. Who the hell was this guy? The Rotwieller that was chained to the fence jumped to his feet, and began to growl. The man looked in his direction and all that could be heard was a low whine as he lay back down. Sully stared at the dog for a moment; usually he barked his head off at strangers, but not this one.

They walked into the office. Sully sat down behind his desk and motioned to another chair. "Sit down."

Adrenalin

The man appeared to be in his early thirties. He smiled, but remained standing. "Thanks. I won't be long. I have a message for you from some friends. You seem to be interfering in their territory and they are not happy. You see you're starting to spread your operation into an area that doesn't belong to you. They left you alone before but now things have changed."

Sully squirmed. "Sure, well..."

"Uh, Uh, I'm not done talking. We are well aware of that fast and quiet Harley Davidson bike that you have been slipping in and out of our territory. We know that your man is down there tonight. He won't be coming back! We also know about the connections that you have been busy setting up with some of the smaller bikers out west. My colleagues are big players in that region, and they don't like competition. They want to send a message to them and to you."

Sully just stared ahead. He always feared that some day the big players would send someone to see him, but he wasn't expecting some well-dressed businessman. How bad could this be, maybe they wanted him to join their organization. He watched as the stranger opened the attaché case and carefully began to place thousand dollar bills in a neat semi-circle on the desk in front of him. He had never seen so many one thousand dollar bills before. For a moment he relaxed and smiled. "I get the message. You want us to join you. No problem. I was thinking..."

The stranger put his finger to his lips and nodded negatively. "You're mistaken. That's not the message that we want to send your friends."

The money had dazzled Sully, so much so that he never saw the nine millimetre pistol slip out of the attaché case. He also never had a chance to reach for the 38 special he had in the drawer. And he never felt the slug that tore into his skull pitching him forward, blood spilling out onto the money.

The stranger exited the office leaving the money that would soon be photographed by some eager news reporter.

This should send a message far and wide. It always costs to advertise, he thought as he moved towards the door. The Rotwieller jumped up ready to bark but he lay back down.

"Smart dog."

He slid into the leather seat of the Lincoln and sped away. He smiled; nice job, he thought to himself. The men he had taken care of were trouble and no one ever screamed for justice. Even the police seldom considered the loss of these individuals top priority.

19

The headlights of Alex's big Buick illuminated the sign, 'Welcome to Dawson Creek', as he and Alfie drove by. Three days of hard driving had brought them to their destination. Alex looked rough, three days growth of beard and his bloodshot eyes made him look as rough as he felt. Alfie didn't look much better but then that was the way he looked most of the time anyway. Alex looked over at him as the city lights flashed through the car's interior.

"We'll get a motel room and call your friend in the morning. You've got his number haven't you?"

"If he's there. He really ain't my friend. I don't even know the guy. I just called the number that the biker gave me and told him that we were coming. I didn't know how long it would take or that we would make such good time. He might not even answer when I call."

Alex looked up, saw a motel with a vacancy light on and drove towards it. "Well, if he isn't there right off, we'll check out the town. There's bound to be some watering holes in a place like this."

The sun shining in his eyes woke Alex up. He lay there for a moment trying to get his bearings. The sound of the toilet flushing brought him around. He looked over at the other bed. The sheets were thrown back and it was obvious were Alfie was. He yawned, scratched himself and got up. His head was aching and his throat was dry. He would have to go out to the car and bring in the case of beer. He was too tired last night. At that moment, Alfie walked out of the bathroom, he was fully dressed. Alex reached over to the nightstand and picked up his keys.

"Here," he said as he tossed them over to Alfie. "Go get the beer out of the car."

"Let's get some breakfast first. I'm hungry."

"Go get the beer damn it!" yelled Alex.

Alex poured the first one straight down. "Ah, that tasted good. My head won't stop pounding until I have my first beer," Alex said as he reached for another.

"That stuff is going to get the best of you man."

Alex stared at him for a moment. "Want one?"

"Hell no, not this early in the day. We should go eat. You look really rough this morning Alex, like you need a shower and a shave."

Alex glared at him. "You sound like my old woman. You don't need to talk, that hair of yours looks like it needs raked." Alex rubbed his chin thoughtfully. "Maybe I do need to clean up some. I think I threw my electric razor in my suitcase. After this though, just look after yourself. While I'm getting cleaned up you can call that guy."

"I doubt that he'll be up."

"It's after nine o'clock."

"By your watch, but this is B.C. time, and they're three hours earlier than us. It's only six o'clock here man."

"Oh, I forgot about this crazy time. I'll get ready and then we'll grab a bite to eat. I saw a restaurant just across the street when we came in last night. We can just walk over."

It was after one o'clock British Columbia time before Alfie finally reached his contact. Alex sat in a chair in the motel room and listened to the conversation.

"Ya, okay, ya, the Copper Creek Hotel. Where is it? Okay, then turn right. We'll see you there about two," Alfie said as he hung up the phone. Turning to Alex he said, "This guy said..."

"Yes, yes, I heard. Two o'clock at the Copper Creek hotel."

Adrenalin

The bar room at the Copper Creek Hotel was empty except for the bar tender and one waiter.

"What'll it be boys," he asked.

Alex looked at him for a moment, deep in thought. "Just bring three glasses and a pitcher of beer." The waiter looked around as if he had missed someone. Alex picked up on his inquisitiveness.

"He's coming," said Alex putting the waiters mind at rest as he headed towards the bar to fill the order.

He wore dark green goggles that covered his face and the tattoos on his huge biceps made him identified him as a biker. He walked in and looked around for an instant before heading over to the table where Alex and Alfie sat. Alex just motioned to the empty chair as he poured beer into the third glass and pushed it towards him. He quickly downed it and Alex refilled it as he motioned for the waiter for a refill.

The biker spoke up. "So you guys just got in from Ontario, eh?"

"My name's Alex and this is Alfie."

"I'm Chad Moore." He looked at Alfie more so than Alex. "Alfie who?"

It was Alex who spoke. "What's the difference? Are you the guy that claims to have seen David Rivers?"

Chad swung around and looked straight at Alex. "Did you bring the money?"

"Maybe."

"Well let's see the green then."

"Not so fast. I'm not paying a cent until I see this guy that you say is Rivers."

Chad Moore's lip curled like a guard dogs. "Don't get smart with me. If I don't see the money, I'm not showing you anybody. You can both go back to Ontario." He got up out of the chair.

Alex quickly realized that his only lead was about to leave. "Wait a minute. Sit down and have another beer. I'll give you a hundred now, say goodwill money. You get the rest just as soon as I see the guy and IF, he turns out to be Rivers."

Moore sat back down. He took the handful of tens and twenties that Alex shoved towards him and poured another drink. "He matches the picture. Maybe a little older, a few pounds heavier but it sure looked like him. He come out of this store at the same time that I was going in with some old geezer."

Alex leaned closer. "I can sweeten the pot another thousand, if it's him."

"I'm listening."

Alex related the chain of events that brought him to British Columbia. He watched the greed in Chad Moore's eyes. "See, the thing is, I don't want the law arresting him and then some candy assed judge or jury turning him loose. I want him to disappear once and for all, understand?"

"That sounds like it should be worth more than that."

"You're not doing it yourself. Chances are you'll have nothing to do at all, except keep your mouth shut. I want the pleasure of shooting the bastard myself! If I miss though, I don't want him getting away. Understand?"

Chad Moore said nothing for a moment. It was hard to fathom what was going on; there was no facial expression at all. Finally, he said, "I'll have to think about that one."

Alex's voice was low but quick as he answered, "No you won't. Your in or else. I don't want you walking around knowing what you do so that you can spill it to the cops!"

Chad was defiant. "Or else what?"

Unlike himself, the expression on Alex's face was very readable. Alex leaned close after casting an eye towards the bartender who was watching them. "I found you, didn't I. I've got contacts, more than you might think. If you want to find out how many, you just get up and walk away."

Chad Moore wasn't sure how much was a bluff, how much was not, but Alex looked mean. This was supposed to be an easy grand, one that he was to get just for fingering a guy. Now, he was getting sucked in and he didn't like it. Still, if he didn't have to do any of the dirty work, he could use another thousand.

"Okay, I'm in but you get this straight, when it comes time for you to pay up, you better have the dough. I have connections too and I'm going to make sure that they know who to start looking for if something happens to me, and believe me, you wouldn't want these guys looking for you!"

Alex sat stone faced. The situation was rapidly approaching the point of no return. It was Alfie that felt very uneasy. The guys Chad was talking about would come looking for you and they didn't need a warrant. He hoped that Alex knew what he was doing. Maybe coming along for the ride hadn't been one of the smarter things that he had done.

"We'll need a couple of rifles, thirty thirties, one with a scope."

"You're talking at least three hundred bucks each, scope or no scope. I know where I can lay my hands on them, I think."

Alex took out a nice fat wallet, the contents of which didn't escape Chad's greedy eyes. "Here's the six hundred for the guns. At that price, I'll expect them to throw in a decent amount of shells. We'll be at the Frontier Hotel, room 107. I'll expect to see you no later than nine tonight."

"I'm not sure that I can get them that quick. If you didn't want them coming from an unidentified source, you could walk into the sporting goods store and buy them yourself. These things take time."

Alex shoved his wallet back in his pocket and drained his glass. "Come on Alfie." Looking at Chad he simply said, "Room 107, nine o'clock."

20

David welcomed Andy's return on Wednesday morning. He and Jim had not been gone as long as he thought, but long enough for him to accomplish all that he needed to do. He had thoroughly explored the cave and gotten all of his gear stored inside his new hideaway. He had sealed the entrance with a large rock so that anyone who passed by would think that it was part of the rock formations that lay along the trail.

It was good to see them. David had not realized until now just how close the friendship between him and Andy had grown. He genuinely missed the little man. The same could be said for the tall outdoorsman, Jim Hawkins, although to a lesser degree.

"It's good to see you guys. Have a good trip?"

"We sure did Davey," Andy grinned. "And a profitable one. The price of gold is up." Still smiling from ear to ear, he handed David a brown envelope. "This here's your share partner."

David opened the envelope bulging with hundred, fifty and twenty dollar bills. David looked up in surprise. "This much?"

"Count it, there's just over twelve hundred dollars there. Not bad after all, eh?"

"Right on. It's a lot more than I expected."

Jim Hawkins laughed heartily. "You're wealthier than your partner. Andy was tipping the gals at the casino right and left. I finally had to drag him out of there."

Andy's face was flush with excitement. "You got to come with us next time we go Davey. I could have set you up with the cutest little gal you ever saw."

David looked at Andy, it must have been exciting but for him, it could be dangerous. Next time might be a long way off. For now he would humour the old fellow. "Sounds like you two had a ball. Ya, next time I'll go."

It was evident that Andy had spent a good deal, as he began hauling packages out of the truck. "I got us a new set of dishes and some new cooking pans, some new blankets, good warm ones. And these are for you Davey," he said throwing a sealed brown box in his direction.

David looked up. "What is it?"

"Open it and see," said Andy grinning.

David tore away at the box and looked inside. "Rubber boots? What the hell do I need rubber boots for?"

"They ain't rubber boots. Pull them all the way out of the package. They're waders. We'll have to cross the river where it's shallow enough to get across in these, unless you want to swim across and work while you're soaking wet. We can start panning on the other side and go all the way down to the cliffs. Look here, I got a pair for myself too."

"Gee thanks Andy. Look, I'll pay for them, I would have had to buy a pair anyway."

"No, I bought them for you. You can buy me and Jim a drink when we go to Barkerville."

"Well in that case let's head for town. I'll buy dinner and some drinks," he said while he thumbed through his money in the envelope. That old guy that he met back in Las Vegas was right. There was still a living to be made panning for gold Not only that, it was peaceful here and the company was good. He hoped that it would stay this way.

Jim spoke up. "Good, I'm famished and since you're buying Dave I think that I'll have the best steak that they serve and a tall cool Ale. I'll be going right back to Dawson Creek after we eat, Judy's beginning to think that I quit the country. You boys can drive in yourselves, that way I can keep going."

They waved at Jim as he drove away, and then headed back to the cabin.

"Ah. I ate too much Davey but that steak was good, cooked just right. That trip that me and Jim made was one of the best and he has to go back up there before freeze-up. I'm going to hold you to your promise boy. We'll have a whale of a time. Say, I forgot to show you the new cribbage board and deck of cards that I bought so that we could pass the evenings away. Did you ever play cribbage?"

"A few times with my dad, he usually beat me though."

"That sounds good to me 'cause I'm no whiz at it but it will give us something to do. It's too bad that they didn't run the hydro wires out this far, a television would sure be nice."

"It would. I thought Jim was talking about buying a generator for out here?"

Andy sat up straight as if he had just awakened from a dream. "He did, didn't he? For that matter I guess we could each throw in a little money and buy one for ourselves, or better yet, let's pan enough to buy one."

"Sounds good to me."

The two drove along like old friends talking about tomorrow and hoping for a bright future.

David was adjusting to this lifestyle. He hadn't had any demons walking into his dreams in the middle of the night since they had moved down to Barkerville. Only on one occasion did the longing for his mother and father leave pangs of remorse. He had accepted the fact that there was no going back, that his lifestyle had changed just as his name had. His folks would always be in his memories and he was grateful to have been raised and loved by two such wonderful people.

The peace and tranquillity of this part of British Columbia quickly grew on him. The friendship with Andy and Jim Hawkins had been his salvation. The fact that he had been swallowed up with such anonymity was of great comfort to him. He no longer kept looking back over his shoulder and feeling the fear of being recognized. His discovery of the cave and his cache of supplies was a safety net that also brought him peace of mind. He awoke thinking of these pleasantries as he threw back the covers and began looking forward to the day ahead.

Andy was already up and came into the kitchen wearing his overhauls pulled on over his long johns. He began to poke away at the cook stove trying to get the still warm embers to burn. He reached down and picked up some kindling and threw it in, looking around he saw David sitting up on the pullout.

"Morning, Davey. We might as well start panning on the other side of the river this morning. We'll see if we can find a spot to ford."

David yawned and swung his feet out on the floor. "What do you mean 'ford' the river?"

"It means that we find a spot that ain't over our waders so that we can get across. You mean that you never heard of fording a river before?"

"Nope, not where I come from, the river was too deep to cross on foot anywhere."

Andy turned around. "I know that they say that the Red River floods a lot, but I thought that there were times that it went down to where you could wade across it?"

David gulped and came full awake. He had forgotten that he had told Andy that he was from Manitoba. This was a wakeup call. What was it they say? The truth is always the same but a lie - - he was jolted back to reality and the fact that he would have to be more careful. "I never fooled around the river back home that much. There was a Lake that my dad always took us swimming at. He always said that the Red River was too treacherous."

"Yes, I heard that too. You were probably wise to listen to your dad."

The morning air was beginning to get cooler now that fall was fast approaching. David and Andy stood on the back porch pulling on their waders. Andy stopped and turned. "I forgot one thing." Andy walked down off of the porch, around to one side of the house and picked up a stick about two inches in diameter and six feet in length.

"What are you going to do with that?"

Andy let out a cackling laugh. "I don't want to step in a hole over my head. I'll just feel along the bottom of the river with this until we find a spot where we can cross. Come on."

It took about three attempts before they finally found a spot where they could safely cross, one that came no higher than their waist. The rest of the day, except for a short break at noon, they worked steadily. The panning was good, better than what the other side of the river shoreline had been yielding. David never got over the excitement of finding the gold in the bottom of the pan. Carefully, he would run his fingers around the bottom and put the gold into the poke bag.

They had put in a full day by the time they crossed the river and returned to the cabin. As they arrived on the back porch, Andy sat down wearily before he began to pull off his waders. "Ah, I think I overdid it today. I must be getting old. I'm plumb tuckered out." He looked around as David stepped out of the waders dripping water all over the porch. He hung them over the railing to dry.

"Why don't you stay out here and have a little snooze. I'll cook something up for us."

Andy struggled to his feet, pulled off his waders very slowly and collapsed back down into the chair. His head nodded and he was almost asleep by the time David entered the cabin.

21

Chad Moore pulled into the Frontier Hotel and drove his bike around back stopping in front of unit #107. Carrying the two rifles wrapped in a blanket on the bike made him nervous. At nine o'clock it was beginning to get dark and they would only be noticed by someone curious, someone like a cop. He was relieved when he looked around and saw no one was following. He foolishly thought the thousand dollars was supposed to be so easy, but the outcome could be deadly. He had made a good buy on the guns and there was supposed to be a lot more money coming, but he didn't like this pair especially Alex.

He was about to rap on the door when Alex opened it. "About time, I thought we were going to have to come looking for you."

"What the hell are you talking about. I'm only five minutes late. What do you expect me to do, come flying down the street with the cops on my tail?"

"Never mind, let's see the guns." Alex barked.

Alex smiled when he saw them, especially the Winchester thirty–thirty, with the scope on it. He turned it over in his hands and rubbed the smooth walnut stock of the gun. He pointed it at the wall and looked through the scope although at this close range he couldn't see anything.

"Nice, real nice. Wait until I get Rivers zeroed in on this, and then pop. What about the ammunition?"

"Out in my saddlebags, I'll go get it."

Alex looked over and smiled at Alfie who was examining the lever action Marlin that Chad had handed him. He looked up at Alex. "I never even shot one of these before."

"Nothing to it, we'll get out away from town and I'll give you a few lessons."

Chad came in carrying four boxes of shells. "That should hold you."

"That's good. What kind of rifle do you have, Moore?"

"I don't. I just come up here to Dawson Creek on my bike. It isn't fitted with a rifle scabbard," he said sarcastically.

"Well get one. If you expect the other thousand that I promised you, you might just have to earn it."

Chad's face got red. "Let's get one thing straight Alex. I'm just going along for the extra thousand and so far, I've seen damn little of the first. If I have to shoot somebody, it's going to cost you five thousand or I'm walking and don't try threatening me again."

"You'll get it if you're the one that shoots him, I'll see to that. I just don't want him getting away. So far, I'm not even sure it's our man."

"Well I want more than a measly hundred bucks that you gave me so far. I want four hundred more before I go anywhere. I'm not getting my ass in a sling for dick all."

Alex began to come back to earth. Chad Moore was getting angry and if he decided to walk away, Alex wasn't sure where to find someone else.

"All right, all right, here's four hundred more," as he fished four hundred dollar bills out of his wallet. "Now I've held up my end, when do I get to see this guy Rivers?"

"I'll have to do some digging around. I haven't seen him since that first day but that old geezer that was with him, I've seen before. He works for Jim Hawkins, I think."

"Who's Jim Hawkins?"

"He guides, traps and gambles some. He owns a lot of property around here, so they say. I don't know him that good, but the guy that I bought the rifles from does, and I'll talk to him."

"Well see what you can find out. If this guy works for this Hawkins he shouldn't be too hard to find. We'll be in the bar at the Copper Creek Hotel around noon tomorrow. Have something for us by then."

Chad Moore got up and left. They could hear his bike bark loudly as it started up and then drove away.

Alfie sat in his chair staring up at Alex who was still standing with the Winchester in his hand.

"Boy Alex, you sure talked rough to that guy."

Alex looked over, silent for a moment as if he was thinking about his answer. "I'm not fooling with that guy, Alfie. If he tries jacking me around, he won't live long. We already have a good idea how to find this guy that we're looking for. It's just a question of whether or not he is Rivers."

Alfie didn't say anything since they had left home. Alex had taken on a whole new personality. He had become much more aggressive, more focussed. He was out for blood, no doubt about it. This thing with David Rivers had become an obsession. Alfie wasn't entirely sure of Alex's motive. Certainly some of it, if not all of it, was to avenge Joey. But it seemed to run even deeper, as if it was a vendetta, like a family feud. Even he was thinking about being careful about what he said around Alex. It seemed that to Alex, everyone was expendable, even Alfie.

Alex and Alfie were busy eating their way through a couple of hamburgers the next day at the Copper Creek Hotel. They paused long enough between bites to wash the food down with beer.

"Do you think that we can trust Chad Moore, Alex?" said Alfie, although he was already pretty sure of the answer.

"Trust him? Hell no! You can't see his eyes through them green goggles that he wears. He swaggers around like he's tough as hell. We'll keep a sharp eye on him. If he crosses me, he'll be sorry."

At that moment, there was the sound of a motorcycle pulling into the hotel parking lot. "Don't you say anything to him that might make him think that we don't trust him. We need him right now and we'll have to put up with him, at least for the time being."

The door opened and, as expected, it was Chad Moore. "Bring me a beer," he said to the waiter as he sat down.

"What have you got for us?" asked Alex.

Chad looked around making sure that there was no one else around before he spoke. "I talked to my buddy. Seems this Hawkins guy is pretty popular around town. He says that the old guy and the kid, the one that you're looking for, were staying in a cabin that this Hawkins owns about half an hour out of Dawson Creek. He also said that Hawkins won another cabin from a guy in a poker game about a month ago and they might be there, he wasn't sure. This other cabin is down at Quesnel, about four hundred miles or so south of here."

Alex shoved the rest of his hamburger into his mouth and chewed vigorously trying to swallow and talk at the same time. "So how do we find out which one they're at?"

"This Hawkins is supposed to be all business. If he has a spare cabin, he'll rent it out see, like to fishermen or hunters. If you were to let on that the two of you just come here from Ontario to do some fishing, and that someone in town told you that he might have a cabin to rent, then we'd know where they were."

"I don't follow you?"

"Well if he says that he has one to rent at Dawson Creek, then obviously, they would be at the other one down near Quesnel."

"Okay. Go see which one he wants to rent."

"Right. I come riding in on a motorcycle from the mainland and ask him that. He probably gets that everyday. From what my source tells me, Hawkins isn't too thrilled with bikers to begin with and he'd get suspicious right off. You both look the part. Tourists come up here fishing all the time. If he thinks everything ain't okay, he won't rent a cabin out to you and he'll clam right up. This guy ain't supposed to be no dummy."

"Just where does this Hawkins live?"

Moore gave specific directions to Jim Hawkins residence, before he left.

Alex and Alfie entered the same sporting goods store where David had purchased his knife and fishing equipment. A half hour later they emerged. Alex looked the part of a tourist looking for a good fishing spot. He was wearing a fisherman's hat complete with a smattering of trout flies and small spinners attached to it, while Alfie could have passed for his son. They had bought rods, reels and tackle boxes and arranged them in the car's back window so that they could be easily seen.

Alex looked over at Alfie. "We better get a couple of long sleeved cotton shirts like most of the yokels around here are wearing. You've got to cover those tattoos on your arms. You know what Moore said about this guy not liking bikers. We don't want to make him suspicious of nothing, see? Besides, it's getting cool here and I could use something warmer than what I'm wearing."

Jim Hawkins had just turned his mules out to pasture and was walking back to the house, when the big black Buick with Ontario licence plates pulled into his yard. Wolf began to bark. "It's all right boy, go up on the porch and lie down." The dog did as he was commanded.

Alex stepped out of his car and looked around. He looked the part of a tourist fisherman, and not a very seasoned one either, judging by the new hat and shirt that he wore. Jim had seen more than his share of city folk who knew almost nothing of life up here in the North Country. Usually, they had read some colourful brochure of huge fish being pulled out of fast running water and had followed their dreams up this way. Often they caught enough fish to take home and brag about.

"Good morning, something that I can help you with?"

Alex put on his best simple smile. "Ya, we came up this way to try our hand at fishing. A fellow at the Copper Creek Hotel said that you might have a cabin that we might be able to rent for a few days or a week and that you could steer us onto some good fishing spots."

Jim scanned the two men all and asked, "What was this guy's name?"

Alex wasn't expecting this question. Chad had said that Jim didn't like bikers. "Don't remember. I don't even know if he said it. You know how it goes, you sit down and somebody comes over and then you have a few drinks, tell a few jokes. Gosh, I can't think of his name." Alex was beginning to sweat.

"What did he look like?"

"Ah, he was tall, quite tall with sandy coloured hair and a goatee. Nice guy he was."

Jim thought for a minute. "Don't sound like anyone I know, but then I meet a lot of people. I do have a small cabin that I would rent out. It's nothing fancy, like the big lodges that you might have seen pictures of, but the fishing is real good there."

"How much?"

"How long do you want it for?"

"Just a few days."

"Fifty bucks a day. It ain't fancy, like I said, there's no hydro, just a wood cook stove and there's outside facilities."

"That's okay, as long as the fishing is good."

Jim smiled. There was something that just didn't set right about these two, something that he just couldn't put his finger on, but business was business. "Good enough. I'll just go in the house and get you a few clean sheets and blankets and then you can follow me down to the cabin."

Jim walked up the steps and unlocked the cabin. He laid the blankets on the cots and walked over and opened the pantry. "All the dishes and pots and pans are in here. You have to wash the dishes before you leave. Just bring the bedding back when you drop the keys off. The firewood is outside. That's the water pump by the sink. Nothing fancy but it beats tenting and that stream out back is full of trout and salmon."

They stepped outside and Alex handed Jim one hundred dollars. Alfie was busy looking the place all over. The sight of a fish jumping excited him. "Hey Alex, did you see the size of that one!?"

"Looks good. We should have some luck here." He turned to Jim. "That guy that told us about you having this place said that he thought you had another cabin further South down around some town that they fixed up like it was back in the gold rush days. Me and Alfie thought that it might be nice to spend a few days down there on the way back home if we could."

"I have one down at Barkerville, which sounds like the one he means. A couple of my friends are staying at that cabin for a while and they'll likely be there for some time. It's more like a small house that one is. This guy that you were talking to sure seems to know an awful lot about me."

Alex looked down towards the ground. "He seemed to know a lot about this whole area. Too bad I didn't catch his name."

Jim looked over towards Alfie wondering if he knew who this talkative person was but Alfie had walked off towards the stream and seemed interested in fishing. It really wasn't important anyway.

Jim drove along back towards Dawson Creek. He had a funny feeling about these two, especially the older one. He really didn't seem that interested in fishing although the other one did. He was glad that he hadn't mentioned that David and Andy were panning for gold. Sometimes, just the mention of finding gold in any amount brought out the worst in people.

Alex began to spread the sheets on one of the cots and then threw a blanket on it. He wasn't use to making his own bed and it showed. His mood was still surly as he turned to

Alfie and said, "You better get busy and make your own bed 'cause I ain't waiting on you."

In silence, Alfie followed suit making up the cot that he was to sleep in. He looked up at Alex as he finished. "I guess that we better catch us some fish for dinner. That's what we came up here for."

Alex snarled. "What do you mean, that's what we came up here for you numbskull. The only reason that we came here is to find out where Rivers is and it's plain that he isn't here. He's got to be down at that other place, the one south of here. We'll stay here tonight and tomorrow to make it look good, and then we'll hook up with Chad Moore and go down there after him."

"If it's him. Aren't you going to go fishing Alex?"

The uncertainty of Alfie saying 'if it's him' disturbed Alex. It better be him, he thought as he looked into the simple inquisitive face of Alfie. "You can go catch some fish. I'll see if I can get this old stove going so that we can cook on it. Don't forget to clean what you catch outside. Take a knife out of the pantry with you."

Alfie got the fishing gear that they had bought out of the car and baited up. He was looking forward to fishing. It had been many years since he fished with a throw line trying to catch mullets in the river back home. He had never been out this way before, never seen such beautiful scenery like the mountains and the steams so clear and sparkling. This part of the trip he was beginning to enjoy.

He had never fished for trout before and so he became intensely interested in catching one. As he began to attach the lure to the line, he began to think of how Alex's intense hatred for David Rivers had so engulfed the man. He had no love for Rivers but he could still remember the sick feeling that hit him in the stomach when Joey had shot that kid. Joey had told him that he was just going to scare the boy. Some scare. Now he had let himself get dragged into another scenario in which someone could get killed. This was different from selling drugs and fencing stolen property. He could end up in jail for a long, long time in this situation. He knew that if he tried to back out now, Alex might kill him. He remembered that look in Alex's eyes when he told Chad that he was 'in or else'. Alex didn't look like he was fooling.

He cast the spinner out across the water. Something hit it, but he wasn't quick enough about setting the hook. The second cast and the excitement of battling a trout made him forget all else. The fish broke water several times before he brought it wriggling up on the shore of the stream. He had never seen a Rainbow Trout up close before. The vibrant colour was something that he had never seen before. He ran back to the cabin. Alex was busy cursing the kindling that he was trying to light. It kept going out and smoking up the cabin.

"Look! I think it's a trout, Alex. I caught it on the second cast."

"Well good for you. Go catch a couple more and clean them. We'll have some dinner, that's if I can get this damn stove lit."

As it turned out, it was Alfie that caught and cleaned the fish and then got the fire in the cook stove going. He also cooked the fish while Alex, still in a foul mood, took his rifle outside and moments later, the sound of bullets could be heard. Alfie set out two plates and placed the fried fish on them before going to call Alex for dinner. As he stepped out on the porch, he saw Alex pointing the rifle skyward. He looked up towards the intended target.

An Osprey had just spread its wings and dropped its tail and was going into a power dive when Alex shot and barely missed it. The startled bird veered off into the sky and soared away to safety.

"Damn it, I missed!" he said to himself and then saw Alfie standing there with his mouth agape. "This scope works good on anything that doesn't move, but it's hard to hit a moving target. When I get Rivers in my sights, I'll have to remember that."

That lump suddenly was back in Alfie's stomach as he said, "Dinner's ready."

The trout was good and even Alex stopped being bitchy as he fell to tearing off the pink flesh and stuffing it in his mouth. "That was good Alfie. Didn't know I was so hungry with all this other stuff on my mind. I just remembered, I told you that I'd give you some shooting lessons. Come on, get your gun and we'll see how it works."

"Right after I clean up the dishes."

"To hell with the dishes, there's more clean ones in the pantry. Just put in the sink and come on."

Alfie was much less enthusiastic about shooting. He had already made up his mind that if he had to shoot at anyone, it would be over their head. He wasn't going to jail for Alex or anyone else, not if he could help it. He levered the shells into the Marlin just as Alex showed him. While Alex watched intensely, he aimed at a tree and squeezed off a shot.

"Dead centre Alfie, if that had been Rivers you'd have nailed him!"

At the edge of the clearing, a marmot sat and looked in their direction. He had gotten curious at the wrong time. Alex whistled, the creature turned slightly and stared right at him, Alex had him in the crosshairs of the scope and he virtually exploded as the bullet ended his life.

"Ha, ha, the scope is dead on. If I get Rivers in my sight he's dead meat."

The target practice continued with Alex urging Alfie to improve his shooting skill. "We better ease off this some Alex. We're wasting ammunition that you might need. Not only that, someone might get curious about why we are really here."

Alex was silent for a moment, then said, "Maybe so. We don't want to bring any attention down on us. At least you know how to load that rifle and shoot it. You probably won't have to though. I want the pleasure of shooting Rivers myself. I want to do that for Joey."

Alfie said nothing. He found it harder all the time to believe that this was all for Joey. Looking at the signs of hatred and revenge that had began to etch deep hard lines into Alex face, he began to understand how some feuds went on for years between families and others over things like race and religion. Sometimes going on for so long that they forgot what initiated it in the first place. No, this was not just because of Joey.

Finally, as the shooting eased off, the birds and the wildlife began to move around again. Alfie looked over at Alex who sat there nursing a beer that he had set down beside him.

"You want I should catch some more fish for supper, Alex?"

At that moment, a doe walked out of the woods. She gracefully lifted her head her large brown eyes looking up towards the two men who remained motionless. Her ears twitched back and forth. She stretched out her long neck to drink from the stream. Suddenly, she jumped high into the air, landed, took two steps and then staggered, her head dropping into the stream which she had just moments ago drank from.

Alex smiled as he lowered his rifle. "That's what we'll have for supper, fresh venison. Go get me a butcher knife, a good sharp one."

Alfie's appetite was not very good that evening. The vision of the deer watching him as the bullet from Alex's gun tore into her caused him to lose his hunger. Alex made up for it though, as he devoured large chunks of steak that he had cooked real rare, the blood still oozing from it. "Eat up Alfie. How often do you get to eat fresh deer meat?"

Alfie pushed back from the table. He wasn't about to tell Alex the real reason that he wasn't hungry, Alex wouldn't understand anyway. "Guess that I ate too much trout at dinner time."

Alex was about to say something when the sound of a motorcycle turning in caught his attention. He brightened right up. "Sounds like Chad."

The heavy footsteps announced his arrival as he walked up the steps and into the cabin. "So they weren't here. I was waiting for you guys to come back and tell me."

Alex tried to speak and he nearly choked as he tried to swallow a mouthful at the same time. "We should have but we were busy trying out the guns that you got us. They work good. I shot this venison and butchered off a chunk and cooked it up myself. Sit down and dig in. There's a lot, Alfie's not hungry. You can have his share."

Chad pulled up a chair and helped himself to a huge portion of venison and began to chew away. Alfie quietly looked at him not really liking what he saw. It was hard to tell much about Chad Moore. Those green wrap-around goggles were almost like a mask. He had a half inch of stubble on his face and he never smiled, not even once. Alex reached down beside him and grabbed a beer from the case on the floor. "Want a beer?"

"Of course I want a beer, thought you'd never ask."

Alex said nothing for a moment. He thought of saying something back but then thought better of it, as he twisted off the cap and shoved the bottle towards him. Chad poured half the bottle down and went back to eating.

"Now that you're here, and we know where Rivers is supposed to be, we can go after him right away."

Alfie turned towards Alex in surprise. "I thought that we were going to stay here another day and fish some and..."

"To hell with the fishing, I told you already that we didn't come here to fish. We came to get Rivers, and that's what I intend to do." Alex turned abruptly to Chad Moore. "Where's you rifle?"

Moore looked up in surprise. "I told you that I wasn't riding around with a rifle on my lap. The Mounties would have my ass. I can pick it up at my place before we leave for Quesnel. That is where the other cabin is isn't it?"

"Down that way I guess," said Alex. "Hawkins said that it was at a place called Barkersville. You know where that is?"

"Yes I know. Just where in Barkerville is it?"

"I don't know," said Alex.

For a moment, Alex sat quiet, just thinking. "I want to get this thing right. I don't want any slip ups. Do you think that you could talk to this guy that first told you about Hawkins having this place at Barkerville and find out exactly where it is?"

Chad Moore looked ahead and said, "Maybe. I will take him out to the bar and offer him a few bucks. A hundred would probably do it." He sat there with just the slightest of a smile on his face, as Alex fished in his pocket for his wallet, fighting to keep his temper in check. Alex was sure that Moore was milking him for every cent that he could get, but Moore had him over a barrel. Alex even managed a smile as he handed two fifty dollar bills to him.

"See what you can find out Chad. I want to know just exactly where this cabin is and how long it takes to get there. I want to catch them by surprise, like first thing in the morning when they're coming out of the cabin. If I can eyeball the one that you think is Rivers by looking through the scope on the rifle, I'll know him right off. If it is him, bang and it's all over."

"And then, I get the money that's coming to me."

"Sure, Chad, it will be my pleasure to settle my account with you, in full."

Something about the way that Alex said those last words bothered Chad Moore. He didn't trust Alex, any more than Alex trusted him. He made up his mind quickly. While Alex had his rifle pointed at Rivers, he would stand slightly behind him and have his rifle pointed at Alex. One wrong move and he would take what was owed him off a dead man. It made no difference really. He didn't like this mouthy son of a bitch. As far as this guy Alfie went, well, he would cross that bridge when he came to it, if he had to. Maybe things would go off without a hitch, but if they didn't, he wouldn't be caught flat-footed.

"What about the old guy with Rivers?" Alfie asked, more out of curiosity than anything. He was regretting the fact that he was involved now that it was coming down to the nitty gritty.

Alex just cast him an annoying look. "Let me worry about him."

Outside on this cool September morning, Alfie could see his breath. Chad Moore was supposed to be back later today with the news of the location of the cabin. Inside the cabin, here at Dawson Creek, Alex was cursing and fighting with the cook stove trying to get it lit to take the chill off the place. Being around Alex was like being around nitro-glycerine; you never knew when he was going to explode.

Alfie picked up his rod and reel and with tackle box in hand, he walked a bit downstream from where the slain deer lay. Two buzzards stood on the carcass ripping away at it with their razor sharp beaks. As he approached, they flapped their wings and for a moment rose above their prize but then they immediately returned reluctant to leave.

The fishing was as good as it had been before. He caught and released several, enjoying the time away from Alex. He spent a couple relaxing hours, dressed out four nice fat rainbows and headed back to the cabin. By then, Alex had the stove going and the place was warming up.

"I got some nice trout for dinner, Alex," he said trying to lighten the mood. Alex looked sullenly at him.

"Big deal, there's still lots of venison left. You can warm some up for me while you're cooking that fish. I'm going out and shoot off a few rounds with my gun. Call me when dinner's ready."

It was late in the afternoon when Chad Moore rode in on his motorcycle. Alex was excited when he saw the forty ounce bottle of whiskey Chad was carrying as he walked in. He sat it on the table and slumped down in a chair.

"Brought you something from town."

Alex produced three glasses, quickly opened the bottle, poured a stiff one for himself and drank half of it with one gulp. "Ah thanks, we was running low on beer. What did you find out in town?"

Chad poured a shot for himself, and shoved the bottle towards Alfie. He looked at Alex. "Found out what you wanted to know. He said that the cabin was about twenty minutes east of Barkerville. Said it wasn't hard to find, that it was the only new house out that way. Any other buildings in that area were just leftovers from the gold rush days and most were falling down. It would probably take between five and six hours to drive it from here."

Alex drained his glass and poured another big shot in it. He smiled. "Show time boys. We'll hang around here until around midnight. What about your gun, Chad?"

"I'll ride my bike into town and get it when we go. You can follow and pick me up there. Don't worry, I'll have my gun and I know how to use it."

The sun was beginning to go down. Alex and Chad were inside the cabin still working on the nearly empty bottle of whiskey. Alfie had drunk very little. He had cooked up some more trout for supper, while Chad Moore and Alex gnawed on cold venison washing it down with the whiskey. Alfie went out and sat on the steps. He once more wondered just how he had gotten himself into this mess. If he hadn't told Joey Gallo that he had seen David Rivers walking towards that railroad bridge that night, maybe all of this wouldn't have occurred. Maybe a small part of the blame was his but not all of it, no way. Joey brought on his own consequences. He was beginning to think the biker's life was not for him anymore. Looking at Chad Moore, he began to see what others saw when they looked at him. At one time it had felt good, the power trip, and one to be feared but now, it was losing its shine.

Maybe he wouldn't go back to Ontario. Maybe he would stay out here in this beautiful country and do something else. He was mechanically inclined; maybe he could even apprentice and get a mechanic's licence. There was that guy that Sully had told him to contact in Vancouver, but getting out of this business that he found himself in, wouldn't be that easy. On the other hand, Sully might not care. Maybe now was the right time to get out, before he got sucked in even deeper.

The sun disappeared and the moon began to rise in the sky. The stars came out as did the creatures of the night, their sounds rustling in the grass. Owls began to hoot and the distant howl of the timber wolf pierced the silence. He heard the door open and the pale light of the coal oil lamp shone dimly as Alex walked out and sat down beside him.

"It's just after nine o'clock. We'll be leaving just after eleven. We have to stop and pick up Chad's rifle and then we'll be off. You can catch some shuteye out here or inside or you can sleep in the back seat of the car on the way down to Barkerville. Chad will sit up in front with me 'cause I'm not too sure of the way."

Alfie said nothing for a moment. He thought that Alex would be stoned out of his mind the way that he had been going at the whiskey but he must have drunk himself sober. Alfie had seen Alex do that once before. Maybe all of the hate inside him had absorbed the alcohol. He grunted, "I think I'll just sit out here until we're ready to go. Chad gives me the creeps. You never know what's going through his mind or what's behind those shades he wears."

"I know what you mean, he's useful though. After tomorrow, we'll be rid of him one way or another. I'm going back inside. Get some sleep if you can, tomorrow could be a long day."

"It's time to go Alfie," said Alex as he shook him.

Alfie woke with a start. He could see Chad Moore. The stubble of beard on his face and those ghastly green goggles, gave him an evil look as he slammed the door. He walked past the two of them and over to his motorcycle. He threw his leg over it and gave the starter a kick. The noise shattered the stillness. He turned on the lights and made a wide circle heading out.

"Come on Alfie. I already put our gear and the guns in the car. We have to follow Chad. Hurry up!"

"Did you lock the cabin, and ..."

"To hell with the cabin, and Jim Hawkins, we ain't come'n back here anyway."

They pulled up onto the road and could see the lights of the motorcycle bobbing along in front of them. Alex floored the Buick trying to catch up. A deer, startled by the noise and the lights, ran across the road in front of them and Alex cursed loudly as he swerved to miss it. "That's all I need," he roared as he raced along.

The lights of Dawson Creek came into view. They followed Chad through town to his flop house, a description that matched the residence perfectly, thought Alfie. Chad parked the motorcycle outside, entered the house, and then reappeared carrying a rifle and more shells. Alex took the keys and walked around to the trunk of the car, opened it and put the gun inside. Alfie had already climbed into the backseat of the car when Alex and Chad hurried into the front seats, ready to go. No one spoke as they left the city limits. They had reached the point of no return

It was still dark when they turned off the highway at Quesnel, and headed east. Barkerville was as dark and quiet as the three men. Only the odd light could be seen in a few houses where the inhabitants were preparing to meet the coming day.

Alfie stirred and woke up. He felt cramped and more exhausted than he had when he fell asleep. He sat there for a moment and then he remembered. He was dreading the answer to the question he was about to ask.

"Are we there yet?"

It was Chad that answered, "Almost. We should be getting close now. When we get to the place you should drive past a few miles, then turn and come back, so that we don't alert them Alex."

The sun was just beginning to show light in the eastern sky. It had been just over twenty minutes since they left Barkerville. They had slowed down so they wouldn't miss the cabin. Another two miles and Chad spoke, "There's a cabin off to the left that could be it. Just drive on a couple of miles or so to be sure. If we don't see any other that matches the description, then that must be it." The next few miles confirmed the fact that there was nothing else along the road, only a few shacks that as yet had not fallen over.

It was difficult to turn the car around as the shoulders of the gravel road dropped away abruptly. As they approached the cabin on the return run, a wisp of smoke rose out of the chimney.

"Looks like someone is stirring around in there," said Chad.

There was excitement in Alex voice. "Okay boys, keep a sharp eye out for a flat spot so that we can pull off."

Moments later, Chad said, "Pull over to the right. I think that there is a spot just behind those evergreens where we can park. It'll hide the car some as well."

Quietly, they exited the car. Alex unlocked the trunk of the car and handed Chad his rifle. Then Alfie took the Marlin that was handed to him. Lastly, Alex pulled out his Winchester. He held it up to his shoulder and looked through the telescopic site, up towards the sky that had now begun to turn blue.

"Make sure that you both have lots of shells and that your gun is loaded," he said as he levered ammunition into the breech of the Winchester. He paused for a moment, looking at the two as if to make sure that they were all set.

"Okay, we'll stay off the road just in case anyone comes along. Don't even walk on the road where someone might catch a glimpse of you. We don't want to screw things up. We may have to wait for some time before anyone comes out of the cabin so just be quiet. I want to get a good look through this scope to make sure that it's Rivers. If it is, it's all over. I'll nail him but good. If I miss him, I expect one of you to nail him. Remember, the last thing I want is for him to get away."

"What about the old geezer?" asked Chad.

Alex thought for a moment. "No witnesses."

Slowly, quietly they walked through the trees, over the rocky ground until they came to the edge of the clearing. About a hundred yards away and about fifty feet below sat the cabin. The glow of a kerosene lantern illuminated the window. As they watched, a figure passed before the window, momentarily blocking the glow from within.

Alex spoke softly, "They're moving around in the cabin. I sure hope that your right about this being Rivers, Chad." Alex said as he rested the Winchester on the branch of a tree and looked through the scope at the back of the cabin.

22

Andy rubbed his eyes as he reached for the coffee pot for a second cup. "Want a refill Davey?"

David looked at his diminutive friend, the grey hair on his head sticking out in every direction, standing there dressed in Levis, with the suspenders pulled on over his long johns. He cut quite a figure.

"No, that's enough for me. Let's see how much gold we can pan today, Andy."

The old man grinned wickedly. "Ha, ha. You must be thinking of getting rich quick so that we can go up to Dawson City and watch them dancing gals."

David pushed back from the table and grinned. "I have been. I guess that I should have gone with you and Jim. Sounds like you had a good time."

"Did we ever. I can't wait to go again. We'll only have another two months at the most before winter sets in and we'll have to pack it in for the season. We'll pan all we can and have us a real hoot for our labour, boy!"

David stood up. "Well, let's get at it then. This shirt feels a little light today. I think I'll put on something a little heavier."

"That fishing vest that you always wear should keep you warm enough."

"My body, ya, but my arms get cold first thing in the morning."

"Well, I'm okay with my Mackinaw on. It keeps me nice and warm. I'm going to step out and pull my waders on. I'll wait for you outside."

Andy carried his waders out and set them down, as he looked for a moment at the sky. It looked as it was going to be a good day. He bent down, began to pull his waders on over his pants and fasten the suspenders over his shoulders, just as David emerged from the cabin.

David looked at his old partner. "I'm glad that I put this heavier shirt on, it's cool this morning." He bent over to pull on his waders.

He jumped as the searing pain of the bullet grazed the top of his shoulder. Surprised, not knowing what hit him; he turned to look at Andy. Blood gushed forth from the hole in the middle of the little man's head. Shock quickly turned to reality. They had come for him. Deep inside, he knew all along that it was just a matter of time. The sound of another shot cut the wind close to his ear and struck the cabin. He propelled into action. He reacted much quicker than what he thought he had. Reaching up quickly he felt Andy's throat for a pulse, as he tried to drag him around the cabin, away from the assault. He knew almost at once that Andy was dead and that the bullet had been meant for him. It was hard for him to let go of the lifeless body and run but self preservation was taking over.

"It's him!" Alex cried. His hands began to tremble as he squeezed off a shot. Someone fell, and for a moment he was jubilant thinking that it was David Rivers, until he took his eye away from the telescopic lens and realized that he had hit the wrong person. Rivers was holding the man in his arms and looking straight at him.

"Jesus!" screamed Alfie, "You hit the wrong guy."

Alex's face was twisted with rage as he pumped another shell into the chamber while screaming, "Shoot him! Shoot him! Don't let him get away!"

Alex took a step or two ahead before firing. He lost his balance and fell forward. Chad and Alfie stopped to help him. "Never mind me! Shoot Rivers you idiots! There he goes!"

Chad dropped to one knee and fired, his shot narrowly missed David, as he dragged the heavy body around the cabin. Alfie fired as well, although he shot high.

He looked back and saw figures scrambling down the grade towards him. One fell and for a moment the other two stopped. David fled in the opposite direction. The rocks and twigs on the ground tore away at the flesh of his feet tearing his socks to shreds. He scarcely felt the pain. He had the advantage of familiarity. Quickly, he outpaced his hunters.

Alex was now on his feet and charging towards the cabin. "Come on you two. We can't let him get away!"

They came around the corner of the cabin. Andy lay there, his eyes still wide open, the blood running down the side of his face from the bullet hole in his skull. The horror shocked Alfie.

"My God...he's dead!"

"To hell with him, Rivers is getting away." Alex ran on another fifty feet in the direction he assumed David Rivers went. He stopped, he was puffing badly.

"Geez. Remember you're heart Alex. You can't stand this pace."

"Never mind me Alfie! Shoot the tires on the truck so that he can't leave if he comes back. One of you guys get out on the road and make sure that he doesn't cross it. If he does, or you see him, fire a shot. The other one, go through the woods and hurry, make sure he doesn't double back. I'll go along the river bank and make sure that he doesn't cross it. Now go!"

Alfie headed for the road while Chad waded into the woods. Alex focused on the river line looking as far as he could down the waterway. Nothing. The hunters were going at a much slower pace than the hunted.

Ahead of them, David was nearing the cave. His feet were cut and bleeding badly but the adrenalin that flowed through his body had just now begun to subside, he could feel the pain. He looked around, puffing hard. There was no sight of the men that had shot and killed Andy. The huge boulder that he had placed on the entrance to the cave was still there. He had not really had enough time to figure how to get in and out of the cave effectively. The rope that he had let himself down into the cave with was not with him now. He looked behind him fearing that he would see those coming after him, so far nothing, but there would be. A meter away laid a huge flat rock.

Quickly he rolled the boulder away exposing the opening. With great effort, he stood the flat rock on edge. Faintly, he could hear voices coming; he had no time to waste. The thought occurred that perhaps he would get trapped in the cave and be unable to get out, but at this point in time, there were few options. He might come to his end just as the skeletons of the small animals he found in the cave. This could well end up being his tomb.

The voices were now getting louder. Slowly he lowered himself into the hole. He braced himself against the walls of the narrow shaft. He reached up and began rocking the large flat rock. It teetered and then fell towards him. The force with which it fell knocked him clear down the hole. Excruciating pain shot up the bottom of his feet as he hit the floor. For a moment, he thought that he might have broken his ankles, but no, it was just the soles of his feet that were burning. He sat on the cool damp floor of the cave for a few minutes, both resting and letting his eyes get used to the darkness. A small shaft of sunlight shone a spot on the floor like a flashlight. He looked up. The flat rock left a very small opening, one that David hoped would not be noticeable to others, notably, those that were pursuing him. Who were they, he wondered? Surely it wasn't the police? They wouldn't have shot Andy, or him, not without at least ordering them to surrender. Bounty hunters were the only thing that he could think of, but then the only bounty hunters that he had heard of were in the old westerns. Someone had told him that there were modern ones who worked for the bail bondsmen. But that was in the States, not here in Canada.

Maybe they had dug up Paulo, in Nevada and were looking for him. It seemed unlikely, but stranger things had happened. Maybe Alex Gallo had put a contract out on him. That didn't seem likely though, not for Alex. Not unless Sully came up with some screwball plan. David didn't really know Sully that well but if anyone back home could hire a hit man, it would be Sully. The fact that someone was after him though came as no surprise. That was why he had found this cave and stocked it with supplies for just such an emergency. He always knew that someone would come looking for him — he was just never sure who that someone would be.

Alex followed the bank of the river until the high cliffs that rose up on both sides impeded his progress. He was puffing badly. He put his hand over his heart and at the same time, he felt in his pocket for his nitrogen spray. He held the vial up to his mouth and pressed twice. It seemed to relieve the pressure and the pain that was around his heart. Common sense should have told him to stop, but that was not an option, not at this point, not when he was this close on the heels of David Rivers. It had been Rivers. He was afraid that this was all a wild goose chase that it would not be Rivers but some look-a-like. But it was David Rivers, not doubt about it. Grabbing his rifle with one hand, he used the other to grasp a small evergreen that grew out of the side of the hill. Puffing and panting, he made his way to the top of the ridge and looking around, he saw Chad Moore emerging from the woods.

"Did you see him?" yelled Alex.

"Nope. All I seen was a small bear."

Alex's face twisted in disgust. "I don't give a damn about no bear. Did you see Alfie?"

"No. I told you. I didn't see anyone."

"Well I'll squeeze off a shot. He can find us."

Several minutes later, Alfie showed up. His face was a pale white from the ordeal but neither Alex nor Chad seemed to notice or care. "Did you guys see him?"

Alex looked at him hopefully. "We thought maybe you had."

"Nope. I looked for him to cross the road but I didn't see anyone, not even a car."

Alex pulled his rifle up to his shoulder and looked through the scope, turning a full 360 degrees as he did. "Damn it. He's got to be here somewhere. It's like the ground swallowed him up."

Chad levelled his gaze on Alex. "It was him all right wasn't it?"

"It was him all right. Just as sassy as a jaybird."

"How about the rest of my money then?"

"After we get him"

Chad became adamant. "That wasn't the deal. As soon as you eyeballed him, you said. Well, you did. I want the rest of my money and I want it now."

For a moment, Alex's brain was bombarded with thoughts. Chad's rifle was loaded and pointed at the ground – just as his was. That and the fact that they still hadn't caught Rivers factored into rationality as he softly spoke. "You're right Chad. You did do your part and the least that I can do is pay you."

He laid his rifle gently on the rocky ground and pulled his wallet from his back pocket. He counted out five one hundred dollar bills. There wasn't much left, maybe a couple hundred. He handed the money over to Chad Moore who took it quickly shoving it into his jacket pocket and fastened the snap. Alex's brain was struggling to keep up with his temper. He knew that he couldn't afford to antagonize Moore at this point in time.

"That makes us square eh?"

"For now. What about the other thousand?"

Alex looked squarely at him. "You haven't earned it yet."

Chad's lip curled slightly, it was one of the few facial expressions that the green shades failed to hide. It was a surly look, mixed with a bit of superiority. It did not go unnoticed and Alex was beginning to seethe inside.

Chad continued, "Have you got it if I do?"

Alex picked up his rifle from the ground and grasped it slowly turning the muzzle towards Chad as he spoke, "You'd trust me for it wouldn't you Chad?"

Alfie silently watched the discussion. He was wishing that he could see the expression on Chad's face at that moment. It would have been interesting. He watched as Chad swallowed hard and smiled inwardly as Chad spoke.

"Sure Alex, I trust you."

Alfie broke into this bit of a stalemate. "If somebody comes along and finds that dead guy back at that cabin, it won't take them long to find the car and start looking for us. We should get out of here Alex."

Alex took his eyes off Moore and looked at Alfie. "Nobody's going anywhere, not when we're this close to getting Rivers. I'm not going to let him get away."

Alfie's voice was full of alarm as he said to Alex. "We really ought to move that car away from where it is. I could slip back, get it and take it up the road apiece. Maybe park it behind one of those old abandoned shacks that we passed earlier."

Alex thought for a moment. This was one of Alfie's better ideas, "Ya, maybe so."

He reached in his pocket and handed the car keys to Alfie. "Park it behind that last shack, the one where we turned around and make sure it can't be seen from the road. You can cut through to the river. Me and Chad will follow the shore line and we'll meet you there. If you get there before us, just wait. And another thing, don't nobody shoot in the air anymore, as you say, if someone finds that old man, we don't want to advertise where we are."

They watched as Alfie started for the car. Chad watched him disappear down the trail. "Maybe he won't come back," he said.

"He'll be back. Let's get going. You walk ahead."

Adrenalin

David sat silently in the cave, feet away from where Alex, Alfie and Chad had been talking. At first, he thought it odd that they would stop at this exact spot. It was a logical place though just as it had been for him the first time. It was the first flat spot that you came to after coming along the river and then climbing up the ridge.

All of the questions he had about who was chasing him had now been answered. And he knew who killed poor Andy. Chad had apparently directed them to this locale. But how, not many people had seen him since he arrived at Dawson Creek and now, down here at Barkerville? Sitting here in the dark, he ran through his mind all of the people he had met. There was Jim Hawkins, that nosey reporter, hmmm, possibly him. There was also the desk clerk at the motel, the folks in the restaurant, that reporter, the salesperson at the sporting goods store, but there was something else, something haunting his thoughts, something that he couldn't quite put his finger on. The voice, Chad's voice, he remember that day at the sporting goods store when he shoved Andy into the door casing and said 'fuck you grandpa'. That was it! But how, why, what was the connection? David recalled how the rough looking biker focused on him. That was the connection and somehow this guy must have contacted Alex and the three of them had come all the way out here apparently to kill him. It now began to fall into place. It shouldn't have come as a surprise, it had been Alfie that saw him heading towards the railroad bridge. He must have told Joey. And Alex, well he had always encouraged Joey into fighting with David right up until the tragedy occurred. He wondered if Alex ever blamed any of this on himself.

The worst part of this was Andy's death. He could still envision his old friend talking and laughing one moment and then the terrible look of panic and fear as the blood haemorrhaged from the wound in his skull. For the first time, David's eyes filled with tears, he felt responsible for Andy's untimely death.

He ran his hand over his shoulder, the blood had begun to dry and the wound was now burning. His feet were also on fire from the rocks, the branch stubble and then the fall to the floor of the cave. He walked slowly over to the edge of the thermal stream that flowed through the cave, stripped off all of his clothing and slowly ventured into the water. He squatted down letting the warm water flow over his body. The water had a therapeutic effect as it soothed his nerves. He climbed out feeling much better and with no towel, he dripped dry.

The heat from the stream warmed the air in the cave. He dressed quickly and began to think about his next steps. The small hole in the rock let in some light for him to see and his eyes adjusted to the condition. He walked over to the backpack that he had left in the cave and spread the contents on the floor. Although he didn't have all of the supplies he might need, he was pleased that he had thought of as much as he did. He reached down picked up the bottle of iodine and poured almost half onto his wound. He winced, as it stung like fury, but it would start the healing process. The can of carbolic salve would be applied later.

His attention returned to finding a way out. He picked up a candle and lit it as he slowly walked towards the back of the cave. The light from the flickering candle penetrated the darkness. The cave went back a long way. He walked for about a hundred yards before coming up against a wall. Water flowed forth from the base of the rock. He looked towards the ceiling, looking for any break, but there was none.

Slowly he retraced his steps hoping that he had missed something. If he had, it wasn't evident. The only way that he knew of to get out was the same way that he had entered, but how to get up to it? He looked at the rope in his supplies but it was practically useless. There was nothing to lasso, nothing for the rope to tie to. He again looked at the steady flow of water. It had to be going somewhere. In all probability, it flowed out into the Cottonwood River.

Adrenalin

His mind ran rampant with questions: where was the water really going; would he have to go under and follow the flow out into the river if that was where it was going; how far would he have to swim submerged to get out; what if he ran out of air in his lungs before he got there; and worse yet, what if it emptied into some underground system. He might go into the water and never come back.

He thought for a few moments and then noticed the small cardboard box that the iodine had come in lying on the floor. He dropped it into the water and watched as it slowly floated down the stream. It flowed along finally disappearing under the rock.

David sat there for several minutes thinking about the possibilities. But there were none, it was do or die. He removed his vest and shirt, took his sneakers from his backpack and tied them to his left belt loop, He picked up the rope and slid it through the belt loops on the right side of his Levi's. He decided that he was ready.

He entered the warm waters of the stream, took a deep breath and went under. Several breaststrokes took him down to the bottom of the stream. Down, down he went until it began to level out. His lungs began to burst for lack of air as he was pulled along by the current. He began to panic just as he had that night in the Thames River. And like that night when all seemed lost, he popped up to the surface of the Cottonwood River like a cork. A scream emitted as he opened his mouth and let the oxygen rush in. He had been right. The thermal stream did empty into the river. There was a small amount of steam that rose from the warm water that rushed into the cold river water, but the high cliffs of the banks obscured it from any casual observer.

It took David a few moments to get his bearings. He turned back towards the cabin, still treading water and happy to be alive, or relatively so. In the direction of the cabin, the flat beach would make it easier to get out of the river. He swam until his feet touched the bottom and then walked out of the water. He was surprised at the energy that he had on this day, maybe some of it was from his level of adrenalin, he wasn't sure. Whatever the reason, it had gotten him to this point, and the day wasn't done.

He sat for a few moments on the bank of the river gathering his thoughts. It had been a desperate measure that forced him to find the exit from the cave, a calculated risk that worked out. He probably would not have known that it existed under normal circumstances. He breathed a sigh. Once more his world had been turned upside down.

He untied the rope. He would need it to get back into the Cave. The sun was beginning to set in the west. There was still a lot to be done this day.

A long straight piece of driftwood was in the water. It was about four inches in diameter and about fifteen feet long. It had not been in the river long enough to begin to rot. He dragged it with him up to the top of the ridge, and then putting it down; he pulled the flat rock back from the entrance to the cave. He struggled once more to stand the rock on its edge. It was dangerous sitting it there like that. It wouldn't take much for it to fall and maim him. Carefully he lowered the piece of driftwood down into the cave. It was just two feet lower than the top of the ground. Bending down, he pushed the pole out of the way and heard it land on the floor below. He took the rope and looped it around the large round boulder that he had originally pushed away from the entrance to the cave, leaving both ends free so that he could pull it into the cave after he was inside. He tugged mightily on the rope. The boulder was heavy. It would hold. Being careful not to move the flat rock, he dropped into the entrance to the cave. The rope burnt his hands as he slid down until his feet touched the floor. He pulled the rope into the cave.

He now had an entrance and an exit. Somehow, he would have to come up with some idea so that he could move the flat rock into place better than that which he was about to do. With the long pole, he tapped on the rock until it wavered back and forth. With a mighty crash it fell flat, once more blocking the entrance. Luckily, it hadn't fallen the other way.

Suddenly, he realized that he hadn't eaten since breakfast. He should have brought more food, but then he hadn't thought that he would need this hideaway so soon. At least he had some canned salmon and some beef jerky. He felt around until he found the package of food. Once in hand, he began to tear away at it. The jerky had a strange salty taste. Blast, it wasn't jerky at all it was a piece of uncooked bacon. He spit it out and in the flickering light of the candle, picked up the salmon. With his Bowie knife, he quickly opened the can. It tasted good. He could have eaten more but he resisted the temptation to open another one, no telling how long he would have to make do with what provisions he had.

His mind came back to the bacon that he had opened by mistake. A plan began to form in his mind but was interrupted as he thought of poor Andy, probably still lying on the ground outside the cabin. He had been so busy thinking of self preservation, that he had forgotten about his friend. He would have to go back and at least put the lifeless body back into the cabin. The thought of what the creatures of the night might do to the body sent chills through him. His thoughts went full circle, back to his own survival. He would bring all of the canned goods that were in the cabin back to the cave.

He reached over and emptied the contents of the backpack out onto the floor of the cave. Tying one end of the rope to the backpack, he ran the other end through his belt loops and over the Bowie knife. He tied both ends securely. Once more, he entered the water, this time he was confident of where he was going. He knew just how much oxygen he would have to store in his lungs before making the plunge. Down he dove, with the rope trailing behind him. The dive didn't seem to take that long now that he was familiar with the exit. He surfaced and kept swimming until his feet touched the shallows of the river. Pulling the rope hand over hand, eventually the backpack came to the surface.

David was soaked clean through. He shivered. It was much cooler now that the sun had gone down. His clothes were wet, but he would get dry ones when he reached the cabin. He paused for a moment as his mind sorted out possibilities. First, he was assuming that Alex and his cohorts had continued downstream, maybe they hadn't. Secondly, there was always the chance that someone else had come to the cabin. Either way, he would have to approach with caution.

Complete darkness had set in and David guessed that it was somewhere around eight o'clock. Somewhere ahead of him, he heard the howl of a wolf. He desperately hoped that the animal wasn't at the cabin, but wolves were not scavengers, not as far as he knew anyway. He reached down and felt the reassuring handle of his Bowie knife.

The dark form of the cabin came into sight as he cautiously approached it. He heard the howl of the wolf once more but it was further away. There were no lights coming from the cabin, no sign of anyone's presence that he could determine. He approached the side of the cabin where he had dropped Andy's body. He discovered that it was still lying there on the ground, apparently untouched.

He walked up the steps and turned the doorknob. It opened easily. Neither he nor Andy had locked it before the attack. He went back to where his old friend laid and picked up the lifeless body up in his arms. Carrying Andy was different from Paulo. He loved this man and the sadness he felt was unbearable. He could feel his own body quiver as he carried Andy into his bedroom and gently placed him on the bed. In the dark, it was difficult but he knew that he could not risk lighting the kerosene lamp. There was no telling if Alex or his crowd were nearby. Suddenly, the emotion of it all got to him. He wept long and low for his best friend.

Coming back and bringing Andy inside had been the right thing to do. It eased his conscience considerably. In the darkness, he said a short prayer for his old friend. That done, he walked through the darkness out into the other room. It was time to carry on. The hard part of losing someone close is that small sense of guilt, knowing that you go on while their time is over. This was that time and for David, he had no time to waste.

He sat the backpack down on the floor near the cupboards and began to fill it with canned goods. In the darkness, his hand came upon a soft package that was sticky on the outside. He held it up to his nose. The smell was rancid. It was some bacon that should have been cooked up some time ago. A plan that he had back at the cave now rekindled itself and this bacon would be put to good use.

He went over to the closet and found his other pair of Levis. Quickly he slipped out of his wet clothes and put on dry ones. Fumbling around in the dark, his hands came to rest on his walking boots. There was a pair of socks shoved deep down inside them. He slipped off the wet shoes and put the socks and boots on. He put another pair of jeans and a dry shirt into the backpack with his wet shoes on top of the canned goods. It was bulging and it was hard to close. He carried the bacon separately. He was about to leave when he remembered Andy's old carbine. He set the backpack down and going by touch he reached into the closet until he felt the cold steel as his hand came to rest on it. He lifted it out and running his hand around the shelf above, found the box of shells. He loaded the rifle and shoved the rest of the ammo into his pocket. He was ready to leave and he had a score to settle.

With the backpack in place and the rifle in hand, he cautiously eased the door open. There was no sign of danger. He slipped out and locked the cabin. It would only be a matter of time before Jim Hawkins came along and he had his own key. He would be in for a most unpleasant surprise.

David walked passed his truck, parked in the drive. The moon crept out from behind the clouds illuminating the Ford pickup enough so that he could see it plainly. All four tires were flat; undoubtedly they didn't want him to be able to escape. He thought of retrieving the rest of his money from inside the camper cap, but he was already overloaded and the way things were going at the moment, he might never have a need for money again. He quickened his pace as he headed for his cave.

The night sounds of the forest filled the darkness as he hurried along. He could hear small creatures scurry about looking for food. As the moon cleared the cloud cover, once again the wolves began to howl. What was it about the moon that caused wolves to howl, he wondered? With all of the sounds of animals, both four and two legged around, the weight of the rifle felt good as he walked along the riverbank.

Finally, he came to the high ridge and began to climb. He set the heavy backpack on the ground and laid the rifle and bacon beside it. Grabbing the large flat rock, he strained once more to stand it up on its edge. He took the rope and slid it through the carrying sling of the backpack and then lowered it down into the cave. Then he retrieved the rope, coiled it and put it over his shoulder. He grasped the huge rock and carefully lowered it down to where it guarded the entrance to the cave. He was tiring but there was one more thing that he had to do this night. Tomorrow he would rest. From this point on, his life would be turned around, possibly forever. He would become one of those creatures that roamed at night and slept in the daytime, away from prying eyes. It would be by necessity, not by choice.

As David walked along the ridge, rifle in hand and the rope around his shoulders, he kept the waters of the river that sparkled in the moonlight in sight. He went in the direction that he believed Alex and the other two had taken. This was unfamiliar territory to him. He was looking for signs of the predators and finally, what he sought, he found. It was the smell of smoke, a campfire. They were close by. Another two hundred yards ahead, he could see the glowing embers of a campfire burning low. He could barely make out the forms of three sleeping men. He moved to within fifty feet of the nearest one. He was positive that these were the ones. Carefully, soundlessly, he opened the bacon and with his knife cut it into three different pieces, which he dropped in three different spots. His work was done. Nature would do the rest. He headed back to his cave.

23

Alfie drove the car off the road and stopped behind the dilapidated shack. The shack appeared to be defying the laws of gravity by simply standing somewhat erect. But there was sufficient scrub brush and weeds covering the area to hide the car from the casual observer. He turned off the engine, picked up his rifle, got out and locked the car. Then he walked the forty yards or so back out to the road to see if it was detectable. Aside from the bent grass that he had driven over coming in, there was nothing visible. He took one last look around and then began to walk in the direction of the river.

The meandering Cottonwood River made the distance from the road to the river much further than it had been from where he left Alex and Chad. The uneven rocky terrain was also much more difficult to walk through. He slipped on some animal droppings and he began to curse as the odour nearly made him sick. He stopped and scrubbed the brown coloured mess off of his shoe and onto the grass.

"Geez, what the hell was that I stepped in?" he said out loud. "It must have been from a bear or a cougar, or some other stinking animal."

The crap was pretty fresh and this was definitely not his back yard. He stopped, looked around and brought the rifle up to where he could fire it, if need be. He walked on, more wary than he had been before. He was not at all comfortable. It was one thing to see the wild animals from a passing car that he enjoyed. Here, on their turf, it was not quit the same.

He looked ahead, anxious now to find the river or Alex and Chad. He picked up his pace, minutes later the river came into view. A sigh of relief escaped his lips. He looked down the shoreline in the direction they would have come but the river twisted and the trees hid everything. He looked around, everything looked the same. He would have to mark the spot so that he could find his way back to the car. He gathered up six large rocks and placed them in a circle. They would be his benchmark.

He listened for any recognizable sound but heard nothing but the sound of the rapids in the river. He began to walk in their direction and about a mile and a half downstream he found them.

"Alfie, did you see any sign of Rivers?"

"I didn't see anyone. I just hid the car behind that old shack like you told me to. You didn't see him either?"

"No. We've been looking high and low but nothing. I'm wondering if he doubled back behind us. We should have seen him by now, especially with you coming from the other direction. Did you look for footprints?"

"Didn't think to, but if there had been some, I'm sure that I would have seen them. So where do we go from here?"

Alex shook his head. He looked bewildered. "I don't know. I was sure that we would have sighted him by now."

Chad stood there looking around. "We should have all drawn a bead on him this morning. If we had, we wouldn't be standing here now with our fingers up our ass!"

Chad had a way of irritating Alex. He was already frustrated for having let David get away. What Chad was saying only made the obvious worse. In hindsight, they should have opened fire on him, but they hadn't. Alfie could see the animosity between Alex and Chad growing by leaps and bounds.

"I'm getting hungry," Chad said, as he looked in Alfie's direction. "You didn't get anything to eat when you went back for the car did you?"

"Does it look like I did?" retorted Alfie. Chad was getting under his hide too. "I just hid the car and came looking for you two."

"So what are we going to do Alex, jump in the car and hightail it out of here?" asked Chad.

"No we're not! That son of a bitch is around here somewhere and I'm not leaving until I settle with him" Alex looked towards the river. "If you're hungry, we'll catch some fish."

Chad looked at Alex with contempt and asked, "How the hell do we catch them? Have you got a fishing pole in your pocket?"

Alex said nothing but walked over to the waters edge and looked intently towards the fast flowing water. He raised his rifle and fired. A rainbow trout rolled belly up to the top of the water, apparently stunned. "Grab him and I'll shoot a couple more."

Chad's lighter came in handy as he lit the pile of kindling that he had gathered while Alfie cleaned the fish. It took a while for the fire to burn down so they could hold the pieces of fish over the hot coals to cook. They sat back eating and even though it was cooked less than perfect, no one complained, it did satisfy their hunger.

Chad turned to Alex. "What's next Captain?"

Alex looked all about before answering, as if he hoped the answer would come into view. It didn't happen. He threw the skeletal remains of the trout into the coals. Still he said nothing, just stared for a moment at the watch on his arm.

"It's just after one o'clock. Rivers has got to be somewhere around here. Maybe he crossed the river, or maybe we just walked past him. The terrain around here is so hilly and there is so much brush, he could be hiding just about anyplace. We should have a dog to sniff him out."

Alfie's ears perked up. "Did I ever tell you about the dog that I had when I was a kid? He was one of those..."

"Not now Alfie! I don't want to hear about some mutt that you used to have. We came here looking for Rivers and this is as close as we've been to him. I don't want him getting by us. Which one of you can swim?"

Alfie's mouth was faster than his brain. "I can swim."

"Good, then you can swim across the river and start looking for any sign that you can pick up, like footprints or broken branches. And pay attention to any place along the bank that looks like someone might have come ashore."

"What would it look like?"

A painful look of disgust crossed Alex's face as he answered, "Just look at what the bank looks like when you climb out. Damn it Alfie, use your head. Quit arguing and get going before Rivers winds up in the next province."

They watched as Alfie waded into the fast moving water until it became deep enough for him to swim. The clothes he was wearing helped to warm his body and protect against the chilly water. The current carried him along as he struggled against it. Finally, his feet touched bottom and he stumbled out of the water using the branches of a small bush to pull him out. He looked back across the river to where Alex and Chad stood watching.

"That river sure is cold," he yelled. For a moment he looked at the spot on the bank where he exited ashore. "I see what you mean, Alex. The grass is all bent over and I pulled some of the leaves off the tree branches."

Alex shook his head slowly, while speaking in a muted tone to Chad. "Sometimes the lights in his head are on but there's no one home."

"That's good Alfie, now just follow the bank back towards the cabin where we found Rivers and look for tracks, or any other thing, that might indicate the direction he took."

"And then what?"

"If you see Rivers, don't let him out of your sight. Leave clues along the way so we can track you if we need to. If you're not back here by five o'clock, we'll come looking for you. Got that?"

"Okay, five o'clock, eh?"

"Right."

Chad stood grinning. He could see that Alex's nerves were beginning to fray. Alex turned to him. "Climb up that tree over there and have a look around. Maybe you can see something moving out there."

"How am I supposed to reach that first branch?"

"I'll cup my hands, you can stick your foot in them and I'll boost you up."

Chad was heavier than Alex thought. It was all he could do to push him high enough so that he could get a grip and pull himself up. Chad climbed high among the branches until he was in a position where he had a good view of the surrounding territory. He could see Alfie searching along the river bank. He also caught a glimpse of a moose coming out of the river about a mile ahead of Alfie. He grinned to himself. He hoped that Alfie could tell the difference between a moose hoof print and those of a man. He looked for movement of any kind, but saw nothing. It was almost as if the ground had swallowed Rivers up.

Alex placed his hand over his brow and looked skyward. "See anything, Chad?"

"Nothing that looks human, what now?"

"Come on down, we'll just have to split up and start looking for him. He has to be here someplace. There are just too many places to hide. He has the advantage. He knows this place better than we do."

Chad left some of his own hide on the bark of the tree as he slid down. He moved around until he felt Alex's hand grab his foot and then he slid down the rest of the trunk. He was puffing as he sat down at the bottom of the tree.

"Ah, I'm not used to this shit man. How long are we going to look for him?"

"You heard what I told Alfie, we'll go in different directions and keep looking. We'll meet back here along about five o'clock. Fire a shot if you see him."

Alex looked around and spied Alfie's rifle lying on the ground. He reached down and picked it up. "I'm going to hide

Alfie's rifle under that little bush. I think we can all find our way back to this spot."

Chad was back long before five o'clock. He was not near as anxious to find David as the other two were. He gathered some driftwood and put it on the warm coals. Supper would likely end up being the same as lunch. He wasn't looking forward to it, but it was better than nothing. It was just after five when Alex showed up. He looked tired and a look of defeat clouded his face.

"Alfie hasn't shown up?"

Chad looked up, the green goggles hiding any emotion. "Nope, not yet anyway. Maybe..."

At that moment a short distance away they could hear the sound of someone walking through the brush. Alex fingered his rifle, a hopeful look on his face, perhaps it was David. No such luck as Alfie came strolling into view.

They sat around the camp fire. Their bellies full and their spirits low. The sun was beginning to set behind the mountains and darkness was rapidly approaching. It was Chad that looked at Alex and said, "What are we going to do next, sleep in the car or haul ass out of here?"

Alex looked at Chad for a few moments before answering. Maybe it was those damn green shades, hiding any expression that irritated him. "We'll throw lots of wood on the fire to keep warm and bed down here for the night. We can start looking for David Rivers first light in the morning. He has to be here somewhere."

Chad leered. "Sure, we'll let the whole country know where we are. How long before someone finds that old man that we shot? Instead of us looking for this Rivers guy, it'll be the Mounties looking for us. You better not let that fire burn too brightly."

Alex knew that he was right. The fire would have to be kept low but he still wasn't going to leave without first finishing his objective. "Okay Chad, we'll keep the fire low and bed down around it. Like I said, we'll resume the search for Rivers tomorrow. If we don't find him by the time the sun is straight overhead, we'll give it up, okay?"

The look that Alex gave Chad was pretty final and Chad knew it. Alfie sat there and said nothing. His thoughts were on the bears, cougars and other things that moved around in the night. He would sleep close to the fire and put a stick or two on it through the night, he'd heard animals were suppose to be afraid of fire.

24

Jim Hawkins was up early. He went out to the barn, completed his chores and went in for breakfast. He sat at the kitchen table while Judy bustled about, buttering toast and turning eggs. She set his plate on the table along with her own and grabbed the coffee pot. She looked at him, he wasn't generally this quiet.

"Why the long face, honey?"

"I expected those guys who rented the cabin to bring back the keys and the bedding yesterday. They still haven't shown. You know, I had a funny feeling about those two right off the bat. Just something that didn't sit right."

Judy brushed a straggly hair out of her eyes. "Maybe you're worried for nothing. Maybe they just decided to stay another day or two."

"Maybe but I think I'll take a run down there and see what's going on. Want to come for a ride?"

"I'd like that. It would be a chance to get out of the house for a while." An hour later, they arrived at the cabin. As they drove down into the yard, Judy exclaimed, "There's a whole bunch of buzzards over by the river. Something must be dead."

"I noticed. There also isn't any sign of their car around. Something doesn't look right."

Jim reached up behind him to the gun rack in the rear window. Grabbing his rifle, he stepped from the truck and fired a couple of shots into the air. The buzzards took flight. He walked over to the creek to see what the buzzards had been feeding on. He strode back towards the truck where

Judy was waiting. She could tell by the look on his face that he was very upset.

"What is it Jim?"

"Was, is the word. It looks like someone just shot a full grown doe and just left it there. I could see where the bullet tore a hole in the carcass, but it wasn't dressed out. That's about all you can tell, those buzzards made a mess of it. It was probably those two that rented the cabin. Come on, let's have a look in the house."

They walked up the steps. The padlock was sitting beneath the hasp, still unlocked. They entered.

"Look at this! Whiskey and beer bottles all over the place and dirty dishes still on the table! They sure left the place in a mess. Come on, we'll clean it up some and throw the bedding in the back of the truck."

An hour later they were headed back to Dawson Creek. For a while, they rode in silence. Judy could tell that Jim was deep in thought as well as being upset and angry. He looked over at her for a fleeting moment.

"I just thought of something. The older guy said that he'd run into this fellow that told him all about me at the Copper Creek Hotel. He told me what the guy looked like, but he didn't sound like anyone I know. I'm going to swing by the hotel for a minute and talk to Joe, the bartender, and see if he can shed some light on this."

Joe was just getting ready for the noon hour crowd when Jim walked over to him. "Jim, good to see you, a little early though isn't it. What'll you have?"

"A little information, Joe. The other day I rented a cabin that I own down the creek a ways, to two guys from Ontario. They just came here to go fishing. One guy was in his fifties and about five ten, beginning to bald, fat face. The other is just young, early twenties with long stringy blonde hair."

Joe gave the bar a wipe and laid his cigarette in the ashtray. "I know the pair. The old guy is kind of surely and does all the talking. The kid don't say much at all, just answers him. Hasn't been that busy at noon time lately, that's why I know who you were talking about. They give you some trouble?"

"Some. Left a hell'uva mess at the cabin mostly, but the older one said that he was talking in here to someone that told him all about me. A real tall young fellow with a goatee and blonde hair, I think he said."

"They were only talking to one other guy that I saw and he don't look like that. He's a good size all right tall and stocky with a brush cut and wears these green wrap around goggles. Never smiles. He rides one of them Harley Davidson motorcycles. He's been in here a few times, acts real tough."

Jim looked puzzled for a moment. He was trying to recall where he had seen someone fitting that description. "Was that guy, the one with thee green goggles, around here about a month ago?"

"I believe he was, you know him?"

"Sounds like the guy that Andy, that old fellow that pans my claims, had a run-in with some time back. Like you said, he never smiles, just looks like trouble coming."

"You got him. That's the guy."

Jim rubbed his chin. He looked at the bartender curiously. "I wonder why that guy tried to throw me off by giving me the wrong description."

"Beats me Jim, but they was just as cosy as could be. It didn't appear to me as if they was just strangers that had set down and got acquainted over a beer. They knew each other all right."

Judy could see the troubled look on Jim's face long before he turned the door handle on the truck and climbed in.

"I knew there was something wrong with those two guys as soon as they came around the other day."

"What do you mean, what's wrong?"

Jim started up the truck, pulled away from the curb and headed towards home. Judy could see the deep lines of concern on his face as he spoke. "The bartender gave me a different slant on the story. He said that the older fellow was talking to some biker when he was in the hotel, a guy that looked like trouble. I don't know what's going on, it doesn't add up. You know, it just seemed funny at the time that those two guys from Ontario show up here wanting to rent a cabin for a few days. Generally, when they come this far, they have a handful of brochures showing them all of the fish that they can catch and they put up at the bigger lodges around here."

"Maybe the lodge prices were too high. Maybe…"

"No, I don't think that's it. They also asked about the other cabin, the one down at Barkerville. And another thing, this is the one that bothers me most. The one that the bartender described as being the informant, he sounds exactly like the one that shoved old Andy around a while ago. The one I told you about, that burly biker with those funny green glasses. It's times like this that I wish there was a phone down at that cabin but there isn't. I'm going to slip down there and see what gives. Do you want to come along?"

Judy could feel the energy coming from her husband. He was going to go all right and so was she. "Sure. While you're doing up the chores, I'll make a lunch up that we can eat on the way. What about Wolf? Should we take him with us?"

"Yes, he likes to ride in the truck and he has a keen sense of smell. He just might come in handy. Maybe all of this is for nothing, hopefully anyway. Still, I just can't shake this feeling."

Wolf was happy riding in the truck. His ears up, eyes alert and pink tongue hanging slightly out of the corner of his mouth, as they drove along. He was a good dog, trustworthy and dependable. Judy was glad that they had brought him along.

Jim looked down at his watch as they reached Quesnel. "It's almost four o'clock. We should be there before five."

Judy smiled, although she was more apprehensive than when they had started out. "It's probably all for nothing. Sometimes you worry too much honey."

Adrenalin

They cruised down the main street of Barkerville. Judy's eyes grew wide as she saw the stagecoach pull up in front of the picturesque theatre with its bright white exterior and the black and red trim. She turned towards Jim, her mouth open with surprise. "You never told me that this little town was this pretty!"

"Yes I did. You just didn't pay any attention when I told you."

"If I had known, I would have made the trip down here before this."

Jim's focus was not on the town, not at this time. "If everything is all right at the cabin, we'll stay overnight here at the hotel and you can look the whole town over tomorrow. I certainly hope it is! For now though we have to hurry along."

He knew instantly that there was trouble. The tires on David's pickup were all flat and there was an eerie silence in the yard. He felt a jolt of pain in his chest at the same moment as his heart skipped a beat. This was what he was afraid he might find. He pulled up parallel with the house and killed the motor. He turned and looked at Judy and could see the fear in her face. He reached behind him and got his rifle from the rack.

"When I get out of the truck, lock it. Come on Wolf, let's go have a look see." Cautiously, man and dog walked up the back steps of the cabin. The padlock was in place and it had been snapped closed. He looked around; everything looked all right except for the truck. That would indicate of course that neither David nor Andy could have gone anywhere. Maybe they were still working but by this time they should have quit for the day. Wolf sniffed at the door and then raised his snout and let out a howl. Jim looked down at him.

"I know boy, it doesn't look good." He walked back to the truck motioning Judy to roll down the window. "Let me have the keys. The place is locked up."

As he put the key in the lock, he looked further over on the porch. The red smear that he saw could have been blood. Again, a chill went through him. Wolf squeezed passed him as he opened the door. Almost immediately, the dog let out a howl. Through the open bedroom door, Jim could see the form lying on the bed. He grasped the rifle firmly in his hand. Reaching ahead, he grabbed the edge of the blanket and pulled it back.

The ghastly sight of Andy staring at the ceiling, the bullet hole in his head and the dried blood that streaked his face was shocking. His premonitions had been correct. He looked around. There was no sign of David, living or dead. Quickly, he ran outside.

"Open the door." he yelled at Judy, who had already begun to do just that. "Andy's inside and he's been shot!"

Her eyes doubled in size. "Is he...?"

"Yes he's dead. It looks as if he's been dead for some time. I want you to take the truck and go back to Barkerville and call the Mounties. They'll probably have to come from Dawson Creek or Kamloops. I'll take Wolf with me and see if I can find David or whoever killed Andy. I have a good idea of who I'm looking for."

Judy's eyes grew wide with fright. "Oh don't do that, wait for the Mounties and then..."

Jim shook his head. "I'll be all right. Just get going, and tell the Mounties when they come that I'll fire a shot every half hour so that they can find me. Now get going!"

Jim watched as the truck pulled away. He re-entered the cabin and pulled the cover back up over Andy's face. Looking around the cabin, it didn't appear as if robbery had been the motive. The only thing that seemed to be missing was most of the canned goods from the pantry. He walked to the door and went out, the dog followed. He left it unlocked so that the Mounties would be able to enter.

"Come on Wolf", he said, as he walked down to the river looking for signs. He hefted his rifle. He had forgotten to get some extra shells. He checked the breech. It was fully loaded.

267

Adrenalin

There were plenty of footprints along the sand and gravel banks of the Cottonwood River, some going, some coming. Carefully Jim Hawkins examined them. They had been made by more than one person. He looked at the smaller footprints. They had been made by someone wearing gym shoes or sneakers. These prints caught his interest because they were made by someone both coming to, and going from the cabin and the prints that were going away were deeper, as if that person was carrying something heavier than when he arrived.

He began to follow the tracks east, Wolf sometimes following and sometimes running ahead, his nose to the ground. Suddenly, Wolf took off in pursuit of something. Jim saw the marmot that his dog was chasing dart beneath some rocks. Wolf stood there; head lowered barking loudly at the rocks where the marmot was hiding.

Jim became impatient. "Come on boy. Leave him alone. We don't have time to play around today. There is much bigger game for you to hunt somewhere up ahead of us."

Two miles later, Jim came to the place where the river ran through the gorge the high rocky ridge created. Both man and dog made their way up to the top. Jim stopped to catch his wind and sat down on a flat rock that was lying there. Wolf began to circle around him and sniff, barking loudly at the same time. Jim just shook his head.

"You sure are after those critters today, boy. You can hunt them all you want another day." Jim rose, looked eastward along the ridge down to where the river began to bend. He could see nothing. He looked at his watch. It had been a good full half hour since he sent Judy to call the Mounties. They should be coming soon. He could hear the sound of a plane approaching in the distance and squeezed off a shot as he said he would. Maybe help was on its way.

25

Alex Gallo awoke cold, shivering, and aching all over from sleeping on the hard ground. His face was covered with three days of stubble whiskers and his mouth had a foul taste. Whether it was from the fish that he had eaten last night or from not brushing his dentures, he didn't know nor care. This whole thing was leaving a bad taste. By now, David Rivers should have been dead and he and Alfie should have been sitting in a beer hall celebrating. But it hadn't turned out that way, not yet anyway.

He looked over at Alfie curled up in a ball, still sleeping. Chad was moving slightly as the rays of the morning sun shone down on his face. Alex walked over, picked up a stick and poked away at the fire hoping to see some sparks flying. There were none, he was out of luck. If he wanted to get warm, he would have to start from scratch. He threw new sticks into the ashes and began to curse.

The sound of his voice woke Chad. He reached over and put on the green shades that were laying close by. He didn't feel dressed without them. With a groan, he got up and walked away from the makeshift campsite.

"Where the hell are you going?" growled Alex.

"For a crap, want to come?"

"Go to hell," Alex snarled as Chad walked behind a clump of bushes.

Alex turned back looking for more small sticks to get the fire going. The ground was white with frost. It was colder than he was used to. He jumped! Startled by a scream that had come from the direction where Chad had disappeared into the bushes. The scream also startled Alfie bringing him to his feet; eyes wide open, in an apparent state of shock.

Adrenalin

"Help! Help! Oh my God!" came the shrieks of terror.

Alex grabbed his rifle just as the brush parted and Chad, bleeding profusely came half running, half stumbling, out of the bushes. Behind him was a full grown grizzly bear, roaring and clawing at the terrorized Chad.

Alex drew the rifle to his shoulder and fired. The bear paused for an instant, roared and stood on his hind legs. The sight was something to fear, never had Alex seen anything so massive. He fired again and again as the bear charged straight towards him. Alex let out a horrific scream as the bear pounced on him. Fortunately for Alex, his shots had hit their mark. The bear was dead by the time it hit the ground. Alex scrambled out from beneath the huge animal. White with fright, he ran about ten feet and stopped. Looking down he could see that his shirt sleeve was shredded and blood was pouring from where the bear had torn the flesh wide open. He looked around in a daze, still unsure of what was going on.

Chad was not as lucky, gone were the green shades. The back of his head and neck were covered in blood where the bear's teeth had ripped into him. His right arm was useless and the muscles exposed for all to see. He was screaming in pain and then, mercifully, he passed out falling to the ground.

Alfie stood there transfixed, unable to think and too terrified to move. It was Alex that first came around.

"Alfie! Alfie! Help, help me over to the river."

Alfie snapped out of it and rushed over to Alex's side. The bear's fall on Alex had also injured Alex's leg causing him to lean heavily on Alfie. At the river, Alfie helped Alex to the ground. Alex laïd his arm in the cold fast flowing water, where it washed away the blood and slowed the flow. Alex laid there for a few moments, slowly regaining his sanity. All the while, Alfie looked anxiously back to where Chad lay half dead.

"You be okay here for a few minutes Alex?" he asked, his voice trembling greatly. "I better go see what I can do for Chad."

Alex became agitated. "Don't go yet. I need you. Take my belt off and put the end through the buckle and slip it on over my arm."

Alfie looked once more in Chad's direction and then bent and did as he was asked.

Alex's face was still very white but his senses seemed to be close to normal. He looked up at Alfie who stood there trembling. "That's good," he said as the belt slid up his arm. "Now pull gently on it until my arm stops bleeding. Ah, geez, easy does it Alfie. There, that's better, the blood is stopping now. Thanks pal. I can hold it tight now myself. You go see if you can help Chad."

Alex lay with his arm in the water. The pain was subsiding some and he knew enough to let the pressure off of the makeshift tourniquet and allow the blood to circulate before tightening again. Finally, he sat up and took a good look at his arm. It still hurt like crazy but now he could see that it looked worse than what it was. The bear's claws had only penetrated to any depth in two places. The other marks were very shallow and the bleeding had stopped all together. He mumbled to himself. "You'll live old boy, it'll take more than this to put you down." He looked up to see Alfie coming back.

"What brought that bear into camp Alex?"

Alex shook his head. He had been wondering the same thing. "Damned if I know. Maybe he smelled the fish that we cooked up last night."

"What are we going to do about Chad? He looks real bad off, like he's going to die or something. We should get him to a doctor."

Alex looked up from his sitting position. "How do you think you'd make out in jail Alfie? They ask a million questions when you take someone all mauled like that to a hospital. Questions like 'where did this take place, what were

271

you doing there, did you have anything to do with that old man that was murdered down that way?' We'll do what we can for Chad but I'm not going to jail for him. I know that he wouldn't do it for either one of us. Now give me a hand to get up and we'll see what we can do for him."

Alfie bent down and Alex put his good arm around his shoulder. Slowly he made it to his feet.

"Can you walk?"

"I think so. I don't think that anything is broken, just bruised where that bear fell on me. He must have weighed a ton. He just knocked the stuffin' out of me."

Alfie moved forward slowly. Alex was getting along better than either of them thought he would. "It was lucky that you put as much lead in that bear as you did. For a minute, I thought you were a goner."

They made their way back to where Chad was laying on the ground. He seemed to be in a coma. Alfie blurted out what was on his mind. "When he comes around he's going to scream like hell. What are we going to do?"

"We'll do whatever we can for him, Alfie."

Alex thought for a few minutes. No one, outside of a few, had seen Chad with them. He hadn't been with them when they rented the cabin at Dawson Creek from Jim Hawkins. And the bartender who might have seen them might not say anything, not wanting to get involved. If he did not survive, he might even get the blame for killing that old man at the cabin near Barkerville. Besides, he had most of Alex's money in his pocket. Alfie interrupted his chain of thought.

"What are we going to do Alex?"

Alex looked solemnly at Alfie. "Well, we can't move him. We have to get him up off of that hard ground Alfie. You see those small evergreen trees over yonder? Go over and break off enough to make a nice deep soft bed for him to lie on."

"Sure, I'll do that."

"Be careful of bears."

The warning was not needed. Bears were the only other thing on Alfie's mind at the moment as he walked towards the evergreens.

Alex watched and made sure that Alfie was out of range. Chad moaned as Alex walked over to him. His eyes wavered as though he were about to regain consciousness. Alex reached down and slid Chad's Bowie knife from its sheath. Chad's eyes fluttered once more and then opened wide. They were grey, seldom seeing daylight without the green goggles. They opened wide. He could see Alex's hand closing on his mouth, smothering any cry that might escape. Only Chad's eyes seemed to scream as the twelve inch blade went deep inside his heart. Chad's face showed that his exit from this world had been most painful.

Alex wiped the knife on Chad's already bloodied shirt and slid it back into the sheath. He rolled the body on its side and quickly withdrew the wallet, all the while watching for Alfie. He took all but twenty bucks and left it in Chad's pocket. He might need a couple bucks when he got to wherever it was he was going. He rolled the corpse back over, face up and looked up to see Alfie walking out of the brush, his arms loaded with evergreen branches.

"Look what I found where that bear met Chad. I smelled it and it sure looks and smells like bacon. Where in the world would bacon come from way out here Alex?"

Alex face took on a look of surprise that quickly turned to anger. "How do you think it got here stupid? That goddamn Rivers must have come up here in the night while we were sleeping and planted it where bears were sure to find it. That's what brought that grizzly down on us. He probably did it as payback for shooting that old buzzard back at that cabin. Geez, I can't believe he was this close and we didn't know it. I'll skin him when I catch him, and I will catch him."

Alfie stood there, mouth open while Alex raged on. He glanced at Chad who was quiet. "I'll go get some more evergreen branches."

Alex struggled to his feet. "Save it. Just after you left to get those evergreens, poor old Chad just let out a low moan, spit up some blood and gave up the ghost. He's in a better place now Alfie. Nothing we can do for him."

"Oh good God." Alfie stared forward and bent down placing his fingers on the throat looking for a pulse. He found none. He shook his head. He didn't really like Chad but what he said aloud was pure truth. "What a way to go."

"It was bad all right. We can blame Rivers for that." Alex loosened the belt tourniquet from around his arm. "Seems the blood has stopped flowing, I'll make it." He slipped the belt back through the loops in his trousers and cinched it tight. He took a look around as if looking for bears, Rivers or any moving object. He saw none

"Come on Alfie, we have to remove anything that looks like we were here. Throw all the sticks on the dead fire. Make it look like Chad was going to light it up this morning when the bear jumped him. Where's his rifle? Never mind, I see it."

Alex picked up Chad's rifle and rapidly shot three bullets into the air. He then walked over, brushed any prints from the gun and threw it down about twenty feet from the body. Alfie looked puzzled. "What are you doing Alex?"

"I'm making it look like he shot the bear and it killed him. He might as well take the rap for killing that old geezer. Now take those evergreen branches and brush away signs that we were here."

"What about Chad? Ain't we going to bury him?"

Alex shook his head in disgust. "Aren't you listening to what I just said? They have to find the body for him to get the blame so that we get away scot-free. Think for a minute."

"It don't seem right Alex, just leaving him here for the buzzards."

"Fine. You stay here and keep the buzzards off of him until the law comes along and then explain it to them."

Alfie felt stupid. This whole business was getting to him. Alex shouldn't have had to explain it to him. Still, it didn't feel right but then that was Alex decision, not his.

Alex stood, waiting for an answer. "Well are you coming?"

"Yes"

"Can you find your way back to the car?"

"I put a circle of stones on the river bank when I walked in. Let's go." They walked away dragging evergreen branches behind them covering their tracks.

The heat from the sun, that was now high overhead, was welcome. It felt good after the cold night and the chill of early morning. They walked well away from the shoreline where their footprints would be evident. They had thrown away the evergreen branches they used to cover their tracks. Alfie's benchmark finally came into view.

"My mark is still there Alex." The stone circle was untouched.

"That's good. We'll throw them in the water so that no one else gets wondering about them."

"What now, Alex?"

"Ah, I've got to sit down and have a rest," Alex said as he unlocked the car and sat on the seat. "You know Alfie, Rivers can't be that far away. Maybe he's watching us right now. I've still got lots of ammo. Look, you put your rifle in the trunk of the car, I want you to drive back into that hick town and get some things."

"Like what?"

"Like food, for one thing, I'm hungry. Get a small case of beans and one of peaches, some cans of meat, like spam or whatever and don't forget a can opener. Get a case of beer and a forty of whiskey. See if you can get a bottle of alcohol or peroxide and some salve for this arm of mine. I want you to get me a shirt too, that damn bear made a mess of this one. And pick up a couple of jackets, nice warm ones. It's starting to get cold up here and we'll be here until I get Rivers."

"What if they don't have all that stuff?"

"Then drive to that other town, Quesnel. Use your head Alfie, if they have most of it, that's okay or buy substitutes, I don't care."

"Why don't you go Alex? I ain't got no licence and 'sides that, I've only driven a car a few times."

"There ain't no traffic on these roads around here. Just drive slow and you'll be all right. I'm not leaving here, I told you, until I collect River's hide." Alex reached into his pocket and pulled out some money handing it to Alfie. "That should be enough. Now get going."

"Where are we going to stay tonight, Alex? I'm scared shitless of those bears."

"We'll sleep in the car if we have to. We'll throw the cans and wrappers in the trunk. The bears won't bother you in here. By the way, when you drive by the cabin, look and see if there's anyone around or any strange cars. If someone finds him, they'll call the law. I'll be here when you get back. Now get going."

26

Jim Hawkins could hear the whir, whir, whir, of the helicopter long before it came in sight. He had heard it moments earlier and had guessed that it had landed at the cabin. Soon afterwards, he heard the recognizable sound of the whirlybird once again becoming airborne. There was no doubt in his mind that it would be the Mounties looking for him. Now, it circled high above looking for a place to land.

Wolf was excited, running and barking as the helicopter began to land. "Stay here boy and be good," Jim said.

The dog looked at the chopper, made a couple of steps towards it and then with haunting eyes, looked at his master and stopped, his tail wagging briskly.

The pilot stepped from the chopper after shutting it down and made his way towards them.

"Mr. Hawkins?"

"That's me."

"I'm Sergeant Ronald Curtis, Royal Mounted Police. We're stationed at Kamloops. We received the call from your wife at our office. My partner, Constable Ron Block is waiting with her at the crime scene. She told me where to look for you."

Jim described in detail what had happened up to this point. "I followed two sets of tracks this far. I'm not sure how far ahead of me they are, or for that matter, if they still are ahead. I'm not sure when the shooting occurred."

The constable looked in the direction that Jim was pointing. "I'm going to enlist your help Mr. Hawkins. You and your dog proceed as you are. I'll go up in the helicopter and see if I can see anything from the air."

Jim watched as the chopper took off. The blast of air from the propeller blew his hat off. He retrieved it and placed it back where it belonged. "Come on Wolf."

The chopper had gone little more than a mile when it circled twice and began to descend. Jim broke into a jog, Wolf beside him. He half expected to hear gunshots, but there were none. As Jim came into view of the chopper, he could see the Mountie looking at something on the ground.

The sergeant looked up as he approached his face stern. "Looks like we found one of the men that you were following, recognize him?"

"My God. He really got mauled" Jim looked over at the body of the grizzly a few yards away. Wolf growled and began to bark. "You don't have to worry about this bear boy. He cashed in."

Again the Mountie asked, "Do you recognise the fellow?"

Jim looked the corpse over more closely. The face was tanned except for around the eyes. "He could be one of them. I can't be sure, with all of that blood and the distortion of the face. If he's the guy that I think he is, he always wore green goggles. You can see how the skin is whiter around the eyes."

"Yes, I see. The back of his head is smashed quit badly. The bear must have hit him from behind. Possibly he was running from it. His rifle's here. There's a shell over there on the ground and there's another. Hmm."

"What's the matter officer?"

"It just looks a little strange. There are no other signs of anyone else here but if that bear hit him from behind, how did he manage to shoot it?"

"Good question. I know that I started out following two sets of tracks but then the ground got rocky and I couldn't be sure."

The Mountie stood there for a moment, his eyes scanning the area. "Let's roll the bear over and see where he's hit." The bear was heavy and smelly. The dog began to bark, crouching down as if he expected the bear to rise up. The bear's massive chest was red with blood.

"It looks like they both lost this round," said Sergeant Curtis.

Jim looked around, first at the remains of the man and the bear, and then at the ground.

He looked at the Mountie. "Doesn't it strike you funny that there are no foot prints here except our own. It's as if someone cleaned the area all around here removing any trace of the conflict that must have occurred?"

"Of course it has. It will be interesting to see if the bullets in that bear came from that rifle. You said that you were tracking two men?"

"I did. There's no trace that I see of another man though."

"Right, we won't touch anything here. I want a forensic team to come down and investigate what could be a crime scene area. It appears as if someone might be trying to tidy up a murder, the one back at that cabin, and pin it on this person. Just how the bear came in to all this could be a bit of a mystery, then again, it might have been something that wasn't planned but just happened. There's room for you and your dog in the helicopter Jim. Come-on, I'll make out a report and dispatch the proper people to come down and look after this back at the cabin."

"Right, my cabin. The old guy that was shot was living there with another young fellow. They were working some claim rights for me on shares."

"Where's this other fellow, the young one?"

"Good question, like where is the other guy that I was following."

"Then you don't know?"

"Haven't a clue."

There seemed to be more questions than answers as they walked towards the helicopter. Wolf had the luggage compartment all to himself. Jim turned and said, "Stay put Wolf. You're getting a ride that few dogs ever get."

Adrenalin

The dog lay down, ears erect and eyes large as the chopper soared up into the air and headed west.

The chopper circled once over the cabin before landing. The spot where the Mountie had landed before had been kept open. The yard now was full of red flashing lights from patrol cars and an ambulance. There were other cars there as well, probably curiosity seekers from Barkerville. The helicopter hovered for a moment and then touched down.

27

Alfie carefully backed the big black Buick out onto the road as Alex watched from behind the weathered shack. Slowly he drove towards Barkerville. It felt strange, driving Alex's car. He had only driven a car a few times in his life. Once when he was fourteen, he and another kid stole a car from a pump at a gas station as the owner went inside to pay. He grinned thinking back. The cops had chased him at high speeds, the other kid screamed with fear as he had put the pedal to the metal until he rolled the car on a gravel road.

No one got hurt that bad. The other kid had a few scrapes on his face. Alfie himself had come out of it with a sore shoulder and six months in a detention home. The defence attorney that had been appointed to defend him pleaded for a light sentence because of his age and absence of any record. He could still see the serious look on the judge's face as he talked about how he could have killed somebody. Alfie gave up on cars after that.

His father died when he was five years old and his mother had brought him up best she could. As a young adult and alone, it wasn't long before he began to hang around Sully's. Much of it was the lure of motorcycles and as soon as he was old enough, he was riding around the city. The first code he learned was to 'keep your mouth shut'. Sully, started to use him to pick up packages and drop them off. He didn't know what was in the packages; at least that was what he was told to say if he got caught. Soon, he was picking up packages at different locations, places where the law wouldn't expect a kid of his age with that much money. He had his first tattoo when he was fifteen and about the same time he began to let his hair grow long. It wasn't long after that Joey Gallo came on the scene. At sixteen, his mother passed away. It was funny; he now felt the remorse and sadness that he should have felt back then. Now he realized what a really hard life she had.

He drove on slowly picking up speed, feeling more comfortable behind the wheel. He passed the cabin where Alex shot the old grey haired man. The place still seemed deserted. He drove on, his mind in turmoil over what had occurred. Briefly, he thought of passing through Barkerville and just going to Vancouver or some other place far away. But he didn't want Alex looking for him. He had no other choice but to complete his errand and return.

He drove down the main street of Barkerville and pulled into a parking spot when he noticed Jim Hawkins and a passenger go by. Hawkins didn't see him.

He had to go to three different stores before he got everything he needed. He returned to the car and started to back out when the sound of a siren caused him to stop. A police car sped by, lights flashing and siren blaring. Slowly he pulled out. He was just starting out when an ambulance swerved around him, the siren going and lights flashing in much the same fashion. He had a good idea where they were heading.

Sergeant Curtis set the helicopter down and Jim stepped from the chopper. Wolf bounded out behind him. Judy rushed over, the questions flying fast and furious.

"Did you find Andy's killers?"

Jim looked at her and didn't speak for a moment. "Well, we're not exactly sure." He paused as he noticed people trying to catch some of the conversation. He lowered his voice and they moved a few yards away from eavesdroppers. "We did find one fellow. We think it was the biker that said I had the cabin for rent."

Judy was intent, her dark eyes flashing. "What did he say?"

"He didn't say anything and he's not likely to. He had a run-in with a grizzly bear. He wasn't a pretty sight. Both he and the bear were dead. Either he shot the bear, or someone else did and made it look as if they killed each other."

"Oh my God!" gasped Judy. "So you didn't see anything of the two men that you thought had come here?"

"No, but I'd bet my last dollar that the guy that the bear killed came down here with them."

"What about David? Did you see any sign of him?"

"Nope. I don't think that we're going to find any of them today. I guess..."

At that moment Jim looked up and saw Alex's big black Buick. He saw the stringy blonde haired driver slow down for a better look and then sped off. Jim looked anxiously at one of the younger Mounties that had driven up in a patrol car. He screamed.

"Hey! Stop that car!"

Without asking why, the officer jumped into his patrol car, turned on the siren and took off in pursuit.

The flashing lights in his rear view mirror caught Alfie's attention. A jolt of fear surged through his body as he saw the patrol car rapidly closing in sirens screaming. He shoved the gas pedal to the floor and took off. His mind flashed back to the day long ago when another police car had pursued him. His palms grew sweaty, his nerves began to override his senses and he could almost feel the car wheels skidding on the loose gravel.

The Buick literally jumped out of its skin as the gas injection into the carburetor exploded. The automobile thundered down the road, the wheels leaving the ground as it crested the hills and rocketed down the inclines before cresting another. Alfie careened the curves. He could hear the blare of the siren and see the patrol car close behind in the mirror. The derelict cabin, where Alex was waiting, came into view, but he was going too fast to stop. At that moment, the car wheel dropped off the edge of the road and Alfie could feel the steering wheel tearing out of his grip and then the sight of a huge boulder. The Buick ploughed into the rock, bringing the car to a stop and sending Alfie flying through the windshield. Almost at the same instant, the car exploded sending a ball of flame high into the air.

The patrol car screeched to a stop a few yards back. The officer reacted quickly pulling out a fire extinguisher from beneath the seat and putting out the flames before they could spread into a forest fire. A second patrol car pulled up just as he got the fire under control. Together, they began to approach the battered body lying several yards away from the crash site. Alfie should have stayed back in Ontario. He would never see home again.

28

Alex Gallo had found a good spot under the spreading branches of a tree after Alfie headed for town. He was exhausted and his arm was throbbing and paining him, but fatigue overrode the pain and he fell asleep. He didn't know just how long he had been sleeping when the sound of a helicopter woke him up. He staggered to his feet. The helicopter was descending close to the spot where they had camped the night before, the spot where the bodies of the bear and Chad Moore lay. It was probably the police in the chopper. Someone must have found the old man back at the cabin and called the law. It came as no surprise. There was a momentary fear that they would start looking for him, that is, unless he and Alfie had covered their tracks good enough to throw them off. At any rate, it was getting late and nobody would start searching this late in the day. For the moment he was safe.

His arm was still hurting and he was hungry. It had also been far too long since he had a drink. Those things would change when Alfie got back. Damn it, what was keeping Alfie? He should have been back here by now.

It wasn't long before he heard the blare of the siren and the powerful roar of vehicles racing in his direction. His heart pounded as he recognized his Buick flying past with a police car in hot pursuit. A sickening feeling came over him as he heard the screech of brakes followed by the sound of metal hitting rock. He saw a ball of flame shoot higher than the tops of the trees, then black smoke. Carefully he approached the road keeping a low profile. Half a mile away, he could see the smoke and make out the flashing lights of the police cruisers. At that moment, a truck passed by. It looked like the same one that Jim Hawkins drove. That figured. It was probably Hawkins that had called the police. It was too far away for him to hear just what was going on, but the prospects of Alfie coming with food and drink diminished.

Although Alex couldn't see what had taken place, he could make an educated guess. If Alfie had survived the crash, he would be in critical condition or in police custody. Either way, Alex found himself out of luck. He had no food, no shelter, and the shirt and jacket that he needed were out of reach. Moreover, the medical supplies along with the alcohol had gone up in smoke.

Everything had gone wrong since yesterday. If that first shot had not missed David Rivers, he would be headed back to Ontario right now. Fate had dealt him a bum hand. He cradled the Winchester in his hand. His jaw tightened with determination, he would endure the pangs of hunger, the pain in his arm and the cold of the night and he would find David Rivers. He would put an end to his life, once and for all. Somewhere, probably somewhere close by, Rivers was hiding. He had been close enough to plant the bait that brought the bear. Sooner or later, Rivers would show himself. When he did, Alex would be there.

He thought of waiting around to catch a glimpse of the wrecker that was bound to show up, but changed his mind. There were too many law enforcement people in the area, and Hawkins might have that dog with him that could pick up his scent. Stealthily, he moved away. He walked westward towards the cabin, close enough to the Cottonwood River so that he could keep his bearing. There would only be a few more hours of sunlight. If he could find some sort of trail he would follow it. It then dawned on him, Rivers had placed that bacon close to them, and maybe he left some tracks.

His pace picked up as he hurried back towards the campsite they had occupied. He came upon the sight. Both the bodies of the bear and Chad were still there and the area was cordoned off by yellow police tape. He looked around. It was odd that the chopper had come down and taken off and that Chad's body was still there? Probably the police would soon be back to claim the body. He would have to hurry to avoid them. He walked towards the spot where Alfie had found the bacon. There were signs of broken twigs but the grass left no impressions. He circled further. Near a rock he found a footprint. The V pattern was different from either his, Alfie's or Chad's, it was a smaller size as well. It had to be River's. It took another few minutes before he found another. The footprint was headed west, angling towards the Cottonwood River. Like a hound dog on a scent, Alex picked up on the ancient art of tracking. His senses perked up, all else was forgotten for the moment. He was on River's trail and he would not stop until he found him.

29

The first rays of light had begun to show when he got back to the cave and slipped into his sleeping bag. Even though the floor was hard, he slept well. Here, there was security from the eyes of the world. The thermal waters kept the cave at a comfortable temperature.

David had slept late that morning. His eyes fluttered as he awoke and looked up. The smallest shaft of light shone down from above where the flat rock left the small opening. He was hungry. He slipped on some clothes and reflected on the events of yesterday. How quickly the serene life that he had been living was shattered. His father had always said that one never knew what tomorrow would bring. He was certainly right about that. The image of Andy's blood spattered face was etched in his mind. The feeling of sorrow quickly turned to anger as he thought of those who pursued him and ended up killing his friend. He wondered how well the bacon worked. Bacon was the one thing that would draw bears quicker than honey. For now though, there was no way of knowing whether it worked or not.

David's eyes quickly became accustomed to the darkness. He could make out his backpack and crawled over to it. The contents that he had emptied in haste the night before lay around in disarray. He picked up a candle and a package of matches. He was sure that at this angle and distance from where the flat rock covered the entrance, the light would not be seen from above. He went back to where the contents of the backpack were strewn. There was a can of beef stew there. He was hungry enough that it still tasted good even without heating it up.

He sat back leaning against the wall of the cave. The spoon on the Swiss Army Knife came in handy. In all probability, every thing that he had brought into the cave would be put to use if he stayed here long. He sat there thinking. It must be late morning, although he wasn't sure. He would have to pass the time until the sun went down. That could be quite some time. He was deep in thought with only the gentle sound of the subterranean stream.

Getting in and out of the cave posed a problem, especially re-entry. His training as a die maker had taught him to think in practical terms. How to construct things came natural to him. Slowly an idea began to take shape. The pyramid shape of an oil derrick was what he needed. It could be strengthened like a ladder with crosspieces on all sides. On the top, he could bind saplings together to form a platform, about five feet from the cave entrance. That would allow him to stand erect while hoisting the heavy rock to one side to allow an opening which he could easily pass through and close. He could visualize the structure and became excited, eager to get to work on the project.

His chain of thought was broken by the barking of a dog. He listened and could hear the sound of a voice overhead. His heart skipped a beat. The dog had sniffed out his whereabouts. For a long time he stood in fear listening to the conversation between man and dog. He listened closer and recognised the man's voice. It was Jim Hawkins. Lucky for him, the dog's master had not mastered the dog's language; otherwise, it would have been game over. Jim was probably on the trail of Andy's murderers. How had he shown up so soon? At first, David thought that Jim might be looking for him, but then, if that had been the case, he might have given a closer inspection to the dog's sensitive nose. Then it dawned on him, Jim must have been following Alex and the others footprints, which was why he continued on down along the river. It was a wakeup call though, he would have to get some animal scent to overpower his own human scent and spread it around the rocks.

Here in the cave, David could feel himself getting hyper. He thought back to the psychiatric ward at the hospital years before. Confinement didn't sit well with him but in the cave it was his own confinement not under the control of strangers. When the sun went down, he would be able to breathe the fresh air and roam the night, just as the night creatures do away from prying eyes. He peeled off his clothes and slipped into the warm thermal waters. It was soothing and relaxing. It made his feet feel good and he could tell that they were beginning to heal.

The remainder of the day he stayed in the peacefulness of the cave patiently waiting for the dead of night.

30

Alex found the tracking to be slow. The footprints were getting harder to find as the sand and gravel gave way to the rocky terrain. Darkness was beginning to close in and Alex was overwhelmed by a sense of defeat. He realized he was too old for this. What was he thinking when he started this hunt? Revenge was going to be so easy. They would find Rivers and kill him. He never thought he would be the only one left. He couldn't believe how he missed Alfie. In a small way Alfie had helped to replace the loss of Joey and ease the pain. Here in the shadows, he longed for the comfort of his home in Ontario. He even thought of Ellen and how maybe things would be different when he went home. His arm was throbbing and all of this was taking its toll on his strength. If only Alfie had made it back, everything would have been better. But it was all gone; his car, the food, the booze and even Alfie himself.

The full moon was beginning to rise and smoke coloured clouds drifted across it, dimming its brightness. He heard a wolf howl somewhere close by and he clutched his rifle. It wasn't wolves that worried him, even though he didn't relish running into any, it was the fear of another bear attack that was making him nervous. The movement of the nocturnal animals made the night come alive.

Finally, it became too dark to pick up the tracks. They seemed to be heading back towards David's cabin. He wasn't keen at all about continuing along the river. God only knew what he would run into. He came upon a huge boulder guarded on one side by evergreens. With the rock at his back, he felt that he could rest without the fear of something coming up unexpected, something like a grizzly. He reached up into the branches of the trees with the barrel of the rifle. A startled roosting bird took a noisy flight, scaring Alex as bad as he startled it, no doubt. He regained his composure and shortly thereafter, he fell asleep.

There was no telling just how long he slept but suddenly he awoke. Faintly, he heard a rhythmic sound, like someone chopping wood. It stopped. He listened. There it was again. He was reluctant to leave his warm and relatively safe spot, but someone was out there in the darkness. Carefully he moved forward and the sound got louder. Suddenly, the sound of chopping ceased. The moon silently moved out from behind the clouds and illuminated the ground. The silhouettes of the pine trees, the dark mountains and the midnight blue colour of the river created a master's canvas in the night. He could see the white foam as it splashed along the shallows. He crouched down low and lay on the ground looking straight ahead to where he had heard the sound. Then he saw it, the form of a man dragging something along the ground. As he watched, the figure moved back to where it had been and stooped as if to pick up something. Alex moved forward towards the shape, quickly, silently.

David had been busy. He found an evergreen about six inches at the base and rose up about twenty feet. The pole was about fifteen feet long and had a four inch top where he cut it off. He would need four in all, but tonight he would cut just one. Leaving the branches in a pile was the easiest way to do things, but the sight of fresh cut limbs would bring suspicion to anyone that noticed them, so he had decided to drop them into the cave. Anything from a two inch diameter up, he would use for the cross pieces, or steps for his pyramid ladder. The smaller bows he would place on the floor and they would make a comfortable bow bed. They would be softer to sleep on than the hard floor of the cave.

He dragged the large pole over to the cave entrance. Leaving it, he retraced his steps. He hacked away at the stump until it was almost flush with the ground. Then he covered the stump with a piece of ledge rock and scattered needles over and about it, hiding it and the wood chips from view. At night, it was undetectable; hopefully it would look that way in the daytime as well. The smallest branches, the one's that would make a nice soft mattress, he carried over and placed them on the ground by the pole. There were two poles left that were about two inches in diameter and about six feet long; they were lying by the hatchet. He went to retrieve them, It would be the last trip for the night.

The ends of the small poles were sharp and pointed where the hatchet had cut them off. He wished that he had bought a small Swede saw. It would have left a nice square end on the poles. It was too late now though. At least he had bought a hatchet and it would have to do. He carried one pole and hatchet in his left hand. The other pole was a little bigger and heavier he carried in his right hand. He began to walk towards the cave entrance. It was getting light now that the clouds had drifted across the face of the moon. David had lost all track of time. The moon didn't follow the same set pattern as the sun so that one could have some idea of the time. It wasn't important anyway. He smiled. He was like the vampires now that he used to go to the movies and watch. They were invincible as long as they returned to their coffins before the sun rose. Now, he had ended up in a similar position but there was a slight difference. With him, he had to return to his cave before man could find him.

Suddenly, a movement caught his eye. Maybe his mind was playing tricks on him. The shadows grew longer, then shorter as the celestial body above moved in and out of darkness. His overactive imagination didn't help either. The shadows might have been imaginary, but the voice wasn't.

"Drop that hatchet!"

David jumped.

"You heard me Rivers, drop it!"

Adrenalin

The moon shone across Alex's face giving it a rather ghostly cast of grey and yellow, his eyes shining wickedly as if he was crazed.

David could now clearly see his whole anatomy, half crouched, rifle in hand pointed at his prey. Strange, David thought, I feel no fear at all.

"So you found what you were looking for Alex. You look as if you've aged a lot, as if life has been hard on you. By the look of that arm, you look like a rag doll that some dog shook the hell out of."

Alex started to breathe heavily. "You think you're smart baiting that damn bear with bacon and setting him on us, don't you? Well he might have killed Chad but I was too tough for him."

David laughed loudly, his voice full of scorn. "Where's your old buddy, Alfie?"

"That's another score that I'm about to...how did you know that Alfie came with me?"

Again the scornful laugh, as David stalled for time trying to think what to do. "I got a lot closer to you than you think I did Gallo. You really aren't that smart."

The last statement infuriated Alex. "You think not, eh. I'm the one with the rifle pointed at you. I knew that I would find you if it was the last thing I ever did. I promised myself on Joey's grave that I'd get you, you murdering bastard."

"There's only one murderer here and that's you. You shot an innocent old fellow that was twice the man you'll ever be. What I did, I did in self defence. Joey didn't leave me any other choice. It was me or him, and I'm still here. The blood of those who came after me is on your hands, not mine."

Alex raised the muzzle of the gun aiming it straight at David's heart. A vicious streak of genuine hatred showed. "You're not here for much longer Rivers. You ripped the throat out of my son like an animal."

"An animal of your creation, Gallo."

Alex sneered. "If I created you, I'll destroy you."

"Even you would give a man a moment to pray and ready myself for the next life, Alex."

The triumphant smile on Alex Gallo's face said it stronger than the words. "One minute, just to see you squirm."

Slowly, David knelt on his right knee. His left leg was straight behind him. He began to pray out loud capturing Alex's attention. Suddenly, it was the same old situation; first Joey, then Paulo and now Alex. They had all tried to collect his hide and now he was once more getting that old feeling, like a volcano starting way down deep inside and then gathered fury and velocity. He could feel the adrenalin surging through his veins as his right hand dropped down to the pole that lay at his finger tips. Like a javelin he hurled it straight at Alex's arm where the bear had mangled. A horrifying scream of pain escaped Alex's lips as he dropped the rifle and grabbed the sharpened pole protruding from his arm like a knife.

With a roar like a mountain lion, David charged his foe. Grabbing the free end of the pole, he pushed Alex backwards towards the high cliff that overlooked the Cottonwood River. Alex felt the ground give way as over the ridge and down, down into the cold waters of the Cottonwood they plunged. The pole snapped as they hit the water, a portion still jutting out of Alex's bleeding arm. Alex quickly realized the fatal nature of the battle. He made a grab for David getting his good arm around David's head. He tried to use his weight to slam David's head into the boulders jutting out of the rapids as the water carried them along.

The overpowering rush of adrenalin that was still ragging through David's body was too powerful. He broke free of Alex's hold. David's hand went down to the Bowie knife at his side. The blade found its mark as Alex let out a horrific scream, his last earthly sound. The Cottonwood River ran red with his blood. Like his son, he had hounded David until his end. The Gallo's would no longer bother David Rivers or anyone else.

The Cottonwood flowed quickly towards the Pacific. If undetected, Alex body would pass Quesnel within the next twenty-four hours and from there who knows. The population west of Quesnel was sparse, maybe his remains would never be found.

David swam to shore. The adrenalin leaving his body this time did not leave him weak. He climbed the ridge and then dropped the remaining poles and branches down into the cave, along with his hatchet and Alex's rifle. Carefully, he looked around for any clues that would disclose his whereabouts. Confident there were none, he lowered himself down into the cave dropping the flat rock behind him. Life as he had known it would never be the same.

31

The day was cool and sunny. The snow in the higher elevations was beginning to accumulate. Each day, it seemed to creep further down the mountainside towards the valley below. The sky was azure blue and the air was thin and clear. The grass and vegetation was still green and still growing slowly. The group of twenty some odd mountain goats browsed here on this late October morning. The kids were pretty well grown, enough that they no longer had to depend on their mothers as they had been when he arrived.

The herd Billy goat raised his head and watched the approaching presence of man. He bleated, alerting the others. There was no stampede or scattering of the herd. They stood and watched with mild curiosity. Here it was difficult to access the mountains; most had never seen a human. Unlike the animals that lived in the valley, they had not developed a fear of mankind.

Seldom had David left the sanctuary of his cave during the daylight. He had often looked high up in the mountains and seen the tiny white dots moving around. He knew that the goats long white hair would provide the warmth and cover that he needed to survive the winter. Unable to go to the store for warm blankets, he had to turn to nature. The meat also would be a welcome change from the steady diet of fish that he had been surviving on these past months. He had deliberated a long time before making up his mind to trek up into the mountains. He was reluctant to fire the rifle that he had taken from Alex. It could draw unwanted attention. He had made the decision that up here, where only the wild goats lived and the eagles soared, the likelihood of anyone hearing the rifle was remote. After all, he did have to prepare for winter. Even though he was reluctant to shoot game, it was necessary.

He looked the herd over carefully selecting a target. Not wanting to shoot a female that could reproduce or some old male that would not be worth eating, he finally zeroed in on a young male about a year and a half old judging by the horns. Slowly he raised the rifle. The shot brought an immediate response. The herd took flight bounding with great agility and speed across the terrain. David looked down at the young billy that he had shot.

He worked quickly. Smoothly he cut the great white coat, sliding the blade of the Bowie knife between the skin and the flesh pulling the hide free. Carefully he scraped all of the flesh from the hide so that it would cure properly. While the hide lay on the ground, he cut several choice cuts from the carcass. Then, wrapping the meat in the skin, he shouldered the load, picked up his rifle and began his descent down the mountain.

Halfway down the mountain, he paused, turned and gazed upwards. A pair of golden eagles soared high above. The remains of the goat would not go to waste, nature would see to that.

The cave had become quite liveable. The pyramid construction enabled a much easier entrance and exit from the cave. David had made a bed and a chair out of two inch saplings. He bound them together with strands cut from the nylon rope. The bed he had covered with bows of pine needles. The goatskin was stretched over it and the sleeping bag was placed on top. Next year he would replace the sleeping bag with another goatskin. To some, it would be an impossible way to live. To David, there was no other choice. The short stay in jail and in the psychiatric ward earlier on in his life had cemented his fear of anything resembling prison. He had to be free, if only in the darkness of the night. He was careful; he left no footprints either in the sand or the snow. Alex had tracked him to his lair, it would never happen again. Anonymity was his best fried.

In the winter, he learned to hibernate just as the bears do, gorging himself with food late in the fall. Sometimes, when he woke in the winter and was hungry, he caught the wily trout, by letting the line flow far into the thermal pool and far out into the river. He would then feast on them and return to sleep. Like the animals that survive the winter he was learning to survive, for if he were to live free, it would have to be in isolation, alone and lonely forever.

ISBN 142511974-3

9 781425 119744